Lethal T

By Helen Christmas

To Juliet

I hope you enjoy this

[signature]

Cover design by Helen Christmas
Photo by Annie Spratt from Unsplash

I dedicate this book to Graham
who played a very special part in its creation.

Prologue

St Richard's Hospital, Chichester June 2015

I turned to DI Fitzpatrick with a gulp, hit with wave after wave of panic as the contents of the press release sank in. But this story, this vicious slant on the truth, had been tainted with everything I had feared.

TEENAGER MUST FACE MURDER CHARGE

> *Sussex Police have detained a teenage boy for a series of actions that resulted in the deaths of two men. The sixteen-year-old (who cannot be named for legal reasons) suffers from severe mental problems which have been verified by a professional team of social workers who dealt with his care since early childhood.*
>
> *On the two occasions he was placed in foster homes, his behaviour was deemed challenging, which at times led to violence. Early warning signs were recorded in 2013 when the police were alerted to an incident. Although no charges were brought, the damage caused inside his foster home could have been life-threatening. He has since been assessed with high functioning autism, but concerns remain that he may develop psychopathic tendencies…*

"They can't print this," I started spluttering, "it's outrageous! How dare he twist the truth, when he was trying to save my life?"

Three pairs of eyes zoomed in on me but of all the people in the room, one face stood out in particular: *Hannah*.

"Tell them," I urged her. "Tell them about Sam!"

"I will," Hannah nodded, "but first and foremost, we need to explain what he witnessed."

A weight closed around my chest, every breath dragged painfully from my lungs while I struggled to grasp this most chilling part of the story.

"The party…" I could hear my voice wobbling, the horror flooding back in a deluge, but they had to know the truth.

Sam.

Suddenly I started crying, as I recalled how this nightmare had begun.
Maisie, Joe and Sam. That's how it began.
We were three kids in a care home, too young to protect ourselves.
Three kids who were inseparable until the night Sam went missing.
And all we had ever wanted to know was what happened to him.

PART ONE
Maisie and Joe

Chapter One

West Sussex, February 2015, Four Months Earlier.

Of all the places my past came back to haunt me, I had never imagined it would begin along this unlit coastal road in West Sussex.

The A259 felt so much safer at night and with none of the surging traffic that besieged the main A27. Caught in the gleam of a crescent moon, the thatched eaves of the Oyster Catcher pub poked above the hedge line. Then without warning, the darkness thickened around me, a wall of trees soaring from both sides.

Hands tight on the steering wheel, I could have sworn the landscape seemed to sway slightly. Perhaps it was exhaustion, a week of troubled nights. Yet it all crumpled into insignificance beside what happened next.

A cap of blonde hair shimmered on the periphery of my vision, followed immediately by the unmistakable outline of a boy. I caught my breath. Hovering in the outer glow of my headlights, there was no question who he reminded me of; a boy of about eleven staring back bolt-eyed, his face frozen in terror.

"It can't be!"

Jamming on my brakes, I heard the squelch of rain water under my wheels before skidding into the opening of an industrial unit. As I switched off the engine, I twisted my head around.

Where had he gone?

Braced on the edge of the trees one second, he seemed to have dissolved into the drizzly darkness. I was taking no chances. Hands clumsy, I dug into my handbag for my mobile and dialled 999.

"Which emergency service do you require?" a robotic voice asked.

"Police!" I started babbling. "There's a young boy wandering about, on the edge of the woods in Climping. He looked scared stiff and it's so dark! Is there any chance someone could check this out?"

By the time the call ended, I was quaking all over, every breath bursting out of me in rapid gasps.

I couldn't have a panic attack. Not now.

But I could barely contain my shock, because that boy - with his blonde hair and an air of fragile innocence visible even in the half-second I'd seen him for -

had jolted me hard.

He looked so much like Sam.

Sam, who had disappeared twenty years ago.

******

An hour later the whole eerie event folded under a blanket of mystery.

They sent out a patrol car. The police had been thorough in their search but as I lingered at the roadside, gnawing my fingernails, my heart thumped against my chest. Watching the spears of torchlight as they cut through the trees, the scene had me gripped, until at last one of the officers approached me.

At least DC Mark Anderson was one of the kinder police officers, and blessed with a manner that set him apart from his superiors.

"Go home, Maisie," he said. "There's no one out there. According to the local police log there have been no reports of anyone missing either. No lost kids, no runaways..."

I felt my spirits sinking. This was not the first time I had called the police out under false pretences. How could I forget? I'd been swayed by a poster I saw many years ago: the NSPCC, advising us never to ignore a child in distress.

'What would you do if you heard next door's child screaming?'

Only a coward would turn up the TV volume on a remote control. Not me, though. I refused to ignore it, terrified to imagine that child being abused in some way.

Just thank God Inspector Burke wasn't around to witness tonight's episode.

"I-I'm sorry," I choked, unable to think of anything intelligible to say, "but I'm sure I saw someone. I swear to you I'm not lying."

Mark raised his eyebrows. He was looking at me intently, which left me wondering what he was thinking. Mistaking a three-year-old's bawling tantrum for abuse might be understandable, under the circumstances... but not this.

"Is it possible you may have imagined it?" he pressed. "I should have asked you sooner, but where have you been tonight?"

I pressed my eyes shut in frustration. "Worthing. Our department held a fostering information evening tonight and I promised I'd help."

"Fostering," the detective constable echoed, "but this is exactly my point. From the very nature of your work, you're in contact with vulnerable children, right? Kids from broken homes, who've been abused or neglected?"

"Not direct contact," I corrected him. "That's the job of the social workers. I work in a hub of administrators and tonight's presentation was to explain the process of fostering to interested parents."

"But you do get to read some of the cases, surely?"

"I suppose so. Typing up reports does give me an insight into the problems

5

families face. Anyway, I left the building at 8:00 by which time it was dark..."

I broke off, a sudden shiver running through me, and as he shuffled from one foot to the other, I could sense his awkwardness.

How could I have got it so wrong?

I was convinced I'd seen that boy. A memory so crisp it flashed up like a beacon, as if those dark, menacing trees had woken some deep-rooted fear. Perhaps I should have stopped to think before I'd called in the police.

With my hand flying to my mouth, I suppressed a sob. "You think my work is affecting my judgement?"

Only the comforting pressure of his palm on my shoulder compelled me to look up. The scent of his aftershave merged pleasantly with the sweetness of peppermints, but something about his kind eyes had an instant sobering effect.

"Come on, there's no need to get yourself into a state now."

I took a gulp of air. "Oh Mark! I-I feel such an idiot! I wish I could explain this but what if you're right? And if so, why would I imagine something so real?"

"Maybe you're over tired?" he suggested, "and I hope you don't mind me saying this, Maisie, but you look wrung out. Are you getting enough sleep?"

Staring back in shock, I mentally pieced together what I needed to tell him.

My nightmares. The suffocating fear I experienced every time I woke, fragments I remembered clearly, although they never quite reached a conclusion...

I told him as much as I could, and it hardly made sense to me even as I was saying it.

"That explains a lot." His voice hung in the deathly silence. "You're probably suffering from sleep deprivation. Didn't you know a build-up of tiredness can make you hallucinate?"

"What?" I gasped. "You're telling me, that boy was nothing but a hallucination?"

"I wouldn't be surprised," he replied. "Now go home and get some rest. In fact, why not take some time off work and recuperate? Any problems, you know you can always talk to me."

I had to praise him for his compassion. Following his advice, I drove on to Bognor Regis, where curling up in my own flat was the only thought that could bring any comfort on this strangest of nights.

My own home, my own space, my own rules.

Clinging to the coast road, I swung past Butlins, its distinctive canopy standing out like peaks of whipped cream against an indigo sky. I could have taken a shorter route through town, but found myself lured towards the seafront.

Rolling beyond the pier, to the Yacht Club, I gazed out to sea. How I cherished the expanse of space; the undulating energy of the waves as they lapped the shoreline. Tonight was low tide. Rows of rocks lined the water's edge like crooked teeth, ripples of wet sand reflecting the moonlight.

Breathing deeply, I tried to suppress the storm of rising emotions. Perhaps tonight's sighting was a hallucination, as Mark had hinted. Yet the boy at the roadside... his chilling resemblance to Sam kept haunting me, because Sam had been very real. How could I forget the care home where the three of us had met?

Maisie, Joe and Sam.

A yawn stretched my jaw, and tugging on the wheel, I spun away from the coast road to complete my homeward journey.

Just thank God they hadn't berated me for wasting police time.

How that would go down with my employees did not bear thinking about: any exposure of my mental state would be a real problem. Working for West Sussex County Council in the childcare and fostering department, my job meant the world to me, and from that thought branched another.

As a girl who had herself been fostered, did they know I was undergoing psychotherapy?

My foster mother had suggested this a month ago, through fear my panic attacks and nightmares would forever hang over me, and sure enough, something dark had been prodding at my subconscious mind lately.

If only I could grasp what it was.

Chapter Two

Hannah Adams. Registered Psychotherapist and Counsellor. West Sussex.
Client: Maisie Bell
6th February 2015

"It's up to you what you want to tell me, Maisie."

The psychotherapist had smiled. A woman in her fifties, Hannah spoke in a way that sent soothing waves over me, her voice warm and breathy.

"All I'm trying to do is gain a deeper insight into the issues you face, so what's been troubling you?"

"Nightmares. They started in my teens. I used to wake up feeling threatened, wondering if they would stop as I got older but now they're back... I feel as if we are in danger again."

"Who is 'we?'" Hannah kept probing. "Is there somebody else involved?"

"Joe. He was my best friend."

"Can you describe him to me?"

Her question drew a smile to my lips. "He was cute but in an ugly sort of way. Joe reminded me of one of the 'Bisto Kids.' Do you remember them?"

Yes, that was my first impression of Joe. Tall, skinny, scruffy with wires for arms and legs. His crooked nose might have been broken for all I knew, and with that broad grin and a chipped tooth, his features were far from perfect.

But none of that seemed to matter at the time.

"I felt lost. I didn't want to talk to anyone, I wanted to hide in the corner with my head in my arms, just wishing those kids would go away."

"Yes, but don't forget you had not long lost your parents."

A lump of pain squeezed my innards. I couldn't suppress it, even though I thought I had expelled all that grief in my last session.

Reliving the hurt of loss, I shrank into a tunnel of darkness that even the brightest of lights could not penetrate.

My real mum and dad were killed in a car crash, see, and so was my little sister, Charlotte. I was in hospital at the time, having my tonsils out. To think, they had driven all the way over to visit me but had never made it home.

How could life be so cruel? I'm over that now, though. It's the stuff that happened since that scarred me forever.

"I loved my parents, they were good to me and I missed my sister terribly, but my grief turned to rage. I was so bloody angry, despite everyone's kindness. Friends, neighbours, all fighting to look after me..."

"And you ended up in a residential care home."

"The authorities got involved," I spat. *"People started to worry about my behaviour, but when the pain of loss is too much to bear, it's easier to switch off your feelings altogether. I became withdrawn."*

I was determined never to suffer that hurt again. Never allow myself to get close to anyone or to love again. It wasn't worth the risk.

Stiffening in my chair, I felt my hands coil into fists, my heart hard as stone. Such a feeling emanated from my childhood. I froze people out. Suppressed every human emotion and made myself unlovable.

"A defence mechanism," Hannah placated, *"not unusual, under the circumstances."*

"I know that, but I never meant to hurt anyone! Everywhere I turned, people went out of their way to be nice to me, and I refused to speak or even look at them. Then finally Social Services stuck their oar in. Decided it was better to put me into care. That bloody care home!"

"So what happened on the day you met Joe?" Hannah pressed.

Pulling my mind back to the scene, I felt the warmth drain out of me, because it wasn't Joe's face that rose from the void but all those other faces. Swarming into my vision like gnats, a whirlwind of hair, eyes and teeth. There was one boy in particular...

"I thought as long as I kept my eyes closed, I could shut them out, but the other kids wouldn't have it. Kept shouting in my face they did, rapping my head with their knuckles. 'Knock, knock, is there anyone in there?' I recoiled into a corner. Squeezed myself into a ball."

God, I could still picture those hard eyes cutting into me, a face twisted with hate.

'Oi, you! I'm talking to you! No one disses me, bitch, d'you get that?'

Squirming in my chair, I knew where this was leading. Joe's intervention. It was that single violent incident that brought us together.

"Go on," Hannah prompted me.

"Joe jumped to my rescue..."

A laugh strained against my chest. I didn't want to repeat his exact words, but even now I could hear his soft, chilling hiss: 'Get away from her, you fucking turd...' and as the tunnels of my mind stretched deep, so the darkest of memories leapt out.

I found myself in a hostile environment, the aggression swelling. All I understood at the time was the blistering impact of that boy's words before everything changed.

"A fight broke out. Everyone was egging them on, a riot of yelling and screaming. That horrible boy had his hands around Joe's throat and I thought he was going to kill him..."

"So what did the staff do, Maisie?"

A blanket of cold wrapped itself around me. Even I was shocked by the way they restrained the little thug. Yanking his arms around his back, they pushed him to the floor face down. One held his arms while the other pinned his legs down.

"The other kids backed off."

A stunned silence.

"I was peering through my fingers and that's when I saw Joe..."

Still as a statue, he had lingered there, massaging his throat. Regardless of his funny features though, he had nice eyes. The way he smiled reassured me; warm eyes, the colour of chocolate. I felt a squeeze of affection.

"He coaxed me out of the corner and took me away from the violence. That's when I knew I'd made a friend."

"Right," Hannah commented. "Well, the whole experience sounds pretty awful. This was a council run home?"

"No, it was private. The man in charge was Mr. Mortimer..."

I bit my lip, swallowing back my fear, since her question had set me thinking. Something else had been going on in that home, something bad, and Joe was one of its victims.

"Okay, so you've told me about the home and the day you met Joe," Hannah's voice penetrated, "but let's go back to the start of your story. The nightmares. You said you felt you were in danger. You and Joe."

"Mr. Mortimer hated him," I said with a shiver. "H-he hurt him."

My blood froze as I said it, an icy chill sliding down my bones. Describing Mr. Mortimer wasn't easy. He struck me as avuncular on our first meeting, with his round face and friendly smile. He was a large man, heavy-set like Father Christmas, but the more I observed him, the more he gave me the creeps.

The chill didn't recede.

All I could picture were his reptilian eyes. He had soft skin, a pale, almost waxy complexion and pink cheeks, fleshy lips. Yet there were times he looked at me as if he wanted to devour me.

"It didn't take long to figure out he was a nasty man."

Chapter Three

The second piece of Mark's advice I chose to follow was to book some time off work. Escaping for a few days would be a treat in itself, but even more so if it were combined with a trip to visit my foster parents.

Resting back in my train seat, I gazed into the distance. A shimmer of green fields streamed past my window, but my thoughts were focussed on Swanley, the grand stucco houses with their red roofs and dormer windows. Mandy and Stewart's house crouched in a quiet cul-de-sac. Picturing the neat privet hedge and walls graced with ivy, I could almost smell the scent of leaves and cut grass. I sighed with pleasure.

It was in this house I had spent the latter years of my childhood.

As the train hummed along the tracks, my eyes began to turn heavy, but something on the other side of the glass jarred me. I sat bolt upright, staring at a blur of forest in the distance. Several dark shapes loomed like an omen. A cluster of mature oak trees. Why did they strike me as symbolic?

A river of cold ran over me as my vision from the other night hurtled back. Turning from the window, I shook my head in denial. Deep in my logical mind, even I knew that boy could not have been Sam. If Sam was alive, he would be the same age as me. A man in his thirties.

Sam, however, was not the only one lingering on the shore of my mind. My therapy had reeled in another person.

Joe.

And seeing those oak trees filled my mind with darkness as I encountered the strangest flashback.

"The laundry room," I whispered to myself.

I could picture the layout of the home clearly now.

A huge house split into two wings. Half for boys and half for girls, with an open-plan communal area, the dining tables where we shared meals. Yet as my mind tunnelled deeper, I saw the steps leading to the basement. Feet frozen on the stone floor, I sniffed the air, thick with the steam of detergent. Lines of sheets hung on drying racks like the sails of a ship, washing machines churning in the background.

Was I imagining things or had Joe locked me in here once? Hellbent on stopping me from going to some party, he swore he was doing it to protect me. I recalled his wiry frame in the gloom.

'Joe, what is it? What's happened?'

Winding my arms around him, I had known nothing of his pain. I heard a sob. Felt his muscles leap as if they had caught fire. Then, as he lifted the corner of his tee-shirt, only then did I see the damage. Never in my life had I seen marks more terrible than the slashes of black bruising like ink stains against his skin... Yet why? If all he was trying to do was protect me?

My eyes pinged open and with the train pulling into the station, I pushed the memory aside. Why those oak trees had evoked such a flashback remained a mystery, although it wouldn't be the first time something like this had happened.

My irrational fear of forests had manifested itself in my teens. Mandy would remember. She had been there.

Suddenly I could not wait to see her, and in the short space of a taxi ride, the sight of their house brought a burst of glee to my heart. Flitting across the lawn, I saw an early sprinkling of crocuses jewel bright against the winter shrubs. I had barely stopped in the driveway when the door flew open; nothing could bring more joy than the beaming smile of my foster mum. Rushing to the door, I cherished the warmth of her arms and for those first few seconds I clung to her.

"Come on in," she chuckled.

As usual the front lounge looked bright and clean. Sunlight poured through the bay windows, illuminating the pastel fabrics. With bleached timber floors and intricate woven rugs, it contained a gentle feminine charm. She had even arranged a vase of fresh flowers on the coffee table.

"My darling girl," she murmured, stroking my hair. She tilted her head to observe me. "You've lost weight. You are eating properly, aren't you?"

"Of course," I blurted a little quickly. "Maybe not as often as I should though..."

I breathed in the essence of pot pourri in the hearth but underlying it, my senses were teased by something far more pleasing. How could I miss that rich and savoury smell wafting from the kitchen?

"Blame it on work. If I get home late, I grab a takeaway but other than that, I live on ready meals. Cooking for one is such a fag."

"Takeaways," Mandy echoed. "It takes minutes to throw together a stir fry."

"I know," I sighed and this time, I stood back to observe *her*.

Now nearing sixty, she radiated goodness, her soft blonde hair threaded with more grey than the last time I'd seen her, but her blue eyes had never lost their twinkle. Having worked all her life as a primary school teacher, she possessed a maternal warmth and as the ultimate recipient of her love, I counted my blessings.

"What's cooking by the way? It smells yum, is it lasagne?"

"As if I'd forget your favourite," she laughed. "Now sit down and take your coat off, I'll open some wine."

My foster mother knew me better than anyone but how could I miss that flicker of concern in her eyes? I sneaked a glance at my reflection.

So maybe my face did look a little gaunt, sharp features, high cheekbones I mistook for signs of maturity. My eyes looked large in comparison. Wide, round and rimmed with black mascara, they gleamed a pale mossy green, fragmented with chips of silver.

"Do you remember what your father used to say?" Mandy's voice hummed from the hallway.

I froze, unaware she had been watching me.

"You were blessed with the grace of an eagle and the fiery locks of a goddess."

My lips curved into a smile, my sleek auburn hair something I had inherited from my real mother. Stewart always was creative with words, and as a teacher of English at the local sixth form college, he had a passion for Greek mythology.

"How is he?" I murmured.

"Stewart's fine!" Mandy breezed. "Keeping himself busy at the allotments but he'll be back at lunchtime!"

As she joined me in the lounge, we settled by the window. I had always loved sitting here, the glow of watery sunshine wrapping us in warmth. I could not resist enthusing about my job; that every child successfully placed with a new foster family brought a flickering ray of hope.

I crossed my fingers, just as enthralled to hear her own stories, from the activities of the Women's Institute to the shenanigans of the council.

"It all gets broadcast on the local Facebook forum," she said. "Which reminds me, I'm glad you got me into social media. Pinterest is my favourite and my recipe board is growing daily."

My smile didn't falter. "Any other boards?"

"Garden Inspiration. I've found some wonderful tips for Stewart. You know how much he loves the great outdoors! In fact, I was thinking we could venture out for a walk later, as the sun's out."

I nodded, the question I yearned to ask now teetering on my tongue.

Mandy tilted her head again. "What? You've got that pensive look about you today. Has something happened?"

"It's hard to explain," I mused, "more *a flashback* really but... I saw a circle of oak trees on my train journey and something about them freaked me."

"Ah," Mandy sighed, "still haven't got over your phobia of forests, then?"

Her words stirred a ripple of anxiety.

"Can you remember when it started?"

Turning her head, she gazed out of the window as if choosing her next words carefully. "We were out on a walk with Terry and Maureen from next door. They had a couple of kids, if you recall, and they'd rescued a dog. So they couldn't wait to take him out..."

"Oh, yes," I said. "It was a collie wasn't it? Fred!"

"That's the one. We took a footpath through the valley where it met the forest. Fred went bounding off towards the gate and there was a track running through the middle but that's when you clammed up. Refused point blank to go in there."

"That's right," I frowned. "Fern and Charlie grabbed my hands and tried to pull me through..." Fragments were starting to creep back now.

"By the time we caught up, you were trembling like a leaf. The kids thought it was funny but even they stopped laughing eventually. I'll never forget your face though. You looked like you'd seen a ghost, convinced the forest was evil and if we went inside something bad would happen."

"Strange," I pondered. "I wonder why."

A shimmy of goose bumps ran over me, but I couldn't stop thinking about Joe again. The sight of those trees had unleashed something, our rendezvous in the laundry room a clue - and somehow the two were connected.

"Looks like your dad's home from the allotments," Mandy announced, and hauling herself off the sofa, gave my shoulder a pat. "Come on. It's nearly lunchtime, so let's go and lay the table."

Sensing I had burdened her with enough of my problems, I followed her into the kitchen. Like every other room, it had a pleasing decor, the peach and cream stencilled walls another example of her creative talent. Laying down the cutlery, I saw Stewart approach the house from the back to remove his muddy boots. His frame loomed behind the glass door panel. A tall man, and broad-shouldered, he glowed with vitality, cheeks ruddy from the cold, his silver hair windswept.

"Hello, Dad," I greeted him as he stomped into the kitchen.

There was no need for more words as he threw his arms around me. Breathing in the familiar essence of his aftershave balm, I felt a surge of affection.

"What a lovely surprise," he murmured. "I've missed you, Maisie."

"Likewise," I said. "It's great to see you."

As the oven door swung open, a cloud of aromatic steam was released into the kitchen. My mouth watered. Braced by the work surface, I watched hungrily, praising Mandy's culinary skills as she hacked through the golden cheese crust.

"That looks delicious and I'm starving."

"Good," Mandy responded. "I'll wrap the fourth portion up for you to take home if you like. You can put it in your freezer."

"That would be great," I smiled. "I'm lucky to have parents like you."

"Oh, stop it!" Mandy fussed, sliding a portion onto my plate. "Cooking doesn't have to be 'a fag' if you plan ahead. I always make double portions."

It was easy to forget my fears as I dived into my lasagne, helping myself to fresh salad and savouring every mouthful. A crusty baguette of garlic bread lingered temptingly in front of me but I resisted it.

Stewart, on the other hand, ripped off a chunk and reaching for the wine bottle, topped our glasses up. His banter was ceaseless as he described his work; his concern about the pressures youngsters were facing in this modern day age.

"I still admire you working in teaching," I remarked. "It must be tough."

Stewart shrugged. "I wouldn't say that, not with sixth formers. I do worry about their safety though, with all this social media and online grooming."

"Dangers we never knew when we were that age," Mandy added, "and I'm just as disturbed by the stories I hear in my school. A ten-year-old pupil posting photos of herself on this 'Instagram' network and getting lewd comments for God's sake! You've heard of internet 'trolls' haven't you?"

"Yes, yes," Stewart intervened, "but grooming children isn't just a modern-day phenomenon. What about Jimmy Savile, eh? Allegations covering a period of fifty years. Kids as young as eight!"

I turned very still, a sense of unease crawling over me. "Then why wasn't he prosecuted sooner?"

"Because of a huge cover up, that's why!" His brows pressed into a scowl. "Accusations are being thrown at the BBC now. Claims that Savile, not to mention other celebrities, had been abusing girls at the TV Centre."

"It's a disgrace," Mandy said, sipping her wine. "Those children were powerless and not one of them could ask for help. People say the authorities knew damn well it was going on yet they did nothing."

"Well, it's all coming out now," Stewart sniffed "and not just celebrities. Have you read about this 'VIP paedophile ring' that's been reported in the news?"

"What?" I looked at him blankly, a tightness spreading over my chest.

"A report sent to Scotland Yard, involving high establishment figures. They'll deny it of course, but weren't MPs equally dismissive of the evidence suppressed about Cyril Smith?"

"Ugh!" I grimaced. "So what about now?"

"Like Stewart says," Mandy answered, "it's only speculation but you can't ignore the rumours. Not after the furore with Jimmy Savile. Police had no choice but to launch an investigation..." A shadow of dread passed across her face. "Maisie, love, did you ever hear of anything like this?"

"Why do you say that?" I gasped.

"The victims were taken out of care homes," Steward finished gloomily.

The atmosphere darkened around the table as I absorbed this. Gazing over the remnants of Mandy's lovely lunch, I could feel a knot tightening my stomach but with so many stories of child sex abuse, I didn't like what I was hearing.

The most scandalous truth was that the children were not believed.

Stewart covered my hand with his own. "Don't dwell on it, love. But you can't deny it's a nasty world out there with lots of youngsters at risk."

"You think I don't know that? It's the reason I work in fostering, Dad..."

"Yes, but what about *you*, Maisie?" Mandy added with caution. "You mentioned your fear of forests but is something else troubling you?"

"I-I can't explain it..." I faltered, "just an overall bad feeling. I mean, why did you suggest psychotherapy, did you think I'd remember something?"

Mandy shook her head. "I thought it would help you. I know you love your job but there is an awful lot missing in your life and not even a hint of romance."

"She's right," Stewart said, without taking his eyes off me. "Most women your age would be settled in a relationship by now."

"But I haven't met anyone I like enough to settle down with," I baulked.

"Sorry," Mandy relented. "We're not trying to put pressure on you but we've sensed for a while you're unhappy and psychotherapy *is* designed to help unlock childhood traumas. Your fear of woods for example, where did that come from? And those awful dreams you used to have..."

"The nightmares are back," I whispered.

My words left a chilling echo. Staring at my empty plate, I caught an exchange of glances between them, a look of shock on their frozen faces.

Then at last Mandy spoke. "Let's leave the washing up for now. Didn't we mention a walk? We should go and grab some fresh air while it's still light."

Even in February the daylight hours were short with long shadows stretching across the lawn. I was nonetheless glad of the exercise.

"I'm sorry to hear about the nightmares," Mandy muttered. She cast me a sad smile. "Maybe this is a good reason to keep up the psychotherapy. Confront your demons and maybe you can move on."

I let my mind empty as I focussed on the environment. We were ambling around a lake where the only trees were the weeping willows, a curtain of soft green foliage drooping over the water's edge.

"How is it going, then?" asked Stewart.

"Okay," I said. "I was reminiscing about my friend, Joe, last time."

"Oh yes," he blustered. "Joe! You used to talk about him a lot..."

But Mandy turned to him sharply, stalling his words in a single stare.

"What do you remember about Joe, Maisie?"

I gazed across the lake, absorbing the tranquility. Ripples raced over the surface but an icy nip in the air made the hairs on the back of my neck tingle.

"Joe was the strong one and looked out for us. Not just me but Sam..."

It occurred to me we had stopped walking.

"It was a hostile environment, the man in charge really creepy, but Joe was the one who suffered. He tried to protect me from something but I can't recall what."

"Who was Sam?" Mandy pressed.

"Sam disappeared," I concluded darkly. "We never did find out what happened to him, but Joe and I swore we would resolve the mystery one day."

Was it too late?

A tiny part of my brain could not suppress the news Stewart had imparted. What if he had said it for a reason?

Victims were taken out of care homes.

Nothing else was said, but in some way, the walk had been pleasantly cathartic, the crisp cold air bringing a glow to my cheeks.

But the day wasn't quite over. Strolling back to our car, we were about to return home when a familiar face swayed into our path. I heard a woman laugh.

"I thought I recognised that coat! I would have spotted you a mile off. How are you, Mandy?"

"Good thanks!" she laughed back. "What are you doing in Swanley?"

"Just passing through..."

Both women embraced, exchanging kisses, before she turned her attention to me. A glow of wonderment lit up her face.

"Maisie? My God, what a beauty you've blossomed into."

"Hello, Sarah," I answered, feeling a smile touch my lips.

Sarah was one of Mandy's closest friends and with a history of infertility, they had attended the same clinic - yet when Mandy and Stewart applied to foster me, they had succeeded - whereas Sarah and her husband had encountered barriers. After three years campaigning to adopt an autistic boy, only now did they know where they stood.

"How are things at work?" she quickly sidetracked.

"Work is fine." I gazed deep into her eyes, uncomfortably aware that it was largely thanks to her, and her role as an adoption reunion counsellor, that I had even landed myself in that job. "I-I've just been a little exhausted and in need of a break."

"Then why don't you and I catch another time," she soothed. "We could book a spa day if you like, it'll do you good. Have you ever been to Champneys?"

"I would love that," I heard myself sigh. "Will you text me?"

******

"I have a report. There is something you need to know about Maisie Bell..."

Thank God for pay-as-you-go mobiles, nothing the police could trace at a later date and no way to link his name to any conspiracy.

There was precious little chance of anyone seeing him here, either. A glimmer of moonlight peered through the clouds but not enough to penetrate the heavy darkness. Lurking on the edge of Binstead Wood, an area steeped in folklore, Cornelius could think of no better place to be having this discussion.

There were even whispers of satanic worship.

"Go on," his associate probed. "I'm intrigued."

That they had tailed her to a specific address on two occasions was not unusual. Only after some research, though, did he discover that house served another purpose: none other than the premises of a practitioner known as Hannah Adams.

He exhaled a long, painful sigh. "Miss Bell is having psychotherapy. You must know how the process works, if she's raking over childhood memories..."

If only she knew. Twenty years had passed since she had been fostered, yet never once had he stopped monitoring her. Now, finally, the tide appeared to be turning.

"What's the problem?" the voice on the other end of the phone mocked. "Don't tell me you're scared she might remember you, Cornelius?"

A cold smile curled his lips as he gazed into the billowing dark woods.

"She might if she talks to the police."

"Oh, come on!" A sniff emanated from the speaker. "There are so many allegations in the news, who's going to know what's true and what's fiction?"

Staring up at the night sky, the man watched the clouds part, allowing a splinter of moonlight to escape. It shone through the trees, as if fated to throw a spotlight on him, and he felt a shiver of fear pass over him.

Chapter Four

I should have been looking forward to coming home. Parking in Annandale Avenue, I saw the imposing brick and cream house awaiting me. Split into four roomy flats, mine was on the ground floor, the door just feet away from where I sat, but at first I couldn't drag myself from my car. Knots of tension gripped me as I stared at it, the light behind the windows mocking me.

What was causing all this anxiety?

Anyone would think a few relaxing days with my foster parents would chase the gloom away but if anything, my world felt bleaker. Mandy was right. I should be settled in a relationship. Yet without even the glimmer of a boyfriend on the horizon, I'd grown accustomed to being single.

I took a deep breath before letting myself into the house. The black and white floor tiles emitted a coolness, the sound of folk music from next door uplifting. Vlodek and Anna had moved here six months ago, a pleasant young Polish couple who spoke little English. Yet somehow we found a way to communicate.

Only as my eyes lifted to the stairs did my muscles turn to ice.

The people here were a mixed bunch; and whilst I had established some rapport with the Polish couple, I had nothing in common with Paula. A single mum on benefits, not only was she grossly overweight but wore a permanent scowl in my presence. Regrettably, it was her three-year old toddler, Jade, whose screams I had reported. But given some of the creeps Paula invited back here, I could not dispel the fear that one of them might be hurting her child.

Fumbling with my keys, I turned away from the stairs.

Over-reacting to Jade's screams was one problem, but I had to consider the repercussions, given my work status. *If I hadn't reported the screaming and Jade had been abused, the outcome would have been far worse.*

Whereas the evil looks Paula fired me I could live with.

This called to mind one final neighbour. An older gentleman lived upstairs too, a man who loathed Paula without question and had not been afraid to voice it.

Safe in the seclusion of my flat, I wondered whether to phone Jess. Jess was my best friend. Blonde, bubbly and as extrovert as I was introvert.

Jess would never forget the day we had encountered Mr Lacey. How the crash of a suitcase being dragged upstairs had halted us in our tracks. But there were no words to describe that frail, spidery old man struggling to lift it. His shoulders shook, the breath exploding from him in loud, laboured gasps.

"Hey! Do you need some help with that?" I called up to him.

Jess had looked at me as if I were crazy, but how could I turn a blind eye?

He was gaunt to the point of emaciation yet his neatly trimmed beard and mane of gold hair gave him a look of refinement. Neither of us could figure out how old he was, either. His tanned, heavily lined complexion suggested a considerable time spent in hotter climates, his eyes nearly hidden in the leathery folds of loose skin.

"I'll grab one end," Jess relented, "and you hang on tight to the other."

It weighed a ton.

"Blimey! What have you got in here, gold bars?"

"Old books," he muttered. "One forgets how heavy they are. I'm a collector."

His eccentric attire comprised a tweed jacket worn with brown cords and most unusual of all, a silk cravat around his neck. He reminded me more of a country squire than a city man.

But that was before he started coughing, a fit so violent, we nearly dropped the handles of the suitcase.

I asked if he was okay, the poor man bent double and groping in his pocket for a handkerchief.

"It'll pass," he spluttered, dabbing his slack lips.

The coughing had subsided but even as he folded his hankie away, a peppering of stains glued our eyes to it.

Rusty red in colour. Blood.

"Are you not well?" I gulped.

"I've not long had treatment for cancer... but please don't repeat that. I was lucky to get this flat, now all I want to do is to move on..."

I don't know who out of the two of us was more shocked, but the atmosphere shifted. Only then did I catch the intensity of his gaze, his dark eyes glinting under his bushy brows.

"You seem like nice people. I don't know much about your neighbours but it would help if they could be bothered to speak English!"

"They're okay!" I protested. "They work in the fields with lots of other East European workers. They're bound to communicate in their own language."

"I admire your tolerance but as for that creature next door..." His gaze flickered to Paula's flat. "You're not friends with *her* are you?"

"Um, we don't really see eye to eye," I whispered.

"No, I can't imagine you would," he smirked. "You do know she entertains men? Call me old fashioned but I deplore people with such low moral standards. Not the sort of environment to bring up a child in. I'm surprised she hasn't been put into care..." An unpleasant laugh followed. "She had the cheek to invite me in. Asked if *I fancied a bit of company* if you know what I mean."

My cheeks turned warm as I battled to figure out how we could escape.

"As if I'd associate myself with the likes of that tart!"

If only Jess hadn't burst out laughing. I could have died, mortified to imagine Paula might be in earshot.

"I'm sorry," he relented, "I can tell I've shocked you. What are your names by the way?"

I felt the scorch of his gaze again.

"Maisie... Maisie Bell and this is my friend, Jessica."

"Well, it's a pleasure to meet you, Maisie and Jessica. My name is Mr Lacey. Or Richard if you prefer."

Oh God. How Jess had giggled in the aftermath of that strange meeting, referring to him as a 'creepy old weirdo.'

If only I could forget the whole ugly business, but the things he'd said about Paula... a shiver of cold swept over me. Baleful and intolerant he might be, although on the other hand, he had endured a dreadful illness, and with no evidence to suggest he was better, perhaps this might account for his sourness.

Tonight, though, my flat felt too large and empty. Something about the hollow sofa screamed for another human to be sitting there and I was missing my foster parents. So I dialled Jess's mobile.

Hearing it go straight to voicemail, I felt another chokehold of bitterness but gulped the feeling back.

It had to be a new man.

With looks to die for, Jess couldn't help being a magnet; her highlighted golden hair tumbled in ripples around her shoulders, complimented by the bluest of eyes. Pushing aside my envy, I just hoped it would work out for her this time.

It didn't matter.

I had a bottle of Sauvignon Blanc chilling in my fridge, but first I needed to unpack. Resigning myself to the task, I dumped my holdall on my bed and unzipped it. There at the top nestled the last portion of Mandy's lasagne, which she had lovingly packed into a box for me. The sight made me smile but as I slid it into the freezer, a heaviness tugged my heart.

With everything in its proper place, I was hankering to unwind now.

So I reached for the wine. A film of dew clung to the bottle, a satisfying glug of liquid as I poured it... and oh, how it slipped down my throat, juicy and fresh, bursting with notes of passionfruit.

Next I switched the TV on, hoping to find entertainment. Catching the tail end of some drama, I stared at the screen blankly without taking in any of it.

The programme merged into the 10:00 News, the usual mundane politics... until one poignant story snapped my head upright.

'*A police watchdog is investigating claims that the Metropolitan Police covered up child abuse... allegations are centred on an apartment block near parliament, where it is alleged that boys in nearby care homes were taken for violent sex parties.*'

This had to be the case Stewart had mentioned.

My hands shook unsteadily as I tipped more wine into my glass.

What was it about these allegations that brought a dark shadow rolling into my mind? Something embedded deep in my psyche flashing up images of trees; the boy by the roadside, the cluster of oaks on my train journey...

Trees. Somehow it always came back to trees.

Nothing could fend off the fear snaking through me. That story seemed to depict everything abhorrent in my dark world, from Sam's disappearance to the cruelty Joe had endured. I couldn't kick out the memories.

So why did they haunt me now?

It had happened twenty years ago, for Christ's sake!

That night, I endured one of my nightmares.

They always started the same way. Trapped in a dark forest, I saw a spidery outline of trees circled above my head.

Next came the voices; a slither of whisperings, rising to a chant, and I started to panic. I sensed an evil encroaching presence.

An icy wind coiled its way through the trees, followed by a procession of hooded figures... but this was the point at which the dream always ended, as if a door guarding my innermost thoughts had been slammed shut; as if whatever lay on the other side was so horrific, even the psychotherapy had failed to extract it.

Chapter Five

Texting Sarah, we agreed to book our spa break before the week was up, yet since bumping into each other in Swanley, she must have detected my low mood. Proposing a day at Champneys was the very escape I needed, a chance to offload, but away from the ever mindful watch of my foster parents.

Drawn to the Hampshire Hills, I was relying on my Sat Nav to direct me to the health spa. Eventually I spied it in the distance; an idyllic expanse of countryside where despite the winter gloom, the honey coloured walls gleamed invitingly.

To my increasing delight, Sarah was in reception waiting for me.

"Maisie!" she called over. "It's lovely to see you! All you need do is check in and we can go straight through to the changing rooms."

"Wow!" I breathed, observing my surroundings, "it's amazing!"

Unable to resist, I pulled out my phone to take some photos. For even the reception displayed perfect symmetry with spotlights twinkling in the ceiling under a glass lantern roof. It highlighted the natural stone flooring, the clusters of sofas arranged in squares around tables, and an abundance of blushing orchids.

"I knew you'd love it," Sarah commented.

She watched in amusement as I took shots from every angle, zooming in on an orchid to capture its intricate beauty.

"That's definitely going on Instagram later."

"Come on, this way," she smiled at me. "Let's get changed and into that pool. It'll be lovely and relaxing in there."

There were even flowers in the changing rooms. Slipping into a complimentary robe, I relished the embrace of ultra-soft fluffy towelling. It made me feel like a child again. Then following Sarah into the corridor, I caught a glimpse of the pool. The crystal blueness took my breath away, and dropping my robe onto a lounger, I could not wait to slide my body into the warm water and start swimming.

Only as I sank into the bubbles of the jacuzzi afterwards did I let my guard slip. Sarah's eyes glittered like emeralds as she observed me. Even in her fifties, she glowed with energy.

"Are you happy doing what you do?" she asked me

"Of course," I placated her.

Closing my eyes, I rolled back my head to let the bubbles swirl around my shoulders, thinking of the opportunities she had presented me with. By the age of eighteen, I was studying for a diploma in marketing but with no clue what I wanted to do for a living. At the turn of the new millennium though, it seemed that business and commerce were the favoured career sectors; the only route for ambitious young people like me to maximise our successes in life.

But there lay the problem. Too money-orientated. I had no desire to be propelled around some faceless company whose only goal was to make profit.

"I can never thank you enough for taking me to that 'Child Protection Conference' in 2005," I added. "If it wasn't for you, I might never have met Margaret. Or applied to work for West Sussex County Council."

Margaret Jones, my current boss, was just one of the many social workers Sarah had befriended. Being part of a huge support network, she knew dozens of like-minded people, including the family liaison officer who had dealt with my own case.

"I've even started helping out at their fostering information evenings. There was one the other week..." An unsettling fear filled my mind as I spoke but it must have shown in my face.

"So why the visit to Swanley?" Sarah probed. "Tell me to mind my own business, but I couldn't help noticing how spooked you looked that day."

"Can I tell you something?" I mumbled. Risking a sideways glance, I shifted over to her side of the tub. "I feel as if I'm going crazy but I called the police on my way home, the other day. I-I haven't even told my folks yet... but I thought I saw someone. A boy stranded on the edge of the woods, who I recognised."

Sarah's face showed no emotion as she stared into the frothing cauldron of bubbles we were immersed in. "Go on."

Pleased to have someone to confide in, I related the whole incident. That Mark had been so intuitive, acknowledging the mind-bending effects of exhaustion.

"A hallucination?" Sarah pondered.

I bit my lip. "It had to be, didn't it? There was no one out there but it frightened me all the same."

"Oh, Maisie! First the nightmares and now this?"

"There's something else," I kept whispering. "I know this sounds even crazier but you know I took the train to Swanley? I was freaked out by some trees. A clump of mature oaks on the edge of a wood. Did Mandy ever tell you about my phobia?"

"She did mention it, yes," Sarah nodded. "Why do you ask?"

"I had a flashback," I answered numbly.

Even the heat of the jacuzzi could not dispel the shivers running over me. Sinking deeper into the bubbles, I coiled my arms around my shoulders.

The resurrection of Sam was one issue – but to think of what Joe had suffered…

Sarah's eyes met mine with a twinkle. "D'you want to talk about it over a coffee?"

As the morning advanced, I found it easier to share my worries. Not only was Sarah a good listener, but the ambience of the health spa induced a tranquillising effect, the restaurant no exception. A gentle glow of light bathed the walls, bringing a shine to the beechwood floorboards.

Picking up the thread of conversation where we had left it, I quickly found myself reminiscing about Joe again - from the memories extracted in therapy to the scene I had relived on my train journey.

"How strange. You talked a lot about this Joe when Mandy and Stewart first fostered you," Sarah told me. "She was quite concerned."

"She never said!"

Eyes lowered, Sarah stirred her cappuccino. "You don't remember? She got in touch with the children's home. Wanted to ask Joe over for tea one day, so they could meet him in person."

"Seriously?"

"If only the man in charge hadn't been so openly hostile..."

"What?" I spluttered.

Her face twisted with the effort of explaining it. "He was reluctant to let Joe out of his sight, on account of his behaviour. Said something like no respectable middle-class family would want anything to do with that boy."

I lowered my cup unsteadily, drops of coffee splashing over the rim.

"What a bastard," I whispered before I could stop myself. "Okay, so maybe Joe was a bit rough around the edges, but he was a nice boy. He did nothing to deserve such cruelty, and that's what I saw in my flashback. He was covered in bruises from a thrashing Mortimer's bully boys gave him..."

"But that's a criminal offence," Sarah gasped, "perhaps the real reason they didn't want to let him out. They were worried he might tell someone."

"Yes, but that's not all," I shuddered. "Joe knew something..."

Pain pierced my heart as I considered what Sarah had told me of Mandy's proposal, the cogs in my mind turning faster.

"I wish Mandy had told me this."

"Maybe she didn't want to build up your hopes," Sarah counselled me. "Given what you saw, it's obvious he needed help but whatever that man said, Mandy wasn't buying it. She was furious! Here they were trying to reach out to another defenceless child... if I remember rightly, they contacted Social Services."

I clung to her stare. "Any idea what the outcome was?"

"Well, this is where it gets complicated," Sarah said. "The social worker assigned to Joe's case said he had left the home. He ran away."

I took another sip of coffee, one part of my mind battling to take this on board, whilst desperately scouring the holes in my memory.

Joe ran away?

"She was an acquaintance of mine and had no reason to lie. What I'm more concerned about though, is the reason your friend ran away."

"Mortimer despised him," I mumbled, thrown back in time to my last therapy session. "Joe could have reported his cruelty but there was something else going on, something creepy and I'm sure it's connected to my dreams; a scene that takes place in a forest..."

"Hmm," Sarah pondered. "That makes sense. Just before your flashback, you saw oak trees and you've had a fear of forests since your teens."

"Yes," I whispered.

As the truth of her words sank in, a ball of fear gripped my stomach. For whatever Joe knew, he had taken a brutal punishment trying to protect me from it. Just the look in his eye had conveyed a warning.

Maisie, Joe and Sam. Maisie.

We were three kids in a care home. And somewhere buried in the dark twisted roots of that care home, lurked the key to all our problems.

"How are you feeling now?" Sarah asked me.

"Better," I smiled. "Thanks for suggesting this, it's a gorgeous place to chill out, and I really needed to have a proper chat."

By the time we reached the spa, I was still thinking about what she had told me, revelations that held me mesmerised.

So maybe life had panned out okay for Joe, after his escape from the care home.

The thought of my parents' intervention stirred ripples of love – but how strange they had never mentioned it. I turned to Sarah and saw her eyeing me curiously.

"I'm fine, really," I reassured her. "Just sat here wondering why so many kids are in care, when there are people out there wanting to adopt them."

Relaxing in the dry heat of the sauna, my muscles softened like marshmallow.

But Sarah didn't answer straight away. Turning my head, I caught a faraway look in her eye, as if her mind was in another zone.

"So how are things with you?" I added. "I gather you were looking into fostering yourself..."

She clutched her robe tighter around her body.

"Connor," she murmured. "Yes, we went through years of assessments to get this far and we very nearly gave up."

"So tell me," I coaxed her. "I've offloaded enough of my problems, now it's your turn. Why did the authorities make it so difficult?"

Chapter Six

Sarah would never forget the grim words voiced by his social worker.

'Connor Wilson. Born in Amsterdam, mother worked as a prostitute and served four years in prison, where she developed a 'class A' drug addiction.'

She exhaled a sad sigh. Having spent a lifetime working as an adoption reunion counsellor, whose principal goal was to help adoptees find their natural birth parents, she was moved by Connor's plight.

Yet how could she tell him?

"Connor was a strange boy. Maybe it stemmed from his autism, but whatever it was, I wanted to help him. He seemed so lost, so locked into himself, he needed careful handling."

"But he was kept in a residential care home?" Maisie breathed.

"Connor's been in and out of residential care homes for most of his life."

That a boy so fragile had been confined in a care home brought another wave of sorrow. In all the years she had worked alongside Social Services, Sarah had come across some tragic cases and Connor's was no exception.

"They chose to hide his identity *because* of his parents. Monsters, both of them, but I'll spare you the details. Irrespective of who they were though, he was an innocent child. Pure and unblemished, the reason Peter and I applied to adopt him. We just wanted to give him a decent start in life."

"Well, that's fair enough! Surely kids are better off *out* of care homes."

"Yes, but there were complications. By the time we approached Social Services, that boy was damaged. There was a time when the authorities would do anything to keep a child with their natural birth parents, but it didn't work out. Connor's mum rejected him when he was six. She just wouldn't bond with him and consequently dumped him straight back into care."

Her face flushed with anger.

As if the poor mite hadn't suffered enough stigma with his autism, she couldn't imagine how deeply this rejection had hurt him.

"Poor kid," Maisie pondered. "So what's he like personality-wise?"

"Different," Sarah reflected. "Quiet, withdrawn, which is understandable, but it's his lack of communication skills that presents a challenge."

She took a moment to reflect. Cold to the point of wooden, maybe Connor's autism could account for his aloofness, but there was more. He had built a wall around himself, so that no one else in the world could hurt him.

"No one could get a response out of him, not a laugh nor even a smile. He didn't like being touched or hugged, which some parental figures find hard, and don't get me started on his more challenging behaviour..."

Maisie nodded intuitively. Working in a fostering environment herself, she was all too familiar with similar cases.

"I feel as if I'm rambling. He may have complex personality issues but he is intelligent. He's achieved high grades in every school he's attended. Loves nature and science, has a yearning to understand the world all around him..."

"But I don't get it," Maisie broke in. "How come you and your husband had to fight so hard to try and help him?"

"I was coming to that," Sarah sighed, wriggling into a sitting position.

Much as she loved the sauna, the heat was beginning to stifle her. Drawn to the glacial shine of the plunge pool, she slid unsteadily off the bench.

"I need to cool down first," she added, dropping herself into the water.

Immersed in the chill, she caught her breath. It felt invigorating, bringing a much needed clarity to her thoughts.

"What were you going to tell me?" Maisie mumbled.

As she hovered on the edge of the plunge pool, Sarah couldn't help but think how innocent she looked. The whiteness of her robe magnified her pureness, the chestnut shine of her hair.

She smiled gently. "You want to know why we were met with resistance? It was because of my husband. He was abused as a teenager."

"No!" Maisie gasped. "I'm so sorry..."

"Don't let on I told you," she continued. "He is very sensitive about it, but as you know, in some scenarios, abuse victims turn into abusers. It took months of psychiatric assessment to convince the authorities he wasn't damaged in that way and as a trained counsellor, he's helped dozens of victims deal with similar emotional traumas. Yet there was still this tiny seed of uncertainty."

Maisie stared back horrified. "That must have been awful for you."

"Yes, but we've moved on. Passed all the medical checks, done the training and we finally got to spend time getting to know Connor. The next hoop we had to jump through was convincing them we could cope. But with parents like his, people feared he was born evil..."

"But every child deserves a chance," Maisie protested.

"That's what we said," she nodded. "It's a shame Social Services needed a little more persuasion."

Moving onto the loungers, Sarah took a moment to compose herself, the spa working its magic.

"Let me tell you what happened in his last foster home," she continued. "You know I mentioned his more challenging behaviour?"

"Go on," Maisie pressed.

Gazing into the distance, Sarah recalled the story. "He has a tendency to hide. It's a type of mental shut-down to avoid social stress, and not unusual in autistic children. From what I heard, he used to spend hours hiding in a tree, even after dark, but on one occasion he went missing for a whole day. His foster carers couldn't cope with the worry."

"Well, I guess that would cause some concern," Maisie argued.

"Yes, but they handled it all wrong..." Conscious of others moving into the area, she tilted her head closer to whisper. "If only they'd tried to empathise with him. Let him build a den in the garden, give him some personal space, instead of trying to control him. That was their mistake. They locked him inside the house."

Denying Connor a chance to detach himself did them no favours. With his stress levels soaring to fever pitch, he must have thought he was being punished for something. And Sarah couldn't help feeling that perhaps, if they had tried to understand him better, the inevitable storm would have been avoided.

Sarah took a gulp. "He lifted the biggest chair in the room and lobbed it against the patio doors. Smashed his way out. I know it sounds awful, but they shouldn't have tried to constrain him. The upshot is the police were called, Connor arrested and that was the end of it. It traumatised the whole family."

"They didn't want him back then," Maisie finished dryly.

A cynical laugh escaped her lips. "No way! But in the meantime, Peter and I had been reading up on the autistic spectrum and everything clicked into place. We convinced the authorities to let us meet him... at least allow him to spend an afternoon with us."

Her heart squeezed inside her chest. Yet with another black mark on his record, Connor's meltdown had been one more factor to add to a long list of negatives. Who would want to foster him now?

"At fifteen, the only prospect left was to keep him in residential care, until they finally considered our application. The day we met Connor, his social worker was present, as if they didn't quite have the faith to leave him alone with us. But we offered him a quiet room to sit in and a stack of National Geographic magazines... and it was amazing how quickly he settled down."

She felt the warmth of a smile spread across her lips. No one expected miracles but giving him that much needed personal space had nudged the barriers away.

"He made no secret of the fact he liked our home, especially the books, and that's what he told his social worker. He didn't want to go back to the children's home."

Even Maisie knew it had taken them three years.

"To think, he was ultimately the one who chose us!"

30

Chapter Seven

I couldn't quite find the words to express my feelings; only that something about Connor's predicament tugged at my heart strings. I confess, it was cases like Connor's that had drawn me to work in fostering in the first place.

"What an amazing story," I remarked, "so how is it panning out?"

"Connor hasn't changed much. He is still very much an introvert."

Mulling over her depiction though, I could not shift my own personal darkness.

Quiet and withdrawn.

I had never forgotten my arrival at the children's home. A day when all I wanted to do was retreat. Shut out all the cruelty in the world.

Doesn't like being touched.

Was this a symptom of his autism or was there a more sinister reason? You see, I too shied away from affection. I feared intimacy. Something I dared not admit to my foster parents.

"You should come over and meet him," Sarah added warmly. "You know you're always welcome to visit us in Rosebrook."

"I'd love to. I hate to think of any child left at the mercy of a care home. So how many times did you see Connor over the years?"

"I lost count," Sarah mumbled. "As you know, it takes many sessions for adults to bond with kids, especially when applying to foster them."

I frowned, unable to fathom what it was about those words that stirred some deep underlying emotion.

Moving around the spa, we spent the last hour to-ing and fro-ing between sauna, steam room and plunge pool.

Yet all the while we were discussing Connor's case, I could not escape the terrors embedded in my own psyche.

******

Hannah Adams. Registered Psychotherapist and Counsellor. West Sussex.
Client: Maisie Bell
6th March 2015

"Come through," Hannah said. "Sit down and make yourself comfy."

After a much needed heart-to-heart with Sarah, it made sense to get another therapy appointment booked sooner rather than later. I had left Champneys on a high note, my mind as lucid as it would ever be, and with none of the emotional baggage getting in the way.

Coaxed into her therapy room, I breathed in the scent of lilies before lowering myself into a reclining chair. Deeply padded with velvet upholstery, this had become a sacred place now. Within minutes I would lapse into a mild hypnotic trance and allow the portals of my inner consciousness to be prised open.

On this occasion I welcomed it.

"I want you to close your eyes," she began, "switch off your mind and relax. Take some deep breaths - four seconds in - ten seconds out..."

The lights dimmed. I heard a swish of paper as she turned the page of her note pad and gradually my heart began to slow.

"Where would you like to begin?"

Where indeed? The nightmares had been disturbing me for weeks now, a resonance that stayed with me, long into the evening, as if the danger had never really gone away.

"Last time, you told me about Joe," she prompted, "your friend in the care home. I got the impression he meant the world to you."

"Joe had a heart of gold," I mused. "Despite his troubled background, he was one of the kindest, bravest boys I ever met. I wish we had stayed in touch."

"So why didn't you?"

"Once I was fostered it was impossible. Kids weren't allowed private phone calls and even if I wrote a letter, there was no guarantee he would get it. In fact, I've only just learned my foster mum tried reaching out to him. She wanted to invite him around for tea but he was barred!"

"And this was down to the man in charge, was it? Mr. Mortimer? You described him as 'a nasty man' and said he hurt Joe."

"That's right," I mumbled.

An icy leaden weight bound me to my chair. I didn't want to think about that flashback, but it insisted on its own presence, an invasive shadow crouching on the edge of my mind.

"There's something else I recalled," I began, and told her the rest.

The million dollar question was why Joe had locked me in the laundry room. More to the point, why had he taken such a brutal punishment?

Describing the scene wasn't easy but I had to force myself to keep talking. An image of his stricken face tore through the void of darkness, a zigzag of black welts.

"He looked so broken that day, as if all the fight had been beaten out of him."

"I'm sorry," Hannah sighed. "You obviously cared very deeply for this boy and yet you were powerless to do anything to help him?"

"Yes," I replied.

"So what would you say to Joe now, if you met up again?"

"I'd ask him what had happened, and how sorry I am he was hurt. Joe and Sam were the only boys I ever really bonded with, you see, but Sam disappeared and I have no idea where Joe went. He ran away, that's all I know. He could be married with kids by now..."

"Yes," Hannah murmured and I could hear the smile in her voice. "There is every chance Joe has moved on, so stop torturing yourself. You can't hold yourself responsible for what happened to him, Maisie. But what about you?"

"Me," I whispered. "What about me? I came out of it okay, didn't I?"

"But did you?" she pushed. "You still harbour painful feelings, or this wouldn't be on your mind to the extent it is. So tell me... when you say 'these were the only two boys you ever bonded with,' does this mean there was no one else you trusted?"

My brow buckled into a frown as I considered her question.

"It's funny you should ask, but I don't think there was, which is something my foster parents brought up too. They can't understand why I'm not in a relationship."

"What about your teens? There must have been a boyfriend or two, surely?"

I'm not sure there was.

Growing up an anxious adolescent, I tended to shy away from boys at my secondary school.

"They were more like friends who happened to be boys. I was so aloof, I didn't have a proper boyfriend until I went to college."

"College... right, so can you tell me how you felt when you first met him?"

Tears pooled behind my eyelids. I didn't want to think about my 'first love' but the memory was rising faster than a tsunami.

"There were lots of nice-looking male students at FE college, and they were so much more mature than the boys I'd met at school. There was one in particular though. Simon."

As I said his name, the man himself leapt into my thoughts. Tall, slender, broad in the shoulders, he moved with a natural loose-limbed grace. Where other boys seemed awkward, Simon behaved as if he didn't give a toss, and it was that easy-going confidence I liked about him.

"We were huddled in the cafeteria when a group of boys joined our table, Simon among them. I remember how excited I was, because all my friends fancied him. He could have had his pick of any one of us but it was me he singled out..."

For all that he seemed not to care about a thing, there was something in Simon that caught me off guard. Oh, those deep blue eyes... the way they shone when I introduced myself.

'Is that your natural hair colour?' he asked me. 'It's stunning.'

I remember laughing. 'Well, yeah! Did you think I'd dyed it?'

Stupid answer! I felt a flood of heat in my face when I should have been swelling with the compliment. Grinning at my coyness, he inched his chair a little closer, the musky essence of his aftershave sending flutters through my stomach.

"He seemed to like the fact I was one of the quieter ones," I said to Hannah. "I mean, I didn't wear much makeup but he said he preferred the natural look and was intrigued when I told him I had been fostered..."

"How fast did the relationship develop then?" Hannah asked.

"You mean did we - we - sleep together?" I faltered.

It happened within two weeks. I had never fancied anyone so much, the way he flirted and laughed with me. Every date brought a warm bubble of anticipation and I loved the way he kissed me. The smell of him, the touch of his skin made my head spin... it was inevitable he would want to take things further.

"At eighteen, I was late losing my virginity, but it was bound to happen one day..." A sob caught my throat. "For someone who claimed to love me though, there was so little tenderness when it did happen."

"Maisie, I hate to pry but can you bear to describe what went wrong?"

A blanket of shame clung to me now. "I've always blamed myself but I-I sort of froze. Every part of me tensed up, my mind in a very dark place..." *I squeezed my eyes shut to block the tears.* "A few kind words might have helped. I wish he had cuddled me, tried to comfort me, but if anything he seemed angry."

His harsh voice barged into my thoughts even now: 'For Christ's sake, just relax will you, can't you at least pretend you're enjoying it?'

I felt wounded.

But as the walls of amnesia started to crumble, so the horror continued to escalate: the way he thrust into me was almost mechanical, as if I were no more than a means to an end.

"I just wasn't enjoying it. There was no emotional attachment. It felt like a part of me had shut down, and I zoned out. Just lay there, waiting for it to be over..."

"But that sounds quite traumatic," Hannah tried to pacify me, "and why do you assume it was your fault? Maybe he wasn't as experienced as you thought."

"Maybe," I sobbed, "but at the end of the day, I was the one who hated it and that's why he got upset. I hurt his pride..."

What I didn't want to tell her was it felt more like consenting to a rape.

A tear squeezed its way out but I wiped it away. To think how I had worshipped Simon, how thrilled I'd been to be going out with him.

"Don't be so harsh on yourself," Hannah persisted. "From what you describe, it strikes me he wasn't that gentle with you."

"No," I whispered. "He wasn't, and that's what killed our relationship."

There was more, I knew that now, but how could I explain it? That on the night in question I was afflicted by a darker fear that had nothing to do with disappointment. More a sense of victimhood. That to me, sex embodied nothing more than power, degradation and pain.

"Do you want to know what was really hurtful?" I choked. "He told his friends I was a rubbish lay."

******

By the time I left I was still tearful, but aware of an overwhelming force of anger. It called to mind everything Sarah had said about Connor building a wall around himself.

Wasn't this exactly what I had done over the years?

Fearful to allow anyone to get close to me, I had grown a shell as thick as a turtle's.

I never wanted to come across as 'needy', but looking back, I'm sure Simon could have handled the situation better and as for the way he insulted me... I should have kicked him in the balls.

Sure, there had been other men in my life, but in the aftermath of that experience, I was lacking in sexual confidence. If a man tried it on too soon, I turned into an ice queen, the one thing I had never wanted to admit to my foster parents.

Because it wasn't so much *I hadn't found anyone I liked enough to settle down with*. I was scared stiff, my single status at thirty-two living proof I was still damaged and lived in fear of intimate relationships.

Chapter Eight

"Are you sure you're going to be okay?" Hannah asked. "You know you can always talk to me. Any more flashbacks, I'm only on the end of a phone."

"Thanks, Hannah." I forced a smile.

Yes, that session had been quite an emotional upheaval.

Except I was no closer to understanding what lay deeper.

Leaving her house, I caught the shadow of a black car lingering on the periphery. It hadn't been there before, and I barely took it in, my mind a maelstrom of personal worries.

Probably Hannah's next appointment.

Then, at last, I switched my mobile back on. Ping after ping, the notifications burst from the handset like machine gun fire. I stared at the screen and sighed at all the missed calls. A second later, it started ringing.

"Maisie!" a voice shrieked from the earpiece. "At last! I must have left a zillion texts! Where the bloody hell have you been?"

"Jess," I spluttered, the guilt coursing through my mind. "How are you? I'm so sorry I never got back to you, but I booked some time off work to visit my family. Then something else came up. I guess I've been a bit pre-occupied."

"And you never thought to switch your phone on?"

I bit my tongue. Of course, I always had it *switched off* during therapy, a matter Jess wasn't even aware of. I just could not bring myself to tell her. Best friend or not, Jess would be desperate to hear all the juicy bits – today's session, for example – and I had a hell of a lot more psychological issues to resolve before I was ready for anything like that. So everything that emerged in Hannah's therapy room would stay under wraps for now.

"You can talk!" I tried to humour her. "When I called you the other night your phone went straight to voicemail. So what's the latest gossip?"

"Oh Maisie..." There was no denying the smugness tucked in her voice. "I can't wait to tell you."

Pausing mid-step, I knew what was coming. "Go on then, who is he?"

"How do you know it's a man?" she laughed. "Ten out of ten though. That hunky jazz musician, Steve, texted me and we had the most amazing date."

"Really?" I said. "Lucky you! Anywhere nice?"

"Steve lives in Portsmouth, a bit of a trek from Bognor, so he only went and booked a romantic love nest in the New Forest! You should have seen it,

Maisie. Marble pillars and chandeliers, champagne in the bedroom, a whirlpool bath... In fact we've only been apart for one night since, and I'm missing him already."

"Sweet," I kept indulging her. "I hope you took some pictures."

"I did. I sent you a couple but you've obviously been too *pre-occupied* to look at them..."

"Oh, stop it," I tittered. "I'll look later! Give me a chance."

"I saw you posted on Instagram," she challenged me. "So what's with the orchids? Where were they taken?"

"Champneys." I smiled with the memory. "I bumped into a family friend in Swanley, who suggested a spa day, and that's the other reason I've been offline. Google it, Jess, it's stunning! We could book a pampering day ourselves for just the two of us."

"I know Champneys. I've been there and you're right, it's heavenly!"

Phone glued to my ear, I kept walking. Just five more minutes and I would be back at my flat. I had to admit it, the sound of my friend's voice felt nourishing, like a breath of fresh air...

"What are you up to tonight then?" I asked. "Fancy popping out for a drink?"

An uncomfortably long pause siphoned all the hope from my heart.

"Um - I'd love to," she faltered, "but I can't. It's Friday night and Steve's got a gig in Midhurst. I promised I'd go along and support him. Any chance we could catch up another time?"

"Yeah, sure," I responded, keeping my voice light.

I didn't want to sound disappointed but the thought of spending another night alone in my flat seemed ever more daunting.

That feeling was exacerbated as soon as I returned home. I had only just stepped into the hallway when Paula almost barged into me. The two of us froze, the air choked with tension.

"Evening, Paula," I greeted her curtly.

"Well, you've got some front," she spat. "You two-faced bitch."

"I beg your pardon?"

Thrusting her head close until it loomed inches from mine, she lowered her voice to a snarl. "I 'eard ya. You and that old fart upstairs. Having a good laugh about me, were ya?"

"You've got it all wrong," I protested. "I wasn't laughing..."

"Yes, you were," Paula sneered. "I 'eard ya! And for the record, I wouldn't entertain that miserable old git if he offered us a million quid, so tell him that the next time you have one of yer cosy little chats..."

With a final glare, she brushed past me and out of the building.

I exhaled a bitter sigh. I loathed confrontations, no matter how small, and the toxic exchange had left me cringing. Perhaps I should have stuck up for her; perhaps I might have seized the opportunity to tell her exactly what I thought of Mr Lacey.

Spiteful, cantankerous, bigoted.

Except he was the last person I wanted to be reminded of right now.

The evening passed in torturous slowness. Devoid of Jess's company, I found myself binge watching old comedies on 'Dave.'

Anything to avoid the news.

At one point I even contemplated taking a walk down to the Waverley, since I was bound to bump into someone familiar.

On the other hand, did I really want to risk being surrounded by strangers? It wasn't the same without Jess, an expert in small talk and always the one to get the conversation rolling... How I wished I could be more like her.

I retired to bed that night with so many thoughts racing around my head.

It was nice to hear from Jess, even if she had rung for no other reason than to boast about her love life. True, she'd made no mention of the steamy sex, but that hadn't stopped it oozing from her voice with every other description.

Champagne in the bedroom, a whirlpool bath.

And how could I forget 'Hunky Steve?' I could picture him at the Waverley on the night their band had played there. Steve with the blue eyes and the pierced ears. Steve who wore his glossy brown hair in a man bun, hassling me for her mobile number.

I felt a prick of envy but it was hard not to fantasise.

Oh, to be swept into a whirlwind romance like Jess. The stuff you read about in fiction, of finding your perfect love.

At the same time the memories drawn from therapy were still haunting me – not just my disastrous first relationship, but the stain of degradation that clung to me every time I thought about intimacy. Why it prevailed even now still baffled me, and for some reason, threads of the conversation I had shared with Sarah drifted back to me.

What dark secrets hid behind the dreams and the flashbacks?

Head heavy from too much wine, I gradually began to doze off. Exhaustion dragged heavily on my mind and my limbs, my chest knotted with anxiety.

The last thing I recalled was Paula's bloated red face - her taunts about Mr Lacey - the echo of Jess's laughter...

Chapter Nine

There was no escaping it. The Pandora's box had been opened a crack, and I could no longer slam the lid down.

The forest began to materialise, more threatening than ever. Trees swayed in the breeze. The sound of whispers pulsated through the darkness, while in another secret corner of my mind lurked an even greater fear.

Those strange hooded figures were coming for us.

A red ribbon fluttered in my mind's eye before something else jolted me. An icy breeze skimmed across my bare stomach, where my dress was rucked up. With the realisation that my body was exposed, a terror sharpened my senses, the whispers beginning to form words.

"For Christ's sake, just relax will you..."

"Simon?"

His voice lapped on the shore of my consciousness, yet it was tangled up in my dream. Sure, it had been very dark when he leant over me.

Staring up above though, I saw nothing but bare branches threaded across the night sky like capillaries, a circle of grasping fingers. Trapped in the forest, I had no idea what I was doing there.... only that it was no longer Simon bearing down on me.

The shape of a hood loomed close. Drawing in a gasp, I crammed my lungs with air as the horror suddenly struck me, and a moment later I cried out.

"No!"

My head whipped sideways, but my arms would not move. Looking down, I noticed the red ribbon again, wound around my wrists to restrain me. The whole forest seemed to shudder, before another whisper lashed through the darkness.

"Silence her!"

Semi-delirious with shock, I felt a palm press over my mouth, followed by the sting of a needle. But that voice was too deep to be Simon's, a voice that chilled me to the bone.

******

I stirred in my sleep, hands clawing at the duvet, until the scene dissolved into a haze of daylight. Staring at my bedside clock, I gasped when I saw what time it was. 10:00? It was rare for me to sleep so late.

Taking deep breaths, I felt relief flood through me. The welcome magnolia walls of my bedroom unfolded around me, but even as my eyes followed the curls of stencilling, fragments of the dream came back.

It had been worse than ever before.

Desperate to use the loo, I flung back the covers and staggered towards the bathroom. As soon as I closed the door I started shaking. Lying beneath those spidery trees, I had never felt more vulnerable. This was precisely the feeling I had described to Hannah.

A feeling of victimhood.

The dream had left me feeling as violated as the night Simon took my virginity, and I couldn't escape the idea that it had originated from something real. My mind was drawn to a party Joe had tried to shield me from; six girls, myself included, driven to a remote place, oblivious of how the event would end.

If only I could recapture the detail.

Stripping off my nightie, I climbed into the bath and turned the shower on, still thinking about my youth. Even then, the concept of sex had unnerved me, listening to my school friends bragging about their conquests.

'How far did you go last night?'

I, on the other hand, flushed at the thought of a boy touching me, never mind 'going the whole way.' I'd never really understood why I shied away from relationships, but deep down something niggled. First the nightmares, now this regression into childhood.

Was it possible we had been drugged? Ferried to some secluded forest where no one could witness what was happening?

Flesh icy with dread, I turned the shower up, relishing the blast of hot water as it bit into my skin. But it did little to calm the tremors running through me. As soon as I stepped out of the bathroom, the fear was back. It clung to the edges of my world like tar, something foul, black and evil.

Eventually, I had to drag myself out of my tortured reverie. With the sun blazing down brightly, there seemed no point wasting the day. The supermarket beckoned, so I gathered up my shopping bags. Planning something nice to cook would be a welcome diversion, but more than anything, I craved a walk along the seafront.

Only the salty fresh air would blow the cobwebs away, and while I was there, I would visit the homeless men camped out in one of the beach shelters.

With that thought, I pushed a tray of frozen sausage rolls into the oven.

Those guys had so little to smile about. It had been a severe winter with sub-zero temperatures, not to mention the cruel frosts, sleet and drizzle. But where others in the town scorned them, I liked to donate food occasionally; my simple philosophy being that if I could ease the burden of misery for a few, it would make a difference in the world, no matter how small.

I allowed myself a grim smile. Whatever life threw at me, there were others far worse off. At least I had a job and a home. Even if I lost everything, there were people who would take care of me. People who loved me.

Yet what did those poor souls in the beach shelter have?

By the time I had my boots on, a savoury aroma was billowing from the kitchen, reminding me of my sausage rolls. Rescuing them from the oven, I tipped them onto a square of tin foil, wrapping them snugly to keep them warm.

There was a bite of cold in the air on Bognor Seafront, despite the onset of March.

I quickened my pace. The white posts at the bottom of the road led to the prom, the blueness of the sea dazzling. Oblivious to passing faces, I followed the line of people snaking along the tarmac. Gulls sat like sentinels upon a column of breakwaters yet today it was high tide. Glancing out to sca, I heard an explosion of froth as the waves hit the shore, and the rattle of pebbles that followed.

Distant voices echoed around me, the shouts of children intermingling. But I didn't linger. Continuing my way along the prom, I concentrated on my goal, heading up the slope towards the beach shelter.

"Hello, there," a voice called across. "Beautiful day, isn't it?"

Ambling over to the shelter, I was cheered by a familiar face; skin weathered from the cold, snowy white hair and a pair of blue eyes twinkling up at me.

"Good afternoon," I replied. "I don't know how you survive in this cold, but here's something to warm you up."

He rubbed his hands together before gazing lovingly at the tupperware box I held out to him. Peeling back the lid, his smile brightened as he breathed in the smell of warm pastry.

"Cor," he mumbled. "Thank you..." and grabbing one of the sausage rolls, he took a hearty bite then passed the box to his mate.

"Bloody marvellous," his neighbour mumbled. "Cheers, love!"

Returning their smiles, I glimpsed the shadow of a seagull soaring overhead. My eyes followed its motion – a scatter of crumbs dispersed in the breeze – and that was when I noticed the third man.

I had seen him before.

A frown twisted my features as for several seconds the men munched in silence, the box passed along the line. The last time I'd visited, he had barely registered. Curled up in a sleeping bag, face hidden, he was oblivious to the

41

world all around him. Yet today he was awake. A navy hoodie shadowed the top half of his face as he slouched on the bench rolling a cigarette.

But in the moment he turned sideways, I experienced a stab of recognition. The shape of his nose had a startling effect; a crooked nose, one that might have been broken. Even with several days' beard growth, nothing could detract from his profile, the chiselled cheekbones, a distinctive ridge to his brow.

"Bless you, Maisie," the first man mumbled, cramming the last chunks of pastry into his mouth.

I heard a sharp intake of breath.

"Maisie. I used to know a girl called Maisie."

The whisper hung on the man's lips.

Heart racing, I stared back wildly, shock anchoring me to the promenade. Only then did I feel the power of his liquid brown eyes as they finally rose to meet mine.

"Oh my God," I gasped.

A riot of thoughts streamed through my head, all of them a jumble.

"You're not... Joe, are you?"

Chapter Ten

At first we couldn't tear our eyes apart, drinking each other in. Twenty years peeled away like onion skin, exposing our childhood past.

"Maisie," he croaked. "What the hell are you doing here?"

"I live here," I responded in disbelief. "So what about you? How did you end up sleeping rough?"

"It's a long story..."

His voice trailed off and rising from the bench he took a first tentative step towards me. His hair looked a little greasy but as dark and untamed as I recalled, his frame still wiry. He had grown a few inches taller, his shoulders broader, yet there was no mistaking Joe Winterton... The same Joe I had befriended in that care home.

He risked a smile and at last my heart began to slow itself.

Oh, that smile.

His face had spread out and become more manly, giving an element of balance to his wonky features, his mouth not as wide, his nose no longer quite so prominent. I desperately wanted to throw my arms around him but something held me back.

"How are you?" I mumbled, unable to think of anything else to say.

He stank of stale cigarette smoke and BO but none of that mattered. My long lost friend had arisen from the ashes, and at a time when I needed him most.

"What happened to you?" I kept mumbling. "You look so thin!"

Fine lines feathered the corners of his eyes, his skin ingrained with dirt, a vision that had me yearning to look after him.

"You two know each other?" a voice chuckled from the beach shelter.

"Yes," I gasped. "Joe and I go way back. We met as kids..."

"We were twelve," Joe reminded me.

"Shall we walk?" I suggested, wary of their scrutiny. "See you later, guys, but we've got an awful lot of catching up to do."

Wandering away from the beach hut, I felt a knot tighten my throat as another emotion surfaced. *Panic.*

It seemed incredible that Joe could materialise like this, after everything I had discussed with my therapist.

So what would you say to Joe now, if you met up again?

Right now, I didn't know what to say. Was it possible I'd somehow registered Joe's presence before today? Might some tiny spark of recognition have stirred my deeper memories? Looking at him now, I felt a chill slip down my spine.

"I-it's lovely to see you again," I faltered.

"Is it?" Joe muttered. "I wish it were under better circumstances."

As he shuffled along the prom, I saw a stoop to his shoulders, the gait of a broken man. An uneasy silence prevailed.

"So what went wrong?" I kept pressing. "How did you end up homeless and in Bognor of all places?"

As the prom widened, the crowds began to thin out at last. Here there were fewer people to take notice of us, and I led him towards a stone bench.

Joe let out a sigh and opening his tobacco pouch, extracted the cigarette he had been rolling earlier. "I've been homeless for a couple of years now, bumming around from town to town. London, Brighton. The authorities move me on, I drift a little further along the coast, and that's how I ended up here."

"I'm sorry. Sounds like you've fallen on hard times."

"Don't be," Joe snapped. "A shit lot has happened since we were kids, Maisie."

"Like what?" His tone was warning me away, but I couldn't help asking. "Tell me."

His rueful gaze met mine. "I'm not like you. You were fostered and I guess it all worked out for you. I mean, look at you! A smart, modern day woman and dare I say it, a beautiful one?" He betrayed a ghost of a grin. "Or is that not PC these days?"

My heart leapt with the compliment. "I had a lucky escape. My foster parents turned out to be wonderful people - and I work in a fostering department myself now with West Sussex County Council."

"Fostering," Joe echoed, "for kids like us?" A whisper of smoke strayed from his lips as he spoke.

"That's right," I said. "Kids who would otherwise be in care homes."

Seeing him again brought such joy, but the memories behind the joy sent my fear bubbling back to the surface. I couldn't push the feeling away.

"Listen," I blurted before I could stop myself. "I've got a flat not far from here. I was about to do some shopping but why don't you walk back with me?"

"To your flat, you mean?"

"Yes! I've got so much to tell you, but somewhere other than here..."

His response however, was not what I expected.

"I don't think so, Maisie. I mean, look at me. I live with the dregs of society..." His words trailed off pitifully, his face pinched with despair.

But I was having none of it. "Whoa, Stop right there! We've only just met after two decades and you're pushing me away? Don't be so humble!"

"I'm being realistic," Joe laughed. "I mean for fuck's sake, what if someone sees us? You don't wanna be seen hanging around with scum like me!"

I gaped at him in horror. "Oh my God, will you listen to yourself? Do you know who you sounded like then? Mr bloody Mortimer!"

A shadow folded over his face.

"Please, Joe," I relented. "Twenty years ago you were my best friend, and there's so much I need to talk to you about. Not just about the past but now."

As soon as he had finished his cigarette, he eased his rucksack onto his shoulders. I watched him warily. Any mention of the dreaded Mr. Mortimer was bound to stir a response in him, and I couldn't help feeling a little guilty.

"C'mon, this way," I coaxed him gently.

To my heartfelt relief, he didn't argue this time.

Strolling towards the pier, we passed row upon row of flats until the road swung into view, drawing us back towards the town centre.

"Not much further," I said as we weaved our path through the pedestrian precinct.

He loped along beside me, head down.

"Are you okay?"

"Yeah, fine," he grunted.

"Well, if you can bear with me, I just need to pop into Morrisons."

Shuffling on his feet, he looked uneasy again. It was revealed in every shifty little side glance as the usual Saturday shoppers thronged past.

"I'll wait outside, save you any embarrassment."

"Oh, Joe!" I sighed. "I wish you'd stop putting yourself down."

"And I wish you'd face facts," he sighed back. He attempted a smile but it didn't quite reach his eyes. "I've been wearing these clothes for weeks and I bet they stink. Ain't you seen the looks on people's faces when they walk by?"

Struck by the impact of his words, I felt my heart sink into my chest. Only now did I notice how ragged his jeans were, his worn out leather combat boots literally falling apart at the seams.

"Apart from that, I need a slash," he added jokily. "So why don't you get your shopping done and I'll be sat on that wall over there."

"Okay," I consented, "just promise you will wait for me..."

With my eyes focused on the wall, I waited for him to vanish into the Gents.

But my mind was no longer on the shopping. Appalled by the state of his clothes, I was hit by a sudden impulse, so instead of walking into Morrisons, I sped to the nearest charity shop.

My eyes flitted madly, picking through the racks of clothes until I spotted the familiar purple mohican that distinguished one of the volunteers.

"Matt," I hissed. "Can I ask a favour?"

"For you, Maisie?" he grinned. "Go on, fire away!"

"Would you mind filling up a sack with clothes for my homeless friend? He's about five foot ten, slim build. Shoe size eight or nine."

I fished out a twenty pound note.

"What sort of clothes?"

"Oh, you know," I pleaded. "Trousers, a couple of shirts, a fleece... maybe some cheap socks and undies from Store Twenty-One over there?"

"Okay..."

Yet he seemed to be dithering. I pushed another fiver into his hand.

"Is there any chance you can drop them round to my flat after work?" I pressed my warmest smile, "and let me know if you need any more cash."

Convinced he understood my request, I peered out of the doorway where luckily the coast was still clear, a chance to submerge myself in the crowds before sneaking my way back to Morrisons.

Deep in my heart, I knew I was doing the right thing. From the instant we reconnected I sensed Joe's shame. It hung off him like cobwebs, and he was right about the way other people judged him. Exiting the supermarket, bags bulging with groceries, I was overjoyed to see him waiting for me. A smile lit his face and without prompting, he offered to carry one of my shopping bags.

"Right, so where now?"

"Not far," I said. "Another five minutes' walk to my flat."

An inner glow spread through me like sunshine and following the route along Station Road, we arrived at the historic crossroads. The Victorian red brick railway station stood on one side, the legendary Bognor Picturedrome opposite and towering between the two, the four-storey furniture repository of 'Reynolds & Co.'

"Just a little further," I said, "and then we cross over."

Keeping the conversation flowing as we walked, I couldn't resist mentioning I worked in Chichester, a beautiful Roman City renowned for its Cathedral – but the accommodation was too expensive for me to live there.

By the time we had turned into Annandale Avenue, I felt the tide of tension had shifted a little. "That's the beauty of Bognor," I added, sliding my key into the door. "It's pleasant enough but affordable."

Gazing up, Joe took a moment to observe the large cream-coloured house before I ushered him indoors. The communal hallway lay in its usual tranquility, apart from the clomp of our feet on the tiles.

Next I unlocked the door to my own flat. "Come in."

"Nice gaff you've got," Joe said.

The discomfiture was back, I could hear it tolling in his voice. His footsteps dragged as he followed me to the kitchen and lingered on the threshold.

"Cup of tea?" I asked, catching his eye again.

He swallowed visibly, the swell of his Adam's apple rising. Lowering my shopping bag to the floor, he gradually disentangled himself from his rucksack.

My heart thumped.

What could possibly be troubling him?

Yes, we were two very different people, nothing could change that.

"L-look," I faltered. "I've got some beer in the fridge and a bottle of wine too but we can save that for dinner..."

"Dinner?"

"You didn't think I was going to send you back to the beach shelter did you?"

His eyes flickered with suspicion as if everything was happening too fast.

"Look, Maisie, I don't wanna be no bother. It's great to see you but..."

"But what?"

Seeing him shrink back into himself, I felt my panic rise like a barometer. A hot tear plummeted down my cheek, but a moment later his expression changed.

"Hey," he mumbled, risking a shaky step forward. "What's wrong?"

"Wrong?" Tears swam before my eyes as I struggled to form the right words. "I-I thought we were friends!"

"We are!" he frowned. "I didn't mean to upset you."

By the time his arm slid around my shoulder though, my inner framework was crumbling.

"You think you've got problems! I may look smart on the outside but I'm falling apart. I have nightmares, panic attacks... seeing a therapist and even that's triggering flashbacks! Flashbacks of the time we were in that care home!"

"Orchard Grange..." The words reeled out of him in horror.

"Yes, Joe," I whimpered, brushing the tear from my face, "and you're the only person in the world I can talk to right now, so will you stop running away."

Chapter Eleven

"Running away," I echoed, hearing the shock in my own voice. "I'm sorry, bad choice of words... but you did, didn't you? That's why you were untraceable."

I had offered him a seat. Perched uncomfortably on the rim of a dining stool though, it seemed obvious he was still bothered by his dishevelled clothes.

"Who told you that?" he said guardedly.

"A family friend. Someone who's been around since I was fostered..."

Absentmindedly, I started picking at a sliver of skin around my thumbnail.

"Uncanny, isn't it? I've been talking about you a lot lately. See, just because I was fostered, don't go thinking I'd forgotten about you. My foster mum made enquiries."

"Is that so?" Joe replied, a flash of challenge in his eye.

"Yes," I nodded. "So what happened after I left?"

"Like I said, it's a long story. I'll probably need one of them beers if you wanna hear it all, but it'll keep for now..." His face relaxed a little. "Never mind me, let's talk about you. I get the feeling life hasn't all been a bed of roses."

"Not really," I confessed.

So he'd turned the conversation around to me again.

It didn't matter. I was determined to prise the truth out of him sooner or later.

"When did the nightmares start?"

"In my teens," I murmured, "and now they're back, which reminds me of something else I wanted to ask. How long have you been in Bognor?"

"Two weeks, maybe three? Dunno. I've been a bit out of it lately..."

Drugs. The implications flickered momentarily, but I dismissed them. Thinking back to my nightmares, they had manifested themselves before then.

"So what's in these dreams? D'you wanna tell me?"

I felt a shiver roll over me. Could I bear to recall the details, especially from last night? Staring down at my thumbnail, I was shocked to see a bead of blood forming, unaware how ferociously I had been attacking it.

Joe followed my gaze and frowned. "Must be pretty bad, then."

"Yes, but the flashbacks are more recent. They relate directly to Orchard Grange. Things *you* might remember..."

His gentle brown eyes clung to mine, carrying in them a mantle of

48

protection I remembered from the day I had met him. He said nothing, though.

"I know that place was hell," I prompted, "but we've got to talk about it at some point."

Sipping his tea in silence, he seemed to mull over my words. I found myself holding my breath, until the buzzer of my door resonated, pulling me unsteadily to my feet.

"Sorry, but I'd better get that..."

"Who is it?" I called, hoping it would be Matt with a bin-liner of clothes.

"It's me!" Jess's voice squeaked across the intercom. "Let me in, will you?"

My heart plummeted for a second time that day. I buzzed her in and went to the door. In the sitting room, Joe was out of sight for now, but I'd have to explain his presence at some point.

"Hi," I greeted her crisply. "No date with Steve tonight?"

"Um, no," Jess faltered. "I've got a nasty feeling he's cheating on me."

"He can't be! What makes you say that?"

Her blue eyes glittered. "Same old! Last night in Midhurst he was acting very weird. Like flinching every time his mobile buzzed, and I'm sure I could smell another woman's perfume on him, so I didn't hang around..."

"Oh, Jess!" I commiserated. "Call him. At least give him a chance to explain."

"I've tried, but he's not returning my calls!" She released a harsh laugh. "Bloody men! You're better off without them, and isn't it time we had a good old girlie catch up? What are you up to tonight?"

I bit my lip. "I've got a visitor and I don't want to put you off, Jess, but now is not a good time..."

Without warning, she pushed the door open a crack. I froze, dreading her reaction, eyes scanning my sitting room like searchlights. But it was too late to throw her off the scent. Joe glanced around, freezing her mid-step; a split second later I tried to tug her away from the door.

"Who the hell is he?" she gasped.

Fighting to control my panic, I nudged her back into the hallway.

"Don't jump to conclusions," I whispered, "Joe and I go way back, but I found him sleeping rough in one of the beach shelters..."

Shock froze her face as she surveyed me. "You'd rather spend an evening with some *scuzzy tramp* than have a drink with your best mate?"

"Shh!" I hissed. "Keep your voice down. Joe is not a tramp. We knew each other when we were in care and I'm dying to know what happened to him..."

"Suit yourself!" Jess huffed with a toss of the head. "Let me know if you change your mind."

I gritted my teeth. "Please, Jess, this is important to me. You can fill me in

49

on your love life any time." Without waiting for an answer, I shut the door.

Unnerved by the interruption, I crept back into the sitting room, but Joe was already on his feet, putting his boots on.

"She's right, you know," he snapped, "it's Saturday night. Don't blow out your best mate on my account."

"Oh no you don't," I forestalled him, "I'm not letting you escape that easily. If it's any consolation, she hasn't exactly been around for me lately. I'm bored with her forever banging on about her love life."

"But look at the state of me," he protested. "I'm a fucking mess!"

I took a deep breath.

"Then why don't I run you a bath? You can have a good long soak, while I get on with the dinner."

Happy he didn't argue, I fought an urge to smile, wandering into the bathroom to turn the taps on. The water gushed forth, a fragrant steam wafting from the tub as I added bubble bath. There was a small fire next to it and a few candles, so I flicked the flame on the gas igniter to light them all.

"Go on in then," I coaxed him, and grabbing a pile of fresh towels, warm from the linen cupboard, I thrust them into his arms. "I'll leave you to unwind and as soon as you're done, just give me a shout, okay?"

"Thanks," he muttered. He tried to smile but it couldn't extinguish the pain in his eyes. "This is bloody good of you, Maisie."

Safe in the knowledge Joe was blissfully immersed in a hot bath, I turned my attention back to dinner. I poured myself a glass of wine, switched on my i-Pod and selected a playlist.

Tonight I'd opted for simplicity: some barbecued chicken pieces from the hot counter and a bag of Caesar salad. But first I needed to pop some potatoes in the oven. The chicken only needed heating up, so I would save that until last.

Thinking back to Joe, I was mentally rehearsing what to say to him. Anything to draw him out of his shell.

Like was it wise to describe my flashback?

I hadn't missed the fear clouding his expression at the mere mention of Mr. Mortimer, but it left me hankering to hear *his* take on the story.

Before I had a chance to ponder any further though, I heard a sharp rap on the window. Certain it would be Matt this time, I wiped my hands on a tea towel and crept out to look.

"Oh great!" I spluttered as he lowered a bin bag at my feet. "I was beginning to think you'd forgotten."

"As if!" he sniggered. "We had an extra delivery."

I raised my eyebrows. "And you got first pickings?"

"There's some proper decent stuff in there," he finished with a wink, "and I didn't skimp on the grundies either."

Beaming with pleasure, I thanked him and closed the door.

A hot bath and clean clothes? I could not wait to see the look on Joe's face.

I wasn't disappointed. By the time he emerged, he was a different person and it was hard to believe the transformation, a far cry from the broken man I had drawn out of the beach shelter. The heat of the water had brought a glow to his skin, his wet hair slicked back, dark as polished oak. Borrowing one of my razors, he had managed a shave, too. Gone was the mat of beard growth, in its place a finely honed jaw. It added an element of ruggedness to his features.

"How do you feel now?" I couldn't resist asking.

"Human," he smiled, "and cheers to your mate for the clothes."

He stroked the fabric lovingly, a burgundy corduroy shirt that fitted him nicely, matched with nearly new black jeans. Matt had chosen well.

"Glass of wine?" I offered, opening a bottle of red.

A cheeky grin lifted the corners of his mouth. "Wouldn't mind a beer."

I felt my heart swell, delighted to see the *real Joe* emerge at last. There had been a spikiness to him earlier, as if an impenetrable barbed wire fence was separating him from the rest of society. It left me desperate to understand what had gone wrong in his life, but for now, we kept the conversation to a light and easy banter, until I dished up dinner.

"This is good," Joe mumbled between mouthfuls, "'bloody marvellous' as Paul would say," a reference, I thought, to one of the men in the beach shelter.

As the evening drew on, I cherished the ambience. We were starting to bond again, the barriers sliding away to revive an inseparable friendship. But the thorny subject of the care home was bound to inch its way into the conversation at some point.

I placed down my fork.

"I never did get round to telling you about my flashback."

Joe turned very still. "This is gonna be about the home, in't it?"

"The laundry room. You took a punishment for trying to hide me there."

"Yeah!" Joe snorted. "That I do remember. Fucking Mortimer!"

His name reverberated with a harsh echo as I topped up my glass.

"But you never told me what he did to you."

His eyes burned black with hate. "He was a vicious bastard. His thug gave me the worst beating of my life, and that's saying something, coming from a rough background like mine..."

I nodded in horror, my mouth dry.

Joe's father, a violent criminal in his own right, had been convicted and sentenced to a lengthy prison term for the unprovoked killing of his mum. To think that a single punch could change someone's life forever...

"They threw me to the floor," he spat, "Mortimer pressing his foot on my legs to hold me down while his thug laid into me with a steel hose. Fuckers warned it was just a taste of what they'd do if I caused any more trouble."

I winced. "What sort of trouble?"

"You don't wanna know," he finished icily.

The room seemed to darken all around us, the atmosphere strained.

"Try me," I pressed. "It might help me to understand some of the stuff that's coming out in my therapy. Mortimer really hated you, didn't he?"

Joe shrugged, but he was no longer looking at me. "I knew stuff. Had me own idea how them homes were being run. Violent places at the best of times, kids being attacked and a lot of 'em were almost feral. Truth is, Maisie, you're either a victim or a fighter and I hate to say it, but you were one of the victims and so was Sam."

"Sam!" I gasped. "You do remember him!"

His eyes slid shiftily towards mine. "That he disappeared, how could I forget?"

"Do you ever wonder what happened to him?"

"Yeah," Joe said. "Twenty years might be a long time but I always had a hunch. Should have kept it to myself 'cos Mortimer had it in for me. I was suspicious of a lot of things but pestering him about Sam really got his blood up."

"So what went on after I left?"

He turned his glass in his hands. "I never imagined things could get worse but they did. All I ever wanted to know was where Sam had gone... but Mortimer started threatening me." His head lifted, the glow of a light bulb reflected in his angry eyes. "If he'd followed it through, I'd be dead by now."

I frowned and picked up my own glass. A lump of fear rose in my throat but I gulped the feeling down.

"You seriously think he was planning to kill you?"

"Yeah. I was trouble, 'a piece of scum,' he called me, and he promised that one day, *he'd deal with me once and for all...* I thought, fuck this! I ain't sticking around here, and that's why I escaped."

Gazing at him now, I wondered what he was trying to hide from me. I was still no nearer to understanding his reason for locking me in the laundry room, nor the secrets he harboured about Sam's disappearance.

"Go on," I pressed him. "You ran away from the home but you ended up on the streets. What happened in the years between?"

"I was coming to that," he said, a smile playing on his lips, "but d'you mind if I grab a smoke first? I'll go outside."

"Go on then," I consented, "but don't be long."

52

Joe kept his head down. Stealing a glance down the avenue, he made a mental note of the cars in the neighbourhood.

The little silver Toyota was Maisie's but a shiny white Nissan loomed behind it. Not just any car, some huge great big bastard of a car with tinted windows, covering almost half of the pavement.

With little room to circumnavigate, he didn't pay much attention to the next car in the row. Black as death, it blended into the shadows, just inches out of range of the nearest lamppost.

Chapter Twelve

Thrown back in time, Joe was finally beginning to remember things about the children's home, his thoughts now focused on Sam.

Who could forget Sam Ellis? If ever a kid was cut out to be bullied, it was him, poor sod. The others assumed he was some 'posh boy', his forehead too high for his dainty features, his widely spaced brown eyes almost birdlike. Small for his age with a cap of blonde hair, he was an easy target for those yobs.

Yet what they did to him was horrible even by their standards. Joe had intervened the day they had his head forced down the toilet, their hoots of laughter pounding in his ears. Even now Joe was haunted by the sight of Sam coming up for air, choking, spluttering with smears of excrement in his hair... Joe feared he might die unless he stopped them.

'Leave him alone, he ain't done nothing!' he screamed, and grabbing the nearest collar, he had flung the offender to the floor.

The smack of Danny Butler's head against the tiles was quite satisfying.

'What's it to you?' he roared. 'Stuck up prick thinks he's better than us and his mum was a fucking whore!'

'Yeah, and so were a lot of kids' mums,' Joe argued, 'it's why they got dumped in care, you dickhead!'

Thinking about it left him quivering with rage.

Joe hated seeing people picked on and Sam was no exception. He had spent his early years protecting his little sisters, never knowing when they would be a target for his father's fists. But regrettably, Brian Winterton was everyone's worst nightmare, and not just because of his criminal reputation. Masterminding a number of armed robberies, Brian was a crazed man who could erupt at the flick of a switch.

Joe knew. Those drunken rages had been the scourge of their lives, and although he didn't like to discuss his own family, he was curious to know about Sam's mother.

'My mum was m-murdered,' the boy said, trembling, and straight away they had bonded.

Joe's lips tightened. Growing up under the constant threat of violence had made him vigilant, but what of his little sisters? Pearl had been seven on the night their mum had met her brutal death and Trixie just five. So it seemed only natural that with no little sisters to protect any more, kids like Maisie and Sam filled the void.

At least Maisie was still here.

Joe felt a chill sweep over him. Hearing her describe her hallucination in vivid detail, he couldn't help but wonder if it was a ghost she had seen.

Yet why would Sam haunt her now?

On reflection, he didn't want to remember Sam with his head down the toilet, covered in shit, but one of the few times he looked happy.

Maisie had been there too, a day they were playing football in the yard. Sam, an ethereal figure in his t-shirt and shorts, knees muddy, smile bigger than a slice of sunshine as they hit a high five.

"I remember," Maisie said. "I was watching in the background."

"Yeah," Joe muttered, "and so was Mortimer."

A twist of nausea gripped his gut. God, how he loathed that man, from his shiny complexion to those pale protruding eyes. The way he ran his tongue over his fat wet lips, his gaze anchored on Sam, made Joe's flesh crawl.

"We used to call him Toad Face," he chuckled but it was a hollow sound.

Yes, he was reminded of a toad, imagining that same tongue reeling out and gobbling Sam up like a juicy fly. How ironic that Sam had been invited to attend a '*party*' that same week. '*A treat for a select few children.*'

"Sam vanished after that party," he whispered aloud.

"I was going about to ask you about those parties..." Maisie intervened.

He fired a stare that stalled her words in an instant.

"Let's not go there. Not now. All I remember is we were under constant surveillance and not just from Toad Face but those goons he hired."

"They started tailing us," she shivered.

"I know, except it didn't end there," he added darkly.

The memory of Mortimer's threats rose like an omen. Here was Joe, desperate to know why Sam had vanished. Maisie had left soon after, but filled with an overwhelming sense of emptiness, he couldn't imagine he had anything left to lose by challenging Mortimer. *Oh, how wrong he had been.*

"I had no choice but to leg it. What else could I do? We were just kids!"

******

He didn't need to tell Maisie the details of his escape. What was the point of mentioning the night he had whacked Danny Butler around the head with a baseball bat to create a diversion? By the time the ambulance arrived, no one had noticed him climbing out of the window.

No, she didn't need to know that.

55

So maybe his dad's violence had rubbed off on him, but Danny survived, didn't he? And this was what this was about. Survival.

"I headed for the first place I could think of. Finsbury Park. It's where I grew up, so there were bound to be a few mates around. I was looking for a pub we used to go to, rough as arseholes, but a place where the old man was quite chummy with the landlord. I took a chance..."

Sure enough, his gamble had paid off.

Albert and his wife, Shirley, had been pretty shocked to see him turning up in the dead of night but wary of his circumstances, quick to hide him in their box room. He didn't even need to ask. His dad's murder of his mum had sent ripples of shock through their community, and as if to compound matters, the lad had been incarcerated in some care home.

So great was his fear that he begged them not to reveal his whereabouts, should the authorities start sniffing around.

"It was only a matter of time before the cops visited. From what I heard, they were concerned about my safety..." He let out a snort. "Safety my arse! I bet Mortimer was bricking it with me on the loose, shooting my gob off! I wasn't stupid. I lay low, 'cos if the authorities had found me, I'd be back in that hell hole before I could blink."

Yes, he had a lot to thank Al and Shirley for. Not only had they offered him a sanctuary, but a reason to carry on living. With a couple of sons of their own, it was good to reconnect with old friends, boys not only older, but streetwise. In fact, it didn't take long before they discovered his true worth and set him to work making counterfeit CDs to flog on their market stall.

"Never touched a computer in my life! Funny in't it? We never had computers at Orchard Grange, or CDs, come to think of it, and the internet was quite new. It was so different back then..."

Maybe the counterfeit CDs had given him a purpose in life but the enterprise stretched further. The next craze to be exploited was video games. Computers and games consoles were incorporating an ever more complex graphic interface into their products, but he managed to replicate these too. By the time he reached sixteen, Joe was in his prime and as clever and worldly-wise as his mentors. Hopeful that Mortimer would have forgotten him by now, it was time to step out of hiding.

"The authorities couldn't touch me at sixteen. No way could they dump me back in care, but whatever else life threw at me, I owed Al and Shirley big time. So as soon as they needed an extra barman, I jumped at the chance, happy to muck in."

Joe spent the next few years riding a roller coaster of highs and lows; work, arguments and girlfriends the usual distractions that came with growing up. If he wasn't sofa surfing in his friends' gaffs, he had his bolt hole at the Black Horse to fall back on. Handy on the nights he worked his shift there.

But everything changed when he captured the eye of a local big shot, George Oldman, a man who was as familiar with his past as Al and Shirley.

"I never forget a face, not even an ugly mug like yours. You're Brian Winterton's boy, ain't yer?"

Speaking with a harsh cockney accent, he had the look of a businessman. His grey pin stripe suit looked expensive, his silver hair slicked back from a large, heavily veined forehead. Joe surveyed him coolly.

"Less of the ugly if you don't mind," he said.

Reflected in the lounge mirror, he could not fail to miss the warning look that flashed across Shirley's face.

"Seen the ol' man lately, 'ave yer?" the stranger smirked.

"No," Joe levelled at him, determined to hold his ground. "He can rot in hell for all I care after what he did to my mum."

There was a beat of silence. Before any further words were spoken, George extracted a business card from his top pocket and lowered it onto the bar top.

"There's more to it than yer think, son. I 'ad all the respect in the world for your mum but when the fuzz came down heavy..." he tut-tutted. "Reckon it were Fran who turned 'im in."

Joe gritted his teeth. "You've got it all wrong. Mum would never do that. She was too scared, and in spite of everything, she loved him. Though God only knows why."

With those words George's face softened. "Well, before you get your knickers in a twist, your dad's been askin' about ya. Wanted to check you was okay and I promised I'd sort it. So my advice to you, lad, is hand in your notice at this dump and come and work for me in one of my bars. Something a bit more upmarket."

To his immense surprise, neither Shirley nor Al put up any protest.

"You go, Joe," Al managed to convince him. "He said he'd find us a replacement barman, and it's time you stood on your own two feet."

Joe couldn't argue with that. He wasn't sure he trusted George but true to his word, the man had clinched him a position in one of the swankiest pubs in Chelsea. It marked the beginning of a new life. One that launched him into the social hub of London, working across a chain of bars and nightclubs.

Having survived the horrors of his childhood, he thought he had hit the jackpot working for George. Okay, so he didn't know much about the man, nor the shadier side of his enterprise outside the pub trade and the rumours he dealt in drugs and illegal gambling, but what did Joe care? An ambitious young man in his twenties, he had money in his pocket, smart clothes, nice cars and chicks practically throwing themselves at him.

Oh yes, that life was the dogs' bollocks while it lasted.

Until that one fateful day George bullied him into applying for another bar job, only this time, he had picked a specific public house in Wapping.

"I'll make it worth yer while, son," he pressed. "Secure this job and I'll see to it you've got a never-ending wallet full 'o cash, as much coke as you can snort up yer hooter and more fanny than you can shake yer cock at."

He might have worn a smile, but Joe saw the glint in his steel blue eyes, a look that warned him *refusal was not an option.*

He fiddled with his tobacco pouch, turning it in his hands as he prepared to divulge the most shameful part of this story. But Maisie had insisted on no secrets.

"That pub didn't even belong to George," he mumbled.

Pity he hadn't known that at the time.

Only when he had secured the job did he discover the proprietor was a former partner of George's – and one who had stitched him up.

"Best you don't say nothing about me," George growled. "Mention my name and you're dead, son. All I want from you is a bit of surveillance."

The truth was that some years ago, George and his partner, Claude Dupont, had built up an extremely lucrative property business in the Costa del Sol. The market had bottomed out in 2005 but when the company went bankrupt, George learned that Claude had been cooking the books and siphoning off a greater share of the profits than he was due.

Joe could not deny how nervous he felt. George had clearly been plotting this for years, just waiting for Claude to invest in a new boozer. But as an unwitting pawn in George's game, Joe had charmed the pants off the landlady, Martha Thomson.

Oddly enough though, she knew a bit about him already, having been a loyal friend of his mother's from way back.

"Broke my heart what happened to Fran," she confided. "Poor cow! Never did understand why she stuck around with that bastard."

Such compassion left Joe trapped in a gut-twisting dilemma. He adored Martha, a lively peroxide blonde whose wicked sense of humour and sharp tongue reminded him of his mum, and it sickened him to think he was working for the enemy.

Yet there was no way he could fight George. Forced to bide his time, he kept his head down, said nothing and within a few months of working at the Golden Fleece, had become well acquainted with Mr Dupont himself. He knew where his office was and most importantly, his wall safe. Deep down, he feared the real reason for his employment and it gnawed at his insides like a cancer.

Obviously George was planning a robbery, one that very much relied upon Joe being in place.

But another month crept by before his suspicions were confirmed.

It was a bitterly cold night in November, bulging clouds darkening the sky, releasing sheet upon sheet of drizzle, the weather so foul that few punters would hang around.

Joe had specific orders to stay late but with Martha cashing up, fate had a crafty way of intervening. The icy, dank weather had brought on the worst of her arthritis and after hearing her griping about her knees all day, he used the situation to his advantage.

"Why don't you let me take the cash up to Mr Dupont's office? I'll pick up your coat and handbag while I'm up there."

"Oh, give over!" she scoffed. "I'm not an invalid."

"C'mon, Martha," Joe pressed, "it'll save you an extra trip up them stairs..." and without waiting for an answer, he had spun from the bar, bounding up to the top floor so fast, he arrived breathless.

Seeing her raincoat hanging up in the cloakroom, along with her red leather handbag, Joe made a swipe for it. He knew exactly what he was looking for, and with precious seconds ticking, he snapped open the clasp to locate the spare keys she had been entrusted with.

"Is that you, Martha?" Dupont's voice droned from the adjacent office.

Joe froze but with no other choice than to face the boss, he stepped boldly up to the door.

"No, it's me. Martha's knees are playing up, I was just fetching her coat."

Dupont watched Joe beadily as he lowered the cashbox onto the desk.

"Tonight's takings," he added. "Is there anything else I can get for you, Sir, before I call it a night? A brandy perhaps?"

A short, thickset man with a permanent suntan, Claude grinned broadly. "That's jolly decent of you, Joe, but nah... You can get off now."

"Okay. Goodnight, Mr Dupont."

Joe lingered just long enough to see him open the cashbox. Long enough to see the hefty piles of notes. Long enough to feel his heart hammering as fast as it had ever hammered when faced with the wrath of his father, or even a beating at the hands of Mortimer.

It had turned 11:30 when he and Martha left, and with the door latch switched to locking mode, she slammed it shut behind them.

Joe shivered. Even now the drizzle hadn't let up. Martha lived only a couple of streets away, but he insisted on walking her home, making sure she was safe indoors before heading for the London underground. He watched her draw the curtains, conscious of the keys in his pocket. It was only a small bunch, but the thought of having them in his possession weighed heavily.

Creeping around the corner in the direction of the tube station, he waited a few more minutes, checked his watch, and on the stroke of midnight, returned to the Golden Fleece. As predicted, George's black transit van lingered on the curb.

Joe slipped Martha's spare key into the side door and sneaked back into the bar. Leaving it ajar, he heard the swish of a van door. George and his men were only a few steps behind him, and the hiss of the man's voice chilled him to the core.

"You stick around and keep a lookout. Just tell me where the cunt is and we'll get on with it."

Joe swallowed hard.

"Up the stairs, second floor, first office on the left," he whispered.

A slick of sweat clung to his face but with no choice other than to pass the keys over, he prayed with all his heart that one of them would unlock the safe.

The next part was a waiting game. Leaning against the bar, Joe watched in dread as each man took it in turns to shimmy up the stairs. All he wanted was for this to be over now. For George and his goons to act fast, grab the dough, dish out whatever beating they had in mind and then maybe they could all fuck off home.

Unfortunately, George had other ideas.

Taking a gulp of water, Joe was alerted to some kind of commotion as a succession of shouts emanated from the top floor.

The next sound took him by surprise.

A blood-curdling howl of pain.

Squeezing his eyes shut, he could not bear to imagine what was happening.

It sounded for all the world like they were torturing the poor fucker.

But the horror he felt then was nothing compared to the icy breeze coiling into the bar as the side door flew open. Joe nearly shat himself. For there, braced in the frame, seething like a Rottweiler, was none other than Martha.

"I knew it," she snarled, "soon as I realised me keys was gone. What the bleedin' hell are you playing at, Joe?"

Limbs quivering like jelly, he stepped towards her.

"Martha, just go," he croaked. "You don't wanna be here."

Martha was having none of it. "You conniving little shit! Get out o' me way!"

Joe stood his ground, banking up his courage, but his words were cut short. Another scream filled the pocket of silence, and he knew there would be no stopping her. Martha took another step and shoved him aside. Then turning towards the stairs, all arthritic pains forgotten, she strode to the top with furious intent.

"No!" Joe gasped. His voice sounded hollow but he had to stop her, his terror surging as he sped up the stairs.

He had only just caught up when she turned to him, fury and disgust in her cold eyes and curled lip.

"D'you know, I should have known not to trust you! Might o' known you'd turn out to be the same as your criminal father!"

"I'm nothing like him," Joe whimpered. "This isn't down to me..."

The next thing he knew was a shot of searing pain as she drove her high-heeled stiletto boot into his foot. Gasping in agony, he stumbled. Too late to stop her charging the rest of the way up the stairs and hauling the office door open. Too late to stop one of George's men turning with his gun and popping out a bullet at point blank range.

She hit the carpet with a thud. Watching from the landing, Joe felt the floor disappear under his feet, waves of horror draining away any last hope. The last thing he saw was the crimson stain spreading through her blouse, a fatal wound that left him in no doubt that she would never get up again.

Chapter Thirteen

"That's terrible," Maisie shuddered, "the poor woman."

"Yeah," Joe sighed. "No one was expecting her to come back nor the alarm going off. My guess is Dupont had a panic button fitted under his desk."

How the police had turned up so fast was a mystery. Perhaps he should have made a run for it, but even though he knew it was too late for her, he couldn't bear to leave Martha lying there alone.

"I got five years."

"Five years?" she echoed. "That's a bit harsh!"

"Is it? When George's gang was arrested, there was no way I could wriggle out. We were up for robbery, GBH and murder. Okay, so I didn't pull the trigger but I might as well have done. I was guilty of aiding and abetting."

He lowered his head, the tears welling. He would never forgive himself for Martha's death. Here was a much loved woman whose sparkling wit and big heart had touched everyone who knew her.

"I was the only who showed remorse," his voice cracked. "Broke down in court and cried but it didn't make no difference. The CPS had a field day. Here was Joe Winterton, son of a notorious villain. They wanted to make an example of me."

"But how did you cope?" Maisie gasped. "In prison, I mean?"

Joe shrugged. *Leicester Prison hadn't been that different from the care home, really. The same pecking orders prevailed, the same bully boys, the same victims. But where he had broken up fights in Orchard Grange, there was no way he could tackle the villains in that place and live to tell the tale. Some of the violence had sickened him, scenes that kept him awake and would forever haunt his nightmares.*

"I became something of a recluse," he said. "Got into drugs, 'cos if ever anything kicked off it was easier to turn a blind eye."

He caught the shock dilating her eyes.

"Drugs?" she echoed.

"Drugs were rife in the nick," he snapped. "It was just a coping strategy as far as I was concerned. Got to survive somehow. Don't think I'm not ashamed of the way I turned out..."

"I wasn't having a go," she tried pacifying him. "When did you get out?"

"2012. Got parole after three years but it felt like a lifetime. By the time I got out, I was well screwed up. Who'd wanna employ me now?"

Hands curled into fists, he felt a froth of anger bubbling.

God, how he loathed George Oldman for the shit he'd got him into, wishing from the blackest abyss of his heart he had never met the bastard.

"Everything was ticking along nicely in the days I was helping Al and his old lady behind the bar. I could have had a half decent life if George hadn't muscled in and fucked it all up."

He might even have found a better way out of the mess he was in, but drugs had weakened him, yet another dark slippery hole for him to fall down. Released from prison an addict with nothing but the clothes on his back, he was moved into a half-way house.

"Unlike prison, there weren't no rules. Blokes used to die in them places from overdoses or getting stabbed in fights. The one I ended up in was an absolute shit hole even by today's standards."

Condemned to live in a festering hovel, inhabited by hard men, and not just former convicts, Joe found himself in a thoroughly hostile environment.

"Getting into crime was the only solution for those wasters, but I thought bollocks to that, it ain't worth it. I'd already had a belly-full of prison!"

Shame it wasn't just their company he had to endure, though.

Mixing with such ne'er-do-wells had brought another chapter of chaos rolling into his life. Because of all the people he might have stumbled across, he never imagined it would be his old nemesis, Danny Butler.

"You must remember him," he said. "One of the hard nuts at Orchard Grange. It started with the message. D'you wanna know what it said?"

"Go on," Maisie prompted him. He met her wide green eyes with a shiver.

"'Scum like you can run but you can't hide and I've got your card marked, Joe Winterton...' That was bad enough, but you know what was even creepier? Some sick fucker had tied a red ribbon around it."

Maisie's face turned ashen. "A-a red ribbon?" she mumbled.

"Yup! Some cruel psychological joke and it proper wound me up! Then a day later Danny showed his ugly mug at the hostel, so I decided to front him out..."

Regrettably it took just one hate-filled glare to light the fuse, a look that told him Danny had never forgotten the night he'd whacked a bat over his head. And no sooner did their eyes lock than the fists started flying. For Joe, in his befuddled, drug induced paranoia, had not only accused Danny of delivering that note but called him every name under the sun.

Pity he had overreacted, because Danny was no longer the nasty rat-faced little shit he had confronted in the care home. Danny had morphed into an even nastier, muscle bound, shaven-headed, neo-nazi thug.

"Bastards kicked the crap out of me," he spat, "three against one, but it marked the end of my days in that hostel. Starting a fight was against the rules. Got slung out I did and you already know the rest..."

"I'm so sorry," Maisie breathed, "but that note! How can you be certain Danny sent it?"

"I'm not sure he did," he muttered, "which leaves one other possibility."

"Mortimer," she concluded.

A feeling of dread crawled over him as she toyed with her wine glass but in the aftermath of his story, their lives seemed even more connected.

How strange they had turned the full circle.

Mortimer. Yes, it all came back to Mr bloody Mortimer.

"Do you wonder if he's still around?" she whispered fearfully.

"It's not impossible," Joe pondered. "That bastard swore he'd get me one day and maybe that's the best thing about being homeless. Not many people know your name. You're not on any electoral roll, nothing like that, no phone number, nothing for them to trace you."

"But you can't spend the rest of your life hiding on the streets," she protested. "What do you really want out of life?"

"Same as everyone, I s'pose, a roof over my head, a job... don't think I chose to be homeless. It's shit! But more than anything, I wanna feel safe."

Her lips lifted into a half smile. "Then surely the best way forward would be to get yourself back on your feet..."

"Yeah," Joe nodded. "Maybe."

The shadows seemed to bend slightly, his mind and limbs turning heavier. Sneaking a glance at the cheap digital watch on his wrist, he was shocked to discover the time: almost one in the morning.

"Anyway, enough about the past, I'd best be on my way now."

Observing him with tenderness, her smile didn't waver. "Don't go. I'm not turfing you out on the streets at this hour. You can stay."

"Are you sure?"

"Of course!" she chuckled. "You're welcome to use the spare room, unless you'd rather crash out on the sofa."

Joe closed his eyes, wondering if he had heard her right...

... and in that single flash of darkness, they were back in the laundry room, the place where it had all begun. He drank in her beauty, her porcelain pale skin and big eyes. At that moment he would have done anything to stop her going to that party.

'Sit tight and don't budge. I'll unlock the door when they've gone.'

A distant voice drifted into his mind, the voice of a twelve-year-old Maisie.

'But what if they find out? You'll be in big trouble.'

'It doesn't matter,' he said, and that was the whole point. It didn't.

Confusion widened her eyes, a look of such innocence, he was damned if he was going to leave things to fate. As far as he was concerned, he had made the right choice and had stuck to it through and through.

Chapter Fourteen

In the cool silver light of Sunday morning my eyelids fluttered open. I was surprised I had slept so well after the turmoil of the evening. Yet none of it had played on my mind, and if anything I felt cleansed, for Joe's backstory, whilst harrowing, had intrigued me.

Creeping into the hallway, I paused by the lounge.

A rectangle of grey light shone through the curtains, unmasking his silhouette. I could have smiled. From the rise and fall of his chest, he was sleeping peacefully, the top half of his blanket trailing on the floor. A grey marl t-shirt clung to his frame, his sinewy arms wrapped around his torso. But I saw a gentle vulnerability in him that stirred me, something out of step with the hostile world he inhabited.

Feeling my way to the bathroom, I closed the door.

Yet Joe's face lingered. Looking back, I recalled the desperate gratitude in his eyes when I had offered him shelter for the night. He'd treated me respectfully, too, taking the invitation as it was meant. Joe was my friend and I trusted him.

Happy to leave him, I wandered back to my bedroom and snuggling under the duvet, switched my mobile on. Spotting three missed calls from Jess, I felt an instant tug of guilt. *Hardly surprising.* Yet how could I ignore her when all it would take on my part was a friendly text to clear the air?

> *Hi Jess, how are you? Sorry to let you down but seeing Joe was such a blast from the past. Give us a buzz later and I'll tell you more xx*

Signing off with a smiley face and heart emoji, I arose to get dressed but my movements turned sluggish, my brain still a little fuzzy.

Thinking about last night again, Joe hadn't divulged as much about the care home as I'd hoped, my mind burning with questions about those parties. But as I drew the curtains, a creak from the lounge jolted me.

Whatever he knew would have to keep for now.

The more pressing issue was how to help him turn his life around, and it once again struck me what a deep and satisfying sleep I'd had, with none of the hooded monsters encroaching.

Yes, Joe made me feel safe, Joe, my friend who had always protected me.

Tiptoeing into the kitchen, I grabbed the cafetiere, tipped in a hefty measure of gourmet roast and filled it to the brim.

Five minutes later, an aroma of freshly brewed coffee coiled into the air. Lingering by the work surface, I was still wondering what to say to Joe, when as if on cue his shadow spilled over the threshold.

I glanced around. "Hey, you! How did you sleep?"

"Very well," he mumbled. "Thanks for putting us up."

"It's no problem."

He was fully dressed now, in jeans and a cable-knit jumper, but as we rested in the lounge, taking alternate sips of coffee, the silence between us swelled. Not an awkward silence, more a *companionable* one, each of us mulling over what to say to the other.

"Good coffee," Joe piped up, finally filling the void.

And as I lifted my gaze, everything snapped into focus.

"Look, I've been thinking... Too many years have passed under the bridge to go our separate ways again. We never did discover what happened to Sam but wouldn't it be good to get to the bottom of it? I don't think I can move on until we do. And at the same time I feel like we should stick together..."

Joe cast me a sceptical look. "Go to the police, you mean?"

"Why don't we just tell them what we remember about Orchard Grange?"

"It's complicated," he argued, "not to mention dangerous if it means going up against Mortimer. We can't prove nothing! I mean who's gonna believe someone like me? Some scuzzy low life who's done time, done drugs, and spent the best part of two years sleeping rough?"

I took a deep breath, hit with a flash of intuition.

This was my moment.

"Don't think I haven't thought about it, but like I said, the best thing you can do is turn your life around. Get off the streets and find work. It's not impossible."

"You can't get a job if you don't have a fixed abode."

"Okay, so I've got a solution to that, too. Stay here with me for a while. I've got a spare room. It needs clearing out and a bit of paintwork, but if you're happy to help me out, then it's yours!"

Joe froze, coffee cup suspended.

You'd think he'd be ecstatic but if anything his face fell, his defences rising.

"That's very kind of you, Maisie," he said, "but have you got any idea what you're letting yourself in for?"

"I-I don't understand," I faltered, "where else will you go? It doesn't have to be permanent, just a chance to get your life back on track. What's the problem?"

He expelled a light laugh. "Do I need to spell it out? A professional woman like you, used to your own space and independence? It won't be like living at the care home, you know, and I'll tell you now, men can be fucking gross. I learned that in the nick. You'll hear me snoring and farting."

"Is that all that's bothering you?" I retorted. "Won't you at least think about it?"

"You're lovely you are, d'you know that?"

A smile spread across his face. A warm, lazy smile, and with his eyes half closed, I felt my heart melt another degree.

"Now is there anything I can get for you? I was gonna pop to the nearest shop to get some razors and a paper..."

"No, it's fine," I said, feeling the breath coil out of my lungs. "Just promise me you'll come back!"

"I promise," he kept smiling.

I was cracking eggs in a bowl for an omelette when I jumped at the sound of my buzzer. Thinking that it couldn't be Joe back already, I rushed out to answer it.

"Jess!" I spluttered in shock.

My friend looked the worse for wear. Never had I seen her azure blue eyes so puffy, despite the concealment of makeup.

"Can I come in?" she begged huskily.

Rooted to the spot, I held the door open, then followed her into my flat.

"It's over. Steve is a total wanker! To think of all the amazing times we had, and it turns out there was another woman all along."

"Sit down," I tried to pacify her. "Can I make you a camomile tea?"

Jess nodded bravely but I could see she was fighting tears.

Slipping out of her long winter coat, she eased herself into an armchair.

"Sorry if I was 'off' yesterday, but I really needed someone to talk to. I never imagined you'd pass up an opportunity for a girlie night out - not for some homeless guy... and I know you've got a kind heart."

"Hey, stop right there!" I interrupted. "I'm sorry if you've been hurt but Joe is a very dear friend and we had lots of catching up to do. It's been twenty years."

Turning towards the kitchen, I allowed the memory to bloom. Joe had always been the tough one, but now I knew his story, it was my turn to defend him.

"You don't know anything about him," I persisted, "but he's got a pure heart! Before I was fostered, I spent a year in a children's home, did you know that? Joe was one of the few boys who actually cared about me."

"Okay, okay," she relented, palms raised. "I didn't mean to offend you but I care about you too, you know."

I fell silent, wishing I could find the courage to say more, but as I placed the mugs on the work surface, my nerves got the better of me. Sure, Jess was my best friend, but I was unused to standing up to her, conscious of her preening herself in the background, just waiting for her turn to offload.

"Go on then. Tell me what happened."

Her eyes swam with tears. "He dumped me - by text!"

Pouring another coffee, I resigned myself to do what I always did in this situation. My friend's heart had been broken, and I had to stand by her.

When the buzzer sounded again, she was still in full throttle.

"Excuse me, do you mind if I get that?" I interrupted.

Anticipating Joe's return, I held my breath... but what a delight to see him there, teetering on the threshold, cheeks flushed from the cold and that winning smile.

The door clicked shut behind us.

At first Jess didn't move, lips parted, desperate to carry on her story. A lull of silence bit the atmosphere before her eyes swivelled to Joe.

"Well, hello," she murmured in intrigue.

I didn't move, braced for her next sarcastic comment. To my surprise though, it didn't come.

"Well, aren't you going to introduce us?"

"What, you don't remember Joe?" I said, fighting to contain my amusement. "My homeless friend who was here last night?"

My homeless friend who she had treated like shit off her shoe.

"No way!"

Her cheeks flared crimson as she struggled to speak.

"Joe, this is Jess," I broke in to save further embarrassment. "My best friend."

"Hi," Joe nodded. "Good to meet you."

"We were just having a long overdue catch up but take a seat. Can I get you another coffee?"

"It's okay, Maisie," he said. "I'm fine. I'll grab a wash and a shave then let me know what jobs you want doing and I'll make a start."

Watching him withdraw into a shell again, I felt the air freeze around me.

Jess on the other hand, didn't budge. Eyebrow raised, she met my eye with a grin and I could see that as far as she was concerned, this 'homeless guy' had suddenly become a lot more interesting.

"Wow," she breathed, in the moment we stepped outside. "He scrubbed up nice didn't he?" Dominating the conversation for the last thirty minutes, she had finally decided to excuse herself. "And you've got him doing odd jobs already?"

I felt a twinge of anxiety, but only as we loitered on the doorstep did the enormity of the situation hit me at last.

It was time to come clean about my decision.

"Look, you might as well know, I've offered to put Joe up for now."

Jess's eyes widened. "Seriously? How do you know you can trust him?"

"Call it intuition," I said, "but I just do."

"Ooh, I get it," she smirked. "So what really happened last night? Come on, fess up. There's something between you two isn't there?"

"Absolutely not!" I gasped. "Joe and I don't have that sort of relationship, we're childhood friends, that's all!"

"Really?"

"Yes, really."

A wicked glint lit her eyes. "Well between you and me, I think he's lush. I know I wouldn't kick him out of bed. Maybe I should snap him up for myself."

"Jess," I breathed. "You are unbelievable."

"What's the problem?" she tittered. "You said you were just friends."

"It'll never work. You're too different."

"How do you know?"

"I know *you*, Jess. For a start, he's got no money. He'd never be able to afford the lifestyle you're accustomed to."

Jess shrugged. "I'm not after money, I want passion."

"And Joe needs a bit of looking after before you get your claws into him. He's had a tough life, so please don't jump on him too soon..."

"Whatever," she sighed and pecked my cheek. "It's been lovely to see you."

The sun felt warm, a beam of light slipping through the clouds and onto her face, magnifying her beauty. I kissed her back. Perhaps she was only teasing me, but something about her interest in Joe sharpened my senses.

"Tell you what," she finished, with an afterthought, "let's go out for a meal one night. My treat to make up for being such a bitch yesterday."

I struggled to take it in. Thinking about the omelette I'd been about to make, perhaps hunger had brought on a sudden dizziness, but the sunlight was dazzling me. Dots swirled before my eyes, and slipping back into the house, I closed the door to find myself in a web of darkness.

With nothing but a splinter of light shining under my door, so deep was the gloom, I could not see beyond the hallway.

Only a creak on the stairs alerted me to a presence - someone lingering above, watching me. I turned with a gasp, fearful it might be Paula again, until the spidery silhouette of a man took shape.

"Mr Lacey," I called up, "is that you?"

He took a slow step, one hand clawing the banister.

"Maisie, my dear, forgive me... I saw you had company." He spoke quietly, a husky scratch to his voice that reminded me of his ill health.

"You remember Jess," I responded, keeping my voice light. "Anyway, how are you? Were you going out somewhere?"

"Arundel," he drawled. "Plenty of fine old book shops in that town." He gave a watery smile. "By the way, I hope my car isn't taking up too much space, it's not easy to park around here."

Picturing his car - that huge diamond white Nissan Qashqai with tinted windows - I chose my next words with care.

"No. Just thank God we're the only ones here with cars."

Descending painfully, he reached the ground floor out of breath. His eyes were dark as flints as they met mine but nothing more was said. Just a polite nod before he continued his way through the hallway and left the house.

******

Braced on the other side of the door meanwhile, Joe knew Maisie had been seeing Jess off, the echo of her words resonating.

Hearing her return, though, brought a vivid flashback of his own, his mind no longer in her flat.

Tight-lipped and defiant, he stood in Mortimer's office, the giant of a security guard towering over him. He could remember how much his arm throbbed, being hauled up two flights of stairs.

'What the hell did you think you were playing at, Winterton?'

Mortimer's voice penetrated his mind like a video recording. Joe gulped back his terror. He should have known he would be in trouble, but the sadistic smirk on his colleague's face had turned his blood to ice, the way he reached into his hold-all, uncoiling a length of steel hose.

Yet none of it seemed to matter. That ordeal was nothing compared to the dread he had felt the previous day; of creeping back to the laundry room and finding the door unlocked, the silent gloom that awaited him when he saw the empty space on the bench where Maisie should have been.

Chapter Fifteen

Dark thoughts festered in the man's mind, fingers drumming impatiently on the dashboard. The recipient of his call failed to pick up, the ring switching to voice mail. Yet did he dare leave a message?

No, this needed careful discussion, a matter so private, no one could possibly know how long he had been pursuing young Maisie.

The reason for her brief disappearance a few days ago remained a mystery, yet he was prepared to let that go. The most likely explanation was that she had visited her foster parents, that respectable couple in Kent, both of them teachers.

A covert smile edged its way into his lips as the memory surfaced. Something special about Maisie had set her apart from the others, but when Stewart and Amanda Reedman had applied to foster her, it had certainly been for the best. Anything to keep her away from that troublesome boy, who would forever be their nemesis.

And how could he forget Joe Winterton?

His heart took on a slow, painful thump. There was an animal cunning about that one he had despised from the start, but the day he interfered with their practices, they had to punish him. The steel hose had been Schiller's idea, and a stroke of true genius. Hard steel delivered severe pain without leaving scars - no proof of what they had done but the bruises, and even they had faded over time.

No, the only lasting damage they intended was psychological, a drip feed of fear and threat.

With a shuddering breath he attempted a fourth call, itching to disclose this latest report... that more recently, a man had been spotted sneaking in and out of Maisie's flat. So who was he?

It was time to step up their surveillance.

******

"Funny how the mind works, in't it?" Joe reflected one morning. "I'm starting to remember things..."

We had just stepped outside the house and I was about to lock the door, but the echo of his words pulled my head upright. "Like what?"

"Schiller. That thug of Mortimer's, his name was Schiller..." He let out a hollow laugh. "Remember the dry white board just inside the door, listing the staff on duty? Whenever Schiller's name appeared someone always crossed the Ls."

"Shitter!" I chuckled back. "Trust you to remember that!"

With our conversation echoing to the sound of laughter, I knew I had made the right decision inviting him to stay. The warm surround of protection he wove around my life was a bonus and I enjoyed his company. Thankfully there had been no more nightmares and as the days ensued, I noticed a change in him too. Giving him a roof over his head had effectively broken the cycle of unemployment, poverty and homelessness.

Actively seeking a job, Joe was happy to do voluntary work to fill up the empty hours. So when Matt needed an extra pair of hands in the charity shop, he had leapt at the chance. Not only did it count as work experience, it reignited a glimmer of self-worth in him.

Unlocking my car, I could hardly suppress my smile when he climbed into the passenger seat next to me. I was on my way to work anyway but had plenty of time to drop him off at the Job Centre first.

"What are your plans today?"

"Who knows?" he said. "I saw a couple of supermarket jobs advertised but you can only apply online."

My heart swelled with pride, since once inside the Job Centre, he would get all the help he needed, using their in-house computer facilities. Who would recognise the forlorn, broken character I had stumbled across in the beach shelter, in this clean-shaven man, his tousled dark hair gleaming?

Turning the key in the ignition, I was sure the road had been clear, but the moment I pulled out, an unfamiliar black car loomed in my wing mirror.

Strange. It definitely hadn't been there before. *Perhaps they were after my parking space.*

As I reached the top of Annandale Avenue, I slowed at the junction. Funnelled into the roundabout amidst a river of moving traffic, I clung to the middle lane. The one notable feature of this roundabout was its shape and size; a sprawling configuration that had earned it the name 'Bognor Square-about.'

Conscious of Joe chattering next to me, I tried to concentrate on what he was saying but a tightness gripped my chest, my heart picking up speed. I was not too late to catch another flicker, a dark ink stain in my wing mirror. The same car was lingering in the middle distance, before I swerved onto Hothampton flyover.

I stole another glance in my mirror and sure enough, the car had chosen the same exit. Black as midnight with heavily tinted windows, this did not appear to be any ordinary car.

It couldn't be following us, surely? Was I being paranoid?

My panic spiralled. The things Joe had divulged about Mr. Mortimer and now Schiller, were not lost on me, the notion of danger...

A sea of cars clogged the dual carriageway. Moving into the outside lane, I put my foot down, praying there were no speed patrols. As long as I drove carefully, I could safely deliver Joe to the Job Centre without detection.

Hands tight on the wheel, I shot around the next mini roundabout, past the park entrance, then back in the direction of town.

Confident I had lost my pursuer, I finally pulled up outside the Job Centre.

Joe seemed oblivious to my anxiety, but seeing him bounce back warmed my soul, allowing me to temporarily forget the black car. Added to the glow in his complexion, his newly-found confidence radiated itself in his smile.

"Good luck," I wished him with heartfelt sincerity.

"Thanks, Maisie," he said and with a final backward glance, strolled up to the door with a spring in his step.

Only when he disappeared inside the Job Centre, though, my heart sank into my chest. The car had not gone. Paused by the entrance of Hotham park, I was sure I could feel the pinprick of eyes zooming in on me. I so wanted it to be a coincidence; that its presence had no bearing on anything else unfolding in our lives.

If I was right, I had nothing to worry about.

But what if I was wrong?

Fear speared through my mind as I considered the ramifications. The driver would have spotted Joe, clear as day, walking from my car and into the Job Centre.

The more disturbing question was whether he had been recognised.

Chapter Sixteen

Hannah Adams. Registered Psychotherapist and Counsellor. West Sussex
Client: Maisie Bell
18th March 2015

A blanket of cloud hung across the sky, the air damp with mist.

But hidden inside Hannah's therapy room, the gloom lifted, replaced by pastel walls and the gentlest of light. I felt the warmth of her smile as it settled on me.

"I had to see you," I began. "I realise it's a little sooner than scheduled."

Hannah glanced at her note pad. "Okay, so why don't you start by telling me what brought you here today?"

"It's Joe. We've found each other again."

Yes, it was definitely time to come clean about Joe.

Hannah's face twisted into a frown, pen poised. "When did this happen?"

I described the day I had bumped into him along the seafront. With a storm of childhood memories brewing, I was surprised we still hadn't discussed them in depth. Yet Joe seemed cagey, his fear of Mr. Mortimer as evident now as it had been in the past and with the hint of a threat still dangling.

"Maybe this is an opportunity to capture your own memories," Hannah said.

"Yes, I suppose so. Seeing him again feels strange but you'd think he could have told me a bit more..."

Hannah seemed unfazed. "It doesn't matter, you're here now and no two people's memories are alike. Just tell it your own way, Maisie, and without anyone else swaying your judgement."

She was right. In every session to date, the memories had belonged to me alone.

"Looking at your notes, the last time we spoke you mentioned a flashback. So I'd like to take you back to the laundry room, the day Joe locked you in. Why do you suppose he did that?"

Joe. I could picture him now, those great big eyes like pools of melted chocolate.

"I was invited to a party," I said, "one he seemed desperate to stop me going to."

Black clouds covered my mind as the past started to creep in. Two identical red party dresses were draped across our beds but oh, the smooth, glossy texture of satin, the matching red ribbons and shiny ballet pumps.

"Ramona and I were the only ones invited," I added dreamily.

Ramona was my room mate. I often wonder what had happened to that pretty black girl with her afro hair and smiling brown eyes. She had definitely been one of the livelier children.

"Mr. Mortimer told us we had been chosen specially to attend this gathering, a treat with some girls from the other homes. Ramona was so excited. He mentioned there would be adults there, people who might want to foster us."

"But Joe tried to stop you going," Hannah's voice echoed.

"As soon as I mentioned the party, he freaked out. Said it was a trap. He'd been to one himself and - and..."

"Go on."

I fidgeted in my chair, restless.

"They were driven to a big country house in the middle of nowhere. In fact, it sounded like a lot of fun to begin with - party food, video games, music and Sky TV... they could watch what they liked. But later in the evening the hosts brought a bowl of punch out. He said it made them sleepy."

"Do you wonder if it was drugged?" Hannah pressed.

"That's it!" I gasped. "He warned me not to drink it!"

I heard a rustle of fabric as she shifted her position. She seemed agitated suddenly, the friction of pen on paper progressing with increasing speed.

"Something happened at the party he went to, something bad, and that was why he tried to stop me going. Ramona was furious. Said there was no way she was going to miss out and that she had already tried her dress on."

I held my breath, almost frightened to continue.

"So Joe had this idea to hide me. We sneaked downstairs to the laundry room and he locked the door. Told me to 'sit tight' and as soon as they were gone, he would come back..."

"But that didn't happen did it?" Hannah's voice tolled on the periphery.

"No. For some reason they cottoned on. Sussed out our game and one of Mortimer's henchmen came down and got me."

"Henchmen?"

This time I was the one who became agitated, twisting and wriggling, a rush of terror sweeping over me. Two scary looking thugs wandered into the spotlight, one dark, one blonde, both heavily muscled men.

"They were employed for security - we thought they looked more like bouncers. The upshot is I was taken to the party after all."

I bit my lip, though it was pretty much as Joe described, a journey that

76

ferried us some distance from London until we arrived at a secluded country mansion.

"A big black car came to collect us. A posh one, like a limousine and there were two girls already in the back seat, wearing identical dresses and red ribbons. The interior of the house was luxurious but I remembered Joe's warning when they brought the punch out..."

"This is good, Maisie, you're doing really well," Hannah said.

Her voice hung in the air with a mysterious echo, fading in and out like a weak radio signal.

What happened next though, took me by surprise, as if a light bulb in my mind had exploded. I was flung into panic, the blackness around me intensifying.

"Have you remembered something else?"

Yes! Something was lapping on the shore of my mind, a sense of weightlessness as if I was floating. It was the memory of the red ribbon that had triggered it. I could hear a whispering sound in the distance.

Spikes of cold shot through me, the vision of a ribbon fluttering past my face.

"Oh my God! I saw a red ribbon in my dream!"

I couldn't explain it but I could sense the danger pouring in, a vortex of all-consuming evil that had no form but threatened to swallow us as we lay there. I knew we were powerless... but was I the only one who saw those spidery branches encircling us from above? Heard the whisper that sliced through the darkness?

'Silence her!'

I imagined a red ribbon restraining me, a hand pressed over my mouth.

"Relax," Hannah urged, "take deep breaths now."

Except I couldn't. My breath was coming faster and faster, a thickening in my throat that brought a cry erupting to the surface.

"Ssh," she kept soothing me. "Don't panic, you're safe, Maisie and no-one can hurt you... but I think it's best I bring you out of your trance now."

Chapter Seventeen

Ten minutes after leaving the Salvation Army headquarters Joe let himself into the house, using the spare key Maisie had arranged to be cut for him. Delivering leaflets for the latest *homeless appeal,* he found the work not only fulfilling, but it served a painful reminder of his own plight.

He couldn't wait to share his news, the prospect of having an interview lined up with a major supermarket a huge step up the ladder for him, the thought of contributing to her bills even better...

So lost was he in his reverie, he was unprepared for the sight in front of him. Braced on the edge of the sofa, chewing her fingernails, Maisie glanced up at him in fear.

"Joe, why have we never talked about those parties?"

The question froze him mid-step and he could no longer dodge the elephant in the room. Unnerved by her expression, he turned to hang his coat up.

"Dunno."

"Yes, you do. You're hiding something."

"What's brought this on?" he asked gently.

"I went to see my therapist," she said in a monotone. "It's amazing what comes back when you're in a mild hypnotic trance, but I remember why you locked me in the laundry room. You took an awful thrashing for trying to protect me but what exactly were you protecting me from, Joe?"

A sudden dread ran into him. "Does it matter? Whatever happened, we can't change it and I don't wanna dwell on the past. We need to move on..."

"I-I can't move on," she shivered. "My work's been affected, my foster parents are worried... they thought the therapy would help get to the root of my traumas."

"Okay, okay," he tried to shush her, "just let me get my coat and shoes off and I'll stick the kettle on. Would it help if you told me a bit about the nightmares?"

His movements slowed as she described them. Joe said nothing, listening mesmerised as she spoke of a sinister dark forest, a ring of trees...

It was when she related the chants that he felt a chill judder down his spine.

"A red ribbon fluttered past my face," she croaked.

Fear filled her eyes, dragging unpleasant memories in its wake.

"Ramona and I wore red party dresses and red ribbons when we went to the

78

party..."

Yes, he too could remember the ribbons they wore.

Equally sinister was the red ribbon wound around that message he had found at the halfway house. A message laced with threat that told him everything he needed to know and, now he thought about it, exactly who was responsible.

No wonder she looked at him as if she had seen a ghost.

"What if that scene in the forest happened on the same night?" she gasped. "They brought a bowl of punch out like you said they would and I tried not to drink it but I must have had some of it. My memories are vague - there's a huge black hole between the end of the party and returning to Orchard Grange."

Joe's hands gripped the kettle tighter as he poured hot water into the cups. It was hard to concentrate on making tea when the words flooding from her lips filled his mind with horror.

"Hannah wondered if the punch was drugged."

Placing the mugs down on her coffee table, he felt his mouth run dry. Deep down in her subconscious mind, a chilling scenario was unravelling.

But could he bear to fill in the blanks?

"Your punishment wasn't just for hiding me." She held his gaze as the final piece of the puzzle slid into place. "But for warning me not to drink it!"

"Yes," Joe confessed. "You're spot on. Now let me ask you something. You remember Ramona being at the party, but did you ever see her again?"

"No," she whispered. "Where do you suppose she went?"

"A different home perhaps? There was more than one and Mortimer owned them all - private homes - I overheard him talking..."

Picturing Mortimer's cold, twisted smile tied another knot in his stomach.

"What do you mean 'a different home?'" Maisie pressed. "Are you saying Orchard Grange wasn't the only children's home you lived in?"

He had been eleven years old when he was put into care, the residents all boys. Lurking on the edge of an industrial estate, that house resembled a prison more than a children's home...

Joe closed his eyes.

Everything had ticked along okay until that party. The matching outfits, a fancy car turning up to collect them, before he and five other boys were spirited away into the unknown. They had been having the time of their life, until the onset of oblivion blurred the rest out...

"So what do you remember?" She was looking at him intensely now.

Joe swallowed deeply. "The boys wore identical outfits too. Loose black tunics and trousers, clothes to chill out in - red neckerchiefs, a bit like the shit you see boy scouts wearing."

Maisie sank deeper into the sofa cushions, her eyes never leaving him.

"Sounds like some kind of uniform."

"Hmm," Joe murmured. "That's what I thought. Trouble is I don't remember much about the party other than what I told you, and then I was moved on to Orchard Grange."

In another dark recess of his mind rose the memory of several days spent in sick bay before that, his brain foggy from the pills they had forced down him, his gut torn with a pain so intense... They told him it was a severe bout of gastric flu, the reason he had to be isolated. But Joe suspected something far worse; *the fear someone had messed with him* evoked a sickening sense of violation.

"Why did they hurt you so bad," her voice ebbed in the background, "if all you were trying to do was warn me?"

"Cos they were up to something illegal!" he snapped. "Consider the effort those bastards went to, to drag you to that fucking party. I had a horrible feeling you were at risk... and Mortimer was hiding something."

"But I don't understand," she balked, "if your suspicions match mine, then how could he have got away with it?"

Joe took a large gulp of tea, relishing the hot liquid as it swilled down his throat. It afforded him time to consider his next words.

"Think about it, Maisie, we never went to school. A lot of kids got moved around, some from different counties, up north and God only knows where... We had no contact with the outside world."

Her face buckled into a frown.

"We were easy prey. Kids whose mums were prostitutes, like Sam's mum. Kids who'd been prostituted themselves. Damaged, messed up kids that men like Mortimer didn't give a shit about!"

"Victims," Maisie whispered, hands shaking as she lifted her mug. "I've always woken up with a bad feeling after my nightmare but just say we *were* drugged? Taken to a forest, somewhere secret. What could have happened that we don't remember?"

"Some place out in the sticks," Joe pondered, "and no witnesses..."

He could only imagine the horror in her mind. Her face was drained of colour, but even with the cat already crawling out of the bag, could he bear to voice his suspicions aloud?

"I knew exactly what sort of man Mortimer was. A predator."

The degradation hit him even now.

"It's obvious why he got into that line of work and I bet those homes were magnets for all sorts. Private homes, so I doubt the authorities got too involved. I don't know about you but I never saw my social worker after I was dumped in that place."

"Did you ever tell anyone he threatened you?" she whispered.

He shook his head. "Nah! Who'd have listened to me?"

"But this is serious, Joe!" Lowering her mug, she gaped at him in panic. "Isn't it about time we reported it?"

"And say what?"

Looking at her now, he so wanted to reach out to her. Hold her in his arms, whisper tender words into her ears, anything to reassure her there was nothing to fear.

Except he couldn't do it. He couldn't lie.

"You're scared," she accused him. "You think there's still danger."

"Yes," he nodded in reluctance, "but let's deal with this one step at a time, eh?"

He risked a smile.

"I've got an interview next week."

Her head snapped upright.

"Wow, Joe, that's great! Sorry if I burst your bubble."

"Don't be. We needed to have this conversation but now we've talked, let's not dwell. Like I say, it's better we try and move on."

Chapter Eighteen

Regrettably, I couldn't 'move on' quite as fast as Joe hoped. Now the Pandora's box was open, and with an eerie thread of possibilities unspooling, I knew where my thoughts were leading.

Was there a way we could find proof of Mortimer's strange parties?

A blackness closed around my mind as my hideous dream crept back to me. For the horror I felt was the same as on the day Mandy's friends had tried to lure me into a forest. As if the worst kind of evil was lurking...

Terrified to face my demons, I hugged a cushion to my chest.

Thank God I had Joe to confide in.

Ever since he had moved in, we had tumbled into a clumsy harmony. Joe had his own friends and he went out sometimes, leaving me to catch up on my own pursuits. Wednesday night I had attended a *Zumba* class for the first time in weeks. What's more, Jess had agreed to meet me, buzzing for gossip about Joe.

But on the nights he stayed in, we watched TV, chatted, shared news and even recipes. And how could I forget the first time he had cooked for me? His pièce de résistance, *beans au gratin* had me in fits; thick slices of toast smothered in baked beans and cheese, heated under the grill, until bubbling and golden.

Even my foster mum laughed at that when I phoned her.

Tonight, however, I was in no mood for humour, given the turmoil my therapy had stirred up.

But I wasn't alone: Joe seemed unable to hide his own anxiety, for some reason. It manifested itself in his face, from the grooves etched in his brow to the way his eyes darkened.

He had not long returned from town. Lingering in the kitchen, slowly unpacking the groceries, I saw his eyes flitting to a newspaper.

"What have you got there?"

"Just something I picked up from the Salvation Army headquarters earlier," he said.

Odd, I thought, flipping the pages apart, *why the Guardian?* He usually read the Mirror. I carried on flicking through until one particular headline caught my eye. My head shot upright.

That story. The allegations Stewart had mentioned weeks ago.

"Claims that the establishment covered up a paedophile ring at the heart of Westminster are finally being investigated, decades after rumours first surfaced."

"I know what you're thinking," Joe snapped. "You must wonder if there's a connection, given what we were talking about."

"To Orchard Grange?" I replied. "My foster dad said the same thing... victims taken out of care homes."

My eyes flashed across the lines of news print.

"It says '*a chauffeur driven car was used to drive them to locations where they were abused.*'"

"I know," Joe broke in softly, "but there's no mention of a country house, is there? Just a block of apartments, so don't get freaked out. It's the wrong decade. This stuff is reported to have happened in the 70s and 80s and to be fair, I don't remember any 'high establishment figures' on the scene, do you?"

I took in the names and shuddered. "No, but it's a horrible story and there are even allegations of murder..." I glanced up. "Isn't this what you suspected all along about Sam? That he might have been killed?"

This time Joe was the one who stiffened. "I didn't wanna say this but Sam's just the sort of boy who'd get picked out by nonces. Mortimer's homes were like buffets for certain types, and we had no way of communicating outside them."

"So what else do you know?" I pressed. "I've told you everything I remember but you must have your own recollections surely..."

******

The light was low, a cloak of shadow embracing him as he allowed his mind to wander into the past. Like Maisie, Joe could not dismiss the news stories out of hand. Someone had come forward with a set of horrific allegations - only one person - but enough to send him reeling back to the savage world of Orchard Grange.

There was noise, so much noise. Children shouting, doors slamming, the bellow of adults ordering them to shut up! Occasionally fights broke out and there was damage, kids stamping up and down the stairs, desperate to get out, objects thrown and smashed. Then came the restraints, the banging of heads against walls or worse... He didn't know if anyone else had suffered a beating the way he had, but it was enough of a deterrent for him to keep his mouth shut for a while.

Whatever had happened to Maisie, though, no one knew the truth. Ramona had gone. Most likely shifted into an unfamiliar home the same way he'd been. Days blurred into each other, the passage of time vague... and then Sam had turned up. Sam, who captured Mortimer's interest, stirring deep waves of dread in Joe.

"What did he say," Maisie gulped, "after Sam disappeared?"

"Spun some bullshit story he was adopted."

A frown knitted his forehead as the words ripped through his mind.

'Sam has a new family now, someone who's chosen to adopt him. Pity the same couldn't be said for you, Winterton, but then who in their right mind would want an ugly little tearaway like you in their home?'

Joe knew when to back off. It wasn't so much the insult but the way he voiced it. Puffed up like a toad, Mortimer towered over him in a way that made him feel worthless and crushed any possible defiance.

No, that would come later...

"I don't believe that!" Maisie intervened. "I remember the process when I was adopted. It took months. Meetings with social workers, bonding sessions with my foster family. When did anyone ever turn up to see Sam?"

"That's just it, no one did," Joe pondered. "Just another one of his big lies to throw me off the scent, except I wasn't buying it."

Sure, there had been 'meetings', but they had nothing to do with Sam's alleged adoptive family. This was around the time Joe had gleaned some notion Mortimer owned several homes. Private homes used to run an undisputedly dodgy business.

"The only person I saw visiting was some smart geezer. I overheard him talking... something about *Government funding*."

"I remember him," Maisie whispered. "Professional, sharp suit, silver hair... at least he was kind."

"Kind," Joe echoed cynically. "Maybe I'd run out of trust by then but I always thought there was something a bit creepy about that guy."

Given Mortimer's loathing, Joe often found himself outside his office, which was where he had first spotted this enigmatic stranger. A man with impeccable charm who had smiled at him.

Maisie leaned forwards. He had just been about to elaborate, but the glint in her eye stalled him.

"And you overheard him talking about Government funding?"

"Yeah..."

"So he was a politician?" she murmured. "Someone in power."

Joe frowned, hardly able to take this in. With his thoughts locked in the past, the memories were swirling faster, a volley of hateful words.

'Sneaking around again, Joe? I wouldn't bother associating yourself with that one, Sir, he's a lying, devious little troublemaker.'

Joe had barely acknowledged the other man at the time. The bigger problem was Mortimer, his spiralling animosity towards Joe - not just for attempting to protect Maisie, but for his unrelenting curiosity about Sam. With no further clue as to whether his friend was alive or dead, Joe could not resist cranking the pressure up.

Where did Sam's adoptive family live?

Was there a way they could contact him?

Joe had relished watching Mortimer squirm, until the day his temper soared to a staggering new level.

"Joe," Maisie prompted. She touched his arm gently. "Is there something else you want to tell me?"

His heart hammered harder. It was so much easier to forget the vile things hissed at him, but as days stretched into weeks, his yearning to know the truth about Sam's disappearance tore against the struggle to keep himself safe from Mortimer's violence.

Mortimer had grabbed him by the throat once, and pressed him against the wall of his office, kicking the door shut.

'Breath one more word about Sam Ellis and I will wring your scrawny neck!'

Next came the night they had him trapped in the boys' toilets.

Schiller had accompanied him, a mammoth of a man in his twelve-year-old eyes. The dark sky pressed down heavily, the other kids in their beds, just a rectangle of light shining around the door frame.

'Time we dealt with you once and for all, you piece of scum...'

If it hadn't been for a cough escaping from the corridor, he might not have lived to tell the tale.

Locking eyes with Maisie, he felt the breath on his lips tremble.

"Joe, I'm sorry, I didn't mean to upset you..."

"You wanna go to the cops, don't you?" he shuddered. "Report the parties, even though we ain't got proof."

"This isn't just about *us* any more though," she argued. "What about Sam? I want to know why he vanished, and as for this story he was adopted, I know someone who could check it out. My friend, Sarah, is an adoption reunion counsellor and an expert when it comes to tracing people."

Joe expelled a sigh. At the back of his mind, he would forever agonise over Sam's disappearance. If it was possible to trace him he would.

But neither could he ignore his nemesis, Mortimer, and the fear he was still at large.

Chapter Nineteen

Rage pounded through the man's head as he studied the images emailed to him. Or more specifically, the image of the man who had been spotted with Maisie.

"We have a problem. Joe Winterton has resurfaced!"

In all the days this worthless vagrant had taken shelter on Bognor seafront, no one had really noticed him. Head concealed under a hoodie, he was not worthy of attention, but freed from the shadows and the facial hair, there was no denying who that face belonged to. The long lens captured every detail, from his misshapen nose to his soulful dark eyes.

Joe bloody Winterton.

"Hardly a wonder he's so pally with Maisie then," his associate sniffed. "They were friends already."

"But he's living with her!" He drew in a deep breath, teeth bared.

One would think they had scared Winterton off long ago but no... they should have guessed that young trouble-maker would appear one day.

"Can you believe he's turned up in Bognor of all places?"

"It must be fate," his ally warned. "You'll definitely have to watch your back now, and the same goes for our watcher."

A slick of sweat moistened the man's forehead.

Seven weeks they had been stalking her. If it hadn't been for that Fostering Information Evening last year, he might never have discovered her workplace. But the trail had eventually led to Bognor, the house she was living in now.

"We can't drop our surveillance. As if it's not enough there's some psychotherapist poking her nose in, recovering God only knows what..."

"Still seeing the shrink then?"

"Yes, but you're missing the point! Those two are bound to talk!"

Staring at the images of Joe, he felt the acid burn of hate. With his long term plan coming together at last, they had been on the verge of ensnaring her. Yet Joe's jagged profile mocked him, filling him with an insatiable thirst for vengeance.

"If only we'd dealt with the little shit beforehand. We should have beaten every last breath out of him..." His voice shuddered to a snarl. "It's not too late."

"Calm down, Cornelius," his associate sighed. "Let's not get carried

away."

He could almost picture the smirk on his face.

"You always suspected Maisie might expose you one day, but if you take any drastic action, if you resort to violence, you know she'll go bleating to the police before we're ready. All Joe needs for now is a warning."

******

London

Thomas tucked away his mobile and crossed the busy main road. To the unfamiliar eye, he looked like any other suited businessman; immaculately groomed and silver-haired. The city was full of them, a place where it was easy to remain inconspicuous. And right now, he was craving a cup of tea.

He breezed into an elegant tea room, favouring this particular establishment as much for the gorgeous young waitresses as for its decor. Palm resting on the door rail, he relished the coolness of polished brass. Large windows with delicate gold etchings looked directly out onto the pavement but Thomas had no desire to sit and people-watch. Instead, he chose a secluded table near the back.

"What can I get for you, Sir?"

He looked at the waitress, holding her gaze for as long as he dared.

Dear God, what a beauty. Smooth skin the colour of caramel and thickly lashed brown eyes... she was enough to snatch a man's breath away.

"Tea for one and some cakes please. What would you recommend?"

"Strawberry slice is good," she said, scribbling down his order, "made with fresh cream, otherwise, have you tried our banoffee cupcakes?" She rolled her eyes heavenwards. "Now they are lush!"

"I'd like to try one of each, then."

With a polite nod, she wandered up to the counter, hips rolling nicely under her tight black skirt. *Fifteen, perhaps? She would have to be if she was working here but oh, that figure...* Thomas shook his head. A man of his status, he shouldn't be thinking like this, but he couldn't help himself. The young had always fascinated him, the innocence of youth, the untrained mind he so longed to nourish.

"What's your name?" he muttered, the moment she returned.

She lowered a pot of tea and milk jug carefully onto the table. "Poppy."

"Poppy," he echoed. "What a pretty name."

A slow, rich smile spread across her face. "Well, thank you, Sir."

The slenderness of her fingers was next to catch his eye, entwined in the handle of his tea cup. Not a chunky white cup like a soup bowl, but delicate bone china infused with a pattern of roses. Such refinement pleased him and, with a political career spanning three decades, he had developed a taste for the finer things in life.

But as Minister for Education in the 90s and a short spell as a backbencher when the opposition were in power, his resounding success as Minister for Social Care had at last granted him a position in the House of Lords.

Yes, he had cause to celebrate, and what better place than this exclusive tea room with its quintessential English charm?

Poppy was back, her deportment calm and meticulous, with none of the rush that so irritated him in those commercial chains. Even the cakes she presented resembled works of art. Their eyes met and her smile lingered.

"Lovely," he muttered. "Thank you."

Whether he was referring to her or the cakes was open to speculation, but how he loved her little titter, the way her fingers crept to her mouth. *Such coyness.*

He looked away. Diverted his stare from her budding breasts. With his newly acquired status, he should be mentally rehearsing the speech he was going to give at next week's press interview.

Thomas Parker-Smythe newly appointed to the House of Lords.

He had all the reason in the world to relish his success, and easily enough to leave Poppy an extra large tip.

"Treat yourself to something special," he said warmly. "A pretty pair of earrings maybe..."

Her last glittering smile was the one that stayed with him; one that would reel him back to this place again and again, powerless to fight it.

******

"Poppy," her mother scolded her. "What have I warned you about flirting with older men?"

"Got a result didn't it?" Poppy argued. "Stop fussing."

"You're going to get yourself into trouble one day, young lady."

But regrettably, Poppy wasn't listening. Fingering the ten pound note her customer had tucked in with the bill, she was glowing with the compliments he had showered her with.

Chapter Twenty

For the next few days, Joe shoved the whole ugly business of Orchard Grange to the back of his mind. As for the mystery of Sam, if Maisie thought she could trace him with the help of her friend then so be it.

He couldn't imagine she'd have much luck, but who was he to stop her trying?

With his brain overloaded, he had left the Job Centre on a high note. To be employed by a major supermarket like Sainsbury's would be a pivotal step if he could get through the interview. He had never imagined he would get even this far but as long as he kept a cool head and demonstrated a keenness to learn and work hard, there was no reason he couldn't clinch it. The sheer nerve it took having to declare his criminal conviction had nearly toppled him. Yet despite his shady past, there were at least some people prepared to give him a chance.

Marching along the pavement, head down, he couldn't wait to get home. Devoting the latter half of the day to helping Matt in the charity shop, time had passed quickly. Yet he could no longer ignore the ache in his calves from the hours spent on his feet.

The secluded cosiness of Maisie's flat drew him like an oasis.

Turning the corner though, he was unprepared for the sight of a blue light flashing in the road. Joe quickened his pace. The fluorescent yellow and green squares of an ambulance were next to register, two wheels parked on the pavement, directly outside the house where Maisie lived.

Charging up to the door, he came to an abrupt halt. The first people to appear in the hallway were the Polish couple, Anna with her distinctive fair hair, her lips frozen in a circle of shock.

"What the hell's happened?" Joe gasped.

An unpleasant bolt of worry speared his insides.

Please God, don't let it be Maisie.

"You know - um - man?"

Only then did he notice Maisie's door was still shut, Anna pointing to the top of the staircase. He almost sagged with relief.

"Oh him! The old boy upstairs, you mean?"

"Is bad," the male half of the partnership muttered.

Glancing at Vlodek - a somewhat fierce looking man whose heavy black brows drew a perpetual frown to his face - Joe wished they could expand. Yet given the language barrier, nothing was forthcoming other than a sad shake of his head.

"He's not dead, is he?" Joe faltered.

"Not yet!" snapped a guttural voice from above.

A thud of footsteps followed, all heads turning as a heavily built woman waddled into view. *This could be none other than Paula.*

"Collapsed and with any luck, the old git's had a heart attack!"

Joe raised his eyebrows. "That's a bit harsh, isn't it?"

He felt the blaze of her eyes and suddenly he was the one under scrutiny.

"Who are you?"

"Joe," he said, keeping his voice light. "I'm a friend of Maisie's."

From the corner of his eye he saw the Polish couple flash another glance at each other. They seemed more relaxed, now they had communicated, offering him a final nod before discretely slipping away. The door clicked behind them.

Paula, on the other hand, held her ground, her eyes pinned to him.

She gave a cold smile. "Really? Bet she said I was a right fat slag."

"No way," Joe chuckled. "Maisie wouldn't say that."

He watched the hostility fade from her eyes.

"Well, for what it's worth, me name's Paula and I live upstairs with me little 'un. What d'you do?"

"I'm trying to find work," he said. "Up until a couple of weeks ago I was homeless but Maisie offered me a roof over my head."

"Girlfriend of yours?" Paula smirked.

"Nope, we knew each other as kids."

He half expected the conversation to fizzle out until her expression turned strangely pensive.

"Don't s'pose you're the owner of a black car, are you?"

"Car?" Joe grinned. "You've gotta be joking. I've only just got a mobile, check this out," and delving into his rucksack, he swiped out a nearly new Samsung Galaxy. "Can you believe it's got a six month contract on it? Guy in the charity shop said I could have it... Sorry, what were you saying about a black car?"

"I've seen it driving up our road a few times," Paula continued. "Hanging about. I'm not being paranoid or nothing but d'ya reckon it could be a stalker?"

"Is someone stalking you?" Joe frowned.

She bit her lip but at the same time could not hide the doom chiming in her voice. "Can't take no chances with me little 'un."

"Well cheers for the warning. I'll keep a lookout. Oh, and for what it's worth, I'm sorry about the old boy upstairs. Maisie did say he was ill."

Leaving the conversation on a friendly note, he turned to let himself into the flat. Just before he stepped inside, he spotted an envelope on the doormat; an envelope with his name on it. Thinking about what Paula said, he felt a prickle of goosebumps.

A black car hanging about, and now a letter?

Something didn't feel right.

After a torturous thirty minutes and later than expected, Maisie returned home at six. At first, he did not hear her. Desperate to distract himself from the shock pounding through him, he had taken to cleaning the bathroom floor like there was no tomorrow.

Crouched on all fours when she crept through the door, he was unprepared for the tap on his shoulder, and jolted in shock at her touch.

"Maisie! You scared the shit out of me!"

"Well, who else did you think it was?" she retorted.

"Never mind," he muttered, sweeping a damp curl off his forehead.

"Sorry I'm late, traffic was hideous. I've been stuck in a nose-to-tail crawl for the last half hour but at least I was able to park... I see Mr Lacey's car is gone."

Joe nodded, catching her train of thought.

"Has something happened?" she pressed.

Moving in the direction of the kitchen to fill the kettle up, she listened in stunned silence as he related the scene he had come home to.

"An ambulance?" she echoed.

"He's been rushed to hospital."

"Oh, hell," she said sadly. "I wonder if the cancer's back..."

A frown crossed her face as she studied him more closely. How could he explain? An icy sweat clung to him that had nothing to do with his endeavours.

"What's up?" she whispered. "Is something else bothering you?"

"No," he shrugged. "I was just worried it might have been you."

Retreating into the spare room, he changed his clothes. No matter how hard he tried not to think about that letter though, its words were burned into his brain as if they'd been branded there.

At first it appeared to be a Salvation Army leaflet; the same leaflet he had distributed for their homeless campaign, where the photo of a man huddled in a sleeping bag struck a nerve. But that was before he flipped it over...

> *Crawl back to the gutter where you come from, scum,*
> *people like you are not fit to live in our society.*

Scrawled on the reverse in red pen, the words played darkly on his mind.

There was only one person who had ever called him 'scum.'

Maybe he should have told her, but there seemed no point, not now he had burned the note in a furious act of rebellion. But with his life finally on an upward spiral, did the bearer of that hateful message really think he was about to chuck it all away? He had something to fight for, now. He wasn't going to give it all up.

A chill nonetheless crawled over him as he examined his new mobile, another reason to be grateful for Matt's savvy.

Thinking back to the last time he had owned a mobile, this nearly new Samsung had opened his eyes to a whole new world. Joe had never given social media much thought but the stuff Matt showed him blew his mind; platforms that joined people all over the world and got them talking. Matt's particular preference was *Twitter*, humorous and brutal in equal measure, trends that raised awareness, not to mention a permanent shitstorm of political argument.

With no hesitation he had installed the app and registered an account.

And whoever was trying to intimidate him could fuck off.

Because 'society' had suddenly become a lot more interesting.

Chapter Twenty-One

It so happened that having a new gadget to play with was not the only pleasurable diversion to take his mind off things. Joining Maisie in the lounge, he put on a brave face as she told him about the text she had just received.

"It's Jess. She asked if we fancied going out for a meal later. Her treat."

At first he was unsure what to say.

"Oh come on! She did offer a while ago but you can never tell with Jess."

An hour later, they were huddled around a table in 'Mamma Mia,' an unpretentious but pleasing Italian restaurant.

Glancing around, Joe nodded in approval. A soft glow infused the chalky walls, the interior rustic and comforting. Best of all, it was located some distance from the town centre, a place he felt secluded.

"We often come here for pizza," Jess said. "Isn't that right, Maisie?"

Their eyes met across the table, bringing a lump to his throat.

It didn't seem that long ago he was surviving on scraps donated by the compassionate few; people who didn't regard him as 'scum.'

Now here he was, mouth watering from the delicious aromas of garlic and pizza wafting from the kitchen. Looking at Jess, it was hard to forget the disdain on her face the first time she had clamped eyes on him. Tonight though, he felt the warmth of her smile and there was no denying her beauty.

"What d'you do for a living?" he couldn't resist asking her.

"I work for a PR consultancy in Chichester," she purred. "It's one of the best jobs I've ever had, since no two days are the same..."

Joe shifted in his seat as she proceeded to describe her role. Being at the heart and soul of the media, they worked with a range of clients from local dignitaries to visiting actors and celebrities. It all sounded very glamorous.

"You are lucky," Maisie broke in. "It's days like today I wonder why I stick with my job. Our media company produced a new video, to raise awareness about child neglect but it upset me! A poor little girl, curled up on a filthy mattress. Looks in the fridge and there's not a scrap of food to be seen..." She exhaled a helpless sigh. "At least it got us talking about our next radio appeal."

"I couldn't do what you do," Joe said. "I would wanna kill people."

"Don't dwell, Joe. A lot of kids get help, you know, hence the appeal. We want as many willing fosterers to come forward as possible."

"Sure," he nodded. "I totally get that."

His eyes flitted nervously as the food arrived, though Jess didn't seem to pick up the exchange. Happy to keep the banter flowing, whilst twittering on about her own successes, she took a delicate bite of pizza.

"Social media, of course, has a huge influence these days," she added.

Joe kept quiet. Reluctant to show his ignorance, he tucked into his carbonara, the spaghetti cooked to perfection with just the right bite, the sauce deliciously creamy.

"How are you getting on with your new mobile, Joe?" Maisie piped up, as if desperate to drag him into the conversation.

Dropping his gaze, he wound another length of spaghetti around his fork. "Okay. Matt helped me set up my email and he's just got me onto this Twitter thing."

"Twitter!" Jess gasped. "Oh brill! What name do you go under?"

He reached for his mobile and launched the app. "Still an unhatched egg with one follower, but what do you think? Darth Joe? Joseph of Winterfell?"

"Oh, go for Winterfell," she joked. "Everyone loves a 'Game of Thrones' fan and with smouldering eyes like yours, you could pass as Jon Snow."

He felt a flush spread across his cheeks, unused to such flattery.

"Jess!" Maisie breathed. "You're making Joe blush."

"Oh come on, you must be used to it!"

"No, but I could *get* used to it," he teased her.

Was she playing with him?

Despite her bravado, he sensed a troubled soul who hungered for attention. Maisie hadn't divulged much about her friend, other than a string of broken relationships. He, on the other hand, had no delusions. Sure, this ravishing girl enjoyed flirting but he couldn't imagine he came close to being in *her league*.

She nevertheless held his gaze. "You need a portrait picture. Let me take a photo, you're looking good and I love that shirt. Black suits you."

Joe shook his head. "No. Please. Let's not bother with it now..."

A finger of cold trailed down his back. Despite the ambience, the food, the smells and the company, he could not forget the venom in that earlier message. It was enough to resurrect his fear, and the thought of being recognised online petrified him.

True to her word, Jess insisted on picking up the bill, though the conversation continued long after they had finished their Frascati. As they debated their preferred social networks, Joe's shoulder muscles began to relax again. He desperately wanted to be a part of their world, if they could just find common ground.

Thinking back to his murky past, he had no interest in joining Facebook.

Conversely, Maisie had shied away from Twitter.

"So maybe we can hook up on Instagram," she suggested.

"Hmm," Joe pondered. "What's that then?"

She explained the platform, and he could immediately see its appeal. Joining a photo sharing network, he could retain the same anonymity as on Twitter.

"Beach shots are my favourite," she kept enthusing. "The way the light shines at different angles, it changes the colour of the sea..."

Scrolling through her photos, he understood her passion; the calmness of the sea at dawn so still it shone like glass - a stark contrast to the next image, a thunderous black sky folding shadows into the waves as they went galloping over the breakwaters.

"And we get amazing sunsets here, especially in winter."

It must have been winter she had befriended those guys in the beach shelter.

Joe sighed inwardly. How he wished he could have paid for tonight's meal, but with two crumpled fivers in his pocket, he could just about run to a round of drinks. So taking the lead, he coaxed both girls in the direction of the Waverley, which ironically stood right opposite the beach shelter he had just been thinking about.

A soft breeze spiralled from the sea, filled with the hiss of waves, the sound evoking memories. Entering the pub through a side door, he held it open. Jess sneaked a glance over her shoulder, a wily glint in her eye as she surveyed him. He caught his breath, wondering how much she really knew of his humble origins.

"So, how are things now?" she began quizzing him. "It's been a while since you've moved in with Maisie – how's the job hunting going?"

"Funny you should ask," he said and keeping his voice low, nudged a little closer. "I've got an interview with Sainsbury's next week."

Jess lifted her eyebrows. "Great! What's the job?"

"You know this online shopping malarkey? They need pickers."

As Maisie joined them at the bar, he paid for the drinks. Two delicate flutes of white wine rested on a tray, alongside a pint of ale.

"It's average pay and I have to roll up at the crack of dawn, but hey, it's a job. Something physical, enough hours left in the day to keep up the voluntary work and I can always apply for some bar work."

"Well done, you," Jess mused. "I impressed you've turned things around."

"I'm not just your average *scuzzy tramp*," he replied with a wink.

"Oh, stop it!" she laughed.

Strangely enough, he was warming to her. Glancing from Jess to Maisie it was amazing how two girls could be so different. They were like the moon and the sun, Maisie the enigmatic one with her closed body language and intelligent, probing eyes. She possessed a hidden beauty. Whereas Jess's glamour undulated off her in waves. Her teasing eyes amused him, her smile

95

soft as summer rain, instilling that first trickle of desire. She had built him up in a way that made him feel ten foot tall and for that, he could only be grateful.

"Good luck with the interview," her voice rose again. "I really hope you get it."

His heart swelled with fortitude. "Well, thanks, Jess and if so, I'll pick up the bill next time we go out."

Chapter Twenty-Two

Maisie could not resist winding him up. Creeping their way home in the inky darkness, he had insisted on escorting Jess to her door first. At least they didn't have to walk very far, with her own seaside apartment situated only a couple of blocks from the Waverley.

On the way back to Maisie's, a light-hearted mood had prevailed.

"I reckon she fancies you," she tittered.

But Joe laughed it off. "Jess enjoys flirting, it comes naturally to her."

"Oh, don't be so negative," she argued and closing the door, turned to hang her coat up. "She sees you as a saviour! Finally she's met a man who doesn't treat her like some blonde bimbo and like she said, you're looking good."

It was a nice fantasy, and stealing a glance at his reflection, he so wanted to believe her. Face glowing with confidence, his hair cleaner and glossier than it had looked in years, there was no question he was a reformed character compared to the ruin of a man she had found in the beach shelter.

Battling ahead with their normal routine the next day, Joe thought nothing more of it. For a start, they needed shopping and like most working people, Maisie usually left it until the weekend. On this gloomy, chilly Saturday, however, the prospect of plodding to Morrisons held no appeal, so she decided to drive to Sainsbury's for a change.

"Just think, you might be working here soon," she indulged him.

"Shh," Joe whispered. "Don't jinx it."

Thinking about her words, though, he found himself wandering from aisle to aisle, paying extra attention to the layout as they filled their trolley with groceries. Joe grabbed a bottle of red. At least he could make a contribution to the shopping now, a thought that slapped another smile on his face. Actively on the hunt for employment, he was finally entitled to a Job Seekers allowance.

"What else do we need?" her voice broke into his reverie. "I was going to cook pasta tonight, unless you prefer pie."

"No, no, pasta sounds good," Joe replied. "We can have the pie tomorrow if you like. I'll do the veggies and some mash. I was just gonna grab a paper."

Rolling their trolley towards the newspaper rack, he quickly scanned the headlines. His eyes were drifting towards his preferred 'Mirror' nestled among the tabloids when something jolted him; a face shimmering on the edge of his vision, a face he could barely bring himself to acknowledge, only it was impossible to look away.

Thomas Parker-Smythe Ascends To The House of Lords.

Joe froze.

He knew where he'd seen that man before, and an icy chill swept over him.

"So what's with the 'Daily Mail' then?"

It was no use. He could no longer silence the alarm bells in his head, having hastily snatched up the paper. Following Maisie back to the car park, the clouds seemed to thicken, adding an ominous dark layer to the sky.

Yet they had no clue of what was to come.

"There's something in it, I could tell by your expression."

"You haven't noticed the face on the cover?" he said, trying to keep his voice light. "It's someone you might recognise..."

Sure enough, the photo rendered her spellbound.

"It's that bloke who used to visit the care home. We were only talking about him the other day, the one who turned up for meetings with Mortimer."

Her eyes narrowed as they flitted over the newsprint. "Thomas Parker-Smythe. Nominated for the House of Lords and celebrating his success..." She cleared her throat. "So he *is* a politician."

"Yes," Joe stated factually.

She turned very still but he could guess where her thoughts were drifting.

A politician.

What was his connection with Orchard Grange? Those covert meetings?

As Maisie studied the photo, he felt an unpleasant roll in his stomach; there was an air of superiority about the man smirking below the headline, a pair of intense blue eyes boring into him.

"Arrogant looking git, isn't he?" he announced coldly.

Maisie gripped the pages harder. "What did you say you overheard them talking about?" she murmured.

"Something about *government funding*. I can't remember the conversation word for word, only that Mortimer was looking for investment..."

He experienced a giddy sensation as he read the article. For listed among Parker-Smythe's accomplishments was his role as Minister for Education in the 1990s; a period during which he had proposed and implemented a policy that provided *'additional funding for residential children's care homes if improved standards of welfare and schooling were to be met.'*

Maisie turned to him with a gasp.

"What?"

"He was Minister for Education the year *we* were at Orchard Grange! I wonder if he knew anything about those parties."

Joe let out a resigned sigh. "Dunno. I always thought he looked a bit smarmy, though, the way he used to hang around afterwards, ogling the kids, chatting 'em up... He seemed a bit 'too friendly' if you know what I mean."

So Thomas Parker-Smythe had ascended to the House of Lords, a man of power.

It felt as if the dark tentacles of the past were reaching out again, luring him towards his demons.

Worse was to come. As daytime dipped into evening, Maisie drifted around the kitchen, mumbling something about dinner. All day long the rain had turned ever more persistent, trapping them inside her flat. Not that Joe was bothered. It gave him an excuse to spend more time exploring social media.

Nothing more was said about the politician whose face had materialised in the paper; but tapping away on his mobile, he couldn't resist checking to see if anything was trending in politics.

Discovering nothing of interest, he was about to put it down when he flinched to the bleep of a media notification.

"What now?" Maisie called. "Sounds like you're getting popular."

Joe blinked as the screen lit up, seeing a surprising number of Twitter icons lined along the top. He zoomed in close, thumb hovering to begin scrolling, but what he saw punched the breath out of him.

"Shit," he spluttered. "What the fuck is this?"

> @the_watchman
> Why are you still here @JosephofWinterfell? I'd like to ram a length of steel hose up your arse. Filthy trouble-making scum bag. Get out of Bognor NOW!!!

Maisie flew into the lounge, and even though he tried to twist the screen away from her, he was too late to shield her from the abuse he had seen.

"Oh my God!"

"Matt warned me about Twitter trolls," he said.

"But I can't understand why you've been targeted."

A surge of fear rose from deep within his belly. He'd done everything right, he thought. He had even taken Jess's advice with regard to his Twitter name, downloading a seemingly harmless wolf avatar.

"JosephofWinterfell," she recited. "So who do you suppose could have posted it?"

"Mortimer," he shivered. "Or someone linked to him. I didn't wanna tell you this yesterday but I found a nasty note on your doormat..."

"I knew something was up," she snapped. "Oh, Joe! What did it say?"

A grubby contaminated feeling coated his insides. "That scum like me don't belong here and to crawl back to the gutter where I belong."

"So someone's trying to scare you off," she gasped.

"There's something else I haven't told you," he said. Tossing the mobile into the sofa cushions, he looked at her in dismay. "D'you wanna open the wine?"

"I guess so," she answered.

He was about to lever himself up but she beat him to it, vanishing in the direction of the kitchen again. An erratic clink of glass followed before she made her way unsteadily back to the lounge.

"What else have you got to report, then?"

A lump of guilt rose in his chest.

Maybe he should have been straight with her.

He told her what he'd heard from Paula, the mention of a black car loitering.

"Oh shit, Joe." Horror widened her eyes, and she seemed to be struggling with her words. "I-I haven't totally been straight with you either, but do you remember when we left the house in my car one morning? I saw a black car pull out behind me. I thought nothing of it but a couple of minutes later it was hanging about near the Job Centre."

"So it was following us," Joe mumbled.

"Yes." She picked up her wine and took a sip. "The question is, how long have we been under surveillance?"

His head drooped low as he clamped his hands over his knees. Ever since moving in, he had felt uneasy, a matter he put down to their traumatic past. It had started with Maisie's flashbacks, a topic that forced him to recall his own memories. Now everything he feared was spinning through his mind like a vortex.

His enemies had recognised him, they knew where he lived, and now they'd aggressively broken into his social network.

Chapter Twenty-Three

For the latter half of the evening, I felt numb. Not long after dinner I switched the TV on to catch the headlines, though to be honest, I wasn't really listening to the news. The stuff happening with Joe had shaken me to the core. Here he was trying to forge a decent life for himself, someone who had more than proven his virtue ever since moving in; not just doing odd jobs around my flat and his voluntary work, but doggedly determined to secure a paid job.

To think, he was so close to turning his life around.

Not surprisingly, he had sunk into an even deeper gloom. Braced in an armchair, his eyes rarely left the TV screen yet the edges of his face seemed sharper. From the corner of my eye I saw him check his mobile from time to time, unable to resist checking whether there were more messages.

I could no longer stay silent. "What are you going to do, Joe?"

He glanced up. "Maybe it's best if I move out."

"Don't say that," I whimpered.

"No, hear me out. I could be putting you in danger just being here! So as soon as I've earned some dough, I'll rent a room somewhere."

"No, Joe," I insisted. "I like having you here, we get on well... in fact I feel a lot safer with you around."

With flickers of candlelight dancing in his soulful eyes, his expression did not change. "So what about now? There's some creep following us about in a black car, messages shoved through the door and now this..." Grasping his mobile he shook it in front of my eyes. "We don't know how long they've been onto us, and did you see the Twitter name *they* chose? The_watchman. That's taking the piss!"

For a second I could not answer. Could not bear to imagine what was unfolding in our lives, nor the invisible enemies stalking us.

But did we dare inform the police?

The idea surged like wildfire through my mind. With our memories combined, surely we knew enough about Mortimer and his 'homes' to blow the whistle by now, especially if a prominent MP was involved? If only we could untangle the lies, it would bring justice for dozens of victims.

Our eyes locked, my heart thumping, but I could not utter the words aloud.

"Don't go," I simply whispered. "You always said there was danger, and you were right, but you leaving isn't going to solve anything. We're in this together."

As the night drew in, Joe rose to his feet, and I remembered the chaos in the kitchen. We hadn't yet done the washing up.

"Here, let me help," I offered, hauling myself off the sofa.

It seemed to lift him out of his melancholy.

Rivulets of water ran down the window pane but my eyes drifted further. Staring through the darkness with a shiver, I wondered if we'd ever be safe, the night of my hallucination hurtling back to me...

But where did Sam go? Could he still be out there, calling to us?

Drifting over to the sink, Joe filled a bowl with hot soapy water while I tidied up. I couldn't help cherishing his presence, my eyes drawn to his hands as they swirled around in the water. Every movement seemed gentle and unhurried. He washed the glasses and rinsed them. The crockery and pans came next. The task took no more than ten minutes and still I sensed the night wasn't quite over.

"Are you sure you're okay?" he asked me.

Turning away from the window, I felt the warmth of his hands on my shoulders. Time seemed to stand still, before he slowly spun me around to face him.

"Did you mean it when you said you liked having me here?"

A sigh of amusement escaped my lips. "Of course I meant it..."

My words withered as his face loomed close, the intensity of his gaze making me falter. He was staring at me in a searching way, and I realised we had never stood this close. But as his warm eyes melted into mine, some undefined emotion flared, lids heavy, the shadow of his eyelashes casting soft spikes.

Unsure how to respond, I battled to find the right words but...

Too late.

His lips lowered onto mine, velvety soft and caressing.

"Joe..." I tried to murmur.

I so much wanted to surrender to his kiss, the scratch of stubble rough against my face, but suddenly we were in the hallway. Unsure how we had got there so fast, the momentum between us grew, until his hands slid around my back and he was pulling me in the direction of my bedroom. The warmth of his mouth felt exquisite, the strength of his embrace sending shivers through me...

Yet something inside me snapped. Deep in my subconscious, a distant warning light started blinking and I caved in, all this fear and sadness running through me, a landslide of crumbling emotions. There was no question Joe was aroused now, the bulge of his erection like a rock pressing against my hip.

"No! No! Stop!"

His eyes widened as he registered the shock on my face, and he backed off immediately.

"I-I'm sorry," I started trembling, "b-but this is all happening too fast..."

"And just when I thought I'd got lucky," he muttered.

I heard laughter in his tone, but it was a hollow sound. The hurt in his expression told me far more.

"Please," I tried to pacify him, "just give me a bit more time."

"Okay," he said, hands raised in mock surrender.

I could see he wasn't buying it though. Poor Joe. In all this time, I was so buoyed up by our friendship, never once did I consider his feelings might change. He was a man, and I should have accepted that - the possibility that he might be feeling more than just friendship.

"Don't rush me, Joe," I begged, "there is too much going on in my head right now to commit to anything."

At last a smile softened his features but a wan smile. "Goodnight, Maisie," he sighed, "and for what it's worth, I never meant to offend you."

The night dragged on. Occasionally I drifted off for an hour, only to awaken immersed in the same weighty darkness. Wrestling with my conscience, I could not stop thinking about Joe. The way he kissed me left my head spinning in circles, the pain evident from my rejection stirring ripples of guilt...

Until finally morning came.

The shape of my wardrobe and dressing table were first to morph out of the gloom as the early light crept through the curtains. Finally the darkness lifted, giving substance to the world, and reaching for my dressing gown, I peered out of the window. A spectacular blue sky stretched above, the rolling motion of the clouds inspiring me to grab some fresh air.

Imagining Joe asleep, I slipped on a pair of leggings, threw a slate-grey hooded top over my head and was out of the door within minutes.

I loved having Joe here, the joy of rediscovering my childhood friend.

But as time elapsed, the dynamics were bound to change. We were no longer children and the sooner I accepted this, the better.

Parking on the seafront, I spent several minutes gazing out to sea. Tears welled in my eyes but I didn't want to think about past relationships any more. Deep in my heart, I trusted Joe. I had confessed this much to Hannah; and the problem wasn't him, it was me.

Stepping out of my car, I was mentally piecing together what I wanted to say to him, though in the current loop of time, there seemed no point over-analysing things. Not when we had a quest to complete, a reason to stick together.

As I strolled along the beach, my eyes following the pattern of foam decorating the sand, I saw a woman in the distance. Golden head bobbing, she pounded along the shoreline with a dog in tow.

I did a double take. That mane of curls reminded me of Sarah.

Sarah would relate exactly to how I was feeling. Sarah, my dearest friend, who I had been yearning to contact before today.

Strands of hair blew across my face but I flicked them away brusquely. For if ever there was a time to contact her, it was now.

Chapter Twenty-Four

"Hi, I need a favour. I hope you don't mind me dumping this on you at short notice but some incredible things have happened since I saw you last..."

"I know," Sarah broke in smugly. "Mandy told me. You bumped into your old friend, didn't you? Joe, from the children's home."

A sigh of relief trickled through me. *Thank God my foster mum had filled her in...* It would save a lot of explaining.

"So how's it working out?"

"Fine," I said, "it's great having Joe here and we've been talking about the children's home but it's brought back more memories. Not just mine but his..."

Gazing out to sea, I felt a shiver as the breeze in the air sliced through me. *How much of Joe's backstory did I dare reveal?*

"I know why he ran away. Like I said all along, he knew secrets about that place but he was threatened... I don't feel safe telling you this on the phone though, is it possible we could meet up again?"

"Of course," Sarah's voice echoed. "But what about you? Are you sure you're alright, Maisie? You sound scared."

"I-I am scared..." I gulped in the sea air, stealing rapid glances in every direction. "I think we're being watched and there's worse. Joe's being bullied online. There was a horrible message on his twitter feed... but that's not the reason I'm calling."

"Go on," she kept pressing.

"Do you remember the other boy I mentioned? My hallucination? Mortimer said he was adopted but Joe's not convinced. I know it's a tall order but is there any way we can find out?"

"Ah, Maisie," Sarah sighed. "I'd love to help. All I need is a name."

A grip of anxiety squeezed my chest as I considered the path I was about to take.

On the other hand, what did I have to lose?

"Sam," I spluttered into my phone. "His name was Sam Ellis."

Ending the call, I felt sufficiently buoyed to approach Joe now. The thought of locating Sam inspired hope. But even as I made my way back to the road, a dark shape seized my attention, and there it was again: a black car lingering by the sea wall approximately ten metres away.

I hastened my step. An eerie tranquillity prevailed but with the road nearly empty, this was my best chance of taking a closer look at it.

If I could just get its number plate.

The gap between us narrowed and I delved for my keys. It took one flick of the button to release the central locking mechanism but as the lights on the side panels blinked, something in the atmosphere changed. A roar shattered the silence as the black car tore away, and by the time I leapt into my car it had gone.

Bursting through the door of my flat, I felt dizzy, unprepared for the sight of Joe waiting in the lounge. He looked terrible. It was likely he had barely slept a wink either, and with his messy bed hair sticking out at odd angles and a shadow of beard growth, his face looked even more drawn and haunted.

"Maisie," he said, his voice tight with anxiety. "Where the hell have you been?"

"Just a walk on the beach," I frowned. "I needed to clear my head."

"Thank God," he breathed, "I've been crapping myself. I thought something might have happened to you..."

Sorrow darkened his eyes as he glanced at me. I desperately wanted to throw my arms around him but considering the way I had so brutally rejected him, I held back, sensing there was more.

"Look, about last night... I'm sorry if I got carried away."

"Joe, please don't apologise," I begged him. "It's nothing personal, I assure you, I'm just a bit screwed up in the head right now... I saw that black car again! I tried to get the number plate but the driver shot off so fast, I never had a chance to get close enough!"

Joe turned away with a snort as he took this in. "Well, that just proves it was following you all along..." He never got to finish.

New notifications came pouring into his mobile at an alarming rate, giving him no choice but to grab it before I did.

"Fuck," he whispered under his breath.

My heart sank as he drifted into the light of the window, his face ashen.

"Not your trolls again?"

"Yup!" Joe spat and holding out his phone, took a screen shot.

@JosephofWinterfell you're nothing but a #waster and a #druggie with a #criminal record. Next time you're in town do everyone a favour and throw yourself under a bus. PIECE OF SHIT!!!

"One from 'The_Watchman' but there's more..."

Without delay he tapped the next notification, and a moment later I heard the breath catch in his throat.

"Oh God, what now?" I whispered in dread.

"This arsehole goes by the name 'ShadowoftheGrange.'"

"As in Orchard Grange?"

"I imagine so," he sighed.

"What does it say then?"

"It don't matter. I ain't gonna to read it to you."

A blaze of anger splashed some colour into his cheeks but I could feel the tension billowing. Whoever was posting these messages had a really nasty vendetta and given time, it was bound to gnaw at his confidence.

"You've got to report this, Joe," I said and moving away from the window, I sagged into the sofa. "Surely Twitter can bar such people."

"Yeah," he sighed, "but for now, I'm gonna keep taking screen shots. Let's see how nasty the fuckers get, 'cos it will all count as evidence. That and this bloody car that's following you!"

"True," I agreed. "I don't understand how you can stay so calm, though. If it was me, I'd be having a nervous breakdown - but speaking of gathering evidence, there's something else I wanted to tell you."

He forced a smile. "Go on."

"I spoke to my friend, Sarah, the one I told you about weeks ago when we were talking about looking into Sam's case."

"And did she agree to help?"

"Yes," I nodded, and numb from our conversation, I had reached a decision. "See, if Sarah can't locate him and there are no traces of him whatsoever, we have got to talk to the police."

Chapter Twenty-Five

Joe didn't bother checking his Twitter feed for the next few days. He appeared calm enough from Maisie's perspective, but he masked his emotions well.

Deep down, he was quaking. No matter how hard he tried telling himself the messages couldn't harm him, they tied his stomach up in knots. But he was damned if he was going to admit that; not when he stood at a pivotal crossroads in his life.

Let the evil fuckers play their sick games.

That tiny seed of defiance thrived in him because a week later, he had something to celebrate; no longer another statistic on the jobless front but the latest employee in Sainsbury's online shopping department.

The first hurdle had been the interview. He would never forget the lingering smile on Maisie's face after she had dropped him off at the entrance.

"Good luck, Joe, you can do it."

Such faith was all he needed for the next phase when he was introduced to the manager, Vicky. In some ways, she reminded him of dear Martha, the banter between them more like a chat over a coffee than an interview. Given the online vitriol he had suffered, it hadn't taken long for the 'trolls' to remind him how sordid his life had once been.

A waster and a druggie with a criminal record.

Joe's heart thumped. As if it wasn't shameful enough to confess he had served time, but he had to come clean. This was a golden opportunity to put right past wrongs and redeem himself - a second chance - and he could not afford to blow it.

Even Vicky said *that took guts* and to his credit, had taken a real shine to him as confirmed in a text next day. Suddenly the world shone brighter and one week after accepting her job offer, he had completed the training, all set to step back into the workplace.

******

For the next week he rode on a rollercoaster of highs and lows. On the days he worked his shift, he set off before dawn, the darkness so heavy it blurred the edges of the world. The fifteen minute walk to Sainsbury's was not an ideal situation. For all the while the town hung in eerie silence, he couldn't shift the fear of how vulnerable he was, especially with enemies on the prowl.

That left one more dilemma to reflect on: Maisie.

Where exactly did he stand with her?

Their chance reunion was the best thing that had happened to him and reliving childhood memories, they had formed an unusual, almost symbiotic relationship. Nothing could change the past. He accepted that. Although her entire focus seemed to be on tracing Sam now.

The trouble was he no longer saw her as that frightened little girl he had locked in the laundry room. *Maisie had blossomed into a beauty and he would do whatever it took to keep her safe.*

Yet ever since the night he had kissed her, she seemed to have withdrawn into a shell. Perpetually trying to convince him that *she was the one who had hangups*, she had so little confidence. What Joe found hardest to swallow, though, was her fear that any intimacy between them would destroy their friendship.

How could she think like that? Or more to the point, why?

Maisie was a stunner, which left him wondering if anyone had treated her badly in life, eroding away her confidence... If that were the case, he thought, then whoever they were they needed their heads kicking in – though he kept these thoughts to himself.

"I've decided to book another therapy session," she announced.

Pottering around, sorting clothes out in readiness to go away, no one but Maisie could have been more congratulatory on his job success.

Yet she seemed determined to stick to her agenda and visit Sarah.

"As long as it doesn't upset you as much as the last time," he commented. "Remember the state I found you in when I got home?"

"Yes, but I'm over that," Maisie shrugged. "At least we talked..."

Her glazed expression told him otherwise. He watched in a dream as she pulled another top out of the laundry basket, draping it over the ironing board.

"Mandy said the whole point of psychotherapy was to unlock painful memories and once purged, I can move on."

"Really?" Joe murmured, his eyes transfixed on her hands as they slid back and forth along the ironing board. "So what you gonna talk about this time?"

"I have to go back to the party scene, where I left it..."

"Maisie," he added gently, "don't torture yourself over this."

His words seemed to trigger a reaction and looking up from the ironing board, she finally met his eye.

"I'm not, but I thought about this last night. Before I see Sarah, supposing I try to figure out what *I* remember? About Sam I mean..."

Chapter Twenty-Six

Hannah Adams. Registered Psychotherapist and Counsellor. West Sussex
Client: Maisie Bell
2nd April 2015

"It's good to see you again, Maisie. How are things since I saw you last?"

"Not too bad," I began. "Joe and I have been talking things over. I wanted to know more about his memories."

"Yes," Hannah nodded. "You were telling me about a party he tried to shield you from but you got upset. I had to bring you out of your trance."

With a shivering breath, I recoiled into my chair. "I-it merged into a scene from one of my nightmares, as if the two are in some way connected."

"Take it steady," her voice ebbed. "Relax and think about where you are now. There is no danger in my therapy room and you are quite safe. Just let your mind wander into the past..."

I concentrated on her voice, the way it undulated, slower, deeper, guiding the rhythm of my breathing, and only then did I let the shadows creep in.

"The last dream was the worst ever," I shuddered.

"You've mentioned a forest before now."

"Yes, a forest... whispers, a procession of hooded figures..."

God, how I loathed having to describe it again, yet somewhere in the mist of memories, the air began to turn cold like an icy weight pressing down on me.

"The red ribbon freaked me out, the ends fluttering in the breeze. I saw a circle of trees above my head and that's when I sensed something evil going on in the forest."

"What sort of evil? Can you bear to explain it?"

"I'll try," I said numbly, "but I was trapped... my wrists were tied. Those figures were coming for us... I felt someone's hand on me and I screamed."

"It was a dream, though," Hannah tried to pacify me. "Isn't that right?"

As I opened my eyes, my breath shook in shallow gasps. The very concept of what was happening in those woods turned me sick to the core, but these leaks in my subconscious had to be clues, didn't they? Joe had almost confirmed it.

"No... I don't think it was. I think we were abused."

"Maisie," Hannah said. "If this is a real memory, it has obviously been *festering for a while. How do you feel now, after telling me?"*

My throat had clammed up. I didn't want to admit to myself those dreams might be based on a real memory, but deep down lingered the horrors Joe spoke of.

"The human psyche is a strange mechanism. Everything that happens is stored in our memories but some things get locked away. Memories so painful, the brain buries them in a place where they cannot harm us. Such a mechanism exists purely to protect you in your conscious state."

"Repressed memories," I murmured. "That's what my foster mum said all along but how does this help me now? Joe spoke of similar things. I know you said I shouldn't let him colour my judgement but he thinks Mortimer ran those homes like a business. One that attracted paedophile networks."

It all seemed much clearer now, my phobia of trees, my fear of intimacy. Was this the reason I felt an aversion? I became so tense, so frozen, it was hard to maintain any sort of trust - flashbacks to when I felt like a victim.

"Paedophile networks," Hannah's voice echoed. "Look, I'm not in a position to guide your thoughts or tell you what I think happened, you need to work through the memories to discover the truth for yourself, but you asked how this helps you now. Why not ask yourself the same question? Where do you go from here?"

"There was someone else," I said, "another boy in our circle. Sam. I'm sure I mentioned him before, but he vanished after one of those parties."

"So let's talk about Sam," she responded. "Tell me what you remember."

"Sam was a strange boy, not like the other kids. The first thing that stood out was his beauty. I mean, a lot of the kids had an almost feral look about them, whereas Sam was just adorable."

His face flickered; clear skin, blonde hair and widely spaced brown eyes. The only flaw I could recall was a jagged scar on his forehead. That aside, though, Sam had an elf-like grace that set him apart – a perpetual gleam of fear in his eyes that lent him a vulnerable look.

"The rougher boys called him a wuss and picked on him without mercy. No one knew much about his background until they discovered his mum was a prostitute."

With the illusion of purity shattered, they set out to make his life hell.

"That's when Joe stepped in. He took him under his wing, same as me."

I could picture the three of us together. There weren't many places to hide since Mortimer had stepped up security, but Joe's room offered us a sanctuary. He shared with two boys, including Sam, after some swapping around. His only other roommate was a seemingly harmless, chubby thirteen-year old they called 'Jabba.'

111

The echo of Joe's laugh resonated. 'Don't mind Jabba. If he's not tossing himself off under a blanket, he's into UFOs and all that weird shit.'

"Joe was such a character," I chuckled, "it was easy to relax in his company and eventually he got Sam talking about himself. He really loved his Mum, regardless of her occupation. Told us about the days she took him to the park and the zoo. They went to the cinema, ate burgers, visited a gaming arcade to play lasers. She wasn't short of money, see. Not your average street worker but high class. Stephanie was her name, her clients rich and powerful men. He showed us a photo..."

Hazy but striking, I would never forget that photo. Stephanie Ellis was a stunner. In fact she reminded me a little of Amanda Holden. But picturing that photo sent a chill crawling over me; more so because of the stories Sam associated with it.

"Did he ever mention who his father was?" Hannah probed.

I held my breath, feeling a lump in my throat.

"Joe and I were gob-smacked when he told us... a High Court judge he referred to as Alistair McFadden QC."

Sam's eyes smouldered with hurt whenever he spoke of him.

'He was a nasty piece of work. Stuck up toff, kitted out in a long gown and one of those stupid wigs, looking down his nose at us like we were crap...'

I understood his outrage. Alistair McFadden had abandoned his mother. Wanted nothing more to do with her from the day Sam had been born.

"I found that really sad," I spluttered. "He could have at least supported them financially but from what Sam said, his mum didn't dare even add his name to Sam's birth certificate. She used her own name, Ellis, and Sam endured a somewhat rocky childhood. He couldn't ignore what his mum did for a living because it affected him too. He told us all his secrets."

I kept my eyes firmly shut, reliving the time we had been friends. The one thing I remembered about Sam, though, is the way he latched onto me. Joe was the tough one but Sam followed me around like a puppy. He looked so scared, the stories he disclosed worse than anything we imagined. And I was curious to know how he got that scar on his forehead...

'One of my mum's punters did that. They were all bastards!'

Pushing back his fringe, I could not help but gasp at the inverted 'V' shape gouged into his smooth skin.

'She told me to stay in my room. Bunged me a video and a bag of crisps to keep me quiet but I couldn't stay quiet, not when there were all these shouts and screeches from upstairs. So I peeked. I know I shouldn't have done, but...'

I heard a sob. Felt my body stiffen as he relayed the story of how this punter had turned on him, grabbed a whisky bottle and smashed it over his head.

When the police and ambulance were called, Stephanie had to lie to protect Sam. Swore he had fallen against a window pane to avoid Social Services taking him away.

'She wanted us to get as far, far away as possible after that. Didn't care about giving up our posh apartment, if we could just start a new life, a different life... and that's when she talked to my father.'

I could picture his little face crunched up with hurt. Anyone could see how much he loathed his father and it came frothing out in a torrent.

'I couldn't stand it either. All those nasty men turning up at night, hurting her. So Mum took a gamble. Visited the Old Bailey and begged to have a word with the judge in private. It was the first time I'd ever met him, but he was horrible... He called her a whore and a slut!'

'Oh, Sam,' *I heard myself gasp.* 'Why do you suppose he was so rotten to her?'

'Didn't want her to bring shame on his family, did he? Said we were an embarrassment... but something changed. She told me out of the blue that he was gonna bung her a few grand to get out of his life for good!'

I remember Joe's shock. He had been braced by the door, keeping a lookout. This was perhaps the most clandestine conversation we'd ever shared, and Joe wanted to keep him talking.

'Jesus, mate, that's heavy. So what went wrong?'

Sam's mouth twisted into a knot of misery, the tears pooling in his eyes.

'Mum was killed next day. Police found her in the back of a taxi with a bullet in her head. Murdered. They said it was a punter but... she was mixed up with all sorts of dodgy geezers and it was rumoured she had dirt on someone.'

I felt the tears welling in my own eyes, and squeezed them shut to hold them in. Poor Sam! To think of that sweet, sensitive soul condemned to such a fate, it must have torn him apart. All Joe and I wanted to do was to protect him then, not just from all the other little toe-rags in there but Mortimer and his creepy guards...

"We did what we could," *I finished shakily,* "but I-I'll never forget one of the last things Sam said to us. Joe and I said we wanted to be detectives when we grew up and that we'd solve his mum's murder..."

Oh, those heart-warming words, his endearing chuckle.

'I bloody love you guys, don't forget that, I want us to be friends forever.'

Yet tragically that never happened.

"Even Joe said he was too pure for the sick games those bastards had in store for him."

And the sickest of those games was the final party they had attended. Once the night was over, we never saw him again.

Chapter Twenty-Seven

London

Heavy clouds filled the sky, the threat of rain ever imminent. With the air turning colder, Thomas quickened his pace, grateful to reach the Pianissimo Tea Room before the first spikes of drizzle hit his trench coat.

Even in this elegant quarter, north of Westminster, an abundance of sleeping bags lurked like slugs in the alleyways. Thomas clicked his tongue, irked by the growing manifestation of homelessness.

Half an hour later, however, he was taking a bite from his miniature black forest gateau, the plight of the homeless forgotten. With another session in Parliament behind him, he could think of no better diversion than to unwind in this lovely café, especially with Poppy meandering between tables.

"Everything okay for you, Sir?"

"Couldn't be better, thank you," he replied, "absolutely perfect."

Oh, that wondrous smile.

It lifted the gloom like sunshine, and even the chandeliers seemed to glow a little brighter. Deep down, he imagined he was one of her more 'distinguished customers,' the way she arranged his cakes on a beautiful tiered platter particularly pleasing.

"I saw you in the paper," she piped up. "What's it like being in the House of Lords?"

Heart leaping with the accolade, he laid down his cake fork.

"Sweet of you to ask, my dear, and it can be very challenging at times but rewarding. We spend half our lives shaping the laws of this country."

"Seriously?" she said. "Must be cool to have so much power."

She would have asked him more, he was certain of it, but a movement from the counter distracted her. Only then did he spot an older woman, eyebrows arched as she flicked her gaze in the direction of another table. An elderly couple perched eagerly, eyes gleaming in anticipation of service.

"'Scuse me, I gotta go," she muttered and with a polite smile, turned away.

Disappointment sagged his shoulders. How he would love to indulge in conversation for a little longer, but with other tables to wait on, it would be wrong of him to monopolise her. Touched nonetheless, he mulled over her question.

Much as he relished his years in politics, those stormy sessions in the House of Commons faded into insignificance these days. All bills had to be considered by both Houses before they became law. Poppy was right.

This was the ultimate seat of power.

With his mind still on Poppy, such thoughts drew his gaze across the café where the gleam of polished floorboards reflected a flicker of motion. Rain streaked the windows, blurring the outside world, but all the while he was fantasising about Poppy, it was easy to forget the austerity that prevailed beyond that door.

Thomas sipped his tea. Wary of her presence, he felt a bubbling anticipation every time she veered close. But the next time he glanced up, she was putting on her rain coat. His heart plummeted. She couldn't be leaving so soon, surely? He hadn't even had a chance to tip her yet.

"Where are you off to?" he called without thinking.

Raincoat draped over one arm, she fished out an umbrella.

"Home. With a bit of luck I'll be in time to catch the 5:30 bus."

Thomas stole a glance at his watch.

"Where do you live?" he probed.

"Vauxhall Park."

An unexpected idea leapt to mind. A somewhat risky one, but not unthinkable if he wanted to keep up their camaraderie.

"Don't go, I was about to call a taxi. Would you like to share it with me? Vauxhall Park is only a little further on from where I live in Pimlico."

"Right," she faltered. "It's good of you to offer but..."

"I'll pay," he added warmly, "if you could just fetch my bill."

It took one more second for the shine to spring back to her eyes.

"Okay, you're on."

Thomas smirked and dipping into his coat for his wallet, he knew he was being brazen. But if he yearned to develop their friendship, his only hope was to get her on her own.

It did not seem long before the taxi cruised into a magnificent Regency terrace, ten minutes that passed in a flash, their conversation unrelenting. Yet how that pretty face came alive when she had slid into the back seat. The way she stroked the upholstery, breathed in the air as if savouring the freshly valeted interior.

He found it difficult to take his eyes off her. As bubbly outside the café as she was in it, she seemed keen to keep the topic on his work status.

"What's rapping then? What laws did you get to change today?"

Thomas smiled inwardly. How rare for one so young to show an interest.

"One of the bills under the spotlight was the National Minimum Wage Regulations. Something that affects girls like you, Poppy."

"Yeah?" Her thickly lashed eyes flared with hope. "So did you agree to it?"

"You mean did we approve the motion? Yes, though not without some resistance. What you have to understand, my dear, is that ever since the minimum wage was introduced, there have been widespread fears millions of jobs would be lost."

"I don't get it."

"Okay, say you're earning £5 an hour. To simplify matters, imagine if a minimum wage of £10 was enforced. Your boss would be tempted to hire half as many people, to make the same profits."

"Oh, right," she mumbled.

Glancing at her reflection in the window, he saw her preening herself. Her brow twisted with the effort of grasping his meaning.

"Perhaps a slightly exaggerated example," he added hastily, "though I'm sure you get the gist. To put your mind at rest, though, the majority were in favour of approving the motion, and I have to praise their enthusiasm in doing so."

As she turned away from the window, a smile curved her lips. Flattered by such attention, he felt his spirits lift. It wasn't just his work she was curious about either, but everything else in life. His hobbies, his marital status...

"Wow! What a awesome place! So which one of those mansions is yours?"

The Regency terrace stretched far into the distance, an endless sweeping façade of houses, punctuated by white pillared doorways.

"Mansion?" he chuckled. "I rent an apartment, my dear. It's in this building here, the one with the red door."

"Oh, wow," she gasped again. "So are you gonna invite me in?"

Thomas froze, perhaps not the reaction she was hoping for, his hubris disintegrating to panic as he considered the ramifications. That her po-faced boss had seen her leave in a taxi with him was the first problem, but he had never once considered the girl's curiosity would extend beyond that.

"Not today, Poppy. My driver will take you home now."

Yet she wasn't listening. Her hand tugged the door handle and the next thing he felt was a breeze flooding into the car. He had to stop her.

"Poppy, please," he insisted.

His voice shuddered as he fought to stay calm.

There was no way he could let her in; not after the rumpus that had arisen the last time he invited a teenager inside his home.

Touching her wrist, he managed to stop her just in time.

"What? It's not like anyone's gonna mind is it? You said you were divorced..." She looked crestfallen.

"I-I am," he said, "but that's not the point..."

He tried to smile, heart racing, as he raked through his mind for an excuse.

"I can hardly bear to tell you this but my apartment is a mess. I've been hiring the services of a housekeeper but had to let her go recently."

A quizzical look illuminated her expression. "Is that it?"

"What, you don't think it's a little shameful? Me, a member of the House of Lords and my home is in disarray? I fear people would lose all respect for me."

"Don't worry!" she laughed. "There's plenty of cleaning firms about and I've not long made some friends who work for a new company. It's called the 'Gleam Gals' agency and yeah, it's a rubbish name."

Her lively titter filled the car, lifting the atmosphere back to a safe level. And for all the while he clung to her incessant banter, she was filling his heart with hope.

"Sounds like the answer to my prayers," he answered dreamily, "a little domestic help would be a Godsend. Do you have their phone number?"

******

"So what's this I hear about Winterton?"

Once again the voice possessed a smooth, mocking quality that infuriated him. Furthermore, it seemed hard to imagine a month had passed since Winterton's return; four weeks of unsurmountable tension. When would it ever end?

"I gather he's got a job, but surely even he has had sufficient warning by now?"

"The problem is he's proving to be a right pain in the arse."

Driving into the South Downs to escape town, he could feel the blood surging to his temples. Even the surrounding views failed to calm him, a secluded spot where no one could witness his outrage.

Hate was too mild a word for it.

The last sighting of Maisie Bell had ended in disaster. If only their watchman could have been a little more discreet, but there was no question she'd seen him. Went swinging up to her car with her keys at the ready and he had only just shot off in time.

Given the possibility their vehicle had been reported that day, there seemed no other option than to abandon it.

"Doesn't look like he's going anywhere soon," he hissed.

"Then maybe you should think outside the box, Cornelius," the caller laughed. "All these benign insults are a waste of time. You need to put yourself in his shoes and strike where it hurts. Think about what would really deter him."

Such words were bound to stoke the flames of his malevolence, and staring across the misty hills, he felt his lips pull back into a snarl.

There was only one deterrent that had ever worked with Joe Winterton.

Except Cornelius was no longer considering idle threats any more. If ever they were to keep him away from Maisie, it was time to up his game plan.

Chapter Twenty-Eight

"You're travelling by car," Joe pondered, "and not by train?"

"It's quicker," Maisie blurted. "I looked it up on Google Maps. The train journey includes two changes."

"So how long are you gonna be away for? You mentioned stopping off at your folks' house on the way back." His eyes wandered to her overnight bag.

"It makes sense," she nodded. "Swanley is only ten miles away from where Sarah lives and it would be nice to see them. So what about you, are you going to be okay on your own for a couple of days?"

"Course," he joked. "I'm a big boy now. I've got my job, plenty of overtime if I want it and I promise not to throw any wild parties."

Her smile brought a glow of colour. "That's not what I meant, but I'm glad you mentioned the job. How's it going?"

"S'okay," he said. "The hours go fast and the walking keeps me fit, I've just got to improve my picking speed."

"They work you hard, then?"

Joe shrugged. "I guess they have to meet the delivery slots, but I am enjoying it. They're a good bunch of people to work with."

"Good," she kept smiling, "because I've got something else to tell you. I saw Matt on the way home and you know he shares a house in Canada Grove? There's a couple of old mountain bikes in the shed left by previous tenants. He said you were welcome to borrow one."

"Aw, that'd be wicked!" Joe grinned. "I can cycle there in half the time!"

Her green eyes sparkled, stirring waves in his heart, and he knew he was going to miss her.

For the next half hour he was immersed in the news when a ping from his mobile alerted him. Grabbing it absentmindedly and assuming Maisie was in her bedroom, he was appalled to see a new message flashing up.

@ShadowoftheGrange
Still on our patch then @JosephofWinterfell you interfering cunt. We have ways of dealing with troublemakers like you if you remember.

"What the f...?" Maisie gasped.

Turning with a jolt, he had no idea she had been shadowing him. The fog in his mind swirled thicker.

"Shit," he spluttered. "I wish you hadn't seen that..."

"But what's the point of me not seeing it?" she argued.

The sob in her voice turned him cold, except he hadn't yet grasped the full horror behind the threat.

"Can't you see it's a retweet? Look what's posted underneath."

Eyes moving to the photo, Joe almost stopped breathing. For there, coiled in a box like a snake, shone the ribbed metal surface of a steel hose pipe.

#Premium_Metals sell ULTRA Tough Stainless Steel Hose Pipe £16.99 (regular price £55) #steelhose #garden #equipment.

A blade of fear tore into him. For anyone else it was nothing more than a promotion for a garden product, but all Joe saw was an instrument of torture - one which his enemies had used to inflict pain on him.

******

"I'll be fine," he placated her for the nth time. "Stop worrying."

Maisie had nearly cancelled her trip in the aftermath of that message but Joe wouldn't hear of it. Anyone could tell how much she had set her heart on consulting Sarah, so why change her plans now?

Winding down her car window, she fixed him with a last wistful stare. "Just promise me you'll be careful and I'll ring you later."

"I promise. Now best get on your way 'cos it'll be dark soon."

Touched by her concern, he watched her car disappear up the avenue. But the way he saw it, he had two choices. Cut himself off from all social media and revert to being a recluse. Or hold his head up high and refuse to let the bastards get to him.

Two hours later, though, he was polishing off a chilli con carne he had cooked when the buzz of the intercom alerted him. He froze. There was no telling who could be calling at this hour and he certainly wasn't expecting visitors.

He raised a trembling finger to the button. "Who is it?"

"Only me," a female voice purred from the speaker.

The familiarity of the voice drew a sigh from his throat and with no hesitation he pulled the door open.

"Jess!" His face split into a smile.

She looked as lovely as ever, in a figure-hugging knitted top, her corduroy skirt swaying around the tops of her high-heeled boots.

"Maisie's not here. She's gone to visit an old friend and call in at her folks' place."

"I know, she texted me..." and without waiting for an invitation, she breezed past him through to the lounge. "So what are you up to tonight? Can't have you moping around on your own all weekend."

Lost for words, he turned to the kitchen, where the first sight to hit him was an untidy pile of washing up.

"Sorry about the mess," he mumbled, "it won't take a minute to clear up. What can I get you to drink? There's some wine in the fridge."

"Now you're talking," Jess smiled, "and congratulations on the new job, by the way."

"Thanks." Conscious of her eyes following him, he grabbed a clean glass. "Take a pew and make yourself comfy."

The clutter of dirty dishes on the periphery was not about to disappear, but Jess sipped her wine while occupying the spot on the sofa Maisie usually took.

"Handy to have a man in the house," she piped up. "Lucky Maisie. You seem very domesticated, she's trained you well."

Swirling the plates in the soap suds, he took a moment to absorb this.

"No. I'm the lucky one. Dunno where I'd be now if we hadn't bumped into each other when we did. She's helped me turn my life around."

"So how do you two get on?" she kept probing. "I mean you live together practically 24/7. Got any plans for the future?"

Still he refused to rise, hands moving faster as he rinsed the crockery.

"There's a lot you don't know about me and Maisie."

"So tell me," she pressed. "Didn't you meet in some children's home?"

"Yeah," he surrendered. "You know she lost her real family in a car crash? Not just her parents but a little sister..."

Jess nodded and there was a sudden jaw-dropping silence.

"Poor Maisie," she relented at last. "The first time I met her I could tell she was sad, someone who carried the weight of the world on her shoulders."

Joe nodded, curious to keep her talking. "How long have you known her?"

"We met at a party three years ago but she's a good listener, someone I could reach out to. I had problems of my own at the time, see..."

Joining her in the lounge, Joe took a gulp of his own wine and guessing there was a lot more she wanted to offload, welcomed the stretch of silence.

"I'd not long been through a divorce from my cheating shit of a husband. See, when push came to shove, he chose the other woman over me."

He felt a pang of sympathy. "Ouch! Did you love him?"

"Very much so. Maybe a little too much but hey, at least I got a seafront apartment out of it. Hark at me going on about myself when we should be talking about Maisie, the perfect friend. Kind, caring and generous with her time. I can't understand why she's still single."

"No," he muttered.

So finally the conversation was getting interesting.

"She attracts the wrong men, and I'm talking about the desperate ones." Caught in the glow of a table lamp, her eyes glittered. "I know it sounds bitchy but I keep telling her to set her sights higher. She's so beautiful."

Yes, beautiful.

"More wine?" he murmured and emptied the last of the bottle into her glass.

"The only men she *does* fancy, though, aren't interested in her. The alpha males of this world, the dick heads, the ones who mess you around. I know I shouldn't tell tales but if a man tries to get her into bed too soon, she runs a mile!"

"Is that so?" Joe sighed, the night he tried to kiss her still haunting him. "Yeah well, women like Maisie deserve a bit more respect. She's not a slag."

A sudden shrewdness narrowed Jess's stare. "No. Maisie needs careful handling. Makes me sad to think of all the problems she's had."

Glancing up, he drank in the ambience of her flat, the pastel colours, the warmth of her table lamps cloaking the walls in a golden glow. It encapsulated everything about her; a mesmerising woman whose fragility he had detected from day one...

Yet there resting on her best friend's sofa, Jess lingered with a smile, and it seemed wrong to be sat here talking about her.

Nursing his empty glass, he released another sigh. "We're out of wine but I don't mind walking you back to the seafront if you want. Do you fancy stopping for a drink at the Waverley?"

A look of merriment brightened her face.

"Okay, Joe, you're on!"

Chapter Twenty-Nine

It had never really crossed my mind what Joe might get up to while I was away, but arriving in Rosebrook before nightfall, I spent a good hour unwinding in Sarah's house.

Our blissful day at Champneys seemed a lifetime ago, the things we had discussed. Joe had been the blink of a memory back then, Sam an even greater enigma.

This was the first time I'd visited Rosebrook, but what a charming town.

A long country road drew me towards the centre, a high street lined with elegant, half-timber buildings. It didn't seem long before I found myself in the neighbourhood where my friend lived - and just as my Sat Nav announced that *in 100 yards your destination will be on the left,* I could not resist grabbing my phone. For there, nestling behind a low stone wall, appeared the prettiest of cottages. Just enough daylight to capture its charm, from the pastel pink walls sliced with beams to a rambling explosion of roses around the porch.

Now that was definitely worth an Instagram post.

#English getaway. Check out this cute cottage Rosebrook #town near #London.

Captured in the fantasy Joe might see it, I clicked the share button, and only then did I think about his safety. He didn't post much on Instagram, and the few posts he did had attracted a couple of likes. He also had a new follower, I noticed, the name 'Silver-Fox' kindling a spark in my mind. Now was not the time to speculate, I would ask him later, but with Sarah's house beckoning, I caught a movement in her window, and couldn't wait to be reacquainted with her.

"Do you know how long it took me to locate Peter's sister?" she levelled at me. "Four years, and even that took some divine intervention!"

Stretching out my legs in front of the fireplace, I absorbed my new environment. The house, whilst not immaculate, had an enchanting interior; mismatched furniture, natural pine shelves sagging under rows of books. Even with a tower of old newspapers accumulating by the hearth, it had a cosy feel, the colour scheme warm with an abundance of cushions and woolly throws.

"Four years?" I echoed.

"That's right," Sarah said, "it's a complex process. We could start by getting a copy of Sam's birth certificate, examine his life, right up to the year his mother died, and you say she was murdered? There must be police records..."

Regrettably, however, we didn't have the luxury of time on our side.

Sam had been missing for twenty years and although it was a joy to share my story - of finding Joe and helping him back on his feet - I dreaded imparting the rest.

"Sam's care would be assigned to a social worker, which can be our next line of enquiry. Find out who took his case on and if possible, make contact. They would have raised the alarm if he went missing."

"You'd think so," I pondered, "unless he *was* adopted, which is the story Mortimer spun to Joe... but he was also very threatening, like he was hiding something."

"In that case, I should talk to the police sooner rather than later and voice your suspicions. What have you got to lose?"

I exhaled a sigh. "I'm not sure we can, not without anything concrete..."

The room seemed to darken around us as I described the more sinister aspects of my story; things I dared not mention out in the open when I had phoned her on the beach. Not just the cyber-bullying or the discovery of a black car tailing us, but the depravities we suspected were hidden in the deep tangled roots of those parties.

Relating it now, I glanced up, wary of Sarah's eyes fixed on me.

"God, Maisie, this is serious," she gasped. "Why an isolated mansion in the countryside? Why not a community centre or somewhere more public?"

"That's what I thought," I said, "but the clues coming out of my therapy sessions are even more disturbing."

Her lips tightened as she took this in. "I'd say you've got plenty to report to the police. I mean how many kids do you reckon must have passed through those homes? Hundreds! Surely some of them will remember the same parties, and what if more victims were to come forward?"

Buckling under the deluge of questions, I was chilled by the path this was leading me down. Did we dare push our suspicions to the next level?

"You're right, but first I need to consult Joe. He's the one being threatened."

"Why though?" she persisted. "Does he really pose such a threat? And as for your missing friend, Sam, I would insist look they into it. All you want is the truth."

"So are you able to help us?" I dared ask.

"Of course," she said, "but like I say, it will take time."

I held my breath, conscious there was another reason she couldn't dedicate herself one hundred percent to our cause; that since our last encounter, she had reduced her working hours to part time, given her extra responsibilities.

How could I have forgotten?

Sarah and her husband had someone else in their lives to consider now and that person was their teenage foster son, Connor.

Wandering into the garden to call Joe, I was unwittingly sidetracked by the silent, hooded silhouette hunched in a deck chair, engrossed in a games console. Caught in the glow of moonlight, this boy could be none other than Connor. I jammed to a halt, unsure what to say. Though it seemed polite to offer the newcomer some form of greeting.

"Hello, there," I piped up.

The figure didn't respond, a profile so sharp, so still, he could have been hewn from marble.

"Ssh," Sarah whispered warily. "Let him finish his level..."

Only his fingers moved, light on the controls as he manipulated his character around the 3D interface. The depth of graphics seemed unbelievably real and I could see how easily one could become addicted. We didn't have to wait long, though. No sooner had he reached some pivotal point in the game than he switched off his Nintendo DS, lowered it to his lap and stood up.

"Hi." He spoke in a monotone, his voice soft.

Catching my breath, I found myself gazing at a face almost as flawless as the character he had been playing. Despite his blank expression, he portrayed an unearthly calmness, his eyes two glowing orbs in the dusk.

"You must be Connor," I said, smiling. "It's nice to meet you at last. Sarah's told me lots about you."

"Yeah, I'm not like other kids, am I?" he put to me. "I'm into more serious stuff like science and all that. Prefer to be on my own."

Given the way Sarah had depicted his behaviour, I would have expected a lot more attitude. This strange, ethereal boy, however, touched a place in my heart I could not define; as if we shared an affinity beneath the stars.

"There's nothing wrong with that," I said, finding my voice at last. "Some people enjoy being on their own and are more introverted than others."

"Where do you live?"

"A town called Bognor Regis. Have you heard of it? It's by the sea."

As he tilted his head to study me, I caught a flicker of interest.

"Do you like the sea?"

"Yeah, beaches are cool. It's like you're sitting on the edge of the world, watching the universe. I think of the moon controlling the tide, you know, a magnetic force that pulls the sea up and lets it go. I read that in a book."

He lowered his eyes, as if bashful to show such passion.

"Connor, why don't you tell her about the trip you had?" Sarah prompted.

"Oh yeah, I got into trouble..." he began, and it was as if a valve had been turned.

Connor talked on, a relentless outpouring. *A day the adults in charge had taken the kids on a day trip. How he hated the crowds. Felt uncomfortable with the constant shifting around from place to place, a confusion that triggered panic.*

On reaching the beach, however, everything changed.

I listened without interrupting, gripped by his narrative. His love of the seaside was infectious, something I could relate to. An area so vast, it absorbed the chaos all around him, the boisterous shouts of the other kids fading into oblivion. Focussing on the sea, he went on to describe the waves, the salty tang of seaweed that smelt of nature itself...

"I ran," he continued reminiscing, his face motionless. "No one wanted to hang around with me anyway, so I kept running..."

The more he talked, the more I felt a stirring of empathy; that for all his life, children and adults hadn't warmed to him; to them he was nothing but an irritant, a boy people only tolerated.

Rushing along the seashore had given him that much needed breath of freedom, but if he hadn't detached himself so far from the group, he wouldn't have lost them.

"What could I do other than hide?"

Reaching a wall of rocks joining the coastal path, he had crept over the other side. There he discovered a quiet place where he could close his eyes, absorb the tranquillity and simply lose himself...

"The sun was setting," he finished. "I glanced at my watch, it was half past five and we were told to be back at the coach by six. But I didn't wanna go back, so I just sat there. Watched the sky and the colours changing."

"I know!" I blurted before I could stop myself, "I love the way the sea changes too. Would you like to see my photos on Instagram?"

It momentarily broke his flow. And all the while his mesmerising eyes clung to mine, I felt an invisible affinity looming again.

"What did you think of him?" Sarah asked me a little later.

She had waited until he retired to his room.

"He's a really interesting kid," I said in earnest, "and didn't you say he had Asperger's? I guess he thinks a little differently."

"I'm glad you understand. I got the impression he liked you too, especially when you were talking about the beach."

"You can always come and visit me you know," I suggested. "It'll be a treat for him to spend some time by the sea. Gives us an excuse to have another catch up."

Conscious it was time to contact Joe, I dialled my land line.

No answer.

Maybe he had popped out for a cigarette... although it wasn't impossible he might have been tempted in the direction of the Waverley.

Chapter Thirty

Jess's heart soared. She had guessed Joe would be on his own tonight, and with Maisie away, what a golden opportunity to get to know him better. Joe was an enigma, a man wrapped in secrecy, and ever since meeting him, how she longed to prise the barriers away and peer deep into his soul.

It was still not quite dark as they advanced down the road towards the sea. Streaks of muted silver-blue light shimmered down from the clouds, casting a gleam across the water.

"Would you like to sit outside?" she asked him casually.

Joe gripped the lapels of his jacket and shivered. "I'd rather sit inside if you don't mind. It's chilly out here."

As he stared out to sea, his profile painted a jagged silhouette in the dusk. He wasn't flawless. His misshapen nose suggested it might have been broken at some point, but the space between the hollow of his throat and jaw gave him an irresistible masculine beauty.

She averted her eyes, following the path of his stare. "Okay, whatever."

He wasn't wrong about the temperature. An icy breeze coiled under the canopy of the seating area, and further out to sea, she saw ripples of foam pulsate against the shoreline. Only when he turned to the door, though, did she catch the frown in his expression, the way his eyes skipped up and down the road.

"Is something wrong?"

Her words melted into a rumble of adult voices as they stepped into the pub.

"No," he snapped. "What makes you say that?"

She surveyed him beadily. "Have you ever heard the expression *forever looking over your shoulder?* It springs to mind every time I see you."

"Yeah, well that's what being homeless does to you. You're an easy target. Did you know one of the guys in the beach shelter got battered?"

She paused with shock, her eyes widening.

"Fast asleep and some prat belted him across the head with a plank of wood, in a totally unprovoked attack. Stuff like that makes you a bit wary."

"So what about now?" Jess challenged as they shuffled up to the bar. "I thought you said Maisie turned your life around."

The woeful expression on his face didn't change. "Maisie's been my saviour but I'm not without enemies. Now, what can I get you to drink?"

"I wouldn't say 'no' to another glass of wine," she smiled coyly.

No one took much notice of them as they crept around to the other side of the bar; a secluded snug room that separated them from the main lounge.

"So come on," she said, resuming their earlier thread of conversation. "How do you really feel about Maisie?"

"What, other than gratitude?" Sipping his pint, he seemed cagey. "Like I say, she dug me out of a very dark place."

"So you said."

He gave a pensive sigh. "You wanna know how I really feel? Same as I felt when I was a boy. All I ever wanted to do was protect her..."

Jess raised her eyebrows.

"If you're asking if we've slept together, then no," he said, "but the friendship we've got is priceless. You obviously know about the care home."

"That's right," Jess pondered and lowering her glass, she found her voice at last. "What happened there, Joe?"

He took another swallow of beer. "Same as happens in all them places. It's a dog-eat-dog world. Some kids are violent, others get picked on and bullied. Just 'cos Maisie was grieving, it didn't stop the little shits giving her a hard time."

"And you jumped to the rescue?" she finished for him.

"Couldn't help myself," he shrugged. "She looked so innocent. I came from a tough background, I was harder, more streetwise. We just bonded."

Jess nodded. "That figures, you being the tough one. You must be hard as nails to survive sleeping rough. I know couldn't handle it, I'd rather die."

She could not resist studying every characteristic; his rugged looks, the swigs of beer he took between sentences. He might appear tough on the outside yet she detected a palpable tension in him.

The next time he raised his head, his eyes gripped hers for a little longer.

"So what's your life story?" she asked him.

Draining his beer, he wiped the froth from his lip, belched softly, then lowered his glass to the table. "I can't talk about it," he murmured, "not here."

Time to hook him in.

"If it's that secret, we can always go back to my place. Carry on the conversation over a coffee?"

******

"My life went pear-shaped when I was roped into an armed robbery."

Jess had been right. He saw no point in refusing her hospitality, and with darkness cloaking the pavements, the prospect of walking home lurked cheerlessly.

Repeating parts of the story he had told Maisie, he drank in his surroundings. Where Maisie's flat possessed a lived-in cosiness, Jess's apartment blew him away. A velvet suite in shades of violet and blue occupied the floorspace. She had filled it with sparkly chintz cushions, but apart from that, she kept it tidy and minimalist. The white walls hung with a single abstract painting; an expanse of solid oak floorboards with nothing but a striped rug to cover them.

"You were banged up," Jess echoed. She squirmed in discomfort. "So this is where the slippery slide began, is it, from prison to being homeless?"

Sipping his coffee, he wondered how much he dared tell her. She was clearly rooting for gossip, but he didn't want to talk about prison, or the drug addiction that had tainted him in its aftermath. For someone immersed in the glamourous world of PR, Jess didn't need to know about the real foulness that stung society.

"Yet somehow you made enemies along the way."

"Yeah," Joe muttered, "but I didn't make 'em in prison. Our enemies go way back..." With an unsteady hand he lowered his cup, careful not to spill a drop on her immaculate glass-topped coffee table.

She touched his hand. "*Our* enemies. This is something between you and Maisie, isn't it, the reason you're scared? Does this go back to the children's home?"

Joe braced himself. *This much was true.*

"I knew stuff. Let's just say those homes were seriously dodgy. Private homes run by very nasty people."

"Joe," Jess nagged him, "don't keep me in suspense. What's the big secret? You can tell me."

"A boy went missing, that's what. Vanished without a trace... Maisie and I have never forgotten him, but she's convinced we should talk to the cops."

"So why don't you?"

"It's risky, Jess, and that's why I'm scared. The man in charge of those homes was an evil fucker and there's every chance he might be onto us."

The silence hung heavy, the seconds ticking. With her face masked in shadow it was hard to read her expression but as Jess nudged a little closer, the subtle feminine scent she discharged was intoxicating.

"What are you going to do, then?"

"Stay out of trouble and keep my head down," he said, "but let's drop it for now. It's been good to offload and thanks for the coffee..."

He shuffled his position as if to rise but Jess caught hold of his hand again.

"You weren't thinking of going yet, were you?" she murmured, "and just when the conversation was getting exciting..."

He lifted his eyes, a smile playing around his mouth.

Was she coming onto him?

It wouldn't have surprised him, given the hints Maisie had dropped, although he couldn't imagine he was her type.

"Sure, but enough about me," he argued. "There must be other things we can talk about."

"Okay," she pondered, "so let me think... I know! Social media! Did you take my advice about your Twitter handle?"

"Joseph of Winterfell," he pondered. "Yeah, I did."

Like he really wanted to talk about social media right now.

But as if to test him, she dipped into her bag for her mobile.

"Well excuse me, but I have got to check this out."

Joe watched transfixed, as she tinkered with her handset. He could not help but notice her lovely hands; pale, smooth with long tapering fingers and perfect nails. Despite her boldness, there was a delicate quality about her that reminded him of a flower. In fact, the more he got to know her, the stronger the attraction grew.

"Ah, there you are, I've found you..." and turning to him with a sparkle in her eye, she raised the handset before a tell-tale 'click' caught him unawares.

"Oh crap," Joe spluttered, "what have you done?"

"I only wanted a photo," she simpered. "Don't be shy!"

An icy chill spread over him as he lowered his head. In her naivety, Jess knew nothing of the online savagery he was being subjected to.

"At least you got my best side," he humoured her, "you ain't gonna post this online though, are you? Please don't."

"Not if you don't want me to," she said. "Shame. It's an awesome picture."

Joe couldn't resist the urge to chuckle. *Jess was such a flirt.*

"What about Instagram?" she kept teasing. "I've followed you but you don't seem to post much."

She just wasn't going to let up. Maybe he didn't use Instagram as much as Maisie – and no sooner had he thought that, she was on his mind. It would bring an extra cheer to his world to know she had reached her destination safely.

So he dug into his jacket for his own phone. "Dunno what to post really, unless you wanna see the walls of our warehouse, or racks of fruits and veggies."

This time Jess was the one who tittered as he opened the app.

Sure enough, the first image he saw was of an idyllic half-timber house with roses around the door. *Rosebrook. Could this be Sarah's house, the place Maisie was staying?* He felt a flickering glow in his heart as he read the caption.

#English getaway. Check out this cute cottage

Rosebrook #town near #London.

Scrolling through the images, however, the next post struck a blast of terror into him. Joe turned rigid, feeling every muscle in his body tighten.

"What?" Jess probed.

"Shit," he gasped. "Not this again..."

A familiar image flashed up. The distinctive steel hose that had taunted him earlier.

#stainless-steel flexible shower #hosepipe #steelhose #metalhose #specialoffer. When the cat's away the mice will play. Time to teach you another lesson JW.

"Joe, what's wrong?" Jess squawked.

Dropping the handset, he raked his fingers through his hair.

How could he even begin to explain?

In Maisie's absence, only he understood the danger, and it was rolling in like a sea mist, threading its way across town.

******

Scooping his phone off the carpet, Jess stared at the screen.

Even after reading the caption, she had no idea why the picture of a steel hose would unnerve him so.

"What is this about?" she kept bugging him. "I don't understand."

He seemed incapable of speech, and she reached out and cupped his face. She tried to recapture his stare but what she saw shocked her. Two dark pools of fear.

"You know I mentioned enemies?" he croaked. "This is down to Mortimer, the man in charge. *Mr C Mortimer...*"

"So what's with the hose?"

Joe shook his head. She could sense the conflict wrestling in him, and wished he would just come clean. It took a few more seconds, but at last the barriers crumbled - the truth tumbling out - he was describing Mortimer's beating in its savage detail.

"Oh my God, Joe!" she whimpered.

Suddenly the world turned black as she took him in her arms. For the next few seconds they clung to each other but all she could feel was the crash of his heart against his chest.

"Maisie's being watched and I get these shitty messages night and day," he whispered, "but it's all connected to that children's home..."

Temporarily breaking apart, their eyes locked. The urge to kiss him had never been more irresistible, and thrown back to the last time they had shared a drink at the Waverley, she sensed the same pull of magnetism.

Only this time she was not going to let him go.

"You can't walk back on your own tonight, not now. Stay the night with me!"

Her lips parted, hovering inches from his own, until at last his expression softened. Their mouths came together in a long, lingering kiss, a delicious flood of passion they could no longer fight.

Chapter Thirty-One

"Come on, Joe, pick up the phone, please," I whined.

Trying his mobile for the third time that morning, I felt my panic levels soaring. That hateful tweet on his mobile was a clear enough warning, and by this time I was beginning to imagine all sorts of ghastly scenarios...

"Hello," he mumbled sleepily.

"Finally!" I snapped. "Why haven't you been answering your phone?"

"Maisie! I didn't expect to hear from you 'til later."

"I tried to reach you last night," I scolded him.

The silence thickened and then I heard it; a squawking of gulls that seemed too loud and then the stifled giggle in the background.

"You're with Jess!" I exploded.

"Don't be cross. We had a drink down the Waverley and..." his voice hung with regret.

"What?"

"That picture," he kept murmuring, "the one you saw on Twitter, it popped up again on Instagram. We only logged in to see if you'd posted anything and I saw your cottage. I was only thinking how nice it looked..."

"Shit, Joe," I breathed, feeling my throat clam up. "I'm sorry. But where does Jess fit into all this? You haven't told her what's going on, have you?"

"Well, I had to explain some of it."

There was another beat of silence, the click of a door closing. Pressing my eyes shut, I could feel my frustration mounting by the second as I pictured her apartment.

"Well?" I said through gritted teeth.

"Look," Joe sighed, "that post scared the shit out of me and I lost the plot, okay? I didn't wanna talk about the care home but it kept cropping up. She's not stupid, Maisie, she's already sussed something went on there..."

"So let me guess," I finished. "You stayed the night with her."

"She offered, and what would you have done, eh? Risk walking home in the dark and get the crap beaten out of you or stay round at her place?"

"Told you she had the hots for you," I sniped.

"Okay, so now you know I haven't been beaten up or murdered, d'you wanna tell me what's been happening in your neck of the woods?"

His face flickered in my mind like a mirage, driving a spur through my heart. Try as I might, I could not suppress the desolation I was feeling, although there was little else I could say to recriminate him.

Pushing aside my anxiety for now, I relived my conversation with Sarah.

There was nothing conclusive yet, but she had promised to sift through the paper trail. If any documents relating to Sam's case could be found, they might lead us to people who remembered him.

"Sounds promising," Joe commented.

Lost in my reverie, I had almost forgotten he was hanging on the other end of the line, listening. I stood up, startled.

"Yes, but it could be weeks before we hear anything, which brings me back to the threats. Even Sarah suggested we should report them."

"I'm not sure," he protested. "How is that gonna help?"

I chewed my nail, knowing the time had come to creep down darker avenues because in truth, he had no idea how worried I'd been with every unanswered call.

"Tell me about this latest threat on Instagram," I pressed him. "You mentioned the same hose image but who would have posted such a thing?"

"Does the name *Silver Fox* ring any bells?"

"A new follower," I gasped. "I saw! But why did you follow them back?"

"I assumed it was one of yours," he answered, "posting the same sort of photos. One that sprung out was them blue and yellow beach huts in Felpham."

I felt a sudden chill snake down my arms. "Felpham. That proves they've been in our area, and there's something about that name that bothers me..."

"Well, I wouldn't have followed 'The Watchman' or anyone to do with 'Orchard Grange,' would I?" he grunted. "Just how many accounts has this bastard got? Unless of course there's more than one of 'em."

"Well, I expect so," I said. "Whoever's trying to intimidate you, I doubt if they're operating alone, which surely gives us even more reason to report this."

I didn't want to voice what I was really thinking but that name, *Silver-Fox*. It called to mind the silver-haired gentleman we had seen in the care home. *Lord Thomas Parker-Smythe*. Could he be one of them?

"Think about it, Joe. Even Sarah said those parties sounded dodgy, and if we tell the police, don't you think others might come forward? We can't be the only ones who remember them."

"Yeah, sure," he murmured, as a jangle of mugs pricked my senses, "but let me think about it... I don't wanna do anything too hasty."

By the time the call ended, I felt a knot in my stomach that had nothing to do with the trolls any more. Frozen in Sarah's kitchen, I could not shift that last lingering image of Joe lounging in Jess's bed.

135

"Everything okay?" Sarah asked. "I take it you got through to him at last."

Drifting over to the work surface where I was standing, she opened a pack of filter coffee. At first all I could do was nod, my thoughts a confused tangle.

"He spent the night with my best friend," I mumbled, finally.

"Oh," she commented. "What's the matter? You can tell me. Is there more between you two than just friendship?"

"No," I croaked, "but there could have been. We shared a kiss. That I could handle, I just didn't want to leap into bed with him straight away. I panicked."

Switching on the coffee machine, she gave me the gentlest of smiles.

"So what were you scared of? Joe, or intimacy? Given your state of mind, I can't imagine he'd harbour a grudge, though. He sounds like a nice guy."

"He is," I said. Tears stung my eyes. "But it's too late, he's with Jess now."

"Oh, Maisie," she soothed. "It's not the end of the world..."

"You don't understand," I kept flapping. "What I feel for Joe is stronger than love and it goes right back to Orchard Grange. We're soul mates, Sarah. He makes me feel so safe, I can't bear the thought of losing him again..." A tear rolled down my cheek, a warm salty stream seeping between my lips.

Sarah cast me a look that extinguished any lingering trace of doubt. "Of course you like him! You sang his praises when he was a boy! Mandy told me, and I doubt if anything's changed. His troubles have made him harder and thornier, but I bet he's soft as marshmallow underneath."

"If only I hadn't rejected him," I blubbered.

"How was he next morning?"

"Gutted. He swore it wouldn't happen again."

"Then at least he's patient," she placated me. "He's giving you time to discover your own feelings, so why not leave things be. Let him enjoy a relationship, it'll run its course, and once it's over, you'll be there for him. Strikes me you've got far more important things to worry about right now."

I could have hugged her, despite the anxiety tunnelling through me.

"I wish I had your wisdom," I said. "You're right, though, in the grander scheme of things it doesn't matter. I mentioned the police too but he wasn't very keen. So maybe I should concentrate on what *I remember* about those parties..."

Chapter Thirty-Two

Hannah Adams. Registered Psychotherapist and Counsellor. West Sussex.
Client: Maisie Bell
16th April 2015

"Now let's see..." Hannah began, sifting through her notes. "Looking over your last five sessions, these memories are beginning to tell a story. Has anything else come to light you want to talk to me about?"

"I guess so," I faltered, hearing the uncertainty fill my voice. "Joe and I need to get to the bottom of all this, but there are so many loose ends."

"How do you feel since you've been reunited? Has it changed anything in your life?"

"Definitely. Having Joe around has brought some stability back and even the nightmares have stopped. But ever since we've been talking, I've been wondering how much we really know... and is it enough to launch an investigation?"

The brush of her fingers turning the pages ceased so abruptly, you could have heard a pin drop.

"An investigation," she repeated. "Do you think you're ready?"

"No, but I think we're getting close."

I didn't want to tell her what was really on my mind; the disturbing online images that directly linked Joe's abusers to Orchard Grange. If I could just dig a little deeper. Unravel those last twisted knots.

"Joe's got a job now, and he's settling down in Bognor very nicely. But a whole new can of worms was opened when we recognised a face in the paper - a man we remember seeing in the care home."

"Then why not focus on him?" she said. "Just let go of your thoughts."

Lapsing into a trance, I felt a creeping coldness. Saw the men lingering in the corridor. One of them was Mortimer, but a silver-haired stranger accompanied him.

Yes, he was the one I wanted to concentrate on, the day his crystal blue eyes had latched onto me. A moth of a memory fluttered...

'Hello, where have you been hiding?'

'Quite lovely, isn't she?' I heard Mortimer drawl. 'Flitting around like a *little mouse, but I'm glad you're here, Maisie. There's a very special party coming up for some of the new girls and that includes you...'*

'Me?' I whispered aloud. 'I-I haven't got a party dress.'

The smug looks they exchanged held the hint of something conspiratorial.

'I've ordered some,' Mortimer kept smiling. 'Lovely new party dresses, which will be delivered tomorrow with ribbons and new shoes.'

His voice thickened, sending an unpleasant roll of fear through my stomach.

'Ramona is invited too...'

As if the company of my roommate would put my mind at rest.

Yet all the while this stranger was lingering, his smile stayed with me, drifting in and out of my thoughts long after his departure.

"Joe warned me not to go," I shivered.

My limbs turned to ice as the scene morphed into the laundry room.

"Yes," Hannah muttered, "I know, but I want to guide you a little further. Joe locked you in. Yet someone let you out. That 'someone' wanted to make absolutely sure you went to the party. So where did they take you? Try to imagine the car and the other girls. Tell me about the journey."

Deeper into the past I tunnelled, my eyes closed. Soft leather cushions embraced me as I sank into the car. The purr of an engine rising.

"It was a posh car. There were two girls in the back already, and they picked up two more. We were about the same age and wearing the exact same dresses."

Oh, the coolness of red satin slipping through my fingers...

"I remember them chattering. I wasn't even sure what they were talking about, only I was too nervous to join in. So I listened. Stared out of the car window..."

I glimpsed the flash of a motorway before the car turned off. Snapshots drifted back to me; a country lane, grassy banks exploding with white cow parsley.

'Where are we going?'

My voice sounded high and girlish.

One of the girls tittered before the voice of the driver interrupted.

'Wait and see.'

Was that the hint of a foreign accent I detected? German, perhaps. The sound echoed like a train swallowed into a tunnel, and I kept my eyes glued to that road... until something else flickered in the mist.

With the car slowing down, we had arrived at a set of wrought iron gates.

"It looked like a country estate! There were horses in the field and hills dotted with sheep b-but..."

"Go on. What else did you see?" Hannah prompted.

"A house, a huge mansion. Neat hedges, a long driveway running up to the entrance."

"So how did the other girls react?"

"They were as amazed as I was. None of us could believe it! What were we doing at this great posh country house in the middle of nowhere?"

Picturing the driveway, I caught my breath; for there, in the distance emerged a cloud of forest. At first it was indistinct, just a green smudge on the horizon.

"Okay, so you were in a car," Hannah prodded, "six of you. You were driven some distance and no longer in London but a country estate."

"That's right," I croaked.

My mind struggled at this point but something else was out there, a vision that manifested itself gradually until it jolted me in its magnitude.

"Maisie, what is it?"

My breath had quickened as I observed the view from behind the car window. The forest shimmered closer but it was no longer the forest I was fixated on.

"A cluster of oak trees."

They rose up without warning. Hugged the fringe of the forest as if guarding it.

"I-I'm starting to remember the party, too. The adults making a fuss of us, admiring our dresses and our hair. They led us into a lovely lounge and we played games, we listened to music. We were dancing and having fun..."

The infectious notes of 'Push the Feeling On,' by the Night Crawlers piped through the room as we gyrated around on the carpet. At the same time, shadows drifted in and out of my mind's eye, a scattering of smiling adults. It was such a surreal atmosphere and something about the merriment seemed forced.

"They were there for a reason. Observing our interaction perhaps, as if to build up some profile for the adoption services?"

Yet the feeling was short lived.

The unexpected sight of Mr. Mortimer twisted a sudden knot of dread in my belly.

"What was he doing there?" I gasped. That was when I spotted the punch bowl. It triggered a timely warning, and I remembered what Joe had said.

'Come on now, girls, drink up. It's nearly time to drive you home.'

His toad-like eyes slithered over me, monitoring every sip I took. In fact if it hadn't been for the squawk of another girl's laugh, he might not have spun around when he did, but for a moment, his scrutiny slipped.

"I tipped the rest of my punch into a flower vase," I said defiantly.

Only when we departed from the house did those trees make their lasting *impression. Their fat, writhing branches formed an ugly silhouette.*

"It was creepy," I choked, my throat so dry I could barely force the words out. "I sensed a presence out there, as if a hundred eyes were following us..."

What I also realised was how quiet the car had become before a raw, paralysing fear consumed me. For there, lingering beyond the oak trees, stood a lone figure, the flutter of a cloak in the gloom.

"A hooded shadow," my voice echoed.

Everything felt like a game now, some eerie fantasy world, where I was the only player. A dreamy silence enveloped me and I felt the strength of that figure's stare. But as the mouth of the forest yawned, a single track was illuminated, twisting its way into the heart, where I knew an even darker thicket of trees was awaiting us.

Little whimpers escaped my throat; I was powerless to stop them.

"No, please... this isn't happening... not now."

"Take it easy," Hannah murmured. "You're safe, Maisie, remember? No one is going to hurt you... time I brought you back now."

But even as I clawed my way back to consciousness, a distant face peered through the darkness. It blew the breath out of me, yet that face... that chiselled profile of the man I had seen earlier. Could he and Mortimer be allies?

******

Heart thumping, I unlocked the door to my flat, unable to believe what my subconscious mind was telling me. The sight of Joe hovering in the lounge stalled me.

"Hi, Maisie," he greeted me. "How did you get on?"

Drifting towards him on autopilot, I wanted nothing more than to hug him. Yet the atmosphere between us felt strained.

How could I explain?

Something felt different since last weekend, and with Joe and Jess in a relationship, I knew the dynamics had shifted.

Pinching the bridge of my nose, I eased myself into the sofa.

"You know we were trying to figure out the truth behind those parties? I regressed as far back into my childhood as I dared."

The frown on his face deepened. "You sure you're up to telling me this? D'you need a glass of wine first?"

I risked a smile. "Sounds like a plan, but only if you'll join me."

The sincerity in his eyes was enough to melt my resolve, and before I knew it, the details were pouring out faster than I could hold back; memories of Mortimer and his silver-haired ally. I had witnessed them colluding in the corridor, but with images of oak trees interwoven into the aftermath of that strange party, I had emerged from the scene even more confused.

"You saw him," Joe pressed.

"Yes, but I'm not sure where he features. I didn't see him at the house or the party, only something creepy came to mind when we were driven to the forest. Everything seemed surreal. I felt sleepy and it was dark..."

I sensed his stare as I chewed the skin around my fingernail.

"I'm glad you're here, though. At least we can talk about it..." Another smile forced its way onto my lips. "So no Jess tonight?"

"Jess is at a works do and I've got an early shift tomorrow." His brow furrowed into a frown again. "Maisie, are you sure you're okay about me and Jess having a fling?"

"Of course," I chuckled. "Why shouldn't I be? You deserve a love life the same as anyone, but is it just a fling?"

"Who knows? Between you and me, I think she's looking for a bit of adventure in her life..." and turning on his heel, he let loose a smile. "So no, I'm not seeing Jess 'til tomorrow. Now where's that wine hiding?"

I felt my heart squeeze.

That sweet, lop-sided smile... the one characteristic that would always endear him to me.

"Great," I responded joyfully. "Then let's get fish and chips tonight. I don't really fancy cooking."

Chapter Thirty-Three

London

Thomas sighed to himself, tucking the news cuttings into his dossier. At least the stories were starting to diminish now. *But what a terrible scandal to blemish the walls of Westminster, and just when he was gaining some prominence.*

Rising to his feet, he checked his reflection. Large bay windows allowed the mid-morning light to flood in, illuminating his features. Despite his sixty-two years, he boasted a full head of hair, as glossy as polished silver, and today of all days he wanted to cling to that confidence.

So when the clock struck eleven he was ready for them.

Lingering by the window, he saw a van pull up, and recognising the pink and white logo assigned to the 'Gleam Gals,' he felt a glow touch his heart.

A week ago, he could not believe his fortune when two girls had turned up at his apartment. Poppy's friends had indeed turned out to be everything a distinguished gentleman could wish for, but never in his life had he expected such beauties.

Abby wore her jet black hair in a tidy bun; Abby whose sweeping black lashes and pink lips reminded him of a pin-up. Tanya, on the other hand, was unmistakably the quieter one with a pale dewy complexion and platinum-blonde hair. But the one feature that mesmerised him was her eyes; large, round and the iciest light blue, their striking impact had stayed with him.

Yes, he had a lot to thank Poppy for, recommending this domestic agency.

"Girls!" he greeted them warmly. "Come on in!"

Abby peeped up saucily from beneath her sooty lashes. "Good morning, Sir, and how are we today?"

"Very well, thank you," he murmured. "All the better for seeing you, my dear. And how is little Tanya?"

A lock of hair had strayed onto her cheek bone and helpless to resist, he spiralled it around his finger to tuck it behind her ear. Staring back brazenly, she returned his smile but it didn't quite reach her eyes, glacially cool, as they swept over his suit.

"Mr Parker-Smythe," she purred with the trace of an East European accent. "You look smart. Are you going out today?"

"I have to be in Westminster by noon," he beamed, "but please! Make yourselves at home. You know where the tea and coffee is and I bought some chocolate chip cookies. If you could just give the place another good sweep and dust..."

The words dried on his lips as the girls exchanged glances, and only then did he notice something strange, almost conspiratorial in their behaviour.

He watched in a dream as they swayed before him in their long, black coats then slowly began to unbutton them. One by one the coats fell to the carpet, a sight that nearly floored him. For beneath those coats were not the pinafores he remembered. Today they were wearing short black dresses, teamed with frilly white aprons and seamed stockings.

"Oh, my darlings!" He gasped with pleasure. "I was only joking when I said I'd love to see you in French maids' outfits..."

How regrettably short was his time with them. Wary of their presence, he engrossed himself in paperwork. Yet they flickered on the periphery like butterflies, one fair, one dark, the essence of every red-blooded man's fantasy.

But given his age and position in Parliament, he dared not be caught staring. His fleeting remark about *French maids' outfits* had never been meant seriously, though he was touched by their efforts to please him. Indulging his little whims reignited a sense of empowerment in him, and when the taxi turned up, he stole a last glance in the mirror.

Satisfied that he looked immaculate, he stepped outside.

But just as the taxi was leaving, a movement sharpened his senses; a shadow so subliminal it would have been easy to miss. Thomas raised his head. And although the youth loitering on the corner appeared preoccupied - hand glued to his mobile, head bowed under the rim of a black hoodie - why was he struck with the impression this person had been waiting for him?

Thomas swallowed, hand clawing at his collar to loosen his tie.

Please not a journalist.

He should have known that as soon as he became a public figure, he would be subject to closer scrutiny. Now here he was, a member of the House of Lords, and there were two girls in his apartment. Two girls dressed up like tarts.

******

"Are you ready for this?" the caller prompted.

"I see no reason why not."

"Then go for it. The wheels have been set in motion."

The man's breathing grew heavier as he pictured his quarry.

Pity he had turned his back on their enterprise, too puffed up with his own flimsy ideology to reap the rewards.

Watching from the sidelines, he had witnessed the man's every career move. Leaping from branch to branch to the top of his tree until he had at last ascended to power.

Yet it was he who would have the last laugh.

"Have you been following the stories in the papers?" he couldn't resist musing. "It appears the authorities are closing in now."

"Good," his accomplice whispered, "the timing couldn't be better. All those high establishment figures, associated with a historic abuse scandal... The police are leaving no stone unturned, and I bet the press will have a field day."

The man's eyes narrowed.

Since falling from grace, he had faded to a ghost of his former self, but now, finally, the balance of power was about to shift.

If all went as intended, the girl would be easy prey soon. Yes, she was the one he had always wanted, a treasured bloom ready to be harvested, and he could not wait to see their long awaited plans fulfilled.

"Only one more obstacle stands in our path," he added sharply.

A prick of anger lanced his thoughts as Joe Winterton arose to haunt him.

"Yes, I know and you've been very patient," his ally placated him. "We've waited too long to allow a skank like him to worm his way into Maisie's life. So let's do what you suggested from the start, shall we? Deal with him once and for all."

Chapter Thirty-Four

What Maisie did not realise was that Joe had been thinking about her too.

Cycling to work before dawn, he would never forget that wistful look when she had returned from her therapy. Yet it wasn't what she had told him that tugged a knot in his chest, as much as what she hadn't.

Pausing at the end of the avenue, he eased his bike onto the pavement to avoid the roundabout. A violet glow infused the sky, melting away the darkness. Despite the lack of traffic, though, the configuration of roads looked daunting. He crossed the Chichester Road with caution before leaping back onto the saddle.

Riding north, he felt a breeze wash over his face, his thoughts creeping back to Maisie.

She couldn't be cut up about him and Jess, surely?

If it hadn't been for that baleful threat on Instagram, she might never have invited him to stay. But with the fuse between them ignited, he couldn't get enough of her now. Neither knew how long the affair would last, but it didn't alter the way he felt about Maisie.

Continuing past the Bognor War Memorial Hospital, he sped up to the main Shripney road without delay. An arc of headlights occasionally split the darkness but as his thoughts wandered, they were drawn inevitably to the threats online.

The trolls were still out there, polluting his Twitter feed with their poison.

The black car, on the other hand, had been markedly absent since Maisie's last sighting, but it all pointed towards some criminal faction.

Staring ahead, he circumnavigated the final roundabout. One more stretch of road and he would reach the pedestrian crossing opposite Sainsbury's.

Then the unexpected belch of an engine broke the tranquillity.

Joe flinched. Seconds ago there had been no one on the road; if there had been, the sound would have emerged more gradually. He could never have known how sharply he stood out, but as the vehicle crept behind him, something else struck him.

Where was the gleam of headlights?

Joe glanced around, then wished he hadn't as the menacing bulk of a transit van emerged from the shadows. A dart of fear pierced his senses and he pedalled faster, but it was impossible to react quickly enough. With one almighty burst of the accelerator, the van cut across in front of him, giving him no choice but to mount the pavement. Wheels jolting over the curb, he could barely think straight.

How the hell was he supposed to dodge a van?

But everything happened suddenly, wheels wobbling as he experienced a horrible loss of gravity. Thrown to the ground, Joe landed heavily, the panic in his mind spiralling, the van driver revving harder...

"Stop!" a scream finally exploded from the opposite side of the road. "What the fuck d'you think you're playing at?"

An aubergine fleece registered, the sight of a colleague belting across the main road. Recognising the heavily built driver known as Colin, Joe heard the blare of a car horn. Saw another rescuer pull into the roadside.

The next time he forced his eyes open, the van had vanished, thank God.

"Christ, mate, are you okay?" Colin spluttered.

Drawn by the commotion, more people began to emerge in the dawning light. A slam of car doors echoed around him like thunder.

"Call the police!" someone hollered. "An ambulance!"

"No - n-no," Joe mumbled, finding his voice at last, "i-it's alright, I'm not badly hurt but can someone help me across the road to the warehouse?"

Giddy with shock, he felt the hands of his colleagues on him, lifting him, and he slowly struggled to his feet.

No, he wasn't badly hurt as far as he could tell.

By the time they escorted him to the warehouse, though, the pain started to kick in. His left knee throbbed from crashing onto the tarmac. Touching the side of his face, he winced at the sting of grazing and when he examined his hands, he saw beads of blood oozing from his palms, glints of gravel embedded in the cuts.

With a resigned sigh, he limped towards the sink where his boss was already waiting. Vicky's face tightened as she sifted through the first aid box; his colleagues must have updated her by now.

"Joe," she began softly. "I think we need to clean up these wounds, don't you? And have you seen the state of your badge?"

Glancing down at his dusty fleece, he could have laughed out loud. His name badge, though cracked and hanging by its pin, was the least of his worries. Turning the cold tap on, Vicky tore a sheet of paper from a roll to dampen it. Rivulets of blood soaked the paper, turning it pink as the truth finally sank in.

"Look, I know what happened," she murmured, her voice so low it was drowned by the commotion in the warehouse. "Colin told me. He witnessed the whole thing from the car park, and you might as well know he's notified the police."

A surge of delayed terror came shuddering down his spine. "The police?"

"Yes," Vicky said, still quiet, "and with any luck those lunatics will be caught and arrested but what about you?"

He felt a lump in his throat but swallowed it back hard.

"I have to ask – and don't take offence – but when you were in prison, did you make any enemies?"

"No," Joe spluttered. "This ain't got nothing to do with prison!"

"Okay," she sighed. "Sorry, but you have to understand my concerns."

Delving into the first aid box, she pulled out a roll of gauze. Joe dabbed away the last of the grit before applying a layer of antiseptic cream.

Vicky's words nevertheless hung darkly.

"Colin swore that van deliberately drove you off the road."

"Bastards shot out of nowhere," Joe whispered. "No lights, no warning... I'm not mixed up with the criminal world though, I swear. The only place I seem to have enemies is in this town."

Holding his stare, she lifted his hand and wound a filmy layer of gauze around his palm. He detected not a hint of recrimination. What stirred him the most was that look of motherly tenderness, a look that filled him with anguish.

His enemies had known exactly where to find him.

For several days he had cycled to work in the early hours, same route, same shifts, and despite the absence of the black car, they had tracked his every move.

An uneasy buzz wheeled around the shop floor as news of his accident spread like wildfire. A short time later the police turned up, the suspense building to fever pitch. But as each and every witness stepped forward, Joe grew ever more nervous, until eventually it was his turn.

"We found the van," one of the officers informed him, "abandoned just off the A27 in Slindon Woods. Turns out it was a hired van from London."

"Have you traced the driver?" he whispered in hope.

"Not yet, but that's our next line of enquiry, as soon as the office opens. We'll also be examining the CCTV footage."

Joe nodded, unused to the law treating him so courteously.

"Mr Winterton," the second officer's voice intruded. "Do you have any idea who your attackers were? If so, it would help our investigation."

Joe froze, eyes flitting to the glass door panel. Enclosed in a tiny office, he couldn't fail to notice other members of staff sneaking past, as if hoping to glean snippets of his statement.

"Yeah, I do. In fact it's time we came clean about what's been going on these past few weeks, but not here..."

"We?"

"This involves a friend," he shivered, "and she needs to be present. But is there any chance we could do this at home?"

Once they had left, the tension around the building began to dissipate. Joe lingered in the cafeteria, his mind and body numb, but he knew he had done the right thing. There were too many people around to piece his story together with any lucidity.

Chapter Thirty-Five

"Hello, Maisie," DC Anderson greeted me.

"Mark," I answered gravely. "It's good to see you again."

Staring at the man in my doorway, I felt a roll of unease. *How many weeks had passed since that eerie sighting of a boy on the edge of the woods?*

At least his blue eyes twinkled, setting my mind at rest.

"Come in and take a seat. This is my friend, Joe."

"It's good to meet you, Joe," Mark said, "and I heard what happened this morning. How are you feeling now?"

Joe raised his head. "Not too bad, thanks."

Perched in a chair at the dining table, he looked smart and composed in his clean denim shirt and chinos. The only blemish was the graze on his cheek, and a swelling of purple bruising.

But Mark wasted no time, lowering himself into the chair opposite. "Well, I'll tell you what we discovered about the van first. According to the rental company, the customer was a large, heavily built man with thinning blonde hair. Spoke with an accent, German they think. Ring any bells?"

An icy chill slid over me as I watched colour drain from Joe's face.

"Schiller," he hissed.

I was catapulted straight back to Orchard Grange.

Mark glanced at his notepad with a frown. "Hmm, that's not the name he gave the rental company, but then it's not impossible he used a fake ID."

As Joe met my eye, an invisible thread of fear pulled between us.

"He goes under many names," he added darkly. "Like *the Watchman*. So maybe it's a good time to mention the trolls..."

Yanking his mobile from his pocket, he placed it on the table before Mark's eyes, and in the minutes it took for him to digest the screen shots, I momentarily left them to make coffee.

By the time I returned, Mark looked stunned.

"Why didn't you report this stuff?"

"That's what I said."

"Yes, Maisie, I know," Joe sighed, "except 'trolling' someone on Twitter in't exactly a crime is it? I didn't think they'd be bothered. Some sick bastard trying to scare the shit out of me."

"So what about the creep tailing us in the black car?" I argued, "which is something else we should have reported..."

It didn't take long to relay our memories, but the faster Joe spoke, the more the atmosphere in the room seemed to blacken.

"We need to look into this," Mark insisted. He had turned very still, his face giving nothing away as he glanced at me. "CCTV cameras cover the main roads around Bognor and the automatic number plate recognition will flag up the number of times this car has travelled in and out of town."

"Good," Joe responded, "cos we know someone's watching us and while we're on the subject of trolls... one goes by the name *Shadow of the Grange*."

"So what's the connection there?" Mark broke in.

"Orchard Grange was a children's home Maisie and I lived in. The owner went by the name of Mortimer, Schiller one of his thugs. Built like a brick shit house he was, German accent - someone who sounds very much like the fucker who tried to run me over this morning..."

"Hey, slow down," Mark spluttered, "I can hardly keep up - but are you saying this case involves both of you? See, I know I shouldn't be telling you this, but talking to my superiors, their immediate concern was of your former conviction, that maybe this had some link with organised crime..."

"Well, they would, wouldn't they?" Joe snapped and lifting his eyes, his gaze rested upon me again. "Now you know why I didn't wanna bother the Old Bill before this. Who'd take some low-life like me seriously?"

"Joe, stop it," I said with a shudder. "At least Mark's prepared to listen to us."

Mark offered me the gentlest smile in response. "So what's your take on this, Maisie? Joe mentioned a children's home... but I'm beginning to suspect something else went on."

Sipping my coffee, I was battling to put my thoughts into words. Joe remained rooted to the spot for now, rolling himself a cigarette. Anyone could see how much that comment from Mark's superiors had stung him, but I was pleased he had stayed put. The abrasion on his cheek flared like a brand, serving a chilling reminder.

"The people who ran the children's home were monsters," I began. "One of my first memories was of a beating they gave Joe with a metal hose. Mortimer sanctioned it. He hated Joe, and all because he tried to protect me. That's how we know they're behind this - the clues are in the tweets..."

Mark froze, a look of dread passing over his face as he finally grasped the horror behind those steel hose adverts. But it inspired me to keep talking.

"It's not the only abuse that went on though, so I might as well tell you now, but you know that night in February when I called the police out?"

"How could I forget?" Mark said. "I'd never seen you look so distraught. You said you were suffering from nightmares - did these relate to the home too?"

"Yes," I shivered, "everything goes back to these strange parties Mortimer organised, and this is what Joe was trying to warn me about."

"The reason they thrashed the shit out of me," he added sourly.

Mark jerked his head upright, a frown crinkling his brow. Watching him warily, I wondered what else might have crossed his mind at this point.

"What sort of parties?" he blurted.

It took several minutes to explain everything I knew. The fact those parties didn't take place in the home was questionable enough; private functions held in a remote country house and far from the eyes of public scrutiny.

The notion we were drugged was the next detail to trigger alarm bells. I told Mark about the punch, and Joe's warning not to drink it, before he had taken the unusual decision of locking me in the laundry room.

"These are my lucid memories, but I should also point out I've been seeing a psychotherapist and a lot more has emerged..."

"Secret parties," Mark muttered aloud, the speed of his pen gathering momentum.

He was struggling to jot it all down, yet at the same time I saw a subtle flush in his face, and his eyes would not meet mine.

"I hope you don't mind me asking this, but are you suggesting the nature of the abuse went beyond physical violence?"

My mouth dropped open of its own accord.

"You've seen the stories in the news, haven't you?"

"The scandal surrounding Westminster? A political hot potato as far as the police are concerned because of the people named, but they have to protect the victims."

"And you wonder if this is connected?" I pressed.

"No, but I see similarities, in so much as vulnerable children were taken out of care homes and driven to highly organised sex parties..." Breaking his flow, he risked a glance in Joe's direction. "And you can relate to this too?"

Joe said nothing but his eyes narrowed, glittering with foreboding.

"Neither of us are a hundred percent sure what happened," I butted in. "Like I say, we were drugged... but there's something else. A friend of ours went missing. *Sam Ellis*. He was taken to one of those parties and we never saw him again."

"A missing child," Mark reflected. Shock tightened his breath as he lowered his pen to the table, and in that moment I knew I had him spellbound.

"I've been wanting to report this for ages," I added, "but without proof we were never sure if the police would take us seriously. Do you see what I'm getting at? Twice I called you out under false pretences, so I had to be sure I got it right this time. I even asked a friend if she could trace him."

"Maisie, you didn't have to do that," Mark sighed, "but I admire your honesty. If it's any consolation, I'd like to run this past my DI if I can just confirm the facts."

His eyes wandered to Joe again, whose silence was beginning to disturb me.

"The first thing the police need to understand is why someone tried to run you over today, Joe. They could have killed you. But if we're looking at attempted murder, there has to be a motive."

At last Joe cleared his throat. "Mortimer swore he'd deal with me one day, and I reckon this is what those threats were about."

"That being the case," Mark said, "these people need to be caught and arrested before they inflict any more harm."

"So what happens next?" he probed.

"Given the amount of information, I think the next best thing would be for you to give formal statements at a police station..."

"Oh no," I baulked, "not Bognor!"

"Littlehampton," Mark reassured me, "and if you like, we can send an unmarked car around to escort you. At least it minimises the prospect of anyone seeing you. Would you agree to that?"

"Sure," Joe said, "I don't think we've got much choice really."

Mark started scribbling again. "You've given me two names to go on, one being Mortimer and the other, this Schiller character, but is there anyone else who could be connected that you can think of?"

I felt the weight of Joe's stare again. But as his fingers fidgeted with his roll-up, he looked so down-trodden, the answer hit me in a flash.

"There might be," I gulped. "Someone who's been in the news recently..."

My lip trembled as Mark's eyes seemed to grow bigger. *Pleading eyes.*

"He's just been admitted to the House of Lords, but we both distinctly remember seeing him at Orchard Grange. Thomas Parker-Smythe. He was very pally with Mortimer - and present when he mentioned the party I was invited to."

Chapter Thirty-Six

If Detective Inspector Burke had been present at the start of the investigation, there was every chance he would not have taken their claims seriously, Mark thought. The first hurdle was Joe's criminal record. Reported as a runaway, he was known to the police for his part in aiding and abetting a brutal robbery, and it was inevitable that in his years behind bars, he would have mixed with some particularly nasty convicts.

His homeless days were a blur, but nevertheless on record.

As for Maisie, she had been right about one thing; his superiors did harbour some concerns about her instability. Referring to her as 'a bit of a do-gooder,' DI Burke upheld the opinion she was 'prone to hysteria,' someone whose judgement could not always be relied upon.

Mark felt a shiver of unease. Back on the night of her hallucination, he had sensed some underlying torment. It lurked in the depths of her eyes; the same haunted look he had observed in many child abuse victims. So the moment a children's home had sprung its way into the discussion, he knew damn well they were looking into something far bigger than a regular *hit and run*.

"So what do you make of all this, Sarge?" he whispered, as they were making their way to the DI's office.

Maisie and Joe had left, escorted back home as promised to protect their anonymity. A glance at the sergeant, who had been present when recording their statements, was enough to tell Mark he was not the only one who felt spooked. A shadow of anxiety passed over the man's face, his lips compressed in a line.

"What they suggest is highly plausible, given the level of victimisation Joe's been through," he muttered, "but I bet you if there's even a sniff of a paedophile ring behind this, Harold will pounce on it like a dog with a bone."

He wasn't wrong. In the instant DI Harold Burke glanced up, his eyes met Mark's with a glitter.

"So let's run over the facts. What we have is a group of privately owned children's homes. Hired thugs to keep the kids under control. Organised parties in a remote house and two youngsters who believe they were drugged. Yet at the crux of the matter, we're looking at the disappearance of a child from twenty years ago."

"That pretty much sums it up, Sir," Mark nodded. "So have you come to a decision with regard to the next phase?"

"Well, Mark, to put your mind at rest," he snapped. "I assure you we're taking the matter very seriously. I know you think my judgement of the victims has been harsh up until now..."

"I didn't intend to malign you," he interrupted.

Yet the DI held up his palm. "For now, I want this kept out of the press. Regrettably, there is little I can do to stop reporters asking about the hit and run, but word has got out. What I fear, however, is that we lack the manpower and expertise to investigate something this momentous, so for that reason, I'm consulting the division in the Metropolitan Police that deals with these cases."

Mark felt his shoulders sag. "You're referring this to the Met?"

"I have no choice," Harold sighed, "and whilst I realise the attack was local, the historic nature of this crime happened in or around London."

"But what about the van driver?" Mark protested. "Not to mention the black car that's been stalking them?"

"You can look into the CCTV footage," Harold placated him. "Obviously we'll gather whatever local intelligence we can, but that's all can I suggest for now."

His face retained its steely resolve, a look which left Mark in no doubt there was nothing else to be gained. Examining the last traces of evidence Maisie had reported was as much involvement as he could hope for, though he could not deny how deflated he felt.

"So what about the victims," he dared ask, "especially Maisie?"

"They are not to be named," the DI barked. "But what I propose is you act as their liaison officer. I must warn you, though, that once the Met get involved, this investigation is out of our hands, especially now she's mentioned a known public figure."

******

Before 12:00 noon that same day, the Metropolitan Police were alerted: a report emailed from DI Burke of West Sussex Police outlining a sustained campaign of intimidation, which had culminated in a near fatal road accident.

As predicted, it wasn't so much the crime of attempted murder that piqued their interest, as the motive. Given the victims' statements, the dilemma rising behind the walls at HQ had taken a sinister twist: with hints of a paedophile ring rearing its ugly head, officers faced the grim task of investigating another child abuse scandal.

"This can't be a coincidence," muttered the Detective Chief Inspector at the head of the investigation. "I'm not suggesting the cases are linked, but we can't rule it out. Now where do we start?"

Detective Inspector Andrew Fitzpatrick glared at the reports, feeling a cold sweat shimmy over him. "I want to track down this *Mortimer* and his accomplice. Can we access the CCTV footage from the van rental company? I know it'll be grainy, but if this is the thug who attempted to mow down Joe Winterton, we could use those images to appeal for witnesses, anyone who might lead us to him."

Fingers steepled on the desk, the DCI nodded shrewdly. "Good, though I must warn you that this Mortimer character is proving to be elusive... There is, however, another man I'd like you to investigate. Thomas Parker-Smythe. It seems these 'gentlemen' were well acquainted in the children's home. So let's see what we can uncover and if any mud sticks, I propose we bring him in for questioning."

Chapter Thirty-Seven

Charing Cross Police Station, The Strand, London
Conducted by officers of the Metropolitan Police
Suspect: Lord Thomas Parker-Smythe
RECORDED INTERVIEW
22nd April 2015

"The time is 10:30," a voice broke through the wall of silence. "My name is Detective Inspector Andrew Fitzpatrick and I am accompanied by Detective Sergeant Mike Havers. For the purposes of this interview, could you give your name and date of birth, please?"

Thomas braced himself. An hour had passed since the police had first approached him, and still he had no idea why. He felt like a suspect already; more so when they had led him into an interview room, the whirr of a tape recorder grating on him.

"Thomas Parker-Smythe," he said, retaining his crisp tone. "Born November 3rd 1954. Now what exactly is this about, please?"

"I am not at liberty to say at this stage, Sir," DI Fitzpatrick answered him, "but I'll start by asking if you recognise this building?"

The photocopy placed before him revealed a sprawling half-timber house. A six-foot fence enclosed the grounds. Thomas frowned. He couldn't put his finger on it, but something about that house breathed an air of desolation, windows so dark they appeared black, concealing whatever unpleasantness lurked on the other side.

But yes, it was familiar.

"Didn't this used to be a children's home?"

"That's right, and did you ever visit this home?"

Peering at it a second time, he felt a river of cold run over him.

"This is one of many private residential homes I visited. They were established to take the pressure off local authorities, though I had concerns about the children's schooling."

"Concerns? And why would that be, Sir?"

The more caressing tone of DS Havers allowed him to relax slightly.

Thomas looked up. "My role was to ensure a reasonable standard of education for all children, including those with behavioural problems. That is why these private homes were set up, to look after the more damaged children in society."

"I see," DS Havers nodded. "So when you visited, who did you speak to?"

Thomas froze, not liking the nature of this question.

"Were you familiar with the owner of the home, Mr. Mortimer?"

"Cornelius!" He released an airy laugh. "Of course, how could I forget? He invested a considerable sum in those homes, and was seeking government funding. My visits were to ensure they were fit for purpose but..."

"Thank you, Sir," the DI broke in, "but can I stop you for a second? When you say 'Cornelius' you are referring to Mr. Mortimer?"

"Yes."

"So is it reasonable to say you were friends?"

"Hardly friends."

"Alright, moving on, did you talk to any of the children? You describe them as 'damaged' but can you be more specific?"

"What sort of question is that?" Thomas bristled.

"Calm down," DI Fitzpatrick cautioned him. "So far you've told us you recognise the home and were familiar with the owner, Cornelius Mortimer. All we are trying to do at this stage is gather information; crucial information that may lead to a wider investigation."

"What sort of investigation?" Thomas pressed, "and why me?"

"Let's just concentrate on the matter in hand, please," Mike insisted. "Do you remember seeing this girl? She was put into care after losing her parents."

The photograph sliding across the table revealed an extremely pretty child; skin pale as porcelain, a dusting of freckles and auburn hair... Thomas swallowed, the ghost of a memory fluttering. He couldn't quite place her, but the fear in those haunted green eyes sent shivers through him.

"Judging by your expression, I think you do."

Thomas shook his head. "I-I'm not sure. There were so many kids in that place, I can't be expected to remember every single one of them."

"But did *Cornelius* introduce her to you?"

"I don't know... Maybe."

The silence swelled like fog. Her face had evoked an eerie sensation but that was all.

"Okay then," DI Fitzpatrick resumed, "what about her friends? Did you ever get to meet any of them, like this boy, for example?"

Before he could draw breath, another image was unveiled. Thomas flinched, jarred by the thin, almost feral face glowering back at him.

"Now that one I do remember," he shuddered. "Always in trouble."

The inspector leaned forwards slightly. "Go on."

"According to Cornelius, he was a proper little tearaway. He referred to him as 'dangerous' and the only reason I remember this is because he warned me about him... yet I struggled to understand why."

The memory left a nasty taste in his mouth.

"Interesting," DI Fitzpatrick muttered. "This 'boy' is in his thirties now and yet you remember him. Funny thing is, he remembers you too. Recognised you in the news and I quote *'he was always turning up at the home for meetings...'*"

With a quickening breath, Thomas studied the boy's eyes, two simmering dark pools of hate.

"What else did he tell you?" he whispered.

"That you harboured an unnatural interest," the DI taunted. *"Staring at the kids, chatting them up, smiling...* said he never felt comfortable in your presence."

"How dare you," Thomas spat. "I was trying to be polite! Some of those kids were abused, as I suspect he was! I saw bruises on his arms, and my only intention was to treat those children with kindness!"

Perched in the chair opposite, the inspector's face hardened like granite.

"You say *you suspected abuse* but did you report any of this?"

Thomas shook his head. "Cornelius had a grudge. Oh, how that boy cowered in his presence. *That's* why I smiled at him. To reassure him not all adults were bad."

"Good," DS Havers said, "you're doing really well, and I apologise if we haven't explained the relevance of this, but all will be revealed soon."

"As I said from the start," DI Fitzpatrick added. "The purpose of this interview is to gather material, which may assist us in our investigation and provide evidence."

"What investigation?" Thomas dared to ask.

"Are you aware of the stories in the news concerning a paedophile ring in Westminster? That children in care were driven to sex parties?"

Thomas felt every muscle in his body turn to ice.

"Yes, I've seen them and before we continue I have to ask... has *my* name been mentioned in connection with these allegations?"

"No. But our enquiry concerns a series of parties that took place in 1995. An era in which you were Minister for Education."

"But this is outrageous," he fumed, "I've done nothing wrong!"

"Okay," the inspector nodded. "Then I suggest we pause the interview at this point. I only wanted to gauge your reaction, Sir, but I see this is distressing you." His eyes narrowed. "Would you like a few minutes to compose yourself? A moment to consider what else you might remember about that year?"

"The time is 11:10," added DS Havers, "and this concludes our first interview."

By the time the officers had returned, Thomas was finding it hard to steady his breathing. The detective inspector was a tall man, whose broad shoulders and burly frame set his teeth on edge. Lifting his head, he was further unnerved by the steel in the man's expression, and the room felt stuffy and airless.

"So," he began, "are you ready to continue?"

Thomas swallowed, his throat dry.

"Would you like another glass of water?" the detective sergeant asked.

"No," he sighed. "I just want this to be over."

DS Havers' serene features and softer grey eyes should have pacified him, but they didn't. The very nature of the investigation tied knots of fear in his belly.

"Interview resumed at 11:20. So going back to 1995, you wanted to know why we called you in for questioning. We have reason to believe Cornelius Mortimer was using those homes to run a highly organised paedophile ring. The girl you saw in that photo is undergoing psychotherapy, and the most serious part of her statement concerns a number of parties Mortimer is alleged to have organised."

Thomas averted his eyes. "What kind of parties?"

"We're not certain; but the one thing we do know is that children were driven to a remote location and drugged. I gather you were present when Cornelius alluded to one of these parties. Do you remember that?"

"No," Thomas snapped, "I don't." Cold with dread, he was unaware of his fingers creeping to his lips as he spoke. "It was twenty years ago, for goodness sake, do you honestly expect me to remember every conversation word for word?"

DI Fitzpatrick raised his eyebrows. "Are you sure? She seemed very certain, not to mention the way you were smiling at her. She claims you were quite flirtatious."

"This is rubbish," Thomas replied. "The product of a delusional mind, and this was extracted under psychotherapy? Recovered memories are unreliable..."

"Lord Parker-Smythe," the detective inspector interrupted, "no charges have been made as yet, but you must understand our concerns. What I would like to raise, however, is your behaviour towards young girls in general."

"To give an example," added DS Havers, "did you know we've received a complaint from the manageress of Pianissimo Café? She's concerned about her daughter, who you've been witnessed chatting up on more than one occasion."

"Oh please!" he drawled. "Not Poppy?"

"Yes, Poppy. A naive fifteen-year-old waitress."

Listening intently, he was wounded to hear how his affections had been misconstrued; from the way he smiled at her, to the more serious accusations of 'ogling her breasts,' his eyes 'glued to her bottom as she walked...'

159

"It's been reported you tip her generously," DS Havers continued, "and that on one occasion you gave her ten pounds."

He would never forget the day he had met Poppy, a day on which he had been well and truly fired up with an inflated sense of power.

"And on another, you invited her to share your taxi."

He closed his eyes. "It was raining! I asked where she lived, which was barely half a mile from my home and the driver dropped me off first..."

A chill rolled over him as the memory came back.

"Such a sweet girl. I enjoyed her company but that's all it was, I swear!"

"Okay, fair enough," the DI said, "but you've had other girls in your home, haven't you? A pair you hire as cleaners."

"Poppy recommended that firm," he muttered in a tiny voice.

"I see," responded the sergeant. "Well, a neighbour caught a glimpse of them through the window, and he claims they did not look like any cleaners he'd come across. What he described were 'two scantily dressed dolly birds.'"

"Oh, for Heaven's sake," he said through gritted teeth. "This is starting to sound like a set up! I didn't ask them to come dressed like that! I suppose you were fed the story I *suggested* they wore French maid's outfits..."

"But was that not the case?" DI Fitzpatrick fired back at him.

"I was joking! Made some light-hearted comment and they took it literally."

"So why didn't you ask them to change?" he shrugged. "I think that's what most innocent people would have done. I'm sorry if it sounds harsh, but we're only trying to corroborate the facts here. Two girls wandering around my home in such costumes is not something I would allow if I were in your position."

"No," Thomas confessed bitterly, "I don't suppose it is."

His heart plummeted, but what could he do? A man on his own, he was vulnerable to their games, two scheming little minxes who had landed him in a right pickle.

"What are you trying to prove, exactly?" he croaked.

Hands clasped on the table, he felt utterly powerless under the spotlight, a writhing worm being pecked at by crows. Aspiring to the House of Lords was his greatest accomplishment. *He might have remembered that hubris always leads to humiliation. He might have guessed his success would be brief.*

"You're portraying me as a lonely old man who preys on young girls. That would fit your purpose well, wouldn't it? You think I'm one of those establishment figures embroiled in your child abuse scandal."

"Will you kindly bear with us, Sir?" DI Fitzpatrick responded coldly. "No one is accusing you of anything at this stage, although I do need to ask you about your past relationships. I understand you've been married."

"Twice," Thomas said, "and do you want to know why my first wife left me? Well, I don't mind admitting it, but she had an affair with my best friend."

"I'm sorry, Sir, I can see this is upsetting you, but why did your second wife divorce you?"

Thomas flinched, an icy sweat prickling him all over.

"You've spoken to her, haven't you?" he shuddered.

"Yes," the man nodded, "and we've learned of a matter that's been a closely guarded secret until now. Is it not the case she stumbled across a naked fourteen-year-old girl in your bed?"

Heart pounding, he lowered his eyes.

Why the hell were they dredging this up, and why now?

"Monserrat swore she was sixteen when we employed her. She offered to do some babysitting, a lonely Spanish girl living in London in need of work experience. How could we refuse? We took her on as an au pair."

"And what was the nature of your relationship?" the inspector pressed.

"It's immaterial," Thomas said. "Whatever my ex-wife told you is no doubt a vastly exaggerated version of the truth."

"Which is?"

"That child was looking for a father figure but developed something of an infatuation. We used to watch Disney films together, and she liked me to read her stories... Once I gave her a cuddle but she was clearly after more."

Acid bit his throat. As with Poppy, he had fought so hard to stop his eyes wandering over that ripening young body. Yet there she was, sprawled in his king-sized bed without a stitch on - long curly black hair glistening like pitch, and as for her breasts... they resembled a work of art.

"I know this isn't easy for you," DS Havers urged, "but please finish."

"I lingered in the doorway and stared. I couldn't help myself..." Facing the officers with a gulp, he was forced to confess the worst. "I heard the bathroom door slam and froze. My wife had been taking a bath and I was too late to stop her walking in. When she reached the bedroom I was still stood there, mesmerised..." He let out a sob. "But that is my only crime! That I stared!"

"I see," the DI nodded, though the disgust in his eyes was evident.

Thomas shook his head. "Haven't you demonised me enough for one day?"

"I sense your frustration," the DI drawled, "and we are not judging you, but we do need to build up a profile. Your name has been linked to a children's home that is central to our investigation, but we won't detain you any longer."

"Interview terminated at 11:55," the Sergeant added. "You are free to go."

Confident Parker-Smythe had left the building, Mike Havers let out a low whistle. "Well, well, what did you think of him, Sir?"

"Arrogant," DI Fitzpatrick said. "Cagey and at times, openly hostile. That's what got my hackles up, as if we had no right to be questioning him."

"But do we have reason to suspect him?"

"He's hiding something. I'll hedge a bet he was lying about Miss Bell's account too, as hinted by his body language. Kept touching his mouth, and did you notice how his eyes started flitting, as soon as we mentioned the parties?"

"Hmm..." Mike exhaled heavily. "Then where do we go from here?"

The DI braced his shoulders. "He didn't reveal as much about Mortimer as I'd hoped, so my next question is why, what is he concealing? I suggest we request a warrant to have his home searched."

Chapter Thirty-Eight

I didn't get to spend as much time with Joe as I'd hoped once the police were involved, though not through choice. My heart ached for him, and in the wake of that terrifying road accident, I had a yearning to wrap him in cotton wool.

But Jess got to him first.

She had been all over him like a rash since that day, showering him with affection, so why would he shy away? With stories of a 'mystery hit and run' splashed across the Bognor Observer, Spirit FM and social media, the horror of his persecution bounced back with a vengeance. Thank God they hadn't revealed his name.

But with a wider investigation looming, I felt little reassurance.

Jess was loving this.

Even Joe had suggested she craved a bit of adventure in her life.

Deep down though, I feared for him, the notion of someone trying to kill him sending wave after wave of panic pounding into me. It seemed wise to leave it in the hands of the police for now. Trust them to do their work. Except they had no idea how every memory associated with Mortimer stirred shivers of dread in me, as if the demons of our childhood were coming for us.

With the situation out of my control, there was nothing I could do. At least, until the following weekend, when an unexpected call changed everything.

"It's Sarah."

"Hi!" I gasped. "I've been meaning to call. How are you?"

"We need to talk," she murmured, "but not on the phone. How about I drive down to Bognor? I could bring Connor with me."

I felt a grip of hope in my heart. The weather had been changeable of late with light rains and a colder than average bite to the air. But today the clouds had thinned, allowing shafts of hazy sunlight to pour down.

"That'd be great. Let's take him to the beach like we promised. Just one question before you set off, though. Has this got anything to do with Sam?"

"I'll explain later," she answered, her voice deepening, "but you know I said I was going to trace his social worker? Well, I found her."

Within the space of two hours we were settled on a stone bench, facing the sea. Sarah wore a faint smile, her eyes on Connor as he bounded towards the shore. It was impossible to restrain him, his boyish frame getting smaller as he moved away from us. Undulating shelves of pebbles created ramparts between the promenade and the sand, but his true fascination lay in the rocks scattered along the water's edge.

"I don't think he's ever seen rock pools like those," Sarah commented, "what a very unusual stretch of beach."

I nodded, my eyes following him as he raced between the boulders. Ragged with shrouds of seaweed, even from a distance their silhouettes looked mysterious.

"Bognor Rocks," I enlightened her. "There's a sign on one of the beach huts further west that explains their history and geography. You never know, he might even find a few fossils down there."

"Great," Sarah enthused. "He'll be in his element."

As the air fell silent, I caught her eye. "So what have you got to tell me? You said you'd located Sam's social worker, though you did seem a bit cagey."

"It's a matter I prefer to discuss face to face," she replied.

Stealing a glance over her shoulder, she scanned the pavement behind the sea wall.

"It's okay, we're well sheltered," I reassured her. "No one will hear us."

"Good," she nodded, "but the reason I didn't want to say too much was down to Connor. You never know when he's listening. Don't get me wrong, he's a nice kid but his surveillance skills are starting to scare me."

She dipped her head a little closer.

"You know I said he likes hiding? Peter made him a den on the landing at the top of the stairs but it doesn't stop him sneaking to other places. I've found him crouched behind our sofa before now."

"Why would he do that?"

A sigh escaped her lips. "Curiosity. He's still hankering to know about his real parents, hoping he'll catch us out. But I didn't dare run the risk of him overhearing anything relating to your friend."

A breeze swept in from the sea, heady with the aroma of ozone. Sarah breathed deeply, as if mentally preparing herself for what she had to tell me.

"So how far did you get with his social worker?" I kept pressing.

"She was scared, Maisie. Between you and me, she did not want it widely known we were probing into Sam's case..."

******

Content that Connor was too busy exploring the beach to care what they were talking about, Sarah began to relax. The spreading rays of sun warmed the bench, the sea air caressing her face, bringing a clarity to her senses.

She had grown accustomed to people shrinking away from her whenever she raked over the past; opening old wounds, dredging up secrets that were better left buried... but whatever enigma surrounded Sam's disappearance, she could not resist doing a little extra digging.

"Her name's Yvonne Draper and she's in her fifties now."

Her eyes drifted back towards the seashore, lids heavy, as the boy flitting in the distance became a blur.

But in her mind's eye, she was seeing a house in East Grinstead, a house that seemed to hide from its neighbours. Untamed shrubs wreathed the windows, masking them in darkness, the porch shabby, the paint flaking in places under a cloak of ivy. Approaching the door, she heard a scurry of paws and barking. Time hung suspended but as the dogs kept yapping, she stood her ground, until at last someone unfastened the latch. A middle-aged man.

Eyeing her with suspicion, he scowled when she asked if Yvonne was at home.

"I knew she was there. Something in the air gave the game away, the hint of a woman lingering. It may have been the smell of hairspray or a movement from the kitchen but I was not prepared to walk away..."

'This will only take a minute or two, Mr Draper.'

The woman who did eventually emerge from the shadows, though, was nothing like she expected. Her eyes possessed an empty look, her complexion so sallow it was as if the very life essence had been siphoned out of her.

"I tried to reassure her that whatever she could tell us would go no further. That we were desperate to trace a missing friend, nothing more."

The shadows in the house seemed to grow as the woman known as Yvonne Draper withdrew into herself like a snail, her voice a shuddering whisper.

"Of course I remember Sam Ellis. Such a sweet little boy, and to think how he lost his mum. No child should have to live through something like that."

"No," Sarah soothed, "and I know how Stephanie died. She was murdered, wasn't she? I am familiar with the case, but it's not the reason I'm here. I am more concerned about what happened to the boy afterwards..."

Backing into a corner, Yvonne seemed incapable of meeting her eye - and instead of addressing the issue of Sam's care, kept prattling on about his early life.

What must it have been like for him growing up with a prostitute for a mother?

What shocking scenes might he have he witnessed in his tender years and who in God's name could have killed her?

Sarah had stood there mesmerised, inclined to let her offload.

"Oh, to die so young," she whimpered, determined to evade the real issue.

"It's rumoured a rogue punter killed her, someone she upset, and that's how he took revenge... that poor child though. How it must have traumatised him..."

Turning towards the window, she started busying herself filling up the kettle. "How rude. I haven't even offered you a drink."

"I'm fine, Mrs Draper, really," Sarah said, "but I'm not here to talk about Stephanie Ellis. I agree her death was a tragedy, it's not that I don't care..."

Yvonne froze. Sarah stared at the back of her grey head with a frown, waiting for her to respond. Yet an underlying tension clawed the atmosphere, the precise opening she had been waiting for.

"Is there any chance we can talk about Sam, though? Surely you know a bit about his life, you were his social worker."

Still Yvonne would not look at her, sinking deeper and deeper into denial.

"He was put into care, wasn't he? A children's home known as Orchard Grange."

Yvonne's face turned white. "Yes, a children's home."

"Do you know how long he was there for, Yvonne?" Taking a brave step forward, she ran a gentle hand over the older woman's shoulder. "You can tell me."

Yvonne's muscles hardened like iron, her face pinched. Sarah couldn't resist feeling a little sorry for her, wondering what she was hiding.

She let out a sob. "Poor Sam was trapped in that place, just waiting for another family member to step forward."

"So did anyone step forward?"

"Who sent you?" Lowering the kettle to the work surface, her hands betrayed a tremor. "Why are you here, and why now?"

"Please," Sarah begged, forcing a calmness into her tone. "I'm not a journalist, I'm just doing this for a friend. She was fostered herself and suffers panic attacks, nightmares, never knowing why Sam vanished. She too was a resident at Orchard Grange and cared very deeply for him."

There was a subtle shift in the atmosphere and the next time their eyes met, Sarah finally saw the shutters roll back, allowing a twinkle of light through.

"Just to reassure your friend," she relented, "someone did come forward to look after him. We always knew Sam had family, and we were right - but it's a secret that must never see light of day and that's all I'm prepared to divulge."

******

"What?" I breathed. "You mean someone actually did take him away?"

Hanging onto her words, I could barely take it in. That final sentence brought a rush of blood to my head, and the ground started spinning.

"Apparently so," Sarah nodded, "though she refused point blank to name them and that in itself is suspicious. I can't help wondering who she's protecting."

"But does this imply Sam is alive?" I frowned.

Sarah's lips tightened. "It's not impossible but I wouldn't build your hopes up until we can find out more. The next obvious step is to research his family tree. See if we can trace those relatives."

"We need to find him," I murmured under my breath.

"Maisie, I understand where you're coming from," she sighed, "but as I said from the start, these things take time. In the meantime, how is the police investigation going? You haven't said much about Joe, either."

I shook my head in frustration. "Joe spends much of his time with Jess these days and she's well and truly got her hooks into him. But the police are monitoring his Twitter account and questioning the politician... There's every likelihood we'll be travelling up to London ourselves soon."

"Then why not concentrate on that for now?" Sarah smiled. "Leave the sleuthing around Sam's story to me..."

I almost smiled back, but in the back of my mind an even scarier thread had started unravelling. "What if our abusers cotton on, though? Sam could be in as much danger as anyone!"

"I'm doing my best, Maisie," she protested, "you have to trust me on this..."

Whatever words followed were gulped into the wind, as a sudden crash of pebbles drew our gaze to the beach. But before she could say another word, Connor sprang into view, golden-brown hair windswept as he struggled up the slope.

"I-I'm sorry," I added hastily, "don't think I'm not grateful."

She caught my eye with a grin, and switched her attention back to Connor. "Having fun?"

"Those rock pools are full of creatures!" he panted, and clambering over the stones, flopped down onto the bench next to us. "Amazing! But I'm starving now!"

"There's a pub near the pier that does fish and chips," I piped up.

A raft of unsaid words hung between us as we walked to the pier. There was no denying Connor's radiance, and in the lingering afternoon sunlight, his cheeks glowed, the knees of his jeans dark from splashes of seawater. I felt a wave of emotion, something similar to what I felt the first time I'd met Sam. His face reflected the same innocence, which brought the glimmer of an idea...

"Look," Sarah murmured in my ear as we ambled up the prom, "I promise I'll do all I can to find your friend. At least the trail is getting warmer, and you could always launch an appeal - if the police agree."

"Yes," I nodded, "brilliant idea, and I know it's difficult..." My footsteps slowed as I contemplated my next words. "So would Connor like to stay with me for the occasional weekend? The fostering department do a three day course in respite care and I'd quite like to sign up for it."

"Maisie, that would be great but it's not as if you owe me."

"Not just for you, for Connor," I added warmly. "Anyone can see how much he's enjoyed himself today. It's the least I can do."

Chapter Thirty-Nine

Police Raid Peer's Home

Two days after that headline appeared, Thomas was still none the wiser.

As anxiety hit, his breath rose in shallow gasps. He had always known that the maxim *innocent until proven guilty* meant little in this savage modern-day world. Yet never once had he imagined it would be himself at the centre of a trial by media. Nothing other than rumours dripping in the ears of prying journalists could have ricocheted like this.

But then, hadn't the press always been the secret weapon of the people?

And that was before social media had spewed its ghastly seed.

Demonised on Twitter, he was shocked to see his name tagged in posts alluding to 'Orchard Grange,' the care home at the heart of a historic child abuse scandal.

> While the @metpoliceuk seek the truth about
> @Thomas-Parker-Smythe children are being abused
> every day in #carehomes across Britain #childabuse
> #paedophile #politicians

He had initially refused to attend a second police interview, a mistake that brought the threat of arrest crashing down like thunder. While appalled to think his home had been searched, it wasn't as if he had much choice in the matter; and from the look of disdain on Fitzpatrick's face, he guessed it was not going to be pleasant.

"Surprised to see us again so soon?" the detective inspector mocked.

A ball of rage clenched the pit of his stomach.

"Isn't it enough you've exposed my personal life? My home has been raided and I cannot step outside without being mobbed by reporters..."

"Lord Parker-Smythe," DS Havers chipped in, "it is the findings resulting from the home search we need to discuss."

"Which are?"

"Quite a collection of press cuttings you saved over the years – and we found a highly significant photo..."

"What on earth are you talking about?"

"For the purpose of this recording, I present Exhibit A, a news article published on September 12th, 1994."

Staring at the press cutting, Thomas said nothing. More than two decades had passed since this had appeared in the London Standard, the day Cornelius Mortimer had proudly unveiled his sixth private home. 'Oak Lands' was a clean white house surrounded by evergreen hedging. His heart thumped as he read the caption, recognising himself in the photo. Suited and smiling, he was about to cut the red ribbon, secured to the gate posts like bunting.

"Oak Lands," DI Fitzpatrick read out. "So is it fair to say Orchard Grange was not the only children's home run by Cornelius Mortimer that you endorsed?"

"True enough," he responded feebly.

"I would now like to ask you about this photograph," he pressed, "one that captured our attention."

"This is Exhibit B," DS Havers announced, "a black and white photo depicting some form of celebration."

Thomas felt the breath freeze in his lungs. Unmistakably dressed in the same suit as he'd worn for the Oak Lands opening, his tie askew, his eyes glazed as if drunk, this photo appeared even more damning. It showed him lingering in a garden, accompanied by a group of men, and there in the centre stood a smirking Mortimer. Towering behind Thomas, one arm clamped around his shoulder, there was no mistaking their camaraderie.

Thomas looked up, heart heavy as he considered the ramifications. A horrible thought was already snaking through his mind, no matter how hard he tried to suppress it.

"What has he told you about me?" he shivered.

DI Fitzpatrick raised his eyebrows. "Told us? We haven't yet had the pleasure of interviewing him. Unless you'd care to inform us where we can locate him..."

"I have no idea where Cornelius lives."

"But you kept a book of addresses," the DI persisted. "We have it here, another relic our team stumbled across whilst rifling through some old boxes."

"I haven't been through those boxes in years," Thomas gasped. "You've got no right to go delving through my personal belongings..."

"Exhibit C reveals an address book," DS Havers stalled him. "Can you confirm this belongs to you, Sir?"

Thomas clenched his fists under the table top. "Yes, it was mine! What point are you trying to make here?"

"It lists every one of Mortimer's homes," DI Fitzpatrick informed him icily. "Orchard Grange being the largest, followed by Willow Court, Beech House, Chestnut Mews, Elm Grove and finally Oak Lands, which you officially opened in 1994. According to records they were dotted around central London, and I

170

gather Mr. Mortimer kept his HQ in Orchard Grange, location of your secret meetings..."

"There was nothing secret about them," Thomas hissed.

"Strange thing is," the other man persisted, "those homes were closed down in 1995. Now why do you suppose that was?"

Thomas shrugged. "He ran out of money. Like I said from the start, Cornelius was after government funding and my only role was to assess the homes."

"Fair enough," DS Havers muttered, "only something else came to light from statements given by the victims. You may recall one of them was a male, someone who identified you from the past. He was twelve at the time, and we cannot name him but he ran away in 1995. The home was shut down weeks after, the kids drafted into council run homes or fostered, as was the girl we spoke of. Seems a little sudden, don't you think?"

"I cannot comment," Thomas snapped, tiring of the whole topic. "It was always my belief they were closed down for financial reasons."

DI Fitzpatrick cleared his throat. "Yes, well that all sounds very convincing. Regrettably, we've seen evidence that suggests otherwise."

His eyes emitted a chilling, knowing glint.

"So finally we come to the contents of your computer hard drive."

Thomas stiffened, helpless to wonder what they had dug up now. As if raiding his home wasn't shameful enough. He eyed them with contempt.

"On what grounds do you have the audacity to search my computer?"

"In cases like these," the DI continued, "no stone can be left unturned. How long have you owned this computer, Sir?"

"Two years," he replied. "I wanted the latest Microsoft operating system since my web browser was out of date."

"We're not referring to your new computer," DS Havers said. "That appears to be clean. This concerns an Apple Macintosh stored in a box in your spare room."

"My old Performa?" Thomas faltered. "It must have been around 1996."

"A time the internet was quite new," Havers added darkly, "before the widespread use of social media, when internet chat rooms and news groups were the favoured networks for discussion."

"What exactly are you referring to?" Thomas pressed.

"A group that calls itself *Babes in the Wood*," the DI enlightened him.

"I know of no such news group," he retorted.

"Yes, you do," DI Fitzpatrick hurled back at him. "You've been a long standing member of this group since 1996. It was set up by someone with the username CM666@hotmail.com. Does that jog your memory? You and I both know of one person with those initials: your friend, Cornelius Mortimer."

"He was not my friend!" Thomas rounded on him. "And I did not join this news group he supposedly founded. Now what is this about?"

The inspector's steel hard gaze turned him cold.

"The clue is in the name. *Babes in the wood.* A secret group established to fuel the fantasies of men obsessed with ritualistic child abuse and with specific reference to sex parties..."

Thomas clutched his tie, feeling sick, and for the first time since this relentless questioning began, he was struggling to know what to say.

"You cannot deny you were a participant," the DI kept goading him. "We've had a computer specialist look into this, and the material was embedded in your browsing history, which brings me on to another matter. Something that did not make pleasant viewing."

"I don't believe this," Thomas whispered, his voice trembling.

"The most disturbing characteristic of this newsgroup," DS Havers intervened, "is that anyone who was a member had access to illegal images. I refer, as you already know, to satanic rituals involving children."

The force of his words twisted a knife in Thomas's gut. "This isn't true."

"If only that were the case. Unfortunately, your hard disc was found to contain hundreds of such images downloaded between 1996 and 2006."

"No," he gasped - he could barely recover the breath to form the words. "I have never downloaded anything of the sort."

"So how did the material end up on your computer?" the DS persevered.

Thomas shook his head. Havers had always come across as the gentler of the two, but now there was an icy edge to the sergeant's tone that chilled him.

"I don't know. It could have been planted."

Even to him it sounded pathetic, but on the other hand...

He recalled the day he had left those girls in his apartment, and was struck by an alarming thought.

"Planted?" DI Fitzpatrick echoed with a smirk.

"Dear God, if only I'd thought to report this," he shivered, "but there is something I haven't told you. The morning I left those cleaners in my home, someone was loitering outside. Some youth dressed in one of those baggy hoodies..."

The DI gave a sniff. "Is that the best you can come up with?"

"I'm not making it up," he answered, the rage swelling in him again. "Can't you at least check it out? Someone is trying to set me up and I wouldn't be surprised if it had something to do with those girls who visited."

"We can talk to them," DS Havers shrugged, "though I should warn you we will have to run further checks. You see stuff like this is rarely just 'planted' on a hard disc. Everything leaves traces, and from the age of your Mac, it appears this material was not added overnight. It's been there for years."

"How do you explain that?" drawled the inspector.

Thomas faced him angrily. "I have nothing else to say on this matter. I did not download those images, nor belong to any news group. So let's get to the point, shall we. Are you charging me? Because before this case goes any further, I have a right to consult my solicitor."

Chapter Forty

"He's been charged," Joe smiled in disbelief. "Police found over two hundred indecent images on his computer. The dirty bastard!"

I did not smile back. Conscious of Jess lingering in the background, I should have relished the seclusion of her apartment. A gentle breeze cooled the air and with its calming interior, this place was fast turning into Joe's sanctuary.

Ever since that harrowing accident, though, he had shied away from the pub.

I could hardly blame him. They might have kept his name out of the press but everyone knew it was him.

"Really?" I whispered under my breath, "so will he stand trial?"

Joe spun around as if he had momentarily forgotten I was there. Slender as a reed, he formed a striking silhouette in the light of the balcony, eyes glued to his mobile as he pored over the latest news feed.

"Dunno," he muttered. "He's pleading innocence but then he would, wouldn't he? It weren't just the kiddie-porn he was into but some newsgroup. You know they found a link to old Toad Face..."

"Shh, Joe," I interrupted. "Don't say too much."

"It's okay, Maisie," Jess purred, moving away from the balcony. "I know who 'Toad Face' is. The guy who ran the dodgy care homes."

Her words sent a dart of fear through me, though I wasn't sure why.

"How much has Joe told you?" I challenged her.

"Don't fret, Maisie, we've got no secrets," Joe butted in. "With all this stuff in the media, it don't take a genius to figure it out."

"And you know I've got your backs," Jess simpered.

"Yeah," I mumbled, feeling a flood of warmth in my cheeks, "except Joe and I are crucial witnesses in this case, so it's important to retain our anonymity."

"Nothing gets repeated outside this apartment," she added smugly.

She held my gaze, and from the spark in her eye, anyone could see the thrill she was getting out of this. I bit my tongue, not wanting to be drawn into her drama. Behind the scenes, however, I knew exactly what was happening. Joe was right. Even before the Met had decided to press charges, stories had found their way into the papers.

Lord Parker-Smythe questioned over child sex abuse allegations.

With a shiver of dread, I averted my eyes. But even with institutionalised child abuse exposed on a massive scale, nothing could be proven until the net closed in on Mortimer, and until that day came there would be danger.

The truth behind Sam's disappearance, meanwhile, continued to evade us all, though after speaking to Sarah, a ray of hope lit our path.

The possibility Sam might be alive.

Furthermore a national enquiry had been launched for other witnesses to come forward. With a powerful social media campaign backing it, would the tentacles of the past find a way of reaching him?

******

Joe, on the other hand, didn't want to build his hopes up.

Waking up in Jess's bed next morning, the trauma of his accident still resonated. *Lying on the ground prostrate, imagining the crunch of his bones under the wheels...* Still, at least he was getting a regular lift to work now.

From the day the investigation had begun, he had kept his eye on the news. CCTV footage released by the van hire company had at least cast a spotlight on his attacker in the car park, but the image was so blurred, his face was barely discernible.

Joe felt his blood run cold. Going by his frame and gait, he knew damn well that man was Schiller. Police wanted to question anyone who knew him, whilst warning the public not to approach him. *He could be dangerous.*

"What are you thinking about?" Jess drawled.

Lying on his back, he stared empty-eyed at the ceiling. She traced the contours of his face, the caress of her fingers calming the beast in him.

"Sorry," he sighed, "got a lot on my mind."

She propped herself up on one elbow, her hair a river of golden waves tumbling over her perfect breasts. He felt the questioning stab of her gaze.

"You're worried about the investigation, aren't you?"

Turning to face her, he ran his fingers through her lovely hair, sweeping it away from her shoulders. *It wasn't a lie.* None of them were expecting the arrest of Parker-Smythe but the news brought little comfort. Unless the net closed in on their real enemies, he was never going to be safe.

"Yeah, well at least the tweets have stopped." He kissed her on the lips. "I 'spect the bastards are lying low, now the cops are involved."

"Then why don't we do something to take your mind off all this?" she whispered seductively, kissing him back.

The message was not lost on him, and he decided to go with the flow.

Pleasurably distracted, he had a lot to thank Jess for, even if this snatch of a romance was only transitory. He wanted to savour it while it lasted, having never imagined they would be together this long. But Jess was such a beauty, he couldn't help being a little in love with her, and as her arms snaked around his back, he knew he wasn't about to step out of her bed any time soon...

From the depths of his mind, however, another thought surfaced. They were due to visit Charing Cross Police Station tomorrow, as Maisie had just confirmed in a text. Jess seemed insistent on driving, and he didn't argue. The police only wanted to pick over the finer details of their statements. So why was he struck with a bad feeling? A sense of no turning back, and that nothing would be the same again?

******

Charing Cross Police Station, The Strand, London

Before meeting the victims, DI Andrew Fitzpatrick and his colleagues had set up an area, in which all intelligence collated had been pinned to the dividing screens. This included a map of London, on which the location of every one of Mortimer's care homes was marked with a circular red sticker.

"Creepy, isn't it?" DS Mike Havers commented. "Looking at it from this angle, they form the shape of a pentagon with Orchard Grange at the centre."

"Maybe it's a coincidence," Andrew shrugged. "What else have we got?"

The next incident board contained pictures of the homes, the lively celebration unearthed from Thomas's home among them. Mike almost shivered as the cold eyes of Cornelius Mortimer seemed to follow him, one of the only photographs they could find of the man, from around 1995.

But as his gaze drifted further, he clocked the CCTV images Joe had been thinking about earlier - and there underneath was a crime report detailing the hit and run in Bognor. It served a chilling reminder of the seriousness and long-term effects of the crimes they were investigating. From the age of twelve, Joe Winterton had battled through life with an ever-prevailing threat of violence hanging over him.

It was substantiated in the blown up screenshots taken from his mobile. Mike winced as the shining metal hose seized his attention; for not only had Schiller beaten him senseless as a child, but more recently he'd tried to kill him...

"Are you still with us, Mike?" Andrew piped up.

"Just reviewing the online stuff," he sighed, "especially the Instagram post. Who'd have thought 'Silver-Fox' would turn out to be our suspect? As if he wasn't in deep enough, he had to resort to that tactic."

"Miss Bell thought it from the start," Andrew snorted, "even if he denies it."

Mike nodded in agreement. Lord Parker-Smythe clung to the conviction that not only had his computer been hacked, but his social media accounts too.

"Anyway, to answer your question, we have statements from everyone we've approached, not just the victims but their friends and relatives..."

The moment he said it, a shadow of dread passed over Andrew's face, jamming the breath in his lungs. For what Joe and Maisie did not realise was another witness had come forward - one whose statement had sent shockwaves through the department - and even the DI was struggling to cope with the horror of it.

"Right," he said. "Then let's see how authentic this latest statement is. We'll start by interviewing Joe, who is without doubt our most reliable witness."

"And Maisie?" Mike added.

"We need to be careful," Andrew cautioned. "The most telling clue is her nightmare, but as for these recovered memories... no court in the land will treat them as substantial enough, although I'd very much like to talk to her therapist."

******

All the while the police were reviewing the evidence, Maisie, Joe and Jess had been steadily making their way to Central London.

Glancing at Maisie now, Joe knew she wasn't thrilled about Jess driving, though he had talked her around. It made sense. Why risk public transport when anyone could be stalking them? Whereas Jess knew London like the back of her hand from the numerous press functions she attended. She'd found somewhere to park just a few minutes' walk from their destination, too.

"Are you alright, Maisie?"

Fiercely protective as ever, he slid an arm around her shoulder. Yet the uneasy feeling that nagged him earlier had not gone away, and judging from her expression, he was not alone.

Taut with nerves, she quickened her step. They paused in Covent Garden, her eyes flitting wildly.

"I feel as if we're being watched," she murmured.

Jess stroked her arm, her expression laced with kindness. "You won't come to any harm," she reassured her, "not with all these people around."

"So what about you, Jess?" She attempted a smile.

"Don't worry, Covent Garden is one of my favourite places, I'll be fine. How long do you think you'll be?" Her gaze wandered back to Joe.

"God knows," he shrugged. "We could be there for hours but I'll text you..."

Her smile faded, their eyes locked. Tilting his face towards her, he planted another kiss on her lips, wary of his heart hammering faster.

Heading in the direction of The Strand, neither of them looked back.

But Maisie was not wrong.

Loitering behind the shrubs on the other side of the railings, a shadowy figure had been monitoring them. With a hood pulled over his head and eyes disguised behind dark glasses, he managed to blend into the foliage undetected.

They were approaching the pillared facade of Charing Cross Police Station now, unaware of his scrutiny.

Yet still the figure did not move, his eyes tailing them to the door, two icy grey slits of pure hatred.

Chapter Forty-One

Joe glanced up, filled with dread, as the sculpted beige walls towered over him.

"What now?" he mumbled out of the corner of his mouth. "Do we just go in?"

"I suppose so," Maisie said, stealing a glance at her watch.

Following her into reception, he inhaled deeply, assailed by painful memories.

It seemed hard to imagine the last time he'd set foot inside a London nick, he was bricking it, wrists locked in handcuffs, about to face serious criminal charges.

Today, though, he wore a jacket and tie, something else Jess had insisted on. If the situation hadn't been so grave, he would have laughed, but shuffling from one foot to the other, he waited anxiously by the desk as Maisie announced their arrival. There was a gentle bustle of activity, various conversations humming in the background. Reluctant to draw attention to themselves, they found a corner in the waiting room where a cluster of chairs seemed to beckon them.

But a moment later, a voice shot across the area. "Maisie!"

Raising his head, Joe felt the tension evaporate from his body at last.

"Hello, Mark," she gasped, rising, "what are you doing here?"

The familiar face of DC Mark Anderson beamed through the blur of bodies as he inched his way across the floor to join them. "I'm here to back you up as part of the local liaison team, since it was me who took your statements. The officers leading the investigation have gone over them, but they want to ask some specific questions..."

"Like what?" Maisie frowned.

He never got to answer. The next man to approach was taller and of heavy build. Judging from his sharp blue eyes and pristine suit, Joe guessed him to be a figure of authority.

"Mark," he began warmly. "I trust you're looking after these two."

Mark's smile did not waver. "Allow me to introduce you to Maisie Bell and Joe Winterton. This, folks, is DI Fitzpatrick, in charge of your case. He'll be joined by a Sergeant but before we proceed, would either of you like a coffee?"

Finally Joe felt he could relax, appeased by their cordiality.

Yet was it too much to hope they had tracked down Mortimer?

Twenty minutes later, he found himself being led into an interview room, where the thought of delivering justice brought a much needed shot of confidence.

"The time is 14:00 hours. This is DS Mike Havers, accompanied by Detective Inspector Andrew Fitzpatrick. Before we begin, would you mind giving your name and date of birth please?"

With the formalities out of the way, Joe shrugged off his jacket, facing the officers with courage. Whatever they wanted to check out, his story had not changed. In 1994 he had been dumped in a care home, aged eleven.

"Can you remember which one it was?" Mike probed.

He observed the photocopies laid out in front of him.

"That one," he said, pointing to an austere grey house. "Willow Court."

The sight brought a wave of sadness, but only in the aftermath of the party had his life taken a horrible turn for the worse.

"I know this is traumatic, Mr Winterton," the Sergeant coaxed him, "but can you tell us what you remember about the party? In as much detail as you can."

He felt the room turn cold as he repeated his story; from being chauffeur driven to some large country mansion to quaffing that glass of punch.

"When you say *spiked*, what were the effects? Did it make you drowsy?"

"Not drowsy. I blacked out."

"What, you don't remember a thing afterwards?"

Joe shook his head.

Whatever had taken place beyond that point was a massive black hole, Willow Court confined to the past, the memories blurring into a new home.

"You were moved to a different home?"

"Yeah, but I don't remember that. Just that one day I came out of sick bay and found myself in another gaff. It was that one. Orchard Grange."

"Okay, can I just stop you there and go back a step. When you say you *came out of sick bay*, why did you end up there? Were you hurt?"

Joe closed his eyes, the shadows in his mind growing darker. "I-I was in pain. They said it was gastric flu but b-but..."

"Take it easy, Joe. You can tell us."

"It was more than pain... it was horrible, excruciating, like - like my innards had been gouged out with a knife. I saw blood on the sheets and started yelling. Next thing I knew there was a load of shouting outside, a commotion..."

With the air in his lungs rushing faster, he was beginning to hyperventilate.

"Steady Joe, you're doing well. Just tell us what was wrong."

"It weren't gastric flu, that was bollocks!" A sob escaped his throat, a sound of utter defeat. "It was something worse that I can't repeat. I 'spect you know."

"There is no need to feel embarrassed."

Joe nodded. "I was only awake for a split second before someone came in and injected me with a needle."

"Injected you? You mean they kept you sedated?"

"I guess so, but that's all I know. Looking back, it seems like a bad dream 'cos before I knew anything else, I was in this new house, a bigger house and there were girls as well as boys."

"But what about the other boys at the party? Your friends?"

"Never saw 'em again, did I? We were moved about, separated, so's none of us could talk about the party... and then finally I met Mortimer."

"The first time you met Cornelius Mortimer was in Orchard Grange?"

"Cornelius?" Joe snorted. "So that's his name! Yeah, I'd seen him before, but he never had much to do with me until the party. Even before that he gave me the creeps. Big and fat with greasy hair and wandering eyes. He reminded me of them strangers they warn you about in TV ads."

"So I gather you saw more of him living at Orchard Grange."

"Didn't take long to suss he was a bad man, given them thugs he hired. Schiller and Mikolov. See, a lot of the kids were unruly and there was violence, but most of it went unnoticed. The only times they intervened, they used force. Restraint for example, pinning a kid to the floor face down, trapping their arms and legs..."

He had never forgotten their fists, hard as manacles, not to mention the bruises left in the aftermath.

"But then I met Maisie and things got a bit better for a while."

"You were close, weren't you? And you said in your statement that she too was taken to one of those parties..."

Joe clenched his fists, feeling the blackness of rage rip his heart open. Repeating his account should have purged him. Yet it never got any easier.

"I had to stop her going. She was so sweet and innocent and the thought of those dirty bastards getting their hands on her... I couldn't stomach it. That's why I locked her in the laundry room, thinking she'd be safe... but they found her."

"So she went to the party," Mike finished gravely. "What then?"

"Dunno," Joe sighed. "I didn't see her for a week and when she did come back she was different. Quiet, lost in another world. I asked her where she'd been but she couldn't remember nothing. It's like her memory had been erased."

"Did you ever voice your suspicions?" the DI frowned.

"No way. Oh man... I doubt if she could have handled it, and I was scared stiff, still black and blue after that beating they'd given me."

Mike flinched but didn't linger on the subject.

"So what about when Sam turned up?" he asked, the question dropped gently into the interview.

Joe exhaled a shuddering sigh. "Sam was like Maisie. Soft as putty with a pretty face... and I don't mean that in a gay sort of way, he just was!"

"How did Mortimer treat him?"

"Like he'd won a prize! Looked like he wanted to devour him."

He took a deep swallow, knowing what was coming. They wanted to ask him about the party they had attended together.

For the first hour they'd tried to enjoy themselves... but if only he'd been more vigilant. He should never have taken himself away, given them a chance to inject him again, because whatever happened that night, Sam had dissolved into the ether.

"I'm sorry," Andrew said, his face a picture of gloom, "but please bear with us, I need to get a picture of the next day. Was it different from the time before?"

"Oh yeah," Joe whispered. "I woke up in my own bed this time and I didn't feel ill or nothing, just drowsy. But something felt wrong, and then the bomb dropped. Sam was gone! Like he'd vanished into thin air."

His head snapped upright as another thought hit him.

"And Mortimer was acting really weird."

"In what way?"

"Agitated... like he had a wasp up his butt!"

"But wasn't he like that anyway?" Mike broke in.

"No," Joe persisted. "Most of the time he pretended to be nice but in a smarmy way. He acted like that to gain the kids' trust, even though some of us had long sussed him out."

It was the not knowing that had been so unbearable. There was no denying Mortimer's face had been ashen that morning, and after a few hissed words, it darkened to a thunderous shade of purple.

Joe leaned forwards, the force of his hatred swelling.

"That guy was a sick, twisted, evil fucker, and the sooner he's locked up the better. Why do you think he set up homes for damaged kids? We were fodder for perverts like him; messed up kids from bad homes. And as for preying on Maisie and Sam... it made my fucking blood boil! I kept asking where Sam had gone. He said he'd been adopted but I never believed any of that shit!"

He didn't need to say more. They knew about the threats, the trolling; Mortimer was a man who harboured grudges, a man intent on hounding Joe to the grave.

******

By the time Mike switched off the tape recorder, a strained silence bit the air. Joe loosened his tie. With emotions running high, so great was his fury, it erupted from him in sparks.

"Are you alright?" Andrew tried to pacify him. "Sorry to have to put you through this again, but it's essential we cover everything."

"I'm fine," he snapped, though his body language said otherwise.

Raking his fingers through his hair, he swept it from his forehead. A mist of perspiration glistened, and his face was flushed.

"So is that it?"

"It is for now," Mike said, keeping his voice soft, "you've told us all we need to know and if anything else comes to mind, you can call us."

"So where's Maisie?" he pressed. "Is she being questioned too?"

"She's in the hands of a female detective sergeant and Mark is with them but yes, they're running over her statement again. Don't worry, she will be treated with the utmost sensitivity."

Joe nodded, pacified. "What happens now, then? You've got our statements, but is it gonna be enough to nail those bastards?"

Mike rose from his chair. "That's what we're here to discuss. Up until now, you're the only witnesses who reported anything sinister about those homes. The question is, are you willing to stand up in court and testify?"

"Bloody right I will!" Joe ranted as he too shot up from his chair, "but what's happening with Mortimer? Have you found him yet?"

Andrew released a sigh. "No, but we're working on it. There has, however, been another breakthrough..."

Joe's mouth dropped open. Mike couldn't wait to gauge his reaction to this disclosure but Maisie needed to be present.

"Let's go and join the others," he added quickly.

Fighting to suppress his excitement, he led him into the corridor, DI Fitzpatrick shadowing them.

Seconds later, Maisie emerged through another door. Judging from her glazed expression, he couldn't help wondering if she had also been informed there was some news.

Yet as Joe wandered closer, a frown crossed her face.

Clouds of tension filled the air as they stared at each other. "Do you know what's going on?" he whispered.

She shook her head.

DC Mark Anderson was next to catch Mike's eye, the suspense stretched to breaking point. Then with no further hesitation, he gave a consensual nod.

"I won't keep you in the dark any longer," Mark announced. "There's someone here to meet you. We were wondering if you might recognise him."

******

183

"Who is it?" Joe spluttered. "Has he made a statement?"

"Just follow me, please," DI Fitzpatrick said.

As he led the way, Joe fell into step beside him, conscious of the others tailing them, until eventually they arrived outside a conference room.

"He's in there," Andrew said, the hint of a smile softening his features.

Joe tugged the door, impatience getting the better of him, but as he strolled into the room, he froze to a complete standstill.

A flawlessly good looking man stood in the centre of the room, awaiting him. Joe took in the square jaw, the high forehead, the widely-spaced brown eyes.

"Do I know you?"

"Yes you do, Joe," he said.

A cold, leaden feeling anchored him to the floor. The whole scene had the unreal quality of a dream.

Risking a glance at Maisie, he heard a gasp.

Shock dilated her eyes as she stood there, gaping at the newcomer. He smiled with undisguised pleasure.

"Maisie?"

Their eyes met in a flash of recognition and suddenly the truth dawned.

"Oh my God, Joe," she gulped, fingers flying to her mouth. "It can't be!"

PART TWO
Sam

Chapter Forty-Two

"Sam?" I breathed in disbelief.

The man staring back bore an uncanny resemblance to the boy we remembered as Sam, but the recognition dawned in stages. First it was his hair, more ash than blonde. Yet where Joe's features had evened out, Sam's had become more magnified.

"Shit," Joe whispered. "Are you for real?"

I watched in a dream as the enigmatic figure stepped forward to embrace him.

"I realise this must be a shock, but when I saw the appeal on social media, I had to come forward. So here I am."

To my relief, Joe hugged him back. I had long sensed his bewilderment, and no sooner did they break apart than he took another long, hard look at Sam.

His eyes burned like lasers, searching deep into the other man's soul. Then, as if to confirm his identity, he brushed Sam's fringe back from his forehead. The unmistakable scar still showed.

"Thank God you survived!" he said with a half smile.

"It's good to see you too, Joe," replied Sam.

I nodded my head, gratified to see Joe appeased at last.

"So where the bloody hell did you go, and how come you're here now?"

"I'm sorry, at least give me a chance to explain."

Lingering in the doorway, DI Fitzpatrick cleared his throat. "Would you like some time alone to be reacquainted?" he asked.

"Yes, please," I nodded in gratitude.

The door clicked shut, granting us some much needed privacy, and with the police out of earshot, I turned my attention back to Sam.

"Joe and I tried looking for you! My friend, Sarah Summerville, even tracked down your social worker, which gave us hope. So what happened?"

Sam lowered his eyes but not before I glimpsed a flicker of shock in them.

"This'll take a while to explain, but it's time you knew the truth."

"Go on then," Joe said. "It's been twenty years."

A shiver of cold crawled over me as if someone had walked on my grave. The night of my hallucination still haunted me, and I could not take my eyes off him.

But could this really be Sam, the friend we thought we had lost forever?

Once the initial shock had subsided, we seated ourselves around the table. Joe took the lead, which suited me fine. I was too numb to speak.

"First thing you should know is what the cops have been grilling me about," he began.

Sam's face turned rigid.

"The night of that fucking party," continued Joe. "I woke up next day and you were gone, so why don't we start there?"

Sam looked uneasy as he drew a long shuddering breath. "Alright. Let's just take this one step at a time, shall we?"

"Sure," Joe frowned, "but isn't this why we're here? They've obviously been picking over our statements to see if they tally."

"I guess you're right," Sam sighed, "and you've waited long enough to hear my story, though I warn you it is not pleasant."

"Just tell us," Joe pressed. "Let's go back in time, to the moment we were driven to that mansion."

"Yeah. Strange place to throw a party for the likes of us, wasn't it?" Sam mused. "Some big house stuck out in the middle of nowhere."

A visible lump rippled his throat as he swallowed.

"We played pool, if you remember. Neither of us knew how, we were just shooting balls into the holes but you said *fuck it, might as well have some* and that's the last thing you said to me before everything turned a bit weird."

"In what way?"

"What? You don't remember leaving the party?"

"I only went for a piss," Joe grunted.

"I think they drugged you," Sam added. "Something happened to you, long before they brought the punch out for the rest of us to drink."

I heard a sob in his voice, and experienced a horrible sinking feeling. Joe froze. But in another secret part of my mind, I remembered him telling me this.

Slipping away briefly, he was drawn into a web of shadows, where he had sensed another presence.

"Mikolov!" Joe spat. "You're right, I crept out to use the loo but it was dark. Enough for that thug to grab my arm and jab a needle in. They knew damn well I wouldn't touch their hooch, so they had to knock me out another way."

He rubbed his arms as if cold.

"It was Mikolov who brought you back," Sam's voice rose ominously. "You might not remember... but you were still in the lounge with us. Sat in a chair, just staring into space like a zombie."

"In other words, I was well out of it."

"Yes," Sam said, "until finally it was our turn. Out came the punch bowl, as you'd already forewarned. I clung to my glass, knowing they were watching.

Mikolov, Schiller, Mortimer...What they didn't know, though, was that with every sip I took, I held it in my mouth for as long as I could, and spat it out."

"But surely they would have noticed," I intervened.

"I hoped they wouldn't, not if I dripped it down my front. Think about it, Joe, we were dressed in black and I doubt if they twigged, 'cos at the same time I was watching the other four, copying their reactions. One by one, they closed their eyes, heads flopping sideways and backwards... I did the same."

"Clever," Joe muttered. "It didn't just make you drowsy, it knocked you out."

"That's what I thought. So if they were planning to drug us, I had to pretend. Fall back into my chair like I was unconscious."

Layers of memory peeled back like onion skin, exposing my deepest terror.

It was impossible not to picture the same scenario; how in the second Mortimer wasn't looking, I had emptied my own glass into a vase.

"What happened after that?" I dared to whisper.

Fear darkened his eyes, filling me with a sense of impending doom.

"We were taken from the house to another place. Those thugs carted us outside. Lifted us into a four-by-four and drove off..."

He turned away, his gaze lowered.

"There were no roads, no cars, just a long muddy track, winding its way uphill. I could barely see a thing. The darkness was suffocating, wheels jolting over the ground, but I could tell we had entered a mass of thick woodland."

My heart pounded faster. "Go on."

"It felt surreal. I'd only swallowed a drop of that stuff but enough to make my head spin, and there was no telling what it was spiked with. A cocktail of sedatives, I guess, memory-loss drugs designed to lower our resistance? It sounds far-fetched, but once we were in that forest, we were laid in a circle, wrists bound with ties, and there were noises, strange whisperings... They seemed to follow us in there. It sounded for all the world like some religious chant."

A frown crumpled Joe's forehead as he caught my eye.

"Shit," he muttered, "just like your nightmares."

His words seemed to trigger a reaction as Sam raised his head.

"What nightmares? Sorry, Maisie, but is this going to upset you?"

"Probably," I croaked. "It's like Joe says, this sounds very much like a recurring nightmare I've been having, but please... carry on with your story."

"It gets worse," he warned.

"I think we know where this is going," Joe sighed. "We've talked about it, so come on, spit it out. We need to know if we were right."

"Okay," he whispered, "so there's this chanting echoing around the woods and getting louder... I saw lights flickering in the trees too and then shapes. Men carrying torches, wearing robes. Hooded robes. I couldn't help thinking it was a dream, except I was awake. Only just, mind, and very drowsy, but enough to know it was real."

"And then what?"

Writhing in his seat, he pushed his fingers through his hair. "I don't know! I'm not sure I can bear to tell you."

"You have to," I pressed. "I've been through enough psychotherapy to know how familiar this sounds, but how the hell did it end?"

Sam shook his head. "If I tell you, nothing will ever be the same again."

"And I'll never be able to live a normal life unless you do," I argued.

"Keep talking," Joe pressed. "So far you've described a procession of weirdos carrying torches and chanting. This all sounds a bit dark, man."

"Those creatures looked barely human," Sam shivered. "I couldn't help thinking they were ghosts or demons, something summoned up by this ritual they were performing..."

"Ritual?" I echoed.

My eyes widened as I stared at Joe.

"You really want to know? One after the other, those hooded things stepped forward and assaulted the boys. Ripping their clothes off, pawing them, going at them like they were pieces of meat... you couldn't imagine anything worse."

Nausea rose in my stomach with the dread of what I was hearing. I had always feared some kind of ritual, but even in my darkest imaginings, I hadn't envisaged this. The words slipping from Sam's lips flashed up vile images, and I was wondering what he meant by 'assault.'

"So it's true, then," Joe interrupted. "They were a bunch of paedos."

"You don't know the half of it," Sam whispered.

"What's wrong, Sam?" Joe asked. "Did they mess with you too?"

He squeezed his eyes shut, his face creased in pain. "I was sobbing, Joe, terrified of this - this creature crouched over me, it was like something out of a horror film. Then I heard a snarl. He told me to keep quiet, otherwise he'd kill me and that's when he pulled out a dagger..."

"What?" Joe spluttered. "He threatened you with a blade?"

"Threatened to slice my penis off... cut my chest open and offer my beating heart as a sacrifice."

"But that's sick! Did you see his face?"

"Not a face," Sam said coldly, "just a silhouette, but an image I will never forget as long as I live. Sharp and hawk-like, beaky nose. You know the peer who was done for kiddie porn?"

"Not Lord Parker-Smythe?" I gasped.

"Yes. I'd seen him before too, at Orchard Grange, and I'd swear on my mum's grave it was the same bloke!"

"But those threats... oh my God!"

"Yeah," he shuddered, "just thank God it never got worse, 'cos a moment later he backed off. Some disturbance in the woods spooked them."

"Disturbance?" Joe choked.

"I thought I saw beams flickering through the trees some distance away, headlights of another vehicle, perhaps? I'll never know. I was just lying there, paralysed with fear, about to lose consciousness, thinking I was gonna die..."

"But are you saying there was someone else in the forest?"

"All I remember is the chaos, how quickly the torches went out. How it was so bloody dark, there was no telling what was going on, but suddenly we were on the move again, leaving the forest. I think you and I were the lucky ones, Joe."

"Lucky ones," Joe bristled. "You reckon someone saved us?"

"I dunno. I passed out," he finished, "and that, my friend, is why I survived to tell the tale. It's not a happy ending, but you need to hear the whole story, the reason you never saw me again after that night."

Chapter Forty-Three

An uncomfortable knot of silence gripped the three of them.

Joe sat frozen in his chair, but even in the darkest recess of his mind, he could not help imagining himself lying there.

One of six helpless boys at the mercy of those monsters.

"Christ, Sam," Maisie breathed. Her eyes flashed with panic, serving a timely reminder of all they had suffered. "Have you reported this to the police?"

"I have now," he shuddered. "All I ever wanted to do was forget the whole ordeal, until the investigation arose, but as soon as the name 'Orchard Grange' came up, I was wondering if the victims might be you two."

"But you haven't explained where you went," Joe said.

At last Sam lifted his eyes. "I was coming to that."

Sadness hung in their depths as they held his gaze, but Joe was beyond feeling sympathy. Sam's story left a minefield of gaping holes, and Joe was not going to leave this room until he had answers.

"Good," he said. "'Cos d'you have any idea how worried we were?"

"I do - but just before dawn the police turned up at Orchard Grange..." He bit his lip. "I thought they were there to arrest Mortimer and his thugs but I was wrong. Turns out some 'estranged family member' had been in touch and asked them to come and collect me."

Joe felt his chest tighten, his thoughts a confused muddle.

All those years cloaked in mystery, and this was the reason he had awoken to find Sam's bed empty?

"It's all beginning to make sense," Maisie gasped. "This is the story your social worker told Sarah."

"And the reason I never came back," Sam said, his voice deep with remorse.

"So who was it?" Joe snapped. "This 'estranged' family member?"

"Well, you're never going to believe this - but it was my father."

"I thought you hated your father," Maisie whispered.

"I did. Especially after the way he treated Mum, but I had to consider his power. Put it this way, I was led to believe that he was the one who requested a patrol went out, seeking out the whereabouts of that party."

Joe frowned, struggling to take it in. "But why the fuck would he do that? After all those years he wanted nothing to do with you?"

"I know. It sounds mental and I thought the same. That he'd be glad to be shot of me. The truth is, though, he was really cut up about Mum's murder, and once he'd found me, he chose to do the right thing. Couldn't get me out of Orchard Grange fast enough, to whisk me up to the Scottish Highlands and into the family fold." He gave a cynical sniff. "I won't pretend I had a great childhood 'cos I didn't. The man was a total control freak, but that's not the point..."

Joe's heart sank. Looking at Sam now, he so much wanted to console him, yet his disclosure felt more like a betrayal.

"Yeah, well that's all very well, Sam, but let's go back to the morning after the party. Maisie and I were scared shitless. You've got no idea what Mortimer was like either, have you? Hassling him about your whereabouts did me no favours, he behaved like a fucking monster!"

"He would do," Sam said, "and I'm sorry, but it all happened so fast."

"So your dad took you away, while Maisie and I were stuck there. But what did you do? Given that stuff you saw going on in the forest, did you actually consider telling anyone?"

"Yes," he said through gritted teeth. "You seriously think I kept quiet? I was in shock! If it's any consolation, I told my social worker." His head hung low, his shoulders crunched with tension.

Yet the over-riding emotion surging through Joe's mind was outrage. "Told her what, exactly?"

"That I witnessed abuse of the worst kind. Satanic, ritualistic, call it what you like, Joe... but that's what it was."

A shivering breath escaped Maisie's lips. "Then why was nothing done?"

"I wish I knew," he responded sadly, "yet by the time I was in Scotland it was out of my control. I was powerless, Maisie, you've got to believe me."

"It's okay," she soothed, "and I do believe you."

A tap on the door signalled an end to the conversation. Although it seemed Sam had not quite finished, his words bursting out in a whisper.

"I was completely isolated and I'm sorry I lost touch with you guys, but that's another story... Something I'll save for another day."

The sight of DS Havers at the door brought a wave of relief, although Joe was still reeling in the horror of Sam's story.

"How are you getting on in here?" said the sergeant with a smile. "Andrew asked me to check up on you."

"We're fine," Maisie sighed. "It's great to see Sam again and I think we've had enough time to get our heads around this."

Joe swallowed back the lump in his throat. 'Fine' was not the word he would have chosen to describe how he was feeling; and whilst seeing Sam alive was a miracle in itself, his story left him cold.

"Excellent," the sergeant nodded, "and I'm sorry if this seems a bit 'cloak and dagger.' It wasn't our intention to shock you, but we had to review Sam's statement before you had a chance to confer. Because believe me, when this case is passed to the CPS they'll pick over every minor detail, including our own procedures."

"Fair enough," Sam nodded.

He kept his expression neutral; though following the sergeant back to the lobby, Joe could not resist hurling a suspicious glance in his direction. He had endured a lifetime of hell escaping the ever-looming menace of Mortimer, and the fact remained that there were a hundred more questions he wanted to ask Sam.

"So this place you were taken," he muttered. "Where was it? You mentioned the Scottish Highlands..."

"Would it help if I showed you this?" Sam said. Reaching into his jacket pocket, he scooped out his i-Phone. "This is where I grew up."

Next he pulled up a photo on Facebook. Joe stared at it, saying nothing at first. All the snapshot revealed was a group of people gathered outside an imposing grey building. Constructed in worn, irregular stones, it conveyed a historic look.

"Galbraith Castle," Sam added. "Home to the McFadden family."

It wasn't the castle that had captured Joe's interest, though. As his eyes wandered along the line of faces, they paused on a tall, powerful looking man. Poised proudly at the centre, not only did he boast a shock of white-blonde hair but a square-jawed face not dissimilar to that of the adult Sam now walking beside him.

But as his eyes explored further, he felt a punch of shock.

The other people held no significance, apart from one tiny figure almost lost in the shadows. *Sam*. This was without doubt the same boy he had battled to protect in the dark days of Orchard Grange, a boy whose widely-spaced brown eyes had haunted him for a lifetime.

"Sam Ellis..." The words fell out of his mouth automatically, and gaping at the man next to him, the truth was finally beginning to take shape.

"I was re-named Samuel McFadden," he added softly.

He never got to say any more. Those last few steps had drawn them back to the area they had first entered, the remaining two police officers awaiting them.

"So what now?" Maisie asked.

"You're free to go," Mark said. "I was about to make my way back to Sussex but I expect you three have got a bit more catching up to do."

"We'll keep you updated," DI Fitzpatrick added warmly, "by email if you like... and I hope you don't mind me saying this, but I'd rather you didn't discuss this case out in the open. There may be journalists sniffing around."

"Other than that, just take good care of yourselves," Mark added.

Only then did Joe notice he was the only one who wasn't smiling.

Gathered on the pavement, they stood like silent statues. Nobody knew what to say at first, and oblivious to the bustle of London life unfolding around them, they did nothing but exchange nervous glances. Sam clutched his i-Phone, the image on Facebook suspended in time.

"Are either of you on Facebook?"

It seemed such a vapid comment.

Maisie risked a chuckle. "I am."

But Joe shook his head, feeling a stir of unease. "No way, mate, I suffered enough trolling on Twitter."

He was no longer looking at Sam, but could still feel the weight of his stare.

"Trolling?"

Joe shrugged. "There's shit loads we haven't told you, but like the DI says, we'd best not talk about it out here."

"Then why don't we go somewhere else?" Sam suggested. "Seems a shame to depart so soon..." Shooting a sideways glance to check the coast was clear, he seemed as wary as Maisie had done earlier. "Do you fancy going for a bite? I know a great place in Covent Garden."

"Sounds like a plan," Joe said to Maisie. "Covent Garden is where we left Jess, so why don't I text her? She'll be wondering where we've been all this time."

"Jess?" Sam frowned.

"My girlfriend," he murmured, unable to fight the smile on his face. "Don't worry, she's well clued up..." and fumbling for his mobile, he prodded out a text:

'Hi ya babe all done can't wait to see ya xxx.'

Though no sooner had he hit 'send' than he noticed Sam still watching him.

"Cool," he muttered. "I look forward to meeting her..." His eyes pierced into Joe's with a glint. "So let's walk. I want to hear your take on this, Joe, and you can talk quietly... but what exactly happened after I vanished?"

Chapter Forty-Four

Trailing along behind, I couldn't hear what they were whispering. But with Joe gesticulating wildly, eyes black with loathing, I guess it had a lot to do with Mortimer. I could understand his outrage.

It was hard to believe that story about Sam being adopted.

So why had Mortimer been so hostile? If this was the truth, as Sam had corroborated, then surely he had little to fear.

By the time we returned to Covent Garden, I was beginning to feel light-headed. The last couple of hours had been an emotional roller coaster, but what a joy it was to see Sam alive.

At least Sarah's detective work had paid off.

My footsteps slowed as I observed the two heads shimmering in front of me; one dark, one blond, the three of us back together.

"Alright, Maisie?" Joe murmured, turning to me. "Jess is gonna hook up with us in a bit, so we might as well head for this place Sam suggested."

"It's just around the corner," Sam said. "I think a long overdue drink is in order, don't you?"

Looking at him now, I felt the warmth of his eyes slide over me and it filled my heart with promise...

A few minutes later, we found ourselves in the basement bar of a stylish Louisiana barbecue and seafood shack. I loved the dark cavernous interior, the exposed brick walls and hardwood floors, but most importantly, it made me feel safe. Shuffling into a corner table, we basked in the shadows, where at last I felt the tension drop from my shoulders.

"Cool place," Joe said, echoing my thoughts, "right away from the main drag, so we can talk."

Sam smiled, quick to order a bottle of Merlot. "This is on me, by the way."

"That's very generous," I mumbled.

It didn't seem long though, before we were back on the subject of Orchard Grange. For Joe, whilst pacified, didn't seem entirely satisfied with Sam's explanation.

"You've got no idea what it was like, forever on the run with Mortimer on my case, and he's still out there. I might be dead now, if it wasn't for my workmates."

"You do know someone tried to run Joe over," I pressed. "That thug

Mortimer hired, Schiller, which reminds me of something else I haven't told you..."

I took a deep breath, my thoughts focussed on the police interview.

What I hadn't described was the CCTV footage taken in my home town.

"Not long after Joe and I met up, we discovered we were being watched. But you know that black car? Turns out it was tailing me long before then..."

Joe looked horrified, urging me to continue. Sinister though it seemed, the ANPR had not only captured its presence in Bognor; but on the days I attended therapy, it was lurking near the junction of London Road and Sudley Road, a quiet residential street, housing several small companies.

"It's where Hannah has her practice," I finished. "My therapist."

"Strange," Sam pondered. "What kind of therapist is she?"

"A psychotherapist. She's been helping me with my emotional issues. Take my nightmares, for example. They started in my teens but recurred again in January."

Sam leaned inwards, keen to catch my eye. "So you said, and I should have asked you before, but what are these dreams about?"

A flurry of goose-pimples ran over my skin. "Staring up at the sky under a circle of trees - chanting - a procession of hooded figures coming for us... but they never really progressed much beyond that point."

"Must be a repressed memory," Sam concluded.

I looked away quickly. Gulping back my fear, I could not bear to dwell on it now. Not after the atrocities he had described.

"Then once I started therapy, I had flashbacks," I added. "Orchard Grange featured a lot, so I knew whatever problems I had stemmed from there."

"God, Maisie," Sam whispered, his face a picture of woe, "I feel for you both but there's something I don't get. Why did Mortimer come after you? Surely I must have posed an even greater threat."

I paused, glancing at Joe. Fuming in silence, he took another swig of wine.

"We'll never know, will we?" he reflected. "You had it easy. Driven up to Scotland and well out of his reach. Maisie went to live with foster parents and I was kept in that shit hole. That was, until Mortimer's threats got so nasty I had to leg it."

With a sigh of frustration, Sam topped up his glass, before his gaze shifted to me again. It was evident Joe's anger was not lost on him.

"How soon were you fostered after the night in question, then? And did it all seem a bit sudden?"

"Yes. It wasn't long after you vanished that Mortimer signed the paperwork. He said I could leave and I remember thinking *was this just another ploy to split me and Joe up?*" With my thoughts anchored on Joe, I met his gaze with a sigh. "You know the rest! I told my foster parents you were in danger and they tried to contact the home but you'd already run away."

"Bloody good job too," Sam muttered.

"Yes, well moving on," Joe intervened, "what I'm dying to know is why you never tried contacting us. It might have helped to know you were safe."

"I understand where you're coming from, Joe," Sam whispered, "and if only it was that simple..." His eyes flashed in the shadows, transmitting a warning. "I never wanted to mention this, and I can't say too much, but my father forced me to sever all connections from Orchard Grange and everyone associated with it, including my two best friends."

"The mighty Judge McFadden," Joe kept baiting him.

"You've got no idea," Sam protested, his voice choked with sadness, "but all he cared about was the McFadden family reputation. I wasn't allowed any contact with the outside world. They kept me hidden. I even thought about writing to you guys, but my father wouldn't hear of it."

A cloud of anguish crossed his face, and it was impossible not to feel a little sympathy. I had long picked up a vein of secrecy from what Sarah had divulged, but everything was starting to click now; *a defenceless boy hauled up to Scotland, cut off from everyone he had ever known.*

The silence hung heavy as we absorbed everything we had told and heard. Lost in my musings, I was aware of a buzz of activity in the background, the clatter of plates, a chime of glasses emanating from the bar as waiters delivered food and cocktails. It left me wondering if we should order something, though no one seemed to be rushing us.

Before I had a chance to say another word, though, I detected movement from above. Joe turned to the stairs and erupting from his seat, waved wildly.

"Jess! Over here!"

Sam followed his gaze as she sashayed over to our table, and how her dazzling smile lifted the gloom like a lantern!

"You're never gonna believe this," Joe grinned, "but we've found Sam!"

Jess's eyes widened in wonderment. "Wow! How cool is that? So you're the boy at the heart of this mystery?"

He eyed her with quiet curiosity, a smile playing around his lips. But with laughter drawn into our conversation, I shuffled across to make room for her.

She'd want to sit opposite Joe of course, leaving me face to face with Sam.

Not that I minded - for as Sam and I locked eyes, I felt the adoration behind his smile. It allowed me to temporarily forget our turmoil.

Joe ordered more wine. We mutually agreed on a Sauvignon Blanc, although with a thirty-pound price tag, it didn't come cheap.

"I'll pay," Joe insisted. "You'll have a glass, won't you, Jess?"

"Thanks, sweetie, but I'm driving us home, don't forget. I wouldn't say no to a Mojito though, with plenty of ice please. Just the one."

"We can always go halves, Joe," I burst in but he raised his hand in protest.

"No, I'll get it! It's the least I can do if Sam's treating us."

The flash in his eye brooked no argument, and finally the penny dropped. Joe wasn't out to impress me or Jess. *Just Sam.* Sam with his fashionable clothes and meticulously styled hair, Sam who exuded status.

"Okay," I relented. "If you insist."

"I suppose we should order some grub too," Sam added, "and no skimping, choose whatever you like."

Scrutinising the menu, we found the choice so overwhelming, he suggested sharing a combo of mixed dishes. Everything sounded scrumptious.

"What happened at the police station then?" Jess leapt in.

"They wanted to go over our statements again," Joe said, "except neither of us expected *him* to turn up..." His eyes flickered in Sam's direction. "Sorry if I seem on edge, mate, but seeing you is a bit of a head fuck."

"So where have you been all these years?" Jess asked with intrigue.

Sam showed no hesitation in giving a potted history, including his eventual escape from the isolation of Scotland. With a hankering to visit his mum's grave, he was unavoidably drawn back to London – but here in London he had been recruited by an estate agent, starting out as a general dogsbody.

"To think," I commented, "all those years and you were that close."

"I'm glad I stuck with the profession," he added. "I'm a partner in my own firm now."

Joe clung to every word, his face alight with curiosity, and Sam seemed just as curious to know about our lives.

Gradually the conversation shifted. Plates of succulent giant shrimp, barbecued ribs and chicken were lowered onto the table, alongside a side dish of lobster mac and cheese. All came with coleslaw, salad and chips. My mouth watered as Joe filled up my wine glass with Sauvignon Blanc, but I hid my smile. No one seemed to have noticed him sneakily ordering from the bar, so he could settle with cash.

"So you all live in Bognor?" Sam mused. "Must be nice to be close to the sea. Any chance I could come and visit you some time?"

"Absolutely," I breathed, with more joy than intended.

His hand lowered to the table and I felt the featherlight brush of his fingertips against my own. Maybe I had drunk a little more wine than I should have, but the effect was quite pleasurable.

"That would be awesome," Sam nodded, "I guess we'll be in touch anyway, with regard to the investigation."

"Come down and visit us soon then," Joe kept grinning, "spend a day on our turf and we'll talk some more."

Chapter Forty-Five

Of all the visitors who passed through the gates of Wandsworth Prison, none stuck out quite like the two middle-aged ladies who had braved the journey to see Thomas.

With her loosely coiled-up blonde hair and pastel tweed suit, Cecelia held her back straight, refusing to cower under the scrutiny of the other women. The smirks and the sneers had unnerved her at first, the occasional spitting insult - but if they were hoping to get a rise out of her, they would be woefully disappointed.

For deep in her heart Cecelia knew her brother was innocent.

"This way please, ladies!"

Davina glanced up at the uniformed prison guard. She, on the other hand, did not look so confident. A fragile brunette in her fifties, her beauty had evoked even greater scorn. Today her perfectly painted lips trembled, and next to Cecelia, the poor lamb looked petrified. As Thomas's long term mistress, it hadn't taken long for the media to transform her into a figure of hate.

Looping her arm through Davina's, Cecelia led the way. The stench of disinfectant clawed the back of her throat, the clang of metal doors setting her teeth on edge. Yet nothing stirred more horror than the ghost of the man who awaited them.

"Thomas," Davina sobbed and breaking away from Cecelia, she stumbled towards his table. "Oh dear God, what's going on?"

"Hello, darling," he greeted her in a weak voice. "Sit down, both of you. It's kind of you to come and visit me."

His deeply brooding blue eyes welled up, spiking her with dread.

"How are you?" she whispered. "I mean, what are you even doing here?"

He suppressed a sob. "They think I'm in league with Cornelius Mortimer, as confirmed by this latest witness - but Cornelius has not yet been arrested."

She exhaled a despairing sigh. "Oh, Thomas! If you don't mind me saying so, you look terrible. I hope they're treating you well in here."

"Yes, but I have to be kept in solitary," he croaked. "Considering the crimes I'm accused of, you must surely realise the implications. Even among criminals, there is no worse beast than a child molester."

"But you haven't done anything of the sort!" Davina spluttered.

Cecelia placed a comforting hand on her own. "Shh, dear, calm down."

Gazing at Thomas, she inclined her head. Being on the remand wing, he was permitted to wear his own clothes, but the cut of his Savile Row suit appeared baggy on him, his face pale and gaunt.

"How anyone could accuse you of something so monstrous I will never know," she breathed, "and as for this latest story..."

"I was nowhere near that forest," Thomas shuddered. "I-I have never in my life been associated with any of Cornelius's parties, b-but to imply I was involved in something so sick as a satanic ritual involving children... that I threatened a boy with a dagger... These are foul, wicked lies."

"But who on earth would accuse you of such things?" Cecelia pressed. "Have you made any enemies recently?"

"I don't know," Thomas said. His voice betrayed a crack and before they could say another word, he started crying.

Cecelia's heart pounded. With everything out in the open, there was no question of turning their backs on him.

It wasn't as if they hadn't all been affected.

As a close family member, Cecelia, like Davina, had been targeted too; from malicious threats in the post to eggs flung at her windows.

"This is terrible," Davina whimpered. "What are we going to do?"

"I'm going to talk to David again," she murmured in a low voice. "The three of us must surely know enough people who can vouch for your good character. Ask your solicitor if he can pin-point the date of this alleged party. We need to check our diaries. Talk to our friends. Find out where you were on the night in question. That is, if you were even in the country."

"Try not to worry," Davina added, a little more gently. "We used to travel a lot in the nineties, remember? I'm convinced we'll find you an alibi."

He raised his eyes, a bundle of desolation. The tears on his face left glistening trails but studying him now, Cecelia began to fear he might be suicidal, and if he was, who could blame him? Whatever else happened, she yearned to clear him of these crimes before their lives were destroyed forever.

"And what of my accusers?" Thomas sniffed. "Do you have any idea who these 'children' are?" Pulling a handkerchief from his top pocket, he blew his nose.

"The police have refused to name the victims," she muttered, "but I can ask David to probe into this. You know my husband, he's a good barrister."

Braced in his chair like a condemned man, Thomas wiped away his tears, took a number of slow deep breaths and forced his head upright.

"Are you honestly prepared to do that for me?" he asked.

"I said I'd try, didn't I?" She gave a cool smile.

"Liars and fantasists, the lot of them," he spat, "and if it's possible to prove my innocence, I will fight this to the bitter end..."

Cecelia watched mesmerised, as his expression turned to stone.

"I want the whole world to know this entire charade was a set-up. And whoever is responsible will pay dearly for what they have done to me."

Chapter Forty-Six

Staring ahead blankly as Jess turned into our avenue, I had barely noticed we were nearly home. It was a dark, clear night, and the stars made sharp pinpoints of light in the sky, yet on the edge of my mind flickered Sam's face.

"Well," Joe said at last, "some day this turned out to be."

"I'm still trying to get my head around it," I mumbled. "I never imagined he would just turn up like that..."

"Back from the dead, eh?" Jess teased. "Amazing how things pan out."

Switching off the engine, I saw her catch Joe's eye in the rear view mirror.

"Cheers for driving," he said warmly. "Fancy coming in for a nightcap?"

She stifled a yawn. "No thanks. I'd best be heading home, I could do with an early night, but let's hook up again tomorrow."

"See you soon, Jess," I added, and sliding out of the front passenger seat, I made myself discreet.

Joe hung back, shuffling into the seat I had vacated. It seemed obvious they wouldn't want to be parted without a kiss first, so I unlocked the door to the house and left them to it. Blinded by the blaze of light in the hallway, I dragged my weary limbs forward.

All I craved now was a cup of tea.

But before I had a chance to gather my thoughts, I noticed the light flashing on my answering machine. I nibbled my lip. Without knowing why, a prick of anxiety sharpened my senses.

"Hi, Maisie, I hope everything's okay with you, but can you call me as soon as you get a chance?"

"Sarah!" I gasped to myself.

Something was wrong. I could hear it in her voice, a note of fear I did not like. So without delay, I dialled her number.

"Hi," I blurted. "Is everything alright? You left a message. In fact, I've only just switched my mobile back on and saw two more missed calls."

Joe lingered in the background. Having finally extracted himself from Jess's embrace, he had taken over the task of tea making.

"Thanks for calling back," Sarah whispered, "but before I say another word, has Joe received any more abuse on his Twitter account?"

"Not that I know of..." I met his eye across the lounge. "He doesn't use

Twitter so much, since the police proceedings began."

Joe's face buckled into a frown.

"Why?" I pressed. "What's happened?"

"Someone's threatened me too, but on Facebook Messenger. *Keep your interfering nose out of things that do not concern you, otherwise there will be consequences. This is your first warning.*"

I clung to the handset, my heart racing.

"Do you want to know what's really creepy, though? They sent an image of that house I visited in East Grinstead. It looks like it's been downloaded from Google maps, but that's not the point. This must have some bearing on me visiting Yvonne Draper, your friend's social worker."

"Sam," I breathed in amazement. Sagging into my chair, I could no longer ignore the irony. "I can't think what they'd be trying to hide now. Sam's alive! We've found him, or rather he found us. He turned up at Charing Cross Police Station today."

"Really?" she responded. "That's great news. Sorry to dampen the mood."

"Don't be. We're just as gobsmacked... but I don't understand. Can you take a screen shot of this and send it to me? We need to inform the police."

"I-it is possible, yes," Sarah shivered, "except there's worse..."

"What's going on?" Joe demanded, and lowering two steaming mugs of tea onto the table, he crashed down into the chair opposite.

"Sarah's been threatened," I mumbled. "Sorry, what were you saying?"

An uncomfortable silence stretched between us. This, I realised, affected us both, so it made sense for Joe to be listening. Staring at him in trepidation, I flipped the machine to speaker mode.

"An hour later," Sarah continued, "there was another message, and that one proves they know where I live. They attached a scanned newspaper article. The story of a fire from two decades ago."

"Oh my God," I reacted. "Did this happen in Rosebrook?"

"It did," Sarah croaked, her voice tight with fear. "Whoever sent this knows its significance. I don't know if Mandy ever told you about the fire at the community centre, but my husband was trapped in the building. He nearly died, Maisie and that's not the worst. It's the wording in the message that alarmed me."

"Go on," I urged her. "What did it say?"

"*Do not contact the police and in case you need another incentive to keep your mouth shut, we know who your foster son is...*" She sounded close to tears. "What if Connor's in danger?"

Joe's mouth fell open. To think we had made such progress today, and now Sarah's family was being victimised as a result – it was enough to turn my blood to ice.

"I daren't involve the law. You can't imagine the stress this is causing."

"I can," I argued, "and I'm sorry I ever involved you, but I don't get why you've been targeted. We spoke to Sam today and he told us everything. There can't be any more secrets we don't know..."

"That's all very well, Maisie, but maybe your enemies don't realise this. Would you mind putting all this in an email for me?"

"Okay," I said. "But who is this person, and how did they find you?"

"I accepted a friend request from someone calling themselves 'Gemma Black.'" A shuddering breath passed through the speaker. "I took a look at her profile, which I now suspect is fake - a nondescript portrait, a couple of posts about tracing a half-brother to hook me in... I didn't think anything of it."

"But I never accept requests from people I don't know," I whispered.

"It's different for you. I'm used to strangers approaching me. It's my job and like I say, she looked harmless, but that was before I got these messages."

"Oh Sarah," I murmured, my heart sinking. "Is there anything I can do?"

Another sigh resonated from the speaker. "Right now, I could do with a break. Peter and I were thinking of going to Devon for a few days to talk things over... but preferably away from Connor. I don't want him to be frightened."

Locking eyes with Joe, I knew what needed to be said.

"Then why doesn't he come and stay with me for the weekend?"

"I was hoping you'd say that," she replied, the relief evident in her voice. "Does this mean you've completed your course in respite care?"

"I've got one more module, which I'll do this week... and all I have to do is keep an eye on him, right? He can watch TV, read books, he's got his Nintendo DS. I'll take him to the beach and if it's low tide we can go fossil hunting."

"Maisie, that would be great, as long as you keep your guard up. Just one more question. Is your friend, Joe, still lodging with you?"

He met my gaze with a shrug. "Is that a problem?" he whispered. "I can always bunk up with Jess for the weekend. Make some space."

I gave a silent nod. "Joe doesn't have to be here, so no worries."

By the time the call ended, I felt light headed.

Just thank God for Joe's diplomacy, given the horror of the situation.

"Come on, Maisie," he added warmly. "It's the least we can do, and I'm sure Jess'll be cool about it. Strikes me we owe your friend big time."

"Thanks," I nodded back. "I knew you'd understand."

What I didn't want to tell him was that in order to allow me to care for a minor, the authorities would want to run checks on him too.

Flopped in an armchair, he had discarded his tie, his shirt splayed open, top buttons undone, exposing little dark wisps of chest hair. Returning his smile, I realised for the first time how happy I was for him, having Jess to fuss over him. Someone who understood his needs, especially at a time like this.

Chapter Forty-Seven

The past was becoming clearer, but the future remained unknown; and Joe in particular, was soon to experience a chain of events that would completely alter his destiny. It began shortly after he had unpacked his overnight bag. Jess was ecstatic to have him to herself for the weekend and in the absence of Maisie, yearned to make their time together extra special. These were the memories he would cherish; a candlelit bath shared in blissful solitude, luxuriating in an ocean of bubbles. As his eyes wandered, he found it hard to contain his smile. She had even positioned a champagne bucket on the side.

"D'you wanna know what Sam said when you and Maisie popped to the ladies?" he began. "Couldn't believe how I'd managed to net myself such a classy bird."

"Cheeky!" Jess tittered. "And what did you say to that?"

"Must be my charm, my good looks, or I've got the gift of the gab. Nah, seriously, I told him every woman likes a bit of rough..."

"Joe!" she breathed, flicking foam at his face. "Don't put yourself down!"

Joe ducked, but not before getting his jibe in. "You didn't fancy him, then?"

"First impression? Drop dead gorgeous! But I've had enough of men who think they're God's gift. All they do is break your heart."

Sinking into the steaming water, she closed her eyes. The soft glow of candlelight enhanced her flawless skin, and she had never looked more desirable.

"So what did you think of him?" she added.

Joe raked the foam from his damp hair, whilst carefully considering his answer. "He's not the Sam I remember. That kid was a nervous wreck when we lived at Orchard Grange. The adult version – well, if anything, he seemed a bit cocky."

"Yeah," Jess murmured, "but he's bound to have changed. Didn't you say he moved to Scotland and lived in some castle? I guess he's had a totally different upbringing."

Joe nodded. Thinking back to their day in London, snippets of conversation crept back to him.

Completely isolated.

Forced to sever all connections from Orchard Grange.

Seeing Sam again felt eerie. Suave and over-confident on the outside he might be, but Joe couldn't help wondering if he was hiding something.

Next day, any last niggling thoughts about Sam were driven from his mind as he worked his shift at the supermarket. Grateful for his regular lifts now, he was even fantasising of having his own car. Such musings catapulted him right back to the old days when he had lodged with Al and Shirley. Al had been the closest thing he'd had to a father figure and had taught him to drive. But that was before George Oldman had swooped in, snatching him from the nest like an eagle.

George had furnished him with plenty of flash motors over the years, but if he'd only known of the devil's pact he was being drawn into, things might have been very different.

He pushed the reminiscences aside, enjoying the company of his colleagues around him. But today was a day when the past was destined to keep haunting him.

A little later, as he demolished a full English breakfast at the Waverley, Jess asked him how the police investigation was going.

Joe mopped up the last of his egg with his toast, and setting down his cutlery, welcomed an opportunity to talk about it. Jess was not personally involved. Jess would not judge people, nor be swayed by the news or social media.

"Well," he began, "one thing I've learned is those homes were permanently closed down in winter 1995. About a month after I scarpered..."

"Strange," Jess gasped. "Do you wonder if you had anything to do with it?"

Joe shrugged. "Since talking to Sam, everything seems fucked up. Mortimer was such a shit to me when he vanished, though according to records they were shut down for financial reasons. Dunno. Maybe he went bankrupt."

Fingers steepled above the shiny wooden veneer of their table top, he stared out of the window, deep in thought. In truth, the police report troubled him. As if there was a piece missing from the puzzle. For if Thomas Parker-Smythe (then a Cabinet Minister) had promised extra funding, surely it would have saved the homes... unless the Government had refused. The educational standards were poor, something Mortimer should have improved upon - yet never really cared about.

Joe on the other hand, would never forget the anarchy in Mortimer's homes.

"I told the cops about Orchard Grange," he resumed. "Fucking great place. They were all named after trees, you know."

Jess's gaze intensified, her eyes shiny with intrigue. "The police have found records of them all?"

"Yeah," Joe mumbled. Fidgeting in his chair, he shuffled up close to whisper. "Those hell holes deserved to be shut down. I can't imagine why anyone would want to invest a penny in them, which calls to mind the politician..."

"You think he had a more *personal* interest?" she murmured.

"Bloody right," he hissed, "'cos he's not exactly squealing. If he's so innocent, why doesn't he shop Mortimer? Makes me wonder if the bastard's got some hold over him."

Jess finished her coffee. "That figures. How do you know all this?"

"The Met have been updating us by email... Well, Maisie's email. I'm not sure they trust my hotmail account. I mean, look how easily those arseholes found me on social media, and the police reports are confidential. We daren't put anyone at risk."

Jess's hand froze around her coffee cup. "What do you mean, exactly?" Her eyes flitted sideways and suddenly she looked uneasy.

Grasping her hand, he exhaled a troubled sigh.

"Let's go back to your flat. This ain't the best place to be talking about stuff like this and like I say, it's confidential."

The intimacy of her apartment had never felt safer. Yet it wasn't Jess who was in danger, so much as Sarah. He had seen the latest update on Maisie's laptop before the weekend; a report that sent ripples of shock through him.

According to police records, there had been no investigation into the homes.

Joe shuddered. Sam swore he had told his social worker everything. That being the case, how come nobody had acted on this knowledge? Sam, a vulnerable eleven-year-old, had borne witness to a horrific scene. Yet none of it was on record.

He spared Jess the details but to think, they could have arrested that bastard, Mortimer, there and then; Sam the only boy who could 'blow the whistle.'

"I wonder if he was telling the truth," he muttered. Relaxing in each other's arms on one of her sumptuous sofas, he stared idly into space.

"About confiding in his social worker?" Jess probed.

"Yeah," he said, "'cos from what I gather, she wasn't exactly forthcoming. Downright cagey, in fact. Unless, whatever Sam said was treated as make-believe! All she confirmed was *he'd been taken away by another family member*, but refused to go into any detail."

"But that's outrageous," Jess spluttered.

Visions of a forest loomed, columns of trees surrounding them like prison bars. Lost in his reverie, Joe felt a knot in his throat. Thinking of Sam's account turned him cold with dread, but with those thoughts, another idea rose to the surface.

There were so many layers of secrecy where Sam's social worker was concerned, especially now Sarah had been targeted.

"How can it be right when kids report abuse, no one ever seems to believe them?" Jess kept digging.

"Who knows," Joe said, "or maybe she was warned to keep her mouth shut. Keep this to yourself but a friend of Maisie was threatened and all because she saw the same social worker, asking similar questions about Sam."

"Spooky," Jess murmured. Heaving herself up onto one elbow, she teased a stray curl from his forehead. "This is beginning to sound like a cover up."

Joe shivered. "I know, that's what I thought..."

"And talking of Sam," she added. "When is he coming to visit us?"

"I'm not sure, to be honest. Let me check WhatsApp."

Prising himself from her arms, he moved away from the sofa to find his mobile. He pulled it from his coat pocket and drifted over to the window to get a better signal.

"Don't look like he'll be down for a few days yet, due to work pressures."

"Oh well," Jess sighed, rising to her feet. "He did say he was an estate agent."

"Yeah, got property deals in the pipeline, clients to see..." He gave a wry chuckle. "Flash git."

His gaze wandered down to the promenade. The sun was out, but a veil of wispy cloud obscured it, sapping the warmth from the air. Just before he turned away from the window, though, something jolted him.

Maisie. It was her hair that gave her away.

How could he miss that unmistakable auburn gleam in the distance? As she ambled along the sand, he spotted the willowy adolescent boy loping along next to her. This could be none other than Connor, Sarah's foster son. They must have gone fossil hunting after all. Rows of rocks squatted like islands along the sandbank in their encircling moats of water. It gave him an idea.

"D'you fancy going for a walk on the beach?" he called to Jess.

Regrettably though, they failed to reach them.

By the time Jess had her coat and shoes on, her hair brushed and her lipstick refreshed, the cloud cover had intensified.

Joe tensed as the air temperature turned chillier.

A tang of salt coiled through the breeze, and he looked up to see a curtain of grey mist billowing in from the sea. He stared in disbelief, the shape of the rocks turning hazy as they were swallowed up by the fog. And all the while it was advancing, everyone on the beach gradually dissolved too, Maisie and the boy among them.

Joe wrapped his arm around Jess's shoulder, unable to explain his feelings... but something about the scene struck him as ominous.

Chapter Forty-Eight

Hannah Adams. Registered Psychotherapist/Counsellor. West Sussex
Client: Maisie Bell
20th May 2015

"I'm glad you came," Hannah began. "Sit down."

Her face appeared relaxed as she held my stare, but I noticed she wasn't smiling.

"I don't suppose the police have been in touch?" I asked her.

"They have," she said. "I spoke to DI Fitzpatrick, who seemed very concerned about your emotional state, given the claims coming out of these sessions. But I gather they're being investigated now."

"That's right," I confessed. "I told them I was having therapy and hoped you'd back me up. Though it seems our enemies know this, too."

"Enemies?"

My mouth turned dry as I recalled our day in London.

Those sightings of the black car hanging around near her house left a chill in me, yet it seemed only fair to warn her...

"I saw the CCTV footage," I finished uneasily.

"Oh well," Hannah murmured. "I am sorry to hear this, Maisie, but to put your mind at rest, I'm happy to assist with the investigation in any way I can."

Her words trickled over me like warm water, massaging away my fears. Whilst relieved it was out in the open, though, this was not the reason I was here.

"Relax now, and let your mind settle. Is anything else troubling you?"

Yes. There had been a major change in our lives, and I wasn't sure where to start. She had made mention of the investigation, but what of the threat to Sarah? My developing bond with her foster son? And everything else paled into insignificance beside the one person who lay at the heart of all this.

"It's Sam."

His name hung in the air, shrouded in secrecy.

"Not the 'Sam' you mentioned in your previous sessions?"

"That's the one," I said, in a monotone. "When Joe and I went to London, we were told another witness had come forward..."

With my eyelids turning heavy, I allowed them to drop like shutters.

Sam was due to visit us soon; the adult Sam, who felt very much like a stranger. Maybe this was my chance to recapture any last lingering memories of the boy I had met at Orchard Grange... before the night he disappeared.

"Sam didn't die. He was taken away to live with someone else."

Shadows gathered in the tunnels of my mind as his story began to emerge.

"First, he relayed his memories of the party they went to. Him and Joe. A scene in a forest where he heard chanting - saw a circle of cloaked figures. There's no way he could have made that up, is there?"

"Impossible," Hannah said. "It's no coincidence how much this sounds like your nightmare, but was he able to tell you any more?"

The memories swirled darker, conjuring up the horror Sam depicted, except it didn't seem right to repeat it.

"What he described sounded like some creepy satanic ritual, but I have to keep it to myself... or at least until the investigation is over."

"Of course," she murmured. "I wasn't prying. Just wondering if this has helped you in any way, or given you those much-needed answers."

The atmosphere around me turned dreamlike as I pictured his face.

"Sam is a crucial witness," I said. "Joe remembers the drugged punch and little else... and the only evidence I can present is my dreams."

"You do have memories, though," Hannah reassured me. "Things you repressed. I have recordings of all our sessions and as I said, I'm willing to vouch for you."

I let the words sink in. Having a professional therapist to back me up brought a moment of relief, and I clung to the hope her knowledge of the human psyche would verify everything I had experienced.

With neither of us talking, it didn't seem long before the stretch of silence dragged. Something else niggled me. It hung on the edge of my thoughts, a path I was reluctant to take, and as I shifted in my seat, Hannah detected it too.

"Go on," she prompted. "Did either of you suspect Sam was in danger before this happened?"

Deep in my subconscious, the fog was beginning to thin and there he was... the half-remembered figure of Sam hovering before me.

"Oh yes," I whispered. "The first time we saw Sam, he looked terrified. Glancing around like a little lost boy, the tough ones sizing him up. I remember them whispering to themselves and sniggering... an ugly sound. Later that day they got him in the toilets, and Joe had to go and break the fight up..."

"You always said he was the protective one, but how did you feel?"

A glow of adoration spread inside me. "I felt just as protective as Joe, and from that day onwards, he clung to us like glue. No one had ever looked up to me the way Sam did, and in a way it made me feel special."

"Special," Hannah echoed. The warmth of her chuckle stirred a smile in me.

"Very much," I sighed. "He absolutely doted on me... I remember how deeply I cared for him too."

"How long did you know him before he left?"

"Not long," I shivered. "A few months, maybe."

"What happened then? Can you recall the day after he vanished?"

Knots in my shoulders tightened as an invisible key unlocked a memory. I knew where her words were guiding me now, and thrown back to the aftermath of Sam's disappearance, I relived the painful days that followed.

Staring at Joe, I had all but forgotten the stricken look on his face that morning.

A sense of friction bit the air.

'Where's Sam?' I hissed.

Noise boomed all around us, the same bun fight we had to endure every morning, kids grabbing for cereals, arguing over whose turn it was to have what... but it all sounded muffled, as if I were hearing the commotion underwater.

'Sam's gone,' Joe shuddered. 'He wasn't in his bed this morning.'

A prickle of cold fear ran over me, leaving a tingling sensation.

'How come? What happened last night?'

He sat very still, his gaze never leaving me. Something in his expression unnerved me, every facial muscle on edge.

'Dunno,' he muttered, finally. 'They drugged me...'

He would have said more, I was convinced of it, but in the blink of an eye the atmosphere shifted. It was no longer the horror on Joe's face that panicked me so much as Mr. Mortimer's intrusion. His pale reptilian eyes flashed across our table, seeking us out, and latched onto Joe, where they lingered.

'What did you say?'

Joe flinched. Even I detected the menace curling into his voice.

'Nothing,' he sneered in defiance. 'Just wondering where Sam is.'

'None of your business, Winterton,' Mortimer snapped, 'but your little friend is quite safe, so there is no further need for you to baby him.'

'So where's he gone?' Joe pressed.

I could have sworn Mortimer swelled several inches bigger, his bulk casting an ominous shadow over us. But how I felt for Joe. The man glowered at him in a way that froze my blood, his face a darkening cloud. I don't think I had ever seen Joe look more anxious either, his spidery arms wrapping around his body like armour.

To our dismay, though, we never did get an answer.

Struggling to survive in that awful place, Joe insisted we had to watch our

*backs now. The trouble was, we were never alone. Schiller, Mikolov, Mortimer...
one of them was always lurking. If we crept into the yard, they followed us. The
kitchen. The lounge. Even the classroom. Invading our space, day in, day out,
they seemed intent on eavesdropping on our every conversation.*

*It didn't take long before Sam's absence began to bite deep. In a selfish way,
I missed the attention he lavished on me - the power of his smile casting a little
sunshine into our lives. With Sam gone we felt unhinged. For despite
Mortimer's excuses, we suspected something more sinister had happened.*

*Recalling it now brought a well of unshed misery to the surface, and I
couldn't fight it. Tears pooled behind my eyelids, my heart hammering in my
chest, and the next thing I knew I was sobbing.*

*"Take deep breaths," Hannah's voice echoed through the darkness. "It's
obvious how much this upset you at the time, but it's over now. You have found
him, so let's fast forward a bit shall we?"*

"I'm not sure what you mean," I sniffed.

"What you haven't explained is your reaction to seeing Sam now."

*Her gentle tone reminded me how well she understood me, her words
instantly sobering. Yet it was hard to piece my feelings into words.*

*"In all honesty, I'm still trying to come to terms with it," I said. "There was
something about the day Sam disappeared that felt uncanny. Joe suspected he
was dead, whereas I held onto the hope he was alive... Yet I don't think either of
us really expected to see him again."*

"And what next?" Hannah coaxed. "Are you going to stay in touch?"

*"Definitely," I said as more recent memories flooded back. "I had a long
chat with my foster parents the other night and they're delighted. In fact, they
can't remember if I even mentioned Sam before this."*

*"I think you suppressed all memories of him," Hannah concluded,
"especially given your emotional outburst just then... but I'm pleased you've
resolved this. It must be good to have your childhood friend back."*

How did I really feel, though?

*Confused, yes, except Sam was no longer that small frightened boy who
wouldn't say 'boo' to a goose. Sam had bloomed into an undeniably striking
man, and if I were to be honest with myself, I had to admit I was dazzled by
him.*

Chapter Forty-Nine

That feeling stayed with me for the rest of the week and it was good to have something positive to focus on. As far as I knew, the wheels of the investigation rolled on in the background. Yet as the police pursued what meagre leads they had, nothing new had transpired.

It drew my thoughts back to Sarah. If only we could report the threats she had been sent, but in our need to protect Connor, it was impossible. My hands on the wheel tightened as I stared ahead at the traffic queue.

I simply could not bear it if anything happened to him.

Connor was an aloof child who seemed unreachable at times, but exploring the beach together had ignited a hidden glow in him. He had been searching the rocks before the sea mist rolled in, palm outstretched to reveal a gnarled grey pebble, unsure what the overlapping spirals were.

'They're fossils, Connor. Rotulara Bognorienis.'

I would never forget his smile, and like the sun peeping around the edge of a rain cloud, it shone from deep within his eyes.

No-one could tell what the future held, but with my mind wandering off on a tangent, I found myself thinking about Sam again.

He was due to visit this Sunday.

Excited, but at the same time jittery with nerves, I could not wait to see him. His idea to book a pub for Sunday lunch delighted me on so many levels, and already I could imagine the four of us in some idyllic country setting.

By the time I let myself into my flat on Friday though, I had no idea what lay in store, and was surprised to discover a text on my mobile.

Hi Maisie, how are you? Looking forward to Sunday but what are you up to tomorrow? Got some time off work and would love a chance to get to know you again. Best wishes, Sam x

It wasn't until next day that reality hit. Still astonished that Sam – Sam, who I'd thought I'd never see again – was due to turn up at my flat soon, I checked my reflection for the fourth time. My newly washed hair gleamed and I wore the tiniest amount of makeup. I had dithered over what to wear, but my burgundy cords were fairly new and teamed up with a cool summer top and black puffa jacket, I looked stylish, whilst not overdressed.

Minutes later, a car pulled up outside, and glancing out of the window, I felt my heart skip a beat.

Could this sporty Audi in kingfisher blue be Sam's car?

Peering around the door frame, I saw him slide out of the driver's side.

"Sam," I gasped with pleasure. "You found my address okay, then?"

Immaculate in mushroom chinos and a brown suede jacket that matched his eyes as well as his walking boots, he sauntered up to the door. At first we just gazed at each other, until at last he broke the spell.

"Hello Maisie. It's good to see you again."

"You too," I murmured. "What have you got in mind for this afternoon?"

"I was thinking..." he faltered, "seeing as we're in West Sussex, I did some research on the area. How d'you feel about joining me for a spin? We could check out some of the local beauty spots."

A tingle of delight ran over me. "Sounds great!"

"Hop in then! We might as well get going."

Slinging my bag over my shoulder, I locked the front door and followed him to his car. Like a true gentleman, he pulled the passenger door open for me. But as I began to unwind in the soft leather seat, it seemed no time at all before we had left Bognor behind and were charging up the A29 towards Fontwell.

"How's Joe?" he asked lightly.

"Fine. He's with Jess as usual."

Observing his neat profile, only then did I wonder whether I should have mentioned Sam's visit to Joe, but it was too late now. One cosy weekend spent in Jess's apartment had turned into something of a habit, but this naturally led to Sam's next question.

"Do I take it they're living together?"

I bit my lip, careful to mask my emotions. "Not quite. Monday to Friday, he lodges with me but I don't think he will be for much longer. She's asked him to move in with her."

Yes, Joe's disclosure had left me slightly downcast.

But like all new lovers, they could barely keep their hands off each other, so I had to accept the inevitable. Why would a young, red-blooded male like Joe want to be holed up with me, watching the same boring TV shows, when he could be indulging in round-the-clock sex with my beautiful best friend?

"Have you figured out where we're going?" I asked, eager to change the subject.

Sam's face betrayed a hint of merriment. "I looked on Google and put a route into my Sat Nav, but I'll let you in on a little secret. I had some help."

"Go on."

"One of my old pals lives in a village called Storrington."

214

"I know Storrington. It's over Worthing way."

"Yes," Sam mused. "I'm going to see him a bit later but I thought we could take a look around the Chichester area."

"Suits me fine," I consented, letting go of my breath at last. "Chichester is where I work, so I know the area well."

It seemed only natural to tell him about my job; the West Sussex County Council headquarters and the busy role I served in their fostering department.

Seemingly fascinated, his questions came thick and fast.

Before I had a chance to draw breath, he was quizzing me about my teenage years, my education. The reason I had chosen this career path.

How courteous to show such an interest, while on the fringe of my mind hung those final reminiscences from my therapy. Sam had doted on me once...

All the while we were talking, I wasn't paying attention to where we were going. Having left the main carriageway some time ago, it struck me how narrow the roads had become with every new twist and turn. But deeper into the folds of the South Downs we ventured, his Sat Nav guiding the way.

"Anyway, enough about me," I said. "What about you? You live and work in London but what about relationships? Are you married or seeing anyone?"

Staring at the road blankly, he gave a wry chuckle. "Just split up with someone, actually. We met on Tinder, the dating app."

"So how does that work?" I asked, thinking it must be easy for him to meet people in a social hub like London.

"You use it to find people with common interests. Compare photos, music and swipe the profiles you like. I thought I'd found a match when she started raving about my playlist on Spotify, but it wasn't to be... We drove each other nuts."

Grappling to take it in, I was staring ahead as he tackled the upcoming bend. Next I spotted the chalk-white walls of a traditional pub looming on the corner, a mass of foliage hugging the windows, complimented by a profusion of hanging baskets.

"Hey, that looks like a nice pub!" he blurted.

"The George," I mumbled under my breath. "We're in Eartham."

"We could go there tomorrow," he enthused. "What do you think?"

The joy in his tone was unmissable and I found myself nodding, thinking we might stop and book a table.

"Sure, why not. Good choice..."

Yet Sam drove straight past and following the country road beyond the pub, we were swallowed into the shade. I blinked rapidly as the woods on both sides of the road thickened, a vortex of trees encircling us. My heart was picking up pace and in the next moment, I nearly stopped breathing. For without warning, he had spun his car into the parking area at the front of Eartham Woods.

"Why are we stopping here?"

"Eartham Woods is part of the South Downs," Sam chirped. "There might still be a few bluebells, according to my mate, James. Shall we take a stroll?"

I gaped at him in confusion before disentangling my legs from under my car seat. Heedless of my rising panic, he jumped out of the driver side, wandering right up to the forest border.

"Well, come on then!" He glanced back with a smile.

With no choice but to follow, I gulped back my fear.

It's just a forest, I told myself. Nothing in there could harm us, and given the number of cars scattered around the car park, it was not as if we were alone.

Slowly but tentatively, I crept up to his side. Thick foliage concealed the footpath. Speckles of sunlight shone through the leaves, dappling the ground, the hum of cars gradually fading, until all I could hear were birds chirping in the overhead branches.

Another step took us onto the path, and that was where I froze - a musty smell of damp wood and leaves pierced my nostrils, evoking an inexplicable terror...

And I was powerless to fight it.

"I-I can't go in there, Sam... sorry but, b-but..."

"Hey, what's wrong?" he gasped. "You've turned as white as a sheet!"

I fought back a sob. "I don't like woods, I've got a phobia."

His face fell, the sparkle in his eyes extinguished.

Okay, so he deserved a little more explanation.

But even as I spoke, my voice shook.

"Woods a-are the place of my nightmares. Even as a kid, the thought of playing in them triggered panic attacks. I guess it goes back to what we were talking about... You've got memories. But mine are buried deep."

"Oh, Maisie, I am so sorry," Sam murmured. "I didn't think."

His voice reverberated with softness, calming the tremors in me. Turning to me slowly, he drew me into his arms. My heart crashed inside my ribcage as I clung to him, but I had to keep talking.

"It's connected to that party. Fragments emerged in my nightmares and then the therapy like - like - a flutter of red ribbon. I never knew they were used to bind our hands but that was before the whisperings and those creepy hooded men..."

"Ssh," he kept muttering. "Try not to dwell."

Pulling apart, I stared wistfully back at him, and as our eyes met, I felt an immediate spark of attraction. Before I had a chance to gather my thoughts, he had dropped a kiss onto my lips; an action so swift, so spontaneous, it left me wondering if I had dreamt it.

"Would you like to go somewhere else?"

"West Dean Gardens isn't far," I said breathlessly, "if you fancy a wander, and I'll even treat you to a cream tea in the restaurant afterwards."

My heart could have burst. When Sam said *he would love a chance to get to know me better* I had never expected him to kiss me. Soaring up Goodwood Hill, we drove past the racecourse, absorbing the views. A wide green valley rolled into the distance, cloaked in swathes of pine forest.

I felt a rush of euphoria. Just a little further lay the hidden gem of West Dean Gardens.

"There it is," I gasped, pointing, "I don't know if your friend mentioned this place but you are in for a treat."

I adored West Dean Gardens, an impressive estate, which managed to look stunning in all seasons, and no sooner had we paid the entrance fee than I began to lead the way through.

A bridge arched over the brook into an area of open parkland, the trees widely scattered. Wandering a little further, I studied his face. There was something about his extraordinary male beauty that stirred me, filling me with an urge to probe into the one part of his story I was still curious about.

"So how did your life really pan out? Growing up in Scotland, I mean, with your father's family?"

I saw his eyes harden. "When I moved into Galbraith Castle, it didn't go down well with the rest of the clan, especially his wife, Mary. Her family owned a whisky distillery. High society snobs with a status to uphold, so in no way did they want to be discredited."

"But why would they be discredited?" I frowned. "You were his son."

"His illegitimate son. My mum was some high class hooker he had a fling with, remember?" A mirthless laugh tore out of him. "Yet here I was, their bastard son, living under the same roof."

"That hardly seems fair," I protested. "I thought he chose to take you in..."

"He did."

"Then what sort of life did you lead, and weren't you a bit lonely?"

"It was hell," he said flatly.

Mood blackening, he went on to describe the attic room he was moved into. Kept out of sight, he spent the next chapter of his childhood in near isolation, where few people even knew of his existence.

As I listened to his account, it froze the breath in my lungs. Home schooled alongside his half-brother, he was permitted no friends, nor had any contact with the outside world, the remainder of his childhood confined to the castle walls.

"Duncan had to watch over me. I looked up to him in a way, though he didn't much like me, and who could blame him? Poor bugger! Father was pretty harsh on him, looking back. He didn't exactly choose to be my minder."

"Oh, Sam, that doesn't sound like much fun," I whispered.

Head bowed, he flicked his fingers through his fringe. Glimpsing his scar again, I yearned to grab his hand, but resisted. It made more sense to keep walking.

"I'm okay about it, really... but can I tell you about this another day? It's not my favourite subject, and there's too much to cover in one session."

The air ran silent, leaving me helpless to wonder if there was anything I could say to comfort him. It took me back to Orchard Grange again, the heartbreaking stories we shared. Yet as we strolled across the lawn, I could not wait to show him the pergola; a spectacular 300ft Edwardian walkway paved in flagstone.

An air of mystery immersed us as we followed the path to the end; the climbing plants twisting around the pillars, a riot of wild roses fragrant against the feathery purple plumes of wisteria.

"Awesome," Sam said, a smile creeping its way onto his face at last. "The structure is incredible and it looks so old. What else is here?"

"I'll show you around the walled gardens if you like."

Following the path from the pergola, we passed through an iron gate. Artistically laid out in classic Victorian design, the high brick walls contained a variety of plants; orderly rows of vegetables and fruit bushes.

"Wow," Sam said, "some place this is. There was a huge great garden at Galbraith Castle, but formal. There's so much more they could have done with it."

Breaking off mid sentence, he turned to me with a grin.

"Do you ever fantasise about living anywhere else?"

"Who doesn't?" I chuckled. "I mean, Bognor's very friendly but it's a town, and I miss having a garden."

Catching his eye, I saw a twinkle of hope. A look that left me fantasising over whether today's encounter could be the start of something more meaningful.

Completing our circuit, we spent the final half hour in the restaurant where, true to my word, I ordered the cream tea for two.

The weather had been kind up until now but as we walked back to Sam's car, the sun slid behind a cloud, darkening the sky. I shivered as an icy breeze cut right through me. Time seemed to stand still and even the birds had stopped singing.

"Looks like rain," he commented. "Best we get on our way..."

On the homeward journey we spoke very little, which surprised me, but we seemed lost in our own private reveries.

Sam pulled up as close to my flat as possible and regardless of the veil of drizzle, he insisted on walking me to the door.

"Sorry to have to leave you," he said, "but I promised I'd call in on James."

"That's fine," I said with a smile. "It's been a great day and I'm looking forward to seeing you tomorrow. So shall I book a table at the George?"

"Sure," Sam nodded. He stroked my cheek with his index finger, his eyes warm. "It's been good to spend some quality time with you, Maisie, but is there any chance we can keep this to ourselves?"

I nodded without a second thought, wondering what Joe would make of our secret liaison. He was yet to grasp the truth of Sam's past, but it was a secret that would keep until tomorrow.

Chapter Fifty

Opening his eyes to a blaze of sunshine, Joe faced the day in high spirits. With Jess sashaying out of her en-suite in nothing but a skimpy towel, he felt his heart swell with love. Somehow he never imagined their relationship would advance beyond a fling, but the passion between them had soared - more so since spending weekends together - and he was stunned she had invited him to move in.

How could he possibly resist?

His only reservation was Maisie. He had never wanted to neglect her, despite her pledge 'she was cool about it.' In fact, when they'd met her last night to share a takeaway, she had been in a surprisingly good mood. The glow in her eyes had uplifted him, and today he wanted to hold on to that optimism.

Come midday though, his thoughts were elsewhere. Maisie collected them from Jess's apartment, as excited about seeing Sam as they were, and she seemed particularly keen to venture out into the countryside.

He caught her gaze in the rear view mirror. "Where are we going then?"

"A nice country pub with a beer garden," she enlightened him. "You'll love it! It's very remote but no one will know us there, and hopefully we can talk."

She didn't need to say more. Mentally running through the police reports, he had tied his mind up in knots wondering what to say to Sam. But all the while they were driving, he drank in the landscape, a patchwork of greens and browns.

Then at last she slowed down, the road twisting sharply where a traditional looking pub awaited them. Joe smiled, drinking in the exterior, while Maisie squeezed her car into a parking space.

"Do you think he's here yet?" he said.

She glanced around, guiding them into the garden to find a picnic bench.

But as if in answer to his question, it wasn't long before a shadow fell across their table, prompting him to look up.

"Well, talk of the devil," he grinned, squeezing Jess's hand.

"Sam!" Maisie gasped.

She looked ecstatic, he thought, unable to tear his eyes away as Sam strolled over to embrace her. Sam briefly smiled at Jess before turning his attention to Joe. Grasping him by the hand, he observed him fondly, his frame blocking out the sunlight.

"How are you doing, mate?"

"Good, thanks," Joe nodded. "Now what d'you want to drink?"

"Let me get the first round," he insisted.

"I'll come with you," Maisie offered. "I was on my way to the bar anyway, to let them know we've arrived."

By the time they returned, the tables were filling up fast, leaving Joe thankful she had booked one. Gazing across the beer garden, he admired the flint wall surrounding it, the lawn fully enclosed with neatly trimmed bushes and overflowing flower pots. Maisie had chosen well.

"I've brought menus," she piped up. "It might be an idea to order soon, it's getting busy in there..."

As her words trailed off, he could not help but notice the flush in her cheeks. Sam lowered their pints to the table then plonked himself opposite, as slick and confident as he'd appeared on their first meeting. Slipping off his suede jacket, he slung it over the bench and took a tentative sip of his pint.

"Good brew," he commented with a nod in Joe's direction. "Now tell me what you've been up to since I saw you last."

As if to break the ice, the conversation revolved around work. Eyes glazing over, Joe had little to add, thinking how mundane his supermarket job must seem next to their high-status careers... until eventually the topic fizzled out. *Thank God.*

Next they ordered lunch.

Everyone chose a traditional Sunday roast, apart from Maisie who fancied scampi and chips. But all the while he had been observing Sam's face, his mind burned with questions, and he was no longer in the mood for small talk.

"Well, here we are again," he said, tapping glasses, "three kids from a care home, not to forget the lovely Jess of course, and a story finally being investigated. There's just one little snag though. The bastard responsible ain't been caught yet, so where do we go from here?" His eyes pierced into Sam's. "Your memories seem sharp, looking back. Sharper than mine. But don't you wonder why none of this was reported before? 'Cos that's what really bothers me."

Sam's brown eyes flickered in Jess's direction.

"Don't worry, I ain't told her nothing sensitive, but we couldn't help wondering why those homes closed down."

"I thought I-I explained," Sam faltered, "I told the authorities everything but that was before my father took me away. What else do you want to know?"

"Dunno really. We were friends, weren't we? I thought we were inseparable. We might have only known each other a few months, Sam, but we had a hell of a lot of history. You'd think we might have talked a bit more about it."

Sam's face tightened. "What is it, Joe, you think my memories are selective? That I don't remember Mortimer? Great fat git and his bully boys. Or do you want me to go back further, relive the gritty details of when you found me in the loos having my head shoved down the toilet? I was the new boy, Jess, a sad little wimp the others wanted to have some fun with, and I don't know if he told you this, but you may as well hear it from the horse's mouth. Joe charged to the rescue. Sorted those yobs out, before they drowned me in shit."

Jess clamped her hand over her lips in horror. "Ugh, that's disgusting!"

"He's right though," Joe sighed. "That did happen and I've never mentioned it to anyone. I didn't wanna embarrass you..."

"It's okay, I get it," Sam tried to pacify him, "but you still want to check me out. You've been looking at the police reports and chewing over my story."

"Yeah," Joe mumbled, "'cos something don't add up."

The stream of conversation was cut short when the food turned up a little earlier than expected. Huge plates rested in front of them, generously layered with succulent roast chicken, crispy potatoes glistening golden brown in a pool of dark gravy and crowned with a giant Yorkshire pudding. Maisie bit into a piece of scampi. A smile touched her lips as she savoured it before her eyes lifted to meet Sam's.

"I think what Joe's dying to know is why the homes were never investigated, especially after those parties. Even the police said they sounded dodgy, and this was before you gave your statement."

"I thought you told your social worker," Joe added in a hushed tone, "but can you remember how she reacted?"

"We need to know, Sam."

Joe braced himself, wary of Sam's darkening glare.

"Okay," he relented. "She sat me down with a mug of hot chocolate and asked if I was hurt in any way, except I wasn't... just traumatised. I genuinely thought I could trust her, so I tried to describe what happened."

"And did she believe you?" Joe said, cynically.

"Looking back, I'm not so sure. She was shocked, obviously. What social worker wouldn't be? I mean how could someone duty-bound to protect kids face up to the scale of abuse going on in that place?"

"Yet none of it was reported," Maisie pressed. "Sam, if anyone in our department had been informed of something like this, they'd act immediately."

He shook his head in dismay. "Maisie, she swore she'd look into it, but the day my father stepped in, I had no control over the outcome. It was left in the hands of the authorities. I was eleven. What possible power did I have?"

Joe raised his eyebrows, hit with a sudden insight. "Yeah, well talking of power, what about your father? What did he do? I mean, he was a judge, wasn't he? You even suggested he sent a patrol out on the night of the party. That being the case, surely he could have pulled a few strings. So what went wrong and why the fuck wasn't Mortimer prosecuted?"

Forking up his potatoes, Sam was beginning to look flustered. "I don't know, Joe," he said through gritted teeth. "It's probably a bit late to ask now."

"Why? You're his son. Don't you think you've got a right to know?"

"Trouble is, Joe, you've got no idea what sort bloke he was, never mind the nightmare growing up in his castle. No one does, apart from me and my half-brother, Duncan."

"Duncan," Maisie echoed. Her eyes flashed in alarm, suggesting she knew more than she was letting on. "I-I'm guessing he was older than you?"

"Yes," Sam sighed. "Duncan, who was assigned to look after me. Duncan, whose duty it was to keep me hidden in an attic room. This is the story I never got round to telling you in London, but for the benefit of the investigation, I'll tell you now."

"Go on then," Joe urged. "Let's hear about Duncan."

Sam released another sigh. "Poor sod was as scared of my father as I was. The old man had a cruel streak, you know, but I couldn't help thinking it was worse for Duncan. He was his real son, his heir, not like me, the annoying little screwed-up half-brother he had to watch over, 'cos if anything went tits up, Duncan took the flack."

"Well, here's your chance to explain," Joe kept prompting him.

"Yeah, right," he muttered under his breath. "I'll explain what life was like. How about all the staring out of the window at the garden, wishing I could go out? I wanted to walk in the snow, taste the fresh air, so on one occasion I sneaked out. Shame some bloody friend of his mum had to turn up. All she did was ask about 'the little blonde boy' playing in the snow..." His lips betrayed a tremor. "Father went berserk. Grabbed Duncan by the throat and banged his head against the wall until he begged him to stop. The man was a psycho. I spent the next years tiptoeing around on egg shells, trying to avoid that shit, and I'm sorry if it sounds cowardly, but I didn't have the guts to challenge him."

"That's terrible," Maisie simpered, "and I realise it was hard, but did you ever ask him if the police followed up your story?"

"Mmm," Sam nodded through a mouthful of potato, "except I never got a straight answer. He told me to forget all about it. *Pretend it was a bad dream, Sam, you are quite safe here...*"

"God," Maisie shivered, "you said he was a control freak but to keep you isolated... even if he did it to protect you, it doesn't excuse him from keeping quiet. Had it been my foster parents, they would be outraged!"

"Knowing what I know now about him," Sam said, "I don't suppose he gave a shit."

223

"Maybe not, but this is important. Don't you think the police will want to question him anyway? They didn't have much joy with your social worker."

Sam froze, his features rigid.

"Stop," he mumbled, "please. I don't want to talk about that bastard any more, and if the police decide to speak to him, then I say bring it on!"

Jess swallowed visibly, reaching for her wine glass. Her plate was not quite empty, but as the atmosphere around the table blackened, she placed her cutlery aside.

"I need another drink," she said. "Anyone else fancy one?"

"Sorry," Sam murmured. "I didn't mean to dampen the mood."

"It's okay," Joe said. "We're the ones who want answers..." His eyes followed Jess as she strolled to the rear doors. Aware that she was allowing them some privacy, he stayed rooted to the bench. "I'll go and help her in a sec, but let's get this discussion wound up and then maybe we can relax."

"I agree," Maisie whispered. "So come on, Sam, what are we going to do about the investigation? Or should I say *lack of it*. If you told your social worker and nothing was done, that's a huge failing on the system."

Sam leaned forward, his features pressed into a frown. "I'm just wondering... would it help if I spoke to her myself?"

"I-I'm not sure that's wise," Maisie faltered.

"No," Joe reflected. "The police might take a dim view of that, and there's enough secrecy surrounding that woman."

"A friend of mine was threatened," she added, "Sarah. The woman I approached to try and find you. She's an adoption reunion counsellor."

The frown on Sam's face deepened. "When did this happen?"

"It doesn't matter," Joe said. "If you've read the police report, you must know how cagey your social worker's being, though I'm fucked if I understand why. What exactly is she hiding?"

Sam rubbed his throat, his other hand tight around his beer glass. "I have no idea, so maybe I should ask her. And if you're worried about the police, then let me contact DI Fitzpatrick. I could ask him to arrange another interview, at the police station again if it's easier."

Chapter Fifty-One

A brief interlude followed as Joe slipped away to give Jess a hand, leaving me face to face with Sam.

From the instant he had appeared in the garden though, it had been difficult to take my eyes off him. An invisible affection loomed. I just didn't want the others to see it. Even in the bar, I felt that same tug of magnetism. A scent of fresh air clung to him, a hint of dew and green leaves. It brought back our trip from yesterday, but in the absence of the others, only now could I take a proper hard look at him.

"Are you okay?" I heard myself whispering.

His complexion seemed ashen, compared to the glow he exuded earlier.

"Fine," he said with a tight smile, "and I know we've got a lot to talk about but it can be painful at times... I hope you understand."

The light squeeze of his fingers reassured me, the resonance of our discussion lingering. Sam didn't like talking about his childhood, and despite his outer boldness, I sensed a tortured soul.

"Here you go," Joe said, lowering another half pint in front of him, "and we've settled our half of the food bill."

The afternoon continued in a bubble of light-hearted banter, the sun on my skin warm. We basked in the tranquillity of the garden, which was no longer so busy now the lunchtime rush had passed. At first Sam looked preoccupied, but in the light of our discussion, seemed eager to contact DI Fitzpatrick. For several minutes, his fingers moved deftly over the keypad as he typed out a message on his i-Phone.

"There," he said. "I've sent him an email with the gist of my request. Hopefully he'll see it first thing tomorrow."

On the other side of the bench, meanwhile, and halfway through a second glass of wine, Jess was turning ever more animated. Sliding her hands around Joe's narrow waist, she snuggled up close for a kiss. I watched in a dream, stirred by such intimacy, wondering what it must feel like to be so in love.

"Are they always like this?" Sam sniggered. "Hey, get a room, you two!"

I caught the gleam in his eye, and was happy to see him smiling again.

Joe on the other hand, looked up warily.

"Excuse me!" Jess giggled. "Drinking at lunchtime always makes me flirty, and it's not as if I haven't offered. When are you going to accept my invitation, Joe?"

"About moving in?" he muttered. "You know I'd love to, baby..."

"So what's stopping you?" Sam interrupted.

As Joe and I exchanged glances, I didn't miss that flash.

Was he having reservations?

He reminded me of a rabbit caught in headlights.

"Nothing," he faltered, "I'm just worried about you, Maisie. I've loved lodging at your place but it's time I moved on. You've put up with me for long enough."

I gulped, hit with a sense of finality. "But I've enjoyed having you."

"There's Connor to consider, too," he pressed. "Wasn't it just the other day you were talking to Sarah about offering more respite care?"

"You're right," I said wistfully, "but don't go thinking I won't miss you."

"Maisie, if you ever need a handyman, you've got my number," he said with a wink.

"That's not what I meant," I snapped. "It'll be strange coming home to an empty flat. Just promise me we can stay friends..."

"Sorry, am I missing something?" Sam broke in. "Who's Connor?"

I stiffened as thoughts of Sarah shot through my mind. "This is an arrangement with my friend, the one I was telling you about..." My voice lowered to a whisper. "Connor is her teenage foster son. He suffers from Asperger's. But with all the pressure she's been under lately, especially the threats, I agreed to look after him for the occasional weekend. It's just to give her a break."

A little later in the ladies, Jess managed to corner me.

"Hey, Maisie," she whispered. "What's up? You're not upset, are you?"

"No, of course not," I said, a smile pinging onto my face. "I'm happy for you both, especially Joe. He deserves something good in his life after what he's been through, but what about you? Is this what you want?"

"Yes," she sighed, "and I know what you're thinking. It will never last."

I felt the breath pour from my lungs, and considered my next words carefully. "Just be nice to him, Jess. He's led a very hard life, compared to what you're used to, I mean he swears and he smokes. Don't forget he was homeless before this."

"Sure," she smiled, "but he's told me he wants to give up smoking and try vaping. Not that it matters. Joe is so adorable, I can't help falling in love with him. He makes me feel special in a way that no other man has, which reminds me of something else I wanted to say to you..."

"Go on," I frowned.

Lifting her blonde head, her eyes developed a shrewd look. "Have you ever thought about seeing Sam a bit more? I reckon he really likes you."

Her words ignited a glow in some hidden corner of my heart. "Really?"

"Call it female intuition," she murmured, "but do you think I haven't noticed the way he looks at you? God, Maisie, what's the matter with you? He's gorgeous. For goodness sake snap him up before someone else does."

I said nothing more, my mind spinning in circles.

Returning to the beer garden, the crowds had all but vanished, the pub becoming emptier by the second. But looking at the men, engrossed in conversation, there was something in Joe's expression that jolted me - an unmistakable flicker of sympathy that suggested they might have been talking about me.

"We were just saying we might as well make a move," he announced.

Illuminated in the sun's rays, Sam threw a glittering smile in my direction. I had always adored Joe for his character, yet Sam radiated an aura all of his own. I felt another wave of excitement, thinking about what Jess had said.

Could Sam be the one?

The mere hint of a romance brought a glow to my cheeks.

"Is it okay if I follow you back to Bognor, then?" he proposed, out of the blue. "I'd love to take a look at the sea..."

"So let's go back to my flat," Jess smiled, catching my eye again. "It's a gorgeous day. We can sit outside on the balcony if you like and enjoy the sea views."

******

Dozing lightly next day, I was drifting on a cloud of pleasant memories, dimly aware of the world awakening around me. Joe had left for work already, so it was doubtful I would see him again until teatime. Given his imminent move to Jess's flat, our reunion had ended on a high note. Relaxing on her balcony, it was easy to forget our troubles, the late afternoon sun hazy, the swish of waves from the beach blending harmoniously with the cry of gulls wheeling in the sky.

Not quite awake, I saw the first gleam of daylight creep around the edge of my curtains.

Yet somewhere under this pleasurable resonance echoed the incessant ring of my landline.

I sat bolt upright.

Shaken from my reverie, I stumbled out of bed to the lounge, but didn't quite make it before the answering machine kicked in.

"Maisie! Have you checked your email?" Sam's voice barked from the speaker. "Read the report from DI Fitzpatrick and ring me as soon as you can."

A chill shuddered from my neck to the base of my spine, the temptation to pick up overwhelming. But struck with a sense that this was unlikely to be good news, I backed away from the phone to switch my laptop on.

The urgency in Sam's voice had shocked me, and sure enough, the first item I saw in my inbox was a message from the police marked CONFIDENTIAL.

I read it again and again until the words blurred into squiggles. No matter how hard I tried to absorb the information, though, I could barely take it in.

'Yvonne Draper, Sam's former social worker, has been found dead in her back garden. Her husband alerted the police at around 6pm yesterday evening after she wandered outside but failed to return...'

I squeezed my eyes shut, fingertips pressed against my temples. A band of pain spread across my forehead, while at the forefront of my mind hung the threads of the conversation we had shared only yesterday.

Sam had been so keen to text DI Fitzpatrick with a view to arranging an interview. I had been sat in the pub garden, watching him - and convinced no further action would be taken on a Sunday, I hadn't given it any more thought.

But what if I was wrong about the police?

Was it possible they had been in contact but our enemies had got to her first?

With shaking hands, I clumsily dialled Sam's mobile.

"I can't believe this," I spluttered. "What the hell is going on?"

"I wish I knew," he said, a choke in his voice, "and before you ask, I spoke to DI Fitzpatrick. He got my message yesterday and agreed to speak to her but regrettably, it's too late now..."

I listened in horrified silence as he relayed the conversation. The story of Yvonne's unexplained death was scheduled to appear on Sussex News tonight but early speculation was pointing in the direction of suicide.

According to her husband she was depressed, suffering terrible guilt over something that had happened in the past. Furthermore, she had been displaying signs of anxiety, paranoia even, convinced her deeds were about to catch up with her.

"They haven't overruled the possibility of murder," he added, darkly. "He found her face down in the garden pond. Drowned. She might have slipped and hit her head on a rock, but it all sounds very suspect doesn't it?"

"Yes," I whispered, "especially after what we were talking about. I wonder if Joe was right though, that maybe she was hiding something."

"Her husband was cross-examined but they've released him, so shaken up he's under medical supervision. Now the police want to question me. I'm worried they're thinking I had something to do with it, but obviously that's not possible. I was with you guys all afternoon, and we went to Jess's apartment... but is there any chance you'll vouch for me?"

"You know I will! But why are they questioning you? There's only one possible person behind this and we both know who that is."

"What are you saying, Maisie?"

"Mortimer." The name fell from my lips with a shiver. "Whatever your social worker knew would have backed up your own story. So how do you imagine the police are going to handle our case now?"

Chapter Fifty-Two

While Maisie spent the afternoon fretting over the devastating news, Joe kept himself busy. *Anything to take his mind off it.* Cleaning, tidying, whilst gathering a few possessions together, he was going to miss the ambience of her home. But within a couple of days, he would be relocating to Jess's apartment, and he distracted himself by thinking about what to cook tonight to make their evening extra special.

Stepping out of the shower later, he rubbed the steam off the mirror. His reflection stared back through swirls of condensation, and pausing to take a look at himself, he wondered what Jess saw in him. His skin looked clear, stretched tautly over sharp cheek bones, his unruly dark hair in need of a cut. Jess insisted she liked it. Yet in the shadow of Sam's radiance, he saw the same *ugly little tearaway* Mortimer had alluded to. His misshapen nose bulged on one side, unsightly as ever. Even though Maisie said *she adored his smile*, his teeth were still chipped and uneven.

Backing away from the mirror, he tried hard not to cave in to such negative thoughts. It brought his mind back to Maisie, whose endeavours to rebuild his self-esteem had been the most precious gift a man could ask for.

So what could he offer in return?

Thirty minutes later, he heard her key turning in the door.

"What are you cooking? It smells delicious..." Her head appeared around the kitchen partition, a smile lifting her lips.

"I'm attempting one of your foster mum's recipes," he quipped, "the one you were drooling over on Pinterest."

She breathed in deeply, savouring the aroma; cod fillets, drizzled in lemon juice, olive oil and rosemary. After wrapping them carefully in parma ham slices, he had left them on the middle oven shelf to bake.

As daytime drifted into evening, though, they could no longer avoid the inevitable. Joe joined her in the lounge where the first thing she did was switch the TV on.

The 6:00 news was imminent but despite the uplifting mood he had created, there was no mistaking the darkness filling the atmosphere.

'Police are investigating the unexplained death of Yvonne Draper, discovered drowned in her back garden on Sunday evening...'

A photo of the deceased flashed briefly before the camera honed in on her house in East Grinstead. Maisie's eyes widened. Tucked in a secluded cul-de-sac, the tangle of untamed shrubs and ivy suggested an air of neglect compared to its neighbours. Any passer-by might even imagine it was abandoned, thought Joe. These people clearly kept themselves to themselves.

"It's the house Sarah visited," she said.

'Her death has raised suspicion. Police cannot dismiss the possibility this may be connected to a wider investigation into historic child abuse that took place in a number of children's homes in the mid-nineties...'

"Shit," Joe muttered under his breath, "she must have been one of the last people to hear Sam's story before he was dragged up to Scotland."

He felt a shiver run deep inside his body. In the aftermath of Sam's statement, it was obvious the police would question her, but what could have gone so wrong? According to Maisie, all she had confessed to Sarah was *someone came forward to look after him*. Yet even Sarah spoke of a deep underlying fear in the woman.

With his thoughts bouncing crazily, the news commentary droned on in the background, until a statement from one of the officers seized his attention.

'It has since emerged that the deceased harboured crucial evidence linked to a case being examined by officers of the Metropolitan Police. A national enquiry was launched in April. Mrs Draper, who had worked as a social worker during the years relevant to the investigation, was to be questioned over a series of allegations made by a witness, aged eleven, at the time the abuse took place...'

"Sam," they gulped in unison.

'A verdict of accidental death has been recorded, but until we obtain further evidence, Sussex police urge anyone who may have witnessed suspicious activity in the area to contact them as soon as possible.'

"Whatever secrets she knew she'll take to the grave," Maisie shuddered.

"Bit of a fucking coincidence though, isn't it?" Joe snapped. "We were only talking about this in the pub yesterday."

"I know, but we were outside," she pacified him, "whispering among ourselves. No one was paying attention and I only saw families on those other tables."

"What about Sam, then?" he added. "What time did he text the old bill?"

"Not long after we finished lunch. You bought him another beer. Yvonne was found dead around six, so how could anyone have known?"

"Apart from Sam," Joe muttered. He spread his hands mid-air. "I dunno, but I can't help thinking someone was out to put the gag on her. She was a vital witness..."

"Or is it possible she couldn't bear the thought of facing Sam?" Maisie butted in. "I mean, all things considered, she let him down badly! I read something in the report about guilt... she was anxious and getting paranoid."

Joe sighed. His imagination raced with a hundred different scenarios, but the timing could not be worse.

"Talk to Sam, then," he levelled at her. "Get his version of events. You seem to be getting on pretty well."

Maisie froze as an awkwardness loomed between them. He could no longer ignore the tension gathering but with all conversation suspended for now, it was time to rescue his fish from the oven.

"Is there something going on between you two?" he challenged her over dinner.

Maisie took a sip of wine. "What makes you say that?"

"Aw, come on, Maisie, don't go all coy on me. We're mates aren't we? I thought we could tell each other anything."

"I'm not sure really," she sighed. "Ever since our meeting in London my head's been all over the place. Sam was such a sweet boy and it traumatised me when he went missing. I talked about him in therapy but we're adults now. Everything feels different."

"Yeah," Joe nodded. "I get that. Though I definitely caught some vibe between you two on Sunday, and Jess picked up on it too. The little smiles, the hand touching... she's very good at reading signals."

"I know," Maisie nodded, meeting his eye at last. "So she said, except I'm not sure how to handle it. There's nothing *going on*, apart from the investigation, but if anything is meant to happen, it will."

"But would you like it to?" Joe kept probing. "Sam worshipped you when we were kids and I doubt if anything's changed."

Her eyes glittered in the candlelight as they clung to his stare. "I can't answer that right now... but what about you and Jess? I mean living together!"

"You wonder what she sees in me?" he joked.

"That's not what I meant."

Joe grinned. *So she'd managed to turn the conversation around to him again but what was her problem?* If she didn't feel comfortable pouring her heart out, he wasn't going to push it. She allowed him a moment to consider his own feelings.

"As far as Jess is concerned, me moving in is the obvious next stage in her book. The last couple of weekends have been great, so I might as well give it a go."

"But do you love her?" she blurted.

"Yeah," he said in earnest. "Course I love her. What man wouldn't? She's pretty, she's sexy and seems to really care about me. I mean, look at this vaping malarkey she's got me into!" Delving into his pocket, he extracted a stainless steel vaporiser Jess had treated him to. "And all 'cos I mentioned giving up smoking..." He let out a sigh, stroking it in his hands. "Fact is, Jess and I are two very insecure people who get on well. Don't forget she's had some shit relationships."

"I know," Maisie nodded, "you both deserve some happiness and I said the same to her... but don't go thinking she isn't lucky, too." Glancing at her empty plate, the glow in her eyes intensified. "That meal was yum! I really am going to miss you, Joe, and I hope you'll pop round for a cuppa occasionally."

"I'd be honoured," he chuckled and with those words, he felt a wrench in his heart. "I know we've spent most of our lives apart, but that doesn't change the fact that you're my best friend, Maisie, and you always will be."

******

I will never know how I managed to survive the rest of that week. The notion of Joe moving out hung darkly on the precipice, but it wasn't until he was gone that the reality hit me like a sledgehammer. My flat felt huge, the silence crushing, and much as I made light of his smoking and swearing, the absence of his company tore a hole in my life.

Sam, in the meantime, had contacted me twice since Yvonne's death, initially to describe his police interview. His mood swung from overwhelming affection one minute, to unbearable remorse the next. Yet despite being exonerated of any blame, he could not suppress his belief that she lived in fear of the investigation after his statement, the courts and media hounding her.

Perhaps her unaccountable death really was suicide.

Except it shrouded our case in yet another layer of mystery.

For how could we be sure it wasn't Mortimer who'd sealed her fate?

Whatever secrets she guarded would never see the light of day now, and as for Sam... I wished I could have done more to console him, the guilt gnawing at him like a cancer. Even if one accepted the possibility of foul-play, how could our enemies have acted so swiftly? Hanging on the phone, I hankered for some sign. Some hint he wanted to see me again and that maybe we could hook up...

Yet it never came, leaving my world bleaker than ever.

Approaching my home two days later, I couldn't imagine things getting any worse. My footsteps dragged. Hands unsteady, I let myself in but in a moment I knew I was not alone. As Paula's shadow loomed at the top of the stairs, I sensed an underlying wave of hostility. Bracing myself, I couldn't help wondering if she had been waiting for me. For every step thudded with menacing intent as she marched down the stairs with her daughter in tow.

Her eyes flickered over me, narrow with suspicion.

"What is it, Paula?" I asked, my voice sapped of strength.

"I wanna know who that weird kid was," she snapped. "The one who was hanging round 'ere the other week."

"His name is Connor," I informed her quietly, "and he is not weird. He's the foster son of one of my closest friends. Why, is there a problem?"

"Got my Jade 'ere to think about, 'aven't I?" she kept sniping. "Don't ya think you should have told me? Saw him in the garden, didn't we, love, 'eadphones on, just staring up at our window..."

My eyes fell to Jade, a subdued child whose doe eyes glanced up emptily as she clung to her mother's legs.

"I asked him what 'e was doing out there but 'e didn't say nothing... Just kept staring and staring. You sure he ain't some psycho?"

Barbs of irritation pricked me but I had to keep my cool.

"Would it help if I told you he's autistic? Kids like Connor are poor at reading signals and maybe he thought you were angry. They tend to shut down when they feel threatened, but I assure you he's completely harmless."

At last the woman appeared to deflate slightly, and ruffling her daughter's hair, drew back a step. I held her gaze, feeling the mood lighten.

"Yeah, well, you still should have told me," she sniffed.

"Yes, maybe I should," I conceded, "but at least you know now, because he might be staying again in a couple of weeks' time."

"Really?" she muttered, "well in that case I got something else to tell ya. D'you remember 'im upstairs?" Her thumb jabbed towards the stairs.

"Mr Lacey. What about him?"

Yet again her eyes narrowed. "He's coming back. Some occupational therapy lot came round to check his flat over..."

Frozen in the hallway, only now did I clam up, a lump forming in my throat. It seemed like an eternity since Joe had reported the ambulance outside, but with everything else unravelling, I had hardly given it any thought.

"You don't look too pleased," Paula smirked. "Can't say I am neither."

I tried to swallow but the lump wouldn't shift.

"Best keep a close eye on that lad you mentioned," she kept taunting, "specially with creepy old dick heads like 'im hanging around."

"Right, well, thanks for letting me know," I said before shutting myself in my flat.

Chapter Fifty-Three

Gazing up in my innocence, I absorbed the darkness I was immersed in, oblivious to its hidden dangers. The bare branches of trees hovered above, a network of black capillaries. The chill of night bit into me, my ribbon flapping in the breeze. But only as I tried to move, did the horror strike me. Trapped in the forest, I started to shiver, and that was when I heard them...

Closer they came, an army of whispers.

Resonating in rhythm, the tone changed. Louder, deeper, it came from the trees, a chorus that turned gradually into chants. I felt another tug of resistance, the cool red satin cutting into me. But as my head twisted sideways, my breath was cut short. Their torches splintered the darkness, a ring of hooded figures illuminated.

Then something changed, a face I had never before spotted.

"Sam?"

Lingering outside the circle, there was just enough light to unmask his tiny face, his eyes stretched wide in terror. I tried to scream, desperate to warn him.

"Run! Whatever you do, get away from them!"

Too late... He was gone before I had a chance to convey my warning, those creepy robed figures converging on him before he was swallowed into the shadows.

"Mandy!" I spluttered over the phone. "Sorry to call like this, but is there any chance I could come home and live with you again? I can't stand it here!"

"Maisie, sweetheart, calm down. Just tell me what's the matter..."

Her voice sent soothing waves over me, but it would take more than a few kind words from my foster mother to thaw the ice in my veins.

"It happened again," I gulped. "I had one of my horrible nightmares."

Pathetic though it sounded, how much of this could I attribute to Joe's absence? There was no denying that from the day he moved in, to the wrench of his departure, I hadn't endured a single one of those dreams.

Once again, though, my world had been flipped upside down, my old anxieties resurfacing. I thought I had come so far but strolling back to an empty flat, even the familiar white bulk of that Nissan spooked me. Joe was gone, Mr Lacey was back and I was stuck in the same negative feedback loop as before.

"I'm so anxious now," I kept rambling. "I can't do this anymore, living on my own, especially after the death of Sam's social worker. The investigation is ongoing and without Joe around, I feel vulnerable."

"I know, I saw it on the news," Mandy sighed. "Just terrible! And wasn't Sam the boy at the heart of all this, the one who disappeared?"

"Yes!" I replied. "He lives in London now, in fact I'd love you to meet him... if I was living in Swanley it would be even easier."

Before I knew it, I was telling her about our blissful excursion around Sussex; a day we spent getting to know each other.

Mandy reacted with a chuckle. "Sounds promising. So what's he like, this Sam? You haven't really said much."

"Blonde, handsome, stylish," I mused. "He was adorable as a boy and his looks have improved with age."

Yes, I cherished his unusual beauty, his high forehead, his shapely mouth.

"Trouble is, he hasn't said anything about wanting to see me again."

"Then maybe he's waiting for you to make the next move," she advised. "Get in touch! Ask him if he's free at the weekend. You're bound to be lonely now Joe is gone, so what have you got to lose?"

"Are you sure that won't seem pushy?" I faltered. "I-I mean, what excuse am I going to use?"

"Oh Maisie," she sighed. "I wish you had a little more confidence. Why not invite him round for a meal? Or if you don't feel comfortable on your own with him, suggest a restaurant. Just phone him! Even if you stay friends, it's better than moping around on your own, feeling sorry for yourself."

******

Knocking off work on Friday, I could not ignore the anticipation bubbling inside me at the thought of seeing Sam again. True to my word, I had called him. Heard the pleasure tucked into his voice when he agreed to meet me.

What I hadn't considered, however, was that he might set off early to beat the London rush hour traffic. It left me no time to change, and the instant I spotted that tell-tale kingfisher blue gleam outside, I realised it was too late.

With no other choice than to welcome him, I hesitantly opened the door.

Inching back and forth to manoeuvre his Audi into what little space remained, his face twisted with the effort of parking.

"Sam!" I called out, wandering across the pavement. "Would it help if I nudged my car up a bit?"

Turning his head sharply, he snapped on a smile, and leaving his car parked lopsidedly for the moment, jumped out to greet me. He too looked as if he had only just left work, the charcoal jacket worn over his polo neck a little too tailored to be casual.

"Hi, Maisie," he said. His eyes wandered over me from my face to my toes. "You look lovely."

My heart swelled with the compliment, drawing a smile to my lips.

"Thanks," I muttered and suddenly my Laura Ashley dress seemed less formal. Spun in a neat daisy cotton print with buttons running down the front, it moulded itself to my figure nicely.

Before I had a chance to say another word, though, a shadow flickered in the doorway. I glanced around. Felt the breath freeze in my throat as the recognition of our observer hit home.

Richard Lacey.

There was a glint in his eye as he smirked at me.

"Well, if it isn't Maisie Bell... How are you, my dear? I see you have a visitor, and I expect my car is in the way."

Sam frowned, as perplexed I was. Mr Lacey looked no different; the same swept back tawny hair and neat beard. Emaciated as ever, his scrawny neck was looped with a familiar silk cravat, his brocade waistcoat better suited to a museum.

"D-don't worry about it," I stammered. "I expect we'll go out later... but how are you? I gather you've been in hospital."

"That's right. Some routine surgery, followed by a nice period of convalescence, but I'm a lot better than I was, thank you." He narrowed his eyes before his gaze rested on Sam. "And who might you be?"

Shocked by such a direct approach, I turned to him.

Yet he exhibited no shyness and faced him boldly. "Sam McFadden. An estate agent from London. But Maisie and I know each other from way back."

"Well, it's very nice to meet you, Sam," drawled Richard Lacey, and without hesitation, stepped onto the pavement, his hand reaching out like a claw.

As both men shook hands, I felt the tension in the air lift. Then with no further argument, Richard obligingly moved his vehicle a few feet.

How strange to see such courtesy.

Thanking him politely, I was on the verge of leading Sam into my flat, but it seemed Richard Lacey had a few more words to say.

"Now make sure you treat her like a gentleman. I haven't known her for very long, but long enough to say she is a very sophisticated young lady."

I felt a blush creep to my cheeks. Sam, on the hand, gave a nod.

"She is indeed," he smiled, clasping both my hands, "and I shall wine you and dine you somewhere nice..."

After briefly stopping in my flat for a coffee, I tingled with the praise he showered my home with. The bookcase and dresser finished in pine were among my finer possessions, my sofa a little worn, though aptly disguised with a velvet throw and an array of jewel bright cushions.

Sam asked if I knew any restaurants within walking distance. So I tentatively suggested Sen Tapas, a stone's throw away from where Hannah was based.

"I love tapas," he enthused and hooking his arm through mine, we set off.

No sooner had we started walking, though, than he asked me how I was coping. I couldn't avoid mentioning my nightmare. His appearance at the end was a chilling twist and hard as I tried to fight it, the notion of Mortimer's evil lingered, the untimely death of Yvonne Draper fated to resurrect it.

Footsteps slowing, I felt the warmth of his palm run down my back.

"I wish I knew what to say," he sighed, "it was the last thing I expected. Maybe we should avoid the subject of the investigation for one night."

Once hidden inside the busy restaurant, Sam gazed at our surroundings in awe. But who couldn't fall in love with this place, the rich Mediterranean colours warming the walls, an overhead lantern casting a golden pool over our table?

He slipped off his jacket and slowly we began to unwind.

"Well, this is nice," he smiled, "just the two of us. Shall we order?"

A delicious smell of garlic and herbs wafted in the air, teasing our appetites, although neither of us felt like eating much. Picking over the menu, we agreed on a mixture of tapas dishes; deep fried calamari rings, sauteed chicken and chorizo with patatas bravas and a tortilla.

I sipped my wine, a fruity red, and with the alcohol loosening my inhibitions, I was definitely in the mood for talking now. Sam seemed eager to know about my upbringing, wondering what it felt like to be fostered. So without hesitation, I began telling him about Swanley, the home I had grown up in, not to forget the wonderful couple who had raised me.

"Mandy and Stewart are such kind people, both teachers, and they couldn't have done more to welcome me. This is where I developed a love of gardens and country walks. In fact, they'd love to meet you..."

Sam raised his eyebrows, fork suspended. "You told them about me?"

"Of course," I breathed. "I don't keep any secrets from them, and while we're on the topic, I asked Mandy if I could move back home."

"But what about your work?" he responded gently. "Didn't you say they lived in Swanley?"

"I don't care," I shrugged. "Living on my own in Bognor doesn't feel safe now."

Reaching across the table, his hand folded over my own. "In that case, have you thought about talking to that policeman friend of yours? There must be some protection they can offer you."

Holding his gaze, I saw nothing but concern, and was relieved to see he understood my fragility.

As we picked at our tapas dishes, I could feel my mood lifting. Sam ordered another glass of red for me, but after sinking a half pint of San Miguel, he switched to soft drinks. The restaurant had become busier in the last hour, which didn't bother me in the slightest. Feeling less self-conscious, I remembered what Mandy said; that even if we stayed friends, it was preferable to struggling through life alone.

Once the bill was settled, I suggested sharing a taxi back, but Sam seemed to prefer walking.

"It's so quiet," he commented. "If this was London, the streets would be heaving on a Friday night..."

His words drew a frown, unleashing a different stream of thoughts.

"How long have you lived in London?" I asked, thinking he had spoken so little about himself tonight.

"Oh God, let me think," he pondered. "At least fifteen years, but don't forget I lived in London before the era of Orchard Grange."

"Of course," I whispered, his personal memories springing back to me. "I've never forgotten the stuff you told us about your mum."

"I-I loved her very much."

With his voice turning husky, I almost wished I hadn't reminded him.

"She was the centre of my universe once, but it all seems like a dream now. Those final years in Scotland nearly broke me. Thank God I flew the nest!" Head down, he inhaled a shuddering breath. "I reckon Duncan would have murdered me if I'd hung around much longer. So as soon as I was old enough to make my own way in life, I just went for it."

"Oh, Sam," I whispered. "I never meant to dredge up your past again."

"Don't be," he sighed. "It needs saying and you're a good listener. Maybe I should get it off my chest. Do you want to know what the absolute tipping point was?"

Without drawing breath, he launched into a memory of Hogmanay, one of the most celebrated events in Scotland. Bowing to tradition, his family had hosted a huge party, one that meant dressing up, getting drunk and dancing well beyond midnight...

"I remember the year my brother was excluded," he finished sadly. "Even I thought that was unfair. I was fourteen then and used to my own company but our father refused to back down."

"Then why didn't he just go?" I gasped in my naivety.

"I wish he had," Sam snorted, "'cos instead of joining in the fun, he was stuck in the attic keeping me company. We watched telly and played a board game but it was like sitting next to a volcano. He looked at me with such hate, I felt something snap that night, but what choice did we have? With Father pissed on whisky, the consequences of letting his guard slip didn't bear thinking about."

I had never expected him to be so blunt. Yet every encounter stoked a flame in my heart, something deeper than sympathy. Marching along the pavements, never once breaking conversation, I sensed a kindred spirit, an invisible connection looming. Finally, we turned the corner into Annandale Avenue.

"Would you like to come in for another coffee?" I suggested.

He glanced at his watch. "It's getting late, but maybe just the one. Then I'd best be on my way..."

By the time we were approaching my home, the sky had darkened to an inky blue. Sam stared ahead, eyes zooming in on the iridescent panels of his car. It shimmered under a lamp post, but in a flash his expression changed.

I glanced at him in alarm. "Is something wrong?"

Dropping down on one knee, he ran his palm over his forehead.

"No!" I heard him hiss under his breath. "Oh fuck!"

Only then did I notice how lop-sided it looked, the front leaning almost drunkenly into the curb.

"Don't tell me you've got a flat tyre," I spluttered.

"Worse," he said darkly. "Some bastard's rammed a nail into it!"

A feeling of shame curled over me.

Sam's car vandalised outside my home? This couldn't be happening.

"Should we tell the police?"

"What's the point?" he snapped. "They've got far more important things to deal with than acts of petty vandalism."

I watched in dread as he examined the damage. With his head drooping low, he looked utterly deflated, his earlier sparkle extinguished.

"Let's go inside," I said softly. "I'll put the kettle on..."

As soon as I had closed the door I crept into the kitchen, leaving Sam in the lounge.

"I don't bloody believe it," I heard him muttering. "Even the spare's knackered. I should have taken it to the garage weeks ago!"

Pacing around like a tiger, his anger wouldn't abate. I wondered if there was anything I could do to comfort him but my throat felt tight with fear.

"What sort of arseholes would do that?"

"I don't know," I sighed, joining him in the lounge, "but please don't stress. There's not a lot we can do at this time of night."

He shook his head, every contour of his face frozen in anguish. "You don't understand. How the bloody hell am I going to get home tonight?"

I took a swallow, unnerved to see him so crestfallen.

"Sam," I proposed, "you can stay here. There's an empty spare room now Joe has left, so why don't you just relax?"

Freezing mid step, he cast a look of woe.

"Are you sure?" he said at last. "I hate to impose."

"Oh, stop it," I berated him. "None of this is your fault. Now sit down and stop fretting, we've had such a nice evening. I'll go and make you a coffee."

Turning from the window to face me, a smile touched his eyes. "I don't suppose you've got anything stronger, have you?"

"I've got some brandy," I smiled back.

Braced with a glass of brandy each, I sensed the tension begin to evaporate.

"I'm sorry about your car," I pacified him. "I can't imagine why anyone would do such a thing, but it's got me worried..."

"Me too," he nodded, "and I know what you're going to say. What if it's connected to the investigation? Think about it, Maisie, every time we get together, something bad happens."

His words turned me cold, a terrible fear snaking through my innards, no matter how hard I tried to ignore it.

"I bet Mortimer had something to with it," I blurted. "Or Schiller."

The words slipped out before I could stop them.

"You think they're still stalking you?" Sam frowned.

"There's no evidence to suggest they're not."

The clues in Joe's tweets had never stopped haunting me, and looking at Sam now, it pained me to imagine he might be their next victim.

Our eyes locked, my heart thumping, yet there was no mistaking that spark. I took another gulp of brandy, my glass almost empty.

Sam took it from my hands and lowering it to the sideboard, looked deep into my eyes. "Shall we have another?" he smiled suggestively. "Forget our troubles for now and think about ourselves for a change?"

His hand caressed my shoulder, and suddenly I didn't want to think about our enemies. Nothing mattered more than this enchanting man leaning over me. So I did what my instincts were telling me. With a trembling hand, I stroked his face, my fingers tracing that lovely jaw.

Then finally our lips came together and he kissed me. It was almost magical, and by the time we broke apart, I felt breathless.

"Maisie," he whispered. His hand stroked my neck, sending shivers through me. "It's been hard to keep my eyes off you since meeting up... I-I just didn't want to jump too soon and spoil things."

"Spoil things?" I echoed.

Nothing could spoil this moment.

Yet as one kiss led to another, his hands began to wander. I felt his lips on my throat moving downwards, fingers tugging my dress buttons as he slowly began to unfasten them. A deep and insistent well of panic rose in me, forcing my eyes shut; except instead of pulling back, I inhaled his scent, the muskiness of his skin like an aphrodisiac. My stomach flipped another somersault, the taste of his lips lingering. The next time he looked at me, I saw an expression of such tenderness, it turned my limbs to liquid.

"Shall we move to the bedroom?" he said softly.

He was letting me take the lead, so how could I refuse him? The gentleness of his touch stirred little flutters in me, and I could feel my body responding.

"Okay," I whispered, my lips betraying a tremor.

"Don't be nervous," he soothed, "I won't hurt you, I promise."

Stroking the sides of his face, I kissed him again with sudden eagerness, my lips parting to find his tongue.

Because deep down, I knew this was what we both wanted, and if I ruined things now, I might not get a second chance, having already scared off Joe.

Chapter Fifty-Four

What happened that night changed everything. Riding a wave of euphoria, I could never have dreamt it would be so good, but if there was anything Sam possessed it was patience. Slowly undressing me, he stroked me all over, his fingers like flames tracing every inch of my body. Following his lead, I marvelled at his physique, the delicate shape of his collar bones sweeping into the contours of his chest.

He had a tattoo on one shoulder and long graceful limbs, a shimmer of golden body hairs in all the right places. Kissing one another between caresses, I felt my arousal climbing, until I could bear it no more... and even then Sam coaxed me on top of him, insisting I took control. We fused together so perfectly, it banished any last traces of victimhood.

Entwined under my duvet in the afterglow, we talked into the early hours, drank more brandy and drifting off peacefully, I enjoyed the best sleep ever.

There were no nightmares, just a warm secure feeling.

What happened with Sam chased my demons away, awakening a hidden sexuality in me I had never known existed...

Waking up next day, I was already lost in an emotional storm. And that was before life took an unexpected new twist.

Reaching across the pillow, I was startled to discover Sam's side of the bed empty, the sheet rumpled and cool.

Where was he? Surely he wouldn't have abandoned me so readily?

I sat up in bed, feeling a tightness in my chest, my initial reaction panic.

Unsure what to do, I scrambled for my mobile. It wasn't in its usual place, which sent me reeling into the lounge. Yet there was no sign of him there, either.

Spotting my mobile on the coffee table, on charge, I took deep breaths, refusing to succumb to the fear creeping over me. His car was gone. Yet as my mind picked over the events of last night it was hard to believe he would just vanish again.

Mercifully, the fear was short-lived - because Sam did return, the buzz of the intercom bringing me swiftly to my feet.

"W-where have you been?" I spluttered.

Although desperate to appear calm, I could hear the tremor in my voice.

243

"Where d'you think?" he tried to humour me. "I called the AA. Had my car towed to a local garage to get my tyre sorted. You weren't worried, were you?"

"You could have told me," I whimpered.

Taking my face in his hands, he smiled down gently.

"You were sound asleep," he protested, "I didn't want to disturb you."

Only when I gazed at the clock did it strike me how late I had slept. Ten o' clock on a Saturday wouldn't be unusual... except it was nearly noon.

Once the preliminary shock fell away, we took time to consider where we were going with this. There was no question last night had been a turning point, the promise of a relationship dangling.

Yet neither of us felt like staying in Bognor.

The memory of Sam's car being vandalised was still raw. Furthermore, we had Joe and Jess to think about, and we wondered aloud whether we ought to contact them.

Of course if we did, they would likely want to hook up again.

"Maybe not," Sam muttered. "We'll only end up chewing over the investigation and if I'm honest, it would be nice to forget about that stuff for a while..."

I couldn't have agreed more, and with the flames of our newly found passion smouldering, I wanted him all to myself. Luckily Sam felt the same way, and with this in mind, he suggested slipping away to his London residence.

All things considered, it turned out to be a good decision.

How I loved Sam's house, a much needed change of scenery. Split into three roomy apartments, two rented, his dwelling covered the ground floor.

Unlocking the front door, he had guided me into the living area. Sunlight flooded the lounge, casting a shine over the parquet flooring. With smooth plastered walls, painted lemon and grey, it had a light airy feel and was well-designed for modern living. An archway led to a corridor, various doors branching into other rooms.

"This is lovely," I murmured, "and so peaceful. It's hard to imagine we're in London."

Wandering to the kitchen at the rear of the house, I saw patio doors leading to a decking area. It overlooked a tidy garden, and as Sam switched the kettle on, leaving me to absorb it all, I couldn't help imagining what it would be like to live here.

"So what d'you fancy doing later?" he murmured, a gleam in his eye. "We could order a pizza, watch movies on Netflix..."

I felt a smile slip onto my face, recalling the wide screen TV in the lounge, embedded in the chimney breast.

"Or maybe have an early night?"

"I wouldn't mind doing all three," I mused.

As he returned my smile, I decided there was no going back. Sam and I were together now, and even with the threat our enemies encroaching, nothing could ruin this happy moment.

Oh, that pivotal weekend... It had kindled the start of a relationship.

As we drifted into Sunday, I found myself lost in the study of Sam's face, still glowing from the pleasurable hours we had spent entangled in each other's arms – and he swore that even if we lived apart for the time being, he would stick by me.

"So what now?" I challenged him. "Much as I love my home, Bognor feels like a very dark place after what happened on Friday."

I had to think about the logistics, though. For however appealing Sam's home seemed, its North London location posed a problem. Touring the city next day, I felt my enthusiasm begin to wane. The tube journey alone from north to south took us forty-five minutes, and adding in the train ride from Victoria, I could be facing a two and a half hour commute each way. My heart sank.

Standing on the platform to say farewell, even I saw the impracticality.

"Just go back to work and act normal for now," he consoled me. "Leave this with me to have a think about and I promise I'll find a solution."

******

Of all the scenarios that might have arisen, though, I had never imagined taking up residence where we did, or that in seven days time we would be waking up in a very different bed. Wrapped in softness, the pillows felt plump, the sheets luxuriously soft. I stretched out my limbs. Wiggled my toes beneath the covers, the temptation to open my eyes growing.

To think, it had happened so fast.

Yet within the space of another week and with barely enough time to gather my thoughts together, I saw my whole life change beyond recognition. One day I would look back on all this, amazed how cleverly we had been reeled in. But everything came to a head the following weekend, when Sam drove down to visit me.

What a glorious day that was, the sun blazing high in the sky as birds flitted in and out of the trees. Delighted to spend the weekend with him, I could not suppress my glee – even more so when he suggested another ride around Sussex. Only this time he was very secretive about our destination.

Following the main road out of Chichester, he took a sudden bend to the right.

"Pook Lane," I said, reading the sign post, "why are we going to East Lavant?"

"You'll see."

He must have known he couldn't keep me in the dark much longer. But reminding me of his role as an estate agent, he mentioned a property near the village, one he had been hankering to take a look at.

"Sorry to talk shop," he said, "but I need to suss this out. It belongs to a colleague, a top lawyer. Charges £250 per hour for his services, mostly in land and property disputes, so he's absolutely minted."

As we drove a little further, the lane opened up into a quintessential English village. A pretty stone bridge crossed the river, clear water trickling over the pebbles, reflecting sparkles of sunlight. My eyes danced, drinking in the houses, the church looming opposite. I loved the open space; the meadows peppered with daisies, the tall but charming flint walls where moss, ivy and clumps of flowers fought for space between the cobbles.

"This is beautiful," I breathed, "and so quiet."

The next time Sam looked at me, his eyes shone with affection. "Now wait until you see the house..."

Crawling steadily onwards, the road was getting narrower. Rows of cottages began to appear, a rank of cars and four-by-fours squeezed into the curb. Traffic wasn't an issue in a tiny hamlet like this, even with access restricted to single file, and as more of its beauty came to light, Sam could barely wipe the smile off his face. We passed the village pub, white walls smothered in wisteria. Clusters of early summer flowers tumbled over a low flint wall and I felt as if my heart could burst.

Yet gradually the houses petered out.

Leaving the village behind, we were hurtling into the countryside before I knew it; green fields lay on one side, a thickly wooded area on the other. But as the walls of trees escalated, my heart began to pump faster. They hugged the road on both sides now, a tunnel of foliage, sapping the light from the sky.

Only then did I feel a shiver run over me and glanced at Sam with a frown.

"It's a bit remote out here, isn't it?"

"Ssh," he tried to console me and with one hand on the wheel, the other sliding around my shoulder, he gradually began to slow down. "We're nearly there."

I kept my eyes shut, reliving the incredible moment that had followed.

When Sam pulled up, my first impression of the property left me speechless. Guarded by a high hedge with the ornamental gates left open, its magnificence was revealed in stages. First we explored the front, an artistically paved area decorated with stone urns. I saw box balls and shrubs in full flower.

"Wow!" he whistled. "Some place this is! Shall we look inside?"

Taking me by the hand, he pulled me towards the door. I glimpsed the fire in

246

his eyes as he delved into his jacket pocket to produce a set of keys, dangling them in temptation in front of my disbelieving eyes.

"This is just his weekend cottage," he kept smiling. "Craig and his wife are after a place in France, so they decided to put it on the market."

"In other words they've asked you to value it?" I finished.

The house itself was breathtaking. There was no other word to describe it. A character flint-and-brick property complemented by climbing pink roses. Two rows of mullioned windows sat pleasingly under a terracotta tile roof, and as for the interior... I couldn't help thinking it resembled something out of a magazine. The rooms were huge with cream walls and oak flooring; a beautiful stone fireplace in the sitting room, alcoves fitted with bookcases.

Spreading my arms wide, I found myself spinning in circles. I was still unsure what we were doing here, but as we explored the property further, admiring the lovely grounds, I could not help noticing how smug Sam looked.

That was when I twigged he was hiding something.

"Come on! What's the big secret?"

"He's not just asked me to value it," he divulged. "It needs a survey. A bit of renovation work, which he also wants me to oversee - nothing major - just tart up the paintwork and mend a few windows, but do you want to hear the best part?"

I held my breath.

"We can use it as a base while the work is underway."

A gasp flew from my lips before I knew it. "You mean we can live here?"

"It'll only be temporary, until it's ready to go on the market, but can't you see how perfect this is?" Caught up in his excitement, he grabbed me in a bear hug and swung me off the ground. "It not only gets you away from Bognor, but what a great place for your friend's foster son when he visits..."

"I can't believe it," I mumbled. "Are you serious?"

"Yes," he enthused, "and wait until you see the garden! That'll need some work too, which can be your project – and another thing. We should invite Joe over to have a look. Maybe we can make use of his handy man skills. Paid, of course!"

I could have laughed out loud but how could I resist the lure of the garden? Fully enclosed, it was in need of a prune but I could not help wondering what it would look like with the addition of a few perennial flower borders.

Immediately I was mesmerised, thinking back to my foster parents' home and the hours they had spent making it beautiful...

Yes, that house had been a dream.

There was no way I could let such an opportunity pass me by. So once agreed, we had sped back to Bognor. Stopping only briefly, I packed a couple of cases, eager to return to East Lavant and spend the night in our lovely new home.

Reality blinked on Sunday, forcing my eyes open, but as the new day dawned I clung to that moment. Breathing deeply, I allowed my senses to tune into my new surroundings, the world still a little blurry around the edges.

Here there was no traffic, just a whisper of wind in the trees and the melodic chirp of birdsong.

And I felt as if I had awoken in heaven.

Chapter Fifty-Five

The first sight of Maisie's new home stole the breath from Joe's lungs. Thinking back, their lives had changed dramatically since that fated reunion in London. Yet never in his wildest dreams had he imagined it would scatter them like this.

His weekends with Jess had sown the seed, until she had boldly asked him to move in. Now here they were, admiring this charming country house.

It all seemed a little too good to be true.

Maisie, on the other hand, looked ecstatic but then, why shouldn't she? Anxious and alone in Bognor, she must have thought she had struck gold when Sam rolled up, her knight in shining armour.

"What do you think, Joe?" asked Sam, snapping him out of his reverie.

Joe blinked, stunned by his surroundings.

"Wicked," he grinned. "How the fuck did you manage to stumble across a place like this, and right on the outskirts of Chichester?"

For some reason Sam did not smile back. "Dealing in property, you 'stumble across' all sorts of places, but at the end of the day I'm helping an associate. I guess one good turn deserves another."

"I see," Joe muttered, following him through to the dining room.

Jess trailed along in his wake, heels clicking across the polished oak floors, as they wandered from the dining room to the kitchen. Crossing the threshold, she stopped dead, her eyes virtually popping out on stalks.

"Oh wowsers!" she spluttered. "Just look at that kitchen!"

Joe followed her gaze. Like every other room in the house, it was huge, and fully equipped with top of the range appliances. Recessed spotlights drew circles of light onto the granite work surfaces. He turned and spotted Maisie again. Adjusting the controls on a slow cooker, she looked up.

"Wonderful isn't it?" she said.

"Cooking a cracking Sunday lunch too, aren't you, my lovely?" Sam purred.

Her eyes glowed. "Mandy sent a recipe for a chicken hot pot. I've never use one of these..." As she lifted the lid slightly, a rich smell of wine, garlic and herbs spiralled into the air. "But let's go outside first. I can't wait to show you the garden."

Captured in the moment, Jess seized Joe's hand, dragging him through the patio doors, where a path led to the lawn. The grounds were undeniably picturesque; hedges crisp against a blue sky, the roses in bloom and a summer house on one side. Yet as Joe's eyes travelled further, he drank in the encircling woods.

The impression of a hidden track lingered on the other side of the hedge, a single oak tree soaring above the laurels. He turned away with a frown. Something about the atmosphere unnerved him, but he could not quite put his finger on it.

Sam, meanwhile, was in full flow, and as if to further justify their landing in such a remarkable home, spoke of the renovation work required.

"Would you be interested in helping out, Joe?" he asked him directly.

"It'd be my pleasure, mate," Joe nodded.

Turning his attention back to the house, he began to scrutinise the exterior more closely. However beautiful it might have appeared at first, the paintwork was flaking in places, and there were clear signs of decay around some of the windows.

"Those frames are gonna need sanding down first and an application of wood filler," he added, pointing to the top window. "Give 'em a couple of coats of gloss and they'll look as good as new..."

"Brilliant," Sam responded. "I hoped you'd say that, and it's paid work. Craig is in control of the budget but would twenty pounds an hour be enough?"

Joe gaped at him in disbelief. "That'd be great! So when can I start?"

"I'll let you know," Sam said. "The sooner the better really. I just need to organise a survey first - consult the owner and get paint samples."

Sam didn't quite meet his eye but Joe clocked that twinkle, delighted he had included someone else in his project.

"So how long do you reckon you'll be living here," he couldn't resist asking.

Settled in chairs around a beautiful walnut dining table, he revelled in the prospect of doing some work on this house.

Sam gave a shrug. "Who knows? Obviously it won't be permanent, but a few months maybe..." He took a swallow of wine, a particularly smooth red. "The only stumbling block is the investigation, especially if there's a trial."

The words tugged Joe's head upright. "Was there any more news about your social worker?"

Sam lowered his eyes but not before Joe caught a flicker of darkness in them. "No, nothing, and sorry if I seem evasive but that business hit me hard. I really wanted Yvonne on side..." A muscle twitched in his jaw.

"Try not to let it upset you," Maisie soothed. "We'll just have to wait until the next police report but for now, let's unwind..." Reaching across the table, she tapped his glass. "Don't you think Sam's done wonders getting us this place? It's only a ten minute drive to my office."

Yes, very convenient.

Fizzing with excitement, she looked happier than he had seen her in a long time, simultaneously hopping in and out of the kitchen.

"I guess you'll be commuting, then," he said to Sam.

Their glasses touched briefly, Sam's expression betraying nothing.

"On and off when time allows, but weekdays I have to be in London."

Joe froze, flicking another glance at Maisie. "What? Does this mean you're gonna be stuck out here on your own?"

"I'll be fine, Joe," she sighed. "I've got work friends nearby, not to forget you two, and you're always welcome to scoot over. I'm only on the end of a phone."

"Yeah, but what about security?" he whispered. He didn't want to come across as paranoid, but Sam's disclosure had horrified him.

"There's no need to worry," Sam consoled him, his hand squeezing Maisie's. "Didn't you see the burglar alarm on the wall? This house is fully wired and fitted with security lights, and if there's the slightest bit of aggro, I'll be down like a shot. It's not like Bognor Regis..."

Dissing Bognor now, was he?

Joe felt a spark of annoyance, but aware of Sam's hospitality - never mind the work dangling under his nose like a carrot - he swallowed back his retort.

"Right," he muttered and gave a lop sided-sided smile. "Look, don't get me wrong, mate, this house is the dog's bollocks. Just promise to keep her safe!"

"Oh, lighten up will you?" Jess scoffed. "Given the choice, I'd swap places any day. Now is it possible we can enjoy our visit here?"

"Can I get you another drink?" Maisie interrupted. "Lunch is nearly ready."

The warmth of her gaze reassured him before she turned back to the kitchen.

Yet as Joe lowered his eyes, a burn of humiliation spread through him. And with Jess not drinking, he knew when to keep quiet.

"Well, it looks like Maisie's fallen on her feet," Jess sniffed as they embarked on their journey back to Bognor. "What a gorgeous place to live, though! It looked like something out of Country Living magazine. Lucky bitch!"

"Is she?" Joe replied. "I'm a bit worried about her if I'm honest..."

Jess rolled her eyes. "Oh, why do you always have to be so bloody cynical?"

"What, you don't think it's a bit sudden?" he snapped. "Sam comes waltzing into her life, the moment our backs are turned, and next thing you know this house turns up, some rich bastard's weekend cottage, and it just happens to be a few miles up the road from where she works?"

"I don't get it," Jess frowned. "What's your problem? We're happy, Maisie's happy. You're not jealous are you?"

Joe sighed, tempted to shake some sense into her.

"No, I'm not jealous, I'm just looking out for Maisie. I was worried when she was on her own in Bognor, but at least she had us around the corner. She's so cut off out here! Something about this set up don't feel right."

Jess smirked. "She's not on her own though, is she? She's got Sam."

He shook his head, at a loss to explain the fear raking over him.

If anyone was suffering from jealousy, it was her; sat around the table, it had oozed from every pore, from her flitting eyes to her sickly sweet compliments.

As if he didn't feel inadequate enough with her constant sniping. But after two short weeks of living together, they were getting on each other's nerves already. His lips tightened. Sad though it seemed, it hadn't taken long for the novelty to wear off. Unaccustomed to his ways, she treated him more like an irritant lately.

Take the day he had emptied his coat pockets on the coffee table, a few till receipts, ATM slips, Rizlas from his smoking days... she had gone apeshit.

His head hung low, a wave of sadness running through him as his thoughts turned back to Maisie. Only now did he realise how much he was missing her. Maisie, who had been so tolerant, never once berating him for his habits.

So maybe Jess hoped to refine him but it was like trying to teach a dog new tricks. However hard he tried, he was never going to fit into her perfect world.

Next day he awoke even more depressed. Much as he loved his passionate weekends with Jess, moving in had been a mistake, and the more sensible part of him had always known this. However hard he tried, he was never going to fit into her perfect world.

What could he do, though, other than to talk to Maisie?

Given she was no longer in Bognor, he could hardly pop round for a cup of tea any more, but he could phone her. Just to hear her voice would be a pleasurable diversion, so without further delay he dialled her mobile.

Except it rang and rang, until finally going to voice mail.

Joe exhaled a heavy sigh, his soul deflated and empty.

He found himself wondering whether there was a decent signal in East Lavant, but there was always tomorrow. Or he could try phoning her at work.

Over the next week, however, he made several attempts to get in touch.

"Oh come on, Maisie, please pick up," he whispered through gritted teeth, but every time he was left with no choice than to leave another message. "Hi, Maisie, it's Joe again... Sorry to hassle you but is there any chance we can meet up? I need to talk to you, so if you get a moment will you text me?"

Maybe she was pre-occupied with the garden or something, but why couldn't she just answer her fucking phone?

His frustration grew, but at the back of his mind, a more devastating ribbon of thought was beginning to unwind itself.

What if she was in some kind of danger?

Chapter Fifty-Six

Poor Joe. Sweet though it was of him to show concern for me, anyone could see how much it had irked Sam. It was as if he didn't trust him. Yet with time marching on, I had someone else to consider: Connor.

Was it really a month since that memorable day on the beach?

My life had changed so rapidly, it was difficult to keep pace with everything, but a promise was a promise. Sarah and I had a long-standing arrangement, and I was not about to let her down.

"I'm sure I mentioned it," I said on the phone to him that evening.

He was due to drive down tomorrow, the advent of a brand new weekend.

"Or would you prefer it if we went back to Bognor for the day?"

"Don't be silly," Sam sighed. "Didn't I say this house would be great for him? I'd just forgotten it was this weekend, that's all."

"So you're okay with it then?"

"Of course! There's loads of space. You'll just have to make another bed up."

I could almost hear the smile in his voice, and a rush of relief poured over me.

The first person to roll up, however, was Sarah. Sam had been delayed, due to traffic congestion on the motorway, and had no idea when he would get here.

Gazing at Sarah, I felt my heart twist.

I would so much have liked her to meet him.

"You're looking very well," she complimented me, "though hardly surprising with all this lovely fresh air and countryside."

Stepping out of the car with Connor, she was quick to embrace me, her eyes feasting on the grounds, just as Jess's had.

"This cottage is stunning! So what have you been up to all week?"

Oh, where to start.

I raked my fingers through my hair before ushering them inside. Making sure they were settled comfortably, only then did I explain.

For the last few days, my feet had barely touched the ground; from a meal out in Chichester with my colleagues, to another taken up with one of our Fostering Information evenings. But at every opportunity, I could not wait to get out in the garden and start pottering. The evenings were light, the air sweetened with the haunting notes of a song thrush, and I felt more in tune with my surroundings than at any time I could remember.

"I know," Sarah mused, "I've seen your photos on Instagram. I'll tell you now, your foster parents are thrilled, and looking forward to a day they can visit."

Her green eyes glittered, drawing my thoughts back to the garden. Filling the empty pots with summer flowers, I had dotted them around the patio to create instant colour, deciding my perennial borders would have to wait.

"Oh Connor, you're going to have a great time," she kept beaming, "not just getting out and about in the countryside but with all this state of the art stuff here, you won't be bored."

She was right. Gazing around the lounge with its deeply padded sofas, huge plasma TV screen and smart speaker, I realised I'd had little time to bask in the luxury of my new environment.

But maybe this weekend would be different.

Connor, meanwhile, looked mesmerised, his eyes growing bigger as I led him up to his room. I had prepared one at the back for him, which lay farthest from the road, but with superb views across the landscape. Giving him time to settle, I left him staring out of the window. The fields stretched into the distance alongside the forest edge, a cloud of encircling woodland, the trees in full leaf.

Hearing the crunch of tyres on gravel, I sped to the door, delighted to see Sam's car. Flinging the door open, I braced myself. But as he strode towards the door to greet me, I almost recoiled. For never had I seen him look so exhausted, his hair lank, eyes wreathed in dark shadows.

"Finally," he muttered under his breath. "Fucking traffic."

"Sam," I whispered in horror, "are you okay?"

My eyes were drawn to his legs, long and supple in casual linen shorts; yet as he moved close to embrace me he discharged a potent tang of sweat.

"Sorry for the delay. I worked late last night, thinking I'd have time to go to the gym this morning, but then I got stuck in that snarl-up."

"I thought you looked a bit stressed," I commented.

Leaning in to kiss me, his lips felt hot against my own. "I am, and the first thing I need is a shower, freshen up a bit. Any chance of a coffee?"

Turning towards the stairs with a wink, I felt my insides turn to goo, the state he had arrived in forgiven.

By the time he had stepped into the gleam of the hallway, he was transformed. His skin glowed from the shower, damp hair a burnished blonde. Still in shorts, he had changed into a crisp white over-shirt, top buttons undone revealing his shapely pectorals. I held my breath, fighting the urge to tug it off him again, but conscious of Connor loitering.

"Well, hello!" he greeted him. His face split into a smile. "You must be

Connor."

Observing him with interest, Connor gave the tiniest nod. "Yes. Are you Sam? Thanks for letting me stay, and I like your house. It's well cool."

Sam's face froze in surprise. "Well, cheers, mate, but I might as well come clean. It's not actually my house. Didn't Maisie tell you? We're doing it up for a client, so he can sell it."

"Yeah, but it is really cool," Connor pressed. "It's even got a basement..." Gazing past the rug at the bottom of the stairs, he pointed to a shadowy corner, the brackets of a trapdoor only just visible. "Do you know what's down there?"

"Knowing Craig, I expect he uses it as a wine cellar," Sam said. He followed it with a laugh. "Have a snoop if you like. Anywhere else you want to explore?"

"What about the woods around here?"

His eyes flared with hope, filling me with unease before Sam quickly responded.

"No, Connor. I'm sorry, but if you're our responsibility, we can't let you go wandering off into the forest. What if you ended up lost?"

I watched in curiosity, happy to see a rapport developing between them.

"But we could still go out for an excursion somewhere," I intervened.

"Good idea," Sam said. "After being cooped up in a car for two hours, I need some fresh air. So let's make a picnic. Goodwood Trundle isn't far..."

He was right. I hadn't given much thought to the dramatic scenery that lingered virtually on our doorstep. Seeing Goodwood Hill brought back memories of our first excursion, only this time we stopped in the car park.

Connor sped ahead but at least we were able to keep an eye on him. Drinking in our surroundings, we found ourselves climbing a path to an area of open hills. They overlooked the racecourse, but the views up here were fantastic, the exposed chalk paths painting diamond white lines across the landscape.

"This is great, Sam," I sighed as we settled into a hollow between the hills.

Surrounded by carpets of wild flowers, I saw butterflies flitting among the petals, and caught myself thinking we couldn't have picked a nicer spot for our picnic.

"You were right about the woods though, imagine if he'd gone missing? According to Sarah, he's got a habit of wandering off and hiding. It's got him into a lot of trouble in the past, never mind causing worry..."

Sam shrugged. "At least this area's public, so he won't get very far without other people seeing him. Just as well. Last thing we want is to call the police out."

"No," I pondered. "We haven't heard from them lately, have we?"

My words hung suspended before I felt a dart of panic.

"Oh, shit," I whispered.

"What is it?" Sam frowned.

"Something's just occurred to me and I'm surprised Sarah didn't mention it... but please don't say anything about Connor staying with us."

Sam jerked his body upright, as if startled. "Why not?"

"I've broken the rules. If anything happened to him I could lose my job over this but with you being my partner, the authorities would normally want to run some background checks on you first..."

"What the fuck for?" he baulked. "It's not like I'm some pervert!"

"Shh," I tried to calm him but it was too late.

Fury blazed in his eyes as he turned and glared into the distance. I had never seen him like this.

"Don't be offended, it's just a procedure for looking after a minor."

"Offended?" he snarled. "I don't think you realise how much I'm offended."

I would have replied, but before I had a chance, his mobile rang.

"Sorry, I have to take this," he snapped.

And without another word, he rose to his feet - stormed over to the other side of the hill, leaving me speechless.

I went in search of Connor.

Fortunately, he hadn't wandered far. A svelte silhouette against the skyline, he stood admiring the view. So I quickened my pace, staggering to the top of the hill almost breathless.

"Alright, Connor?" I panted.

"You can see the sea up here," he observed shrewdly. "I think that's Bognor over there, but what's that big body of water inland?"

Following the direction of his finger, I made an educated guess. "That must be Chichester Harbour where the boats come in. It's got a lovely coastline and a little further west is Portsmouth. See that fuzzy shape in the distance? I'm betting that's the Isle of Wight."

"Right," he muttered, snapping his head around. "So where's Sam?"

Clasping the lapels of my cardigan, I pulled it tighter around my chest. "Taking a call on his mobile. I expect it's something to do with work..."

I closed my eyes, of a mind to let him stew. I would have to face him at some point, but my heart filled with sadness as I pictured his angry face.

Unfortunately, his mood didn't improve, not even on the journey back. Risking a sideways glance, I hardly recognised him any more, his face set like stone.

"Who was on the phone, then," I asked quietly.

"It was the surveyor," he said, his voice clipped and cold.

"But that's good, isn't it?" I pressed, wary of Connor in the back seat.

Sam shrugged, saying nothing more, and our journey ended in an uncomfortable knot of silence.

Once we were back in East Lavant, I switched the kettle on. Even Connor had turned quiet, which put me on edge. It seemed obvious he had picked up the tension between us and it stifled the air like a thunder cloud.

At a loss as to how to break the deadlock, I found it hard to believe Sam could be like this. Tears burned my eyes but I blinked them back, determined not to let him drag me down. He seemed to have completely withdrawn into himself.

Yet why? What had I done to make him flip so suddenly?

Busying myself in the garden for an hour, I even managed to engage Connor in some of the hedge pruning. But as evening approached, I could bear it no longer. Sam stood in the lounge, staring out of the window, and with Connor preoccupied in his bedroom for now, it was time to confront him.

"Look," I sighed. "I think it's best if Connor and I go back to Bognor after all. I can tell we've outworn our welcome..."

"Don't go," I heard him whisper.

Turning away from the window, he no longer looked angry.

He looked haunted.

His eyes swam with tears as they rose to meet mine, yet they harboured a terrible darkness.

"Sorry. I'm behaving like a complete arse, I know, but I've been stressed as hell. Can we forget what happened and enjoy the rest of our weekend?"

How could I not forgive him - the relief rolling over me so immense, I almost tumbled into his arms.

With the friction discharged, the evening evolved into a bubble of merriment. Sam and I threw a meal together in our lovely kitchen. Happy to entertain Connor, whilst curling up on the sofa together, we scrolled through a list of movies. The choice was endless, until we eventually agreed on a James Bond film.

Next day, however, Connor was due to return home.

Sam had insisted on driving, keen to make a day of it and find a pub to stop for lunch. The thought of finally introducing him to Sarah excited me and for that reason, I suggested we could meet her halfway.

By early afternoon, we had hooked up in a place just off the motorway near Crawley, and like me, Sarah seemed utterly bedazzled.

"It's so good to meet you," she said, "after everything Maisie's told me."

"You too," Sam smiled, "and I was touched by your efforts to find me. There is something I would like to ask you though..."

She stared at him. "Go on."

"You met Yvonne Draper, didn't you?" His eyes lowered, a cloud passing over his face. "How was she?"

Observing the exchange, I saw the smile drop from Sarah's face. Time seemed to stand still, the atmosphere melancholy before she had even opened her mouth to speak.

"She was terrified, Sam. Defensive, as if fearing she would come to some harm. She told me that someone came through for you, but the identity of that person had to remain a secret."

"My father," Sam sighed. "I get it! Like fathering an illegitimate child was his darkest of secrets..." His lips tightened.

"I'm sorry about what happened to her," she added numbly.

An image of the house in East Grinstead flashed in my mind, evoking unpleasant memories of her death. She must have lived in fear as to how she would cope in the midst of such a sinister investigation.

"What else did she tell you?" Sam urged. "I don't suppose she mentioned any of the stories I reported, did she? The stuff about Orchard Grange?"

Sarah held his gaze. "None, I'm afraid. She seemed more concerned about your early childhood, losing your mum... but it was a distraction. I'm sure she was hiding something but I didn't press her. She was too scared."

"I see," Sam murmured. "Well thanks, anyway."

"So how was Connor?" she digressed. "Did he behave himself?"

"He's a nice kid," Sam said. "Very perceptive, not to mention inquisitive, and I've enjoyed getting to know him."

"Thanks so much for entertaining him," she added warmly.

At last a smile sprung to his face. "No problem," he finished. "He's got a good rapport with Maisie and welcome to visit again any time."

Chapter Fifty-Seven

Joe meanwhile, was becoming ever more frustrated until there was only one thing for it. If he wanted to speak to Maisie, he would have to phone her workplace.

"Joe," she gasped, "what a nice surprise! How are you?"

The sound of her voice brought a lump to his throat, but there was no time to explain. "Sorry to call you at work but I need to talk to you. Any chance you could meet me on your lunch break? I can get to Chichester by train..."

They kept the conversation brief but luck was on his side. By one o' clock they were hidden on the top floor of ZiZi Italian, just a stone's throw away from the Council office. Maisie looked radiant, her eyes shining in the shadows.

Ordering two beers, Joe threw a cursory glance over the menu, though food was the last thing on his mind.

"It's good to see you," he muttered. "Where have you been?"

"Just rushing around trying to get a million and one things done. It's good to see you too, Joe..." They touched glasses. "Connor stayed at the weekend, which was a bit nerve-wracking but it went okay. So how are things with you and Jess?"

"Not good," he confessed. "I dunno what to do any more, Maisie."

"Joe," she murmured. "What's happened?"

A fist of misery clenched around his stomach.

"We've drifted apart," he began telling her.

He could hardly believe it himself; how quickly the veneer had crumbled away. Those romantic weekends were nothing but an illusion. The real Jess was needy for love, forever seeking compliments yet draining his emotional energy like a vampire.

He thought he had given her his heart, so why couldn't it be enough, when all he craved in return was a little affection, just an occasional kind word?

He took another swallow of beer but the pain didn't shift.

"She makes me feel like shit," he muttered, "and as for her colleagues..."

He didn't want to elaborate. No more than he felt like admitting the rift it had caused. But no sooner had he begun than Maisie's expression grew serious, her eyes filled with worry, searching deep into his soul.

"She introduced you to her workmates?"

His face hardened. Was it only last week she had dragged him along to

Fontwell Racecourse for one of their corporate hospitality dos? Clean-shaven, hair neatly trimmed, he had genuinely thought he looked smart in a cool blue cotton shirt, worn loose outside his black chinos. So why insist on a suit?

"A fucking suit for Christ's sake!" he hissed under his breath. "Me, in a suit!"

With an enduring passion for horse racing, though, he had nonetheless made an effort. Polite to her colleagues, he had advised them on form, shared tips and even garnered a few wins for the condescending bastards when they bothered to listen. He might have forgiven their attitude, if it hadn't been for that snooty MD drawing Jess aside for a 'quiet word.' But he had overheard the woman clear as day, sniggering about him outside one of the betting stands.

'Still doing your bit for charity, are you, dear? Now, I know we do a lot of PR work to help the homeless, but it doesn't mean you have to sleep with them.'

"No!" Maisie gasped in disgust. "That's nasty! What's more it sounds like Jess told her boss you'd been homeless before she met you."

"Yeah," Joe sulked, "and if her boss had been a bloke I'd have punched 'im."

Perhaps he should have confronted her but no... He had absorbed the brunt of that insult and it felt like swallowing broken glass.

"Are you ready to order?"

Joe looked up, conscious of a smiling young waiter hovering.

"Okay, I'll have some bruschetta, please," he replied, "and another beer."

"I'll have the same," Maisie nodded, "but no more beer, just a side salad..."

Passing the waiter her menu, she turned back to Joe.

"So what are you going to do? I hate to see you so unhappy, but you need to talk to her..."

"What's the point?" Joe snapped. "All she expects from me is gratitude."

"But I don't understand," she continued. "I always felt there was some magnetism between you two, that your 'differences' turned her on. You, the rebel lover who put some excitement into her life..."

"Maybe," Joe pondered, "but Jess doesn't want a lover, she wants a lap dog. Someone who follows her around, telling her how wonderful she is and making her feel like a princess. I fell for her big time, but I'm not sure I can handle it any more."

Maisie looked away with a sigh. Her words came slow and measured. "Joe, if this doesn't work out, you can always move back into my flat, you know."

"Are you serious?"

"Of course. The letting agreement runs until the end of the year and I assume you've still got a key?"

His heart leapt. All he craved was a listening ear; that if he hadn't managed to speak to her soon he would explode.

"Thanks, Maisie, you're a life saver."

"We're friends, Joe," she said in earnest, "so why suffer in silence? I wish you'd said something to me earlier, though."

"I tried," he blurted, "but you haven't been answering my calls."

The words seemed to freeze her in her chair. "What calls?"

"I've rung you loads of times," he persisted. "The week after we visited that cottage of yours, which reminds me..."

He broke off, his heart pounding with dread.

Did he dare bring up the house in East Lavant?

Something felt wrong, and try as he might to dismiss it, he could not forget Sam's stony face. It still bothered him.

"How's it going with the renovation? Any chance of me coming over and getting some work done, or do I get the feeling Sam's stalling?"

"I'm not sure," Maisie shrugged. She drained her glass, lowering it unsteadily to the table. "He's spoken to a surveyor but nothing seems to be happening very fast and he's been so stressed lately."

Joe touched her hand, choosing his next words carefully.

"But what do you really think of this set up? I wasn't kidding about security."

"I know," she sighed. "I was touched by that, but Sam seems to have everything under control. The house is so lovely, and I've done a fair bit in the garden..."

"Sure," he interrupted, "but what about you and Sam? You don't see much of him, do you, which I find a bit strange."

"You don't trust him, do you?" she said, her brow creasing into a frown.

Finally.

Joe exhaled. He clocked the desolation in her eyes and it spiked him with guilt but at least now it was out in the open... it was time to confront her with what he really thought about Sam.

"No," he whispered. "I don't. I'm sorry but he seems different."

"What's that supposed to mean?"

The waiter returned, lowering plates of bruschetta, salad and drinks onto the table, but the fuse had been lit. He could no longer stay silent.

"What I mean is he's got Sam's looks, Sam's scar and Sam's memories but it's like someone else's personality has been poured into him."

She stared at him open-mouthed. "People do change, Joe."

"Yeah sure, but something niggles and I hate to say it but I can't warm to him. He's not the friend I remember. Sam was one of them boys you either loved or loathed. Those who loved him wanted to protect him - like we did - when everyone else in Orchard Grange wanted to kick the shit out of him."

"God, Joe," she whimpered. "What are you saying?"

"Nothing," he finished, "I don't feel love or hate, just indifference. Something that makes me wonder if he's damaged in some way."

At last she nodded. "I think we all are to an extent, but those stories about his life in Scotland... I can't tell you how much they disturbed me. Maybe you're right. He has changed. But neither of us can imagine the effect it had on him, growing up in isolation like that."

"Hmm," Joe pondered.

Even as she spoke, his thoughts branched wider. *Isolation*. The word jarred him, while spooling into his mind came the threads of a new horror.

"Isolation. That's a point. Supposing it's rubbed off on him? What if he's trying to isolate *you*?"

"But why would he do that?" she protested. "We're all friends!"

"I know but I've gotta confess I am suspicious about that house. I mean is it even on a mobile network? I've left voicemails, sent texts..."

At first she said nothing, eyes lowered as she delved into her salad. For the first time since meeting her, he saw a defiant look. It seemed obvious she would do anything to defend Sam.

Then finally setting down her fork, she dipped into her bag for her mobile.

"Okay, let's see... Hmm, I haven't had any voicemails, other than from work, and you say you left a message?"

"Several," Joe said.

The frown was back, distorting her lovely features as she checked her texts and messages. Joe braced himself.

"That's odd. No texts either, not even from Jess..."

Her head shot upright, a sudden flash in her eye.

"D'you know, that's even stranger. Jess would have sent a hundred texts, especially now I'm in a relationship! She'd be digging for all the gossip!"

"So give her a bell." He forced a smile. "Ask her if she's been blanking you and if she denies it, then we'll know something's up."

"I don't know what you're suggesting," she smiled back, "but a simpler explanation could be that something's wrong with my phone?"

"Shouldn't you check it out, then?" he pressed. "I mean, why would our calls be barred?"

"I will, but in the meantime, try not to worry. As a last resort you can always reach me at work like you did today. It's been lovely to see you."

Joe held her stare, filled with a sense their time was nearly up.

"Just look after yourself, Maisie, that's all I care about, and as for Jess... I'll keep you posted, okay?"

******

263

Joe's fears were not unfounded. It was impossible to imagine what was really unfolding behind the scenes; that before the week ended the final chapter of Mortimer's plan would be activated, with terrible consequences.

Little did they know he had taken to spying from the depths of the forest, fingers curled like talons around his binoculars. Seeing his target wandering into view behind the lenses carved a sadistic grin onto his face. So innocent, so pure, as she attended to her flowers but oh, how nicely everything had panned out!

So Maisie and young McFadden were together.

In the grander scheme of things, it was perfect. Joe, Maisie, Sam, the only three nemeses left who could destroy him... Sam had always posed the greatest threat but it brought immense satisfaction to think that in a very short while he would be rid of all three of them.

A vibration from his mobile sharpened his senses; and for a moment he had almost forgotten where he was hiding. Retreating into the forest like a hunted fox, he welcomed the canopy of foliage, secure in its enveloping darkness.

"What?" he whispered. "Is it time to prepare for the ritual?"

"Not yet," the voice on the other end hissed. "We promised we'd do this at the end of the week, and there is work still to be done."

Cornelius ground his teeth, tiring of excuses. With the police investigation effectively stalled for now, and Thomas Parker-Smythe awaiting trial, it was only a matter of time before his cover was blown, and then what? Twenty cursed years he had waited for this, the one last ritual to complete the circle.

Yes, this would herald his ultimate rise to power and immortality.

"You are testing my patience," he warned the caller.

"Please..." he urged, his voice a shuddering echo. "Just hold tight, we're very nearly ready, but Joe Winterton still poses a threat."

"Yes," he murmured icily, "I gather he visited the house."

"W-what..." his ally started stammering.

"I saw him, just as they were leaving the village. Him and that sassy girlfriend of his, and I would prefer it if they didn't return."

"Then isn't it time you relocated Karl Schiller? He can't run the risk of staying anywhere for too long or people might notice him... especially now his work in East Grinstead is done."

"Indeed," Cornelius growled, "then let's deal with Winterton once and for all. You never know when he might come snooping again."

Chapter Fifty-Eight

By the time Joe was approaching Jess's apartment it was gone six. Filled with dread at the thought of facing her again, he had deliberately delayed his journey. Even as he let himself in, knots of tension pinched his shoulders. But whatever little confidence Maisie had restored, Jess was bound to drag him back under.

Could he honestly stomach another slow drip feed of venom tonight?

He held his breath.

"Hi," she murmured sweetly, "you're late! Where have you been?"

He froze to a halt, wondering whether he was dreaming. Poised before him, smiling, she looked ravishing in a summer dress with its soft flowing fabric and V-neckline.

"I went to Chichester," he said numbly.

She tilted her head to one side. "Any particular reason?"

"Just wondering if there were any jobs over that way..."

This wasn't entirely dishonest. Just before leaving ZiZi's he had asked the waiter if there were any vacancies, but with nothing to offer at present, he had been pointed in the direction of a recruitment agency; one that specialised in the pub and catering trade. He had decided to check it out.

"I also met Maisie for lunch."

The smile fell from Jess's face. "Really? So how is she?"

"Okay," he shrugged, turning away from her. "Have you called her lately?"

"Yes," she insisted, "except her phone always goes to voicemail."

Joe switched the kettle on, feeling a chill sweep over him.

So it wasn't only his calls failing to reach her.

Jess, on the hand, seemed unruffled. "I expect she's snowed under! Too busy doing up that gorgeous house to be bothered with the likes of us, not to mention 'Golden Boy Wonder,' though I don't suppose it'll be long before we meet up again."

Joe bit his lip, not liking the acid creeping into her voice; though it seemed she had plans of her own, sidling up to him, hips swaying in a manner that turned his knees to jelly. He could guess what was coming. Her eyes shone with desire, as she curled her arms around his waist, pulling him close.

"I know I can be a bitch sometimes, but I do love you."

Her body rubbed against his, the fresh clean smell of her intoxicating.

"What's this in aid of?" he murmured.

"I thought you might like an early night," she purred, "seeing as we're busy tomorrow evening... Or have you forgotten our dinner party?"

Joe's heart plummeted. *Of course*. She had invited some friends over, hankering to show off. Glancing around, he thought the apartment looked spotless, windows sparkling, the air infused with an underlying scent of furniture polish, which could only have been the result of Jess's cleaner visiting.

"Geoff is a writer I've known for years," she reminded him. "He used to have a column in the Observer... until they started their own 'arts magazine' and Imogen's writing a novel. She's always on the lookout for a good story."

"Are you sure you want me to be here?" he teased.

"Oh, stop it!" she scolded. "You're a good cook and it's not as if we're short of stories to entertain them with, so don't worry. It'll be the best evening ever!"

Twenty-four hours later, Joe was wishing he could escape. He'd thought he could handle people from all walks of life, yet once immersed in Jess's circle, he felt completely out of his league.

Carefully arranging her guests around the dining table, she poured the wine. Joe, meanwhile, observed them subtly. Imogen reminded him of a china doll. With her jet black hair pinned up, her flawless features combined pale skin, round blue eyes and a small pouting mouth. Geoff, too, radiated an aura of self-confidence. He had the same wiry physique as Joe, yet stood a couple of inches taller, his slicked-back hair lighter, a beard so defined it might have been laser-cut.

"Are you having a glass, Joe?" Jess's voice pierced into his thoughts.

Cautious of drinking too much too early, he politely requested a beer before joining them at the dining table.

"Gorgeous apartment this, isn't it?" Imogen drawled. Eyeing him beadily, she moved her head a little closer. "So come on, Joe, what do you for a living?"

"I work at Sainsbury's," he said, "in the online shopping department. It's part time, so I've got plenty of hours to do other stuff - like my one day a week in a charity shop, which is voluntary - but I'm also looking for some bar work."

Nodding in encouragement, Geoff sipped his wine. "Great. It's good to keep yourself busy, have you worked in any other bars?"

"Oh, yeah," Joe sighed and feeling himself relax slightly, went on to describe some of the stylish establishments he had worked for in Chelsea.

"Sounds like you've had an interesting life," Geoff's wife mused.

"It's the one type of work I've got most experience in," he added proudly.

Raising his eyes, he was aware of Jess slipping in and out of the kitchen, preparing to serve her starter; tempura prawns carefully arranged on a bed of

Asian salad with spring onions. Still, at least she looked happy, her face aglow.

Overwhelmed by such hospitality, her friends relished their starter. By the time Joe had finished his beer, though, Geoff seemed eager to ply him with wine. So he gratefully accepted a glass of the same white the others were drinking.

"What's happening in your line of work then?" Jess plugged them.

"Glastonbury Festival's coming up," Imogen beamed, "we're running an article and I'm so excited about the line-up. Let's just say - watch this space!"

"Oh, give us a hint," Jess pressed. "Who have you got in mind?"

Setting aside her cutlery, she and Geoff exchanged glances. Joe did not miss the wolf grins spreading across their faces.

"You need to see what's trending on Twitter," he said. "But George Ezra is a rising star and definitely one to watch. Three o' clock Saturday, Pyramid Stage."

As the conversation ensued, Joe cleared away the plates. He had never attended a festival, no more than he'd heard of half the artists they were name-dropping as if they were close personal friends. Dimly aware of their banter, he lingered in the kitchen to plate up his main course; an aromatic Thai green curry with stir fried vegetables and rice. Jess had agreed it would go nicely with her starter.

As the conversation continued over dinner, he listened with half an ear as they carried on rhapsodising about who was who in the media. Jess seemed unrestrained in her passion, ever keen to keep the topic on the world of journalism.

Pouring herself another glass of wine, she fluttered her eyelashes at Geoff.

"So tell me, what makes a top-selling story?"

"Nothing beats a sex scandal," he announced boldly, "and the sleazier the better, especially when it involves people at the top."

Excitement flashed in her eyes as they met Joe's across the table.

"It's all about envy," Geoff shrugged, "when people achieve success, like celebrities, the public might look up to them, but we can't help taking immense pleasure in their downfall."

"Really," Jess said, "that's an interesting point... isn't it, Joe?"

Heart pounding in his chest, he had a horrible feeling where this was leading.

"Don't," he whispered sharply, "not now."

This time it was Imogen's turn to pounce. "Ooh, what's going on here?"

Joe cringed in his seat, filled with a sense that he had suddenly become a lot more interesting than George sodding Ezra.

How could Jess do this?

"You must have read the stories about Lord Parker-Smythe?" said Jess, relentless in her hunger to impress them.

"Go on," Geoff smiled brightly.

"Joe knew him! He was a resident in one of those children's homes..."

"Jess, please," he said through clenched teeth. "I can't talk about it."

"Who says?" she protested.

"The police," he snapped, feeling the blood rise in his face. "That's who. He's gonna be standing trial soon and until that day, I'm not allowed to breathe a word, not to you, not to anyone..." Catching Geoff's eye, he clung to his gaze with hope. "I'm sorry, but you're journalists. Surely you understand?"

Geoff smirked. "It's okay, Joe, I know where you're coming from and on that note, I think we'd better change the subject."

Jess looked crestfallen, but what did Joe care? The way they'd devoured his main course like there was no tomorrow, it wasn't as if he hadn't entertained them.

Whisking away the plates, she hurled him one of her bitchy looks before retreating to fetch dessert. With nothing else to say on the matter, he sank into his chair, little realising that the evening was about to take a turn for the worse.

Jess returned, and carefully setting down her platter of mango, papaya and passion fruit, served with organic coconut ice cream, she opened another bottle.

The conversation filtered into small talk, Jess and Imogen feverishly sharing celebrity gossip, while Joe sank into a glass of fine red, courtesy of Geoff.

"The best celebrity moment this year has got to be the Bruce Jenner story," Imogen giggled. "Or should I say *Caitlyn*, after transitioning into a woman."

Geoff leaned across the table, his face lit with intrigue, and as Jess fiddled with her mobile, she found a photo on Instagram.

"Oh - my - God," she murmured, her lips twisting into a smile. "Now that is some transformation. Amazing to think that she's gone public with this new image."

Joe suppressed a yawn, wondering how much more of this nauseating spiel he was expected to put up with. But with the conversation edging towards Instagram, he snatched up his own phone. Loading the app, he couldn't resist a peek, secretly wondering whether Maisie had posted anything.

The first image he saw pulled all the breath from his lungs.

Trees. Winter trees, definitely oaks. They lingered in the mist like ghostly figures, skeletal branches clawing the sky, a black and white image so creepy, he could not believe Maisie would have posted it.

Fighting to retain his composure, he took another swallow of wine.

Yet the more he scrolled, the more unsettling images emerged before his disbelieving eyes and not just trees, but forests; dozens of them, the photographs taken in all seasons. One image in particular turned his blood to ice.

A circle of bare branches hung silhouetted against a night sky... so evocative of her nightmares.

"Fucking hell," he murmured, forgetting he was in company.

His thumb froze on the next image. It appeared to be a sponsored link, but who in their right mind would want a flickering torch powered by electricity?

Stopping mid-sentence, Jess gaped at him. "What's up with you?"

"There's something really weird going on with Maisie's account," he said. "I'm not messing around, but there's no way she'd have posted this shit!"

"Oh God, not this 'troll business' again," she sighed.

Joe could not move, the jeer in her tone grating on him. "This is no troll," he said coldly. "This is serious. I wonder if her Instagram has been hacked..."

"Maisie?" Imogen piped up. "I haven't seen Maisie for ages. How is she?"

"Maisie's fine!" Jess bristled, her eyes boring into Joe. "And why are you so obsessed with her Instagram all of a sudden?"

"Why shouldn't I be?" he snapped back, realising even as he spoke that Jess knew almost nothing of her friend's psychological issues.

"Actually, there's a fake app I've heard of," Geoff intervened.

Looking at Joe with raised eyebrows, he grabbed the wine, sloshing another hefty measure into their glasses.

"I'm certain it's got something to do with Instagram."

"Okay, so how does that work?" Joe asked.

"The pictures and posts in feeds don't even look like the user's account, but apparently it downloads spyware. Google it."

"Spyware?" Joe echoed. "Does that mean... Oh, Jesus." He broke off, knuckles whitening as he gripped his glass.

Was it possible Maisie's mobile had been tampered with?

If so, it yielded their enemies a formidable advantage.

"What?" Jess frowned.

"This ain't just about creepy pictures on Instagram," he whispered, his voice deep with dread. "Neither of us have been able to get hold of her. What if this app's given someone total control over her phone?"

As Jess lounged back in her chair, the look on her face was nothing like he'd expected. Surely she should be worried? Yet he caught a glint of amusement in her eye before she glanced back at her audience.

"Sorry. You can't blame him for fearing the worst. He's not unfamiliar with the criminal underworld..." She pursed her lips. "Are you, Joe?"

Joe frowned. "Maybe not, but that's hardly the point..."

Yet it seemed she had not quite finished with him. Locking eyes with Imogen, her words seemed designed to prompt a reaction.

"Criminal underworld?" Imogen gasped in wonderment. "Seriously?"

"Yeah," Joe sighed. "It's not something I'm proud of but some of them bars I worked at in London were run by a local kingpin..."

"A gangster!" Imogen spluttered. "Oh, tell me more, please... I'm dying to find out how organised crime works. It's for my novel."

"She's writing a gangland thriller," Geoff grinned, keen to join in. "So come on then Joe, put her out of her misery will you, and maybe we can move on."

Joe took a shuddering breath. The thought of dragging George Oldman into the conversation made him feel sick to the core, but with the alcohol flowing freely, he was beginning to lose his inhibitions.

"What can I tell you? The guy who recruited me was a legend, and like all the bigshot crime lords he was rich, powerful and very much feared."

"He's the reason you went to prison, wasn't he?" Jess oozed.

Disbelief widened Imogen's eyes. "You went to prison? What for?"

"Got sucked into an armed robbery," Joe muttered darkly, "but let's not go there..."

"But that's awesome!" she laughed with glee.

He hadn't known it before it happened, he hadn't even sensed the inferno building up inside him, but it was this comment that ignited it. Studying their faces, he could see them virtually salivating over his past.

"You just don't get it, do you?" he shouted, banging his glass down.

Slops of red wine spilled onto the table cloth, Jess glaring in outrage, but suddenly he didn't care. He'd had enough.

"There was nothing 'awesome' about it! A woman was shot dead, just for being in the wrong place at the wrong time, thanks to that psycho!"

Jess reached for his hand, but he wrenched it away irritably.

"It still haunts me! And all the while people like you are getting off on this... sensationalising crime like it's some - some *sick entertainment*, there's families out there grieving! Have you ever thought about that?"

The atmosphere buckled into a stony silence. Jess looked as if she were about to burst into tears, but Joe was past caring. With an overwhelming urge to get away from them, he shot up from the table, knocking his chair over, before storming off to the bedroom utterly devastated.

Chapter Fifty-Nine

Lying on top of Jess's double bed, he gulped in deep breaths. The seconds ticked slowly but he could still hear them out there, murmuring in hushed tones, the occasional tinkle of a wine glass.

He wondered whether he should go back.

Except it was too bloody late to apologise, the damage had been done.

They didn't stay long, but hearing them leave brought a roller coaster of emotions to the surface. In those final few minutes the fog in his mind had cleared and only then did he grasp the truth behind Jess's obsession. *What she had done to him.*

Closing his eyes, he braced himself for the bomb to go off, and this time he was ready for her. It began within minutes, the slam of a door, the crashing and banging of plates echoing from the kitchen.

Joe counted to ten before dragging his weary limbs into action.

Sure enough, the moment his shadow fell over the threshold, she spun around, her face flushed with anger.

"How could you?" she hissed. "I have never been so humiliated..."

"So how do you think I felt?" he said icily.

"What the hell is that supposed to mean?" she retorted, ramming another plate into the dishwasher. Disdain twisted her face, and the look did her no favours.

"First, you bring up Lord Parker-Smythe," he spat. "Sex scandal, my arse! You couldn't wait for me to spill my guts about the case! And as for that shit about my past, just be honest, Jess. You don't love me! All you want from me is some titillating gossip to feed your journalist friends. Well, I'm sick of it!"

"Joe, that's not true," she whimpered.

Dropping the mug she was holding, she flinched in shock as it bounced on the floor and smashed. Joe glanced away. The look in her eyes was almost pitiful.

"How can you say that? I invited you into my home, gave you a love life most men would kill for and this is the way you treat me?"

"I never asked for any of it," Joe seethed. "You offered it to me on a plate. We have to face facts, Jess. We're not compatible and it's time I left."

His hands shook as she tried to corner him and he backed away.

What could he do, other than run while he had the chance?

She had sunk her claws in deep but shredded his heart in the process.

"Joe, please!" She was begging now. "Where are you going to go?"

"Does it matter?" he sighed. "Maybe I'll find a bench in Marine Park Gardens, but there's no way I'm spending another night with you. It's over!"

Without wasting a second, he scoured the apartment for his most important belongings and threw them into his rucksack. Returning to the bedroom, where he had already stuffed as many clothes as he could fit into a carrier bag, he made a grab for that too. The rest he would have to leave. All the while he was packing, he could hear Jess bleating in the background. But he wasn't listening. Heart crashing wildly, he threw on his jacket, never more determined to escape.

"You ungrateful bastard!" she screamed in his wake. "I hate you!"

Maybe they were the last words he would ever hear from her, but he didn't look back. Footsteps light, he flitted downstairs to the exit, stepping into the darkness where the cool summer air embraced him.

Creeping his way along the sea wall, he heard the soft swish of waves in the distance. The thought of returning to the beach shelter rose temptingly... but of course, Jess knew nothing about Maisie's key nestling in his rucksack.

At last he allowed himself a smile.

Didn't she say he could move back in if things didn't work out?

So he turned away from the seafront, yet to embark on the long walk up Victoria Drive that would ultimately lead him to her door.

It took less than fifteen minutes, and as the large brick and cream house reared up in front of him, he felt his heart lift.

Oh, how he had missed her flat, the soft lamps, the pretty colours and its cluttered, lived-in cosiness.

Jess's seaside apartment might be luxurious but it lacked character. Minimalist and sterile, he had never felt at home there; the way she snapped his head off every time he left a fleece lying around living proof he could never have fitted into her perfectly-ordered world. Exhaling a sigh, he slipped his key into the door, and with the neighbourhood basked in shadow, took a moment to observe his surroundings.

The first thing that struck him was an unfamiliar silver camper van where Maisie used to park. The absence of her car brought with it a groundswell of fear. Letting himself in quietly, he wondered how she was faring.

Asleep in her idyllic cottage probably, unaware of the hidden danger.

First thing tomorrow, he would call her, but not just to update her on his own crisis. She needed to know about the images he had seen on Instagram.

With no work until Friday there was little he could do other than settle down for now. Crashing out in Maisie's spare bedroom, fully clothed, he had endured a somewhat restless night, but with so many troubled thoughts brewing in his mind, sleep did not come easily.

Before the next day dawned, however, Joe would learn their enemies might be a little closer to home.

Reluctant to call Maisie's mobile, he phoned the Council. The chances were he wouldn't be able to reach her any other way. Yet he heard no ring tone, no sign his phone was even connecting.

Joe stared at the screen. With thoughts of fake apps rising darkly, never mind spyware, he was beginning to question the status of his own handset.

Spyware.

Such a concept left a bitter taste but it seemed unwise to ignore Geoff's warning. Spyware suggested infiltration on a deeper level, something more sinister than he could deal with. That left only her landline.

"Good morning, Chichester District Council?"

Torn from his musings, he asked to be put through to the Child Care and Fostering department. Yet Maisie couldn't be reached there either.

"I'm afraid she's in a meeting until lunchtime. Shall I take a message?"

The situation left him floundering, but what could he say? He had urged her to get her phone looked at but with no further communication since Monday, there was no telling if she had done it.

"No, it's okay, thanks, I-I'll call back later," he spluttered.

Holding his breath, he waited for the receptionist to hang up but as the phone fell silent, he pressed it to his chest. He had a hundred things on his mind, but something else had just clicked.

Spyware.

He couldn't shake off the memories of the things they had talked about; meetings with Sam, the invitation to visit their cottage... Maisie had read out the postcode. It once again drew his attention to the house in East Lavant, its secluded country setting, and a wave of dread rolled over him.

Forcing down a cup of strong coffee, he grimaced at the lack of milk. Yet he couldn't sit here agonising forever. For a start he needed supplies, and furthermore, had a yearning to visit Matt in the charity shop.

Maybe kill an hour at the Job Centre?

It would do no harm to look for a second job; lunchtimes, evenings, anything to fill the gaps between his early morning shifts at Sainsbury's.

Except one hour blurred into three. If only he hadn't allowed himself to get waylaid chatting with Matt, he might have arrived at the Job Centre a lot earlier. But with the next couple of hours gobbled up with job hunting, followed by shopping, it was late afternoon before he turned back.

Marching past the railway station, he noticed the time on the clock tower, shocked at how almost a whole day had disappeared.

Eventually he reached the house. Weighed down with groceries, he lowered the bag onto the pavement to find his key. But before he could draw another breath, his eyes stopped dead. For there lurking outside stood a familiar white Nissan in place of the camper van he had spotted earlier; if he remembered rightly, this belonged to her neighbour.

It seemed a lifetime ago since the old man had been carted off in an ambulance.

Once inside, desperate for a cup of tea, he knew he wouldn't be able to relax until he had touched base with Maisie. So he tried once again dialling her workplace.

"I'm sorry but Maisie's finished for today. She's just left..."

His heart sank like a stone.

She must have knocked off early.

"Did you try calling earlier?"

"I did," Joe murmured, "but don't worry, I'll ring again tomorrow."

A sense of desolation folded around him like a cloud, and as if to add to his anxiety, he knew damn well there wasn't a landline in the cottage.

Packing away his groceries, his thoughts raced wildly.

He could try her mobile again, but was it worth the risk?

With a deepening sigh, he pulled out his vaporiser. The touch of cool steel under his fingertips brought a pang of sadness. A gift from Jess, this was undeniably one of her kinder gestures. Yet the way she had behaved since left no room for regrets and right now, he was hankering for a smoke.

Drifting out onto the pavement, Joe pressed the button to release the fragrant vapour. For several seconds he inhaled deeply and it didn't seem long before a shadow filled the doorway.

"Oh, it's you," a female voice rose. "Long time no see!"

Joe turned, and clocking the whale of a woman observing him, pressed a smile onto his face. "Hi there! Paula, isn't it? How are things?"

"Alright," she said, shuffling her way through the door to join him. "Can't keep up with who's living here no more. Old git upstairs is back but the Poles have gone and there's some other foreign bloke living there now. So where's yer mate gone?"

He folded away his vaporiser. "Maisie's gone to live with Sam now, her new boyfriend. They're staying in a house near Chichester."

"Oh, I get it," Paula smirked. "Wouldn't happen to be that tall, dishy blonde fella I saw hanging around a few weeks ago?"

"That'll be the one," Joe said. Mood sinking, he kicked a stone on the ground.

"Got a flash car an' all. I'm well jeal' but I see everything from my flat..." A smile lit her eyes as she glanced at him. "I'm a bit of a people watcher, you know. Don't s'pose yer wanna come up and have a butcher's?"

In the end he saw no point refusing. Without her presence, Maisie's flat seemed empty and soulless, and he couldn't deny that the events of recent days had shaken him hollow.

"I've just split up with my girlfriend," he mumbled.

After following her upstairs, it was a relief to offload to another human being, apart from Matt, whose crude laddish jokes had done little to ease his depression.

"Sit down," Paula instructed gently. "I'll make us a cup of tea. You look like you could do with one and you can tell me all about it."

It was hard to explain his feelings. But from the very first spark at the Italian restaurant, to her unashamedly hunting him down while Maisie was away, he could see now just how calculating Jess had been. Casting her net, hooking him in.

What a fool.

"I was besotted," he kept rambling. "Maisie did say she was a man-eater."

Gazing around Paula's flat, he felt a warm, oozing camaraderie. Contrary to his expectations, she had done it up nicely. Thick rugs covered the floor, her chairs squashy and inviting. Wind chimes and dream catchers dangled in her window, radiating sparkles of colour, and there were potted plants everywhere.

"I think I know who you mean now," she nodded. "The only friend I've seen of Maisie's is that blonde tart."

"Mmm," Joe sighed. Sipping his tea, he felt the last of his tension evaporate. "So what about you, what's your situation? You've got a kid, haven't you?"

And so her story unfolded. Being overweight had always been a disadvantage, but with low self-esteem, she was a magnet to a certain type of man: the sly and controlling sort. Falling pregnant to a small time drug dealer, Scott Stone, she thought she had landed on her feet. *Engaged to be married and expecting a baby.* Yet within months, Scott had revealed his cruel streak. Battering her senseless, kicking her whilst pregnant – as a result of which she ultimately ended up in hospital – he was charged with assault. So after a short spell living in a women's hostel until Jade was born, Paula had moved to Bognor, determined to protect herself and her baby daughter.

"There's some right bastards out there," Joe said through clenched teeth.

"Yeah," she finished. A shadow darkened her eyes. "He swore he'd hunt me down too, and I know I can be lairy at times but all I care about is my little 'un..."

Boosted by her company, Joe lost track of time again. The evenings were light, the sun spreading a golden gleam over the walls, and before he knew it, she had dug out a big bottle of cider.

"Fancy something stronger than tea?" she teased, waving the bottle in front of him. "You don't have to rush off, do ya?"

"Nah," Joe sighed. Flicking a glance at his watch, he was surprised to discover it was nearly seven. But with little to entertain him, there seemed no point bolting back to Maisie's flat. Less so if he couldn't even contact her. "What do you usually get up to on a Wednesday night then?"

"Not a lot," Paula grunted, "I was gonna go out on the pull, seeing as Jade's at her auntie's, but I'm not sure I can be arsed now. How about you?"

Joe gave a shrug, accepting a glass of cider.

At the same time, a distinct rumble reverberated from his belly, reminding him that he had barely eaten all day. He was gagging for a drink, but on the other hand, was it wise to get hammered on an empty stomach?

"Fuck it, let's get a takeaway," he muttered. "My treat."

Her face lit up like she had won the lottery. Joe took a moment to observe her, feeling a surge of sympathy. The sad truth was that they were both survivors, but where he had moved forward with his life, thanks to Maisie, what did Paula have to fall back on other than handouts?

They ordered an Indian, and within half an hour it had been delivered to the house. Paula rushed downstairs to fetch it, leaving Joe in her flat. Moments later he heard her footsteps thumping back upstairs before a profusion of warm, spicy smells coiled around the door, teasing his senses. Light headed with hunger, not to mention the glass of cider he had consumed, he followed her into her kitchen to dish up.

"Thanks for this," Paula beamed at him. "You're a real decent bloke, you know. Wish there were more like you around."

Joe lowered his eyes, feeling a flush creep up his neck. Despite her obesity and slovenly appearance, she had a nice smile. It shone from deep within her eyes, a balm to his bruised ego, and for the first time in a long while he was enjoying himself.

"This looks great," he said, disregarding her compliment, "and I'm starving. Where are we gonna eat it?"

"On our laps, of course," she huffed, dragging a couple of trays off the top of her fridge. "We're not in Buckingham bleeding Palace."

Joe laughed, amused to wonder what Jess would think if she could see him now. Tucking into onion bhajis, followed by chicken korma, rice and daal, rolled into an enormous slab of naan bread, he no longer had to be on his best behaviour.

A far cry from tiptoeing around at her poncey dinner party.

However tantalising the food was, though, his appetite had diminished somewhat and he could barely manage half of it. He pressed his hand over his mouth and belched. Washed down with another pint of strong cider, he was beginning to feel a little drunk... though not as pissed as Paula.

Switching on the TV, she began howling with laughter at some comedy, but Joe wasn't paying attention. Conscious of the time slipping by, he sensed a need to depart now, and much as he had loved getting to know her, he couldn't hang around all night. The lure of Maisie's flat was growing stronger, somewhere quiet where he could just chill and gather his thoughts.

"Need a hand clearing up?" he offered. "I'd best be on my way soon..."

"Aw, d'you have to go?" she sulked. "I'll wash up later."

"Yeah, sorry," he said, "but I've got stuff to do and calls to make."

She seemed reluctant to let him leave, though. Beady eyes pinned on him, there was no mistaking the leer creeping over her face. Shuddering to imagine where the night was leading, he took a deep breath, then struggled out of his arm chair.

The room spun, forcing him to grasp the table top. Paula too staggered to her feet. Swaying where she stood, she took another clumsy step towards him.

"Giz us a kiss then," she slurred. "S'been a great evening..."

But in the moment she puckered up to him, she appeared to lose her balance. Joe grasped her waist to stop her falling but it was useless. His willowy frame was no match against her eighteen stone bulk. Buckling under her weight, they tumbled to the floor in a heap, taking the table and its contents down with them. Piles of boxes, DVDs and Jade's toys went crashing to the ground. And all the while he was wrestling under Paula, she was rolling around, still hooting with laughter.

The rumpus went on for a few seconds. That was until the atmosphere shifted without warning.

First came the pounding of a fist on the door.

Next roared a voice; a more terrible sound than Joe could take in, and it exploded in his head like thunder.

"For God's sake shut up in there, you accursed animals!"

Every muscle in his body froze but that voice... it chilled him to the core, drawing him unsteadily to his feet. Despite the chaos all around them, Paula too seemed to detect the tension.

"Whassup?" she breathed.

"Shit," Joe whispered. "Who the fuck is that?"

Drawn to the door as if hypnotised, he couldn't help himself. He had to check who was out there, regardless of the paralysing fear devouring him.

Flinging the door open, he gasped at the sight of the emaciated old man standing there. Haggard in the face he might be, those big puffed out cheeks he imagined wasted away, the lips slack and twisted.

277

"You," he shuddered under his breath.

Joe's courage crumbled like an avalanche. He knew he should run, but he could not move. Twenty years rolled back like a black mist revealing the face of a monster.

Mortimer.

Despite his heavily lined, tanned face, the rich gold hair framing it, and the beard, those were Mr. Mortimer's eyes, and how they had changed. Hidden in a nest of wrinkles, they clung to his stare, crazed with hatred and skewering deep into his soul.

Chapter Sixty

If Joe had been thinking more clearly, he would have called the police there and then. But Joe wasn't thinking clearly. He was in deep shock, and after consuming a considerable amount of cider, felt as if his brain had gone on strike.

Hand glued to the door handle, he slammed it shut; but the vision of his enemy left him petrified, his breath coming in laboured gasps.

Paula stared at him aghast. "You're not scared of that old twat are you?"

"Shh," Joe whispered. "H-he's not who he says he is... Oh fuck. Oh shitting fucking hell." His voice shook as he struggled to breath.

And all the while he was floundering, precious seconds ticked by. A creak on the stairs made him flinch, a scurry of footsteps. The slam of the front door followed, leaving a baleful echo.

"Whoever he is, sounds like he's legging it," Paula said tartly.

Finally her words triggered a response. Joe sprang towards the window, but a moment too late and just as the sound of an engine burst into life.

"Bollocks," he spluttered.

Contrary to expectation however, it was not the white Nissan he saw belting up the avenue but the silver van from the previous night.

Cursing his slowness, he turned to Paula. "Who does that van belong to?"

"Guy who moved in downstairs," she frowned.

"What guy?" Joe shouted in panic. "You said he was foreign but what's he look like? Wouldn't happen to be some big bastard would he?"

Shock sprung to her eyes as she staggered over to the window to join him.

"What's going on, Joe? You're starting to scare me."

"Schiller," he whimpered.

How was it possible he could have wound up in a house with his most feared enemies?

"There isn't much time to explain, but that man next door..."

"Mr toss pot Lacey?" she drawled.

"His name is Mortimer," Joe snarled, "and he's a fucking nonce! Maisie and I met in a children's home. Orchard Grange, an evil place..."

Paula's face turned ashen. He would have said more, if it hadn't been for the unexpected buzz of his mobile.

A text.

Wrenching it from his pocket, he scrolled to his messages. Yet a cold suspicion ran its way through him before he had even read it.

Dear little Maisie, all alone and being watched, not a word to the police you scumbag or she dies in agony.

He stared at the screen, heart leaping in his throat, any last hope of nailing those bastards truly screwed. How could he ignore their warning? Deep in his mind, a horrific fear had been unravelling; that it wasn't just Maisie's phone contaminated with spyware.

Battling his inner turmoil, Joe spent the night with Paula for two reasons. His initial instinct was to run but one glance down the stairs drew his fearful gaze to the neighbouring flat. A strip of light shone under the door.

Schiller had tried to kill him once.

There was no telling if he was down there, crouched in waiting, but it was obvious that it would be safer to stay put... at least for now.

The second reason was for Paula's benefit. After opening his heart to her, anyone could see how tense she had become, and now it was down to him to protect her. Satisfying her desires (as well as his own) allowed him time to think about his next move; a plan that would involve careful tactics.

It might have been necessity rather than want, but he was surprised by how good it was. Having never imagined anyone could compare to Jess, with her beautifully toned body, he savoured the warm folds of flesh pressed against him.

This was a real woman, and she certainly knew how to please.

Waking up next morning, he eyed her sleepily, her big thighs like cushions wrapped around him as they indulged in an early morning romp.

Eventually he got dressed and crept to the window. The sun hung suspended beneath a layer of filmy cloud, painting feathers of pink and flame orange across the sky. Such a beautiful sunrise would have soothed his soul, if it hadn't been reflected in the silver panels of the van parked outside.

He expelled a gasp. "Looks like they're back."

And was that a movement he glimpsed behind the glass?

Sure enough, a figure ballooned in the driver's seat and he knew he was not alone. He felt the chill of another man's stare even from the height of Paula's window.

"I-I've got to get to London," he stammered, "dunno how, though..."

As he backed away from the window, Paula took his place. Wrapped in a flowery satin robe, she tugged it tighter around her body.

"Maybe I can distract him," she smiled saucily.

Joe frowned. "No, Paula, you can't put yourself in danger."

"Can't I?" she taunted and turning to him with a lewd smile, slid back the folds of satin to expose her ample breasts. "Try me! I'll go down and chat 'im up a bit and while I'm out there, you can hop it."

With a quaking sigh, he thought she had lost the plot. "You can't be serious! Don't get involved in this, Paula, those are dangerous fuckers."

She shrugged off his warning, the gleam in her eyes growing brighter.

"You do know there's a fire escape outside the kitchen, don't ya?" she added. "All you gotta do is sneak down to the back garden and if yer fit enough to climb over the fence, them gardens in the next row of houses bring you out onto Longford road. It's right opposite the station."

At last he smiled back. Her face glowed with pride, and he could not resist throwing his arms around her.

"Thanks, Paula, you're a diamond!" he laughed, smacking a kiss on her mouth. "But for God's sake look out for yourself."

Slipping into the kitchen, he felt his heart swell with the effort she had gone to, first by letting him stay over and now this... and with that thought came a stir of compassion as he wondered what advice he could offer her.

"Listen, Paula," he murmured. "It sounds like you've had a shit life, but it doesn't have to be this way. I was sleeping rough when Maisie found me but I still managed to get a job and turn my life around."

"Yeah, right," Paula said, rolling her eyes, "but it's different for you. There ain't no way I can get a job, 'til Jade starts school. I'm on benefits and get me rent paid, but soon as you start work you lose all that. What's more d'ya even know how much a child minder costs? Hundreds! Sad fact is, mate, I'm better off not working than working right now, and that's how it's gotta stay."

"I'm sorry," he whispered, "I wasn't having a go..."

"I know." She reached up to stroke his cheek. "Now get away while you can."

******

Paula watched in suspense as Joe tiptoed down the metal staircase. Her eyes traced his every twist and turn, until he had made it to the bottom.

Quietly closing the door, she felt a shudder of disgust. The things he had revealed about her neighbour turned her cold.

That nasty old git had always spooked her, but a kiddie fiddler...

She ground her teeth. Her thoughts crept to her precious three-year-old daughter, and without wasting another second, she stormed out of the house.

Sure enough, the camper van was still lurking. Paula's eyes narrowed and taking a deep gulp of air, she wandered up to the window.

"Can I help you?"

Tilting his head, the driver surveyed her icily. Despite his bulk, he possessed hard, angular features. His thinning blonde crew cut exposed a bulging forehead and the coldest of blue eyes.

"Go away!" he growled in a guttural German accent. "You are of no interest to me, woman."

"Alright, keep yer hair on," Paula snapped. "Not that you've got much but I wanna know what you're up to. Loitering outside our house!"

The man emitted a sniff of amusement. "It is none of your business!"

"Well, that's where you're wrong," she sneered and stuffing both hands in the pockets of her voluminous satin gown, she held her head high. "I've got a little girl, mate, and for all I know you could be some paedo!"

The man's eyes flared with menace as he leaned over the window edge. "What did you say?"

Paula stood her ground. "You 'eard!" she taunted. "Or did my ex send you? I ain't daft. This ain't the first time I've seen some weirdo hanging around. Now bugger off 'fore I call the cops."

Her heart hammered harder but what did she have to lose? Recalling Joe's story, she was not going to be intimidated, least of all by this repulsive thug.

For several seconds, they were trapped in a nail-biting stand-off, until she remembered that pervert he was working for. Taking a cautious step backwards, she appeared to retreat. *Let him think she was scared*. Except the last thing she did was extract her mobile and raising it high in the air, took a photo.

Thrilled by her own bravery, she watched with pleasure as fury reddened his face. The flash of his teeth was the last she saw of him before he fired up his engine and screeched away.

******

Joe, in the meantime, knew nothing of the risk she was taking. Following her instructions, he crept his way across the gardens of the houses lining Longford Road and no longer caring who saw him, hot-footed it to the railway station.

A minute was all he needed to buy a ticket, the train to London already on the platform.

It was due to leave in three minutes. But as he ambled along the platform, looking to board a carriage, he could hardly believe his luck. For there, just ahead of him, loped a familiar youth dressed in black. Joe grinned to himself. There was only one guy whose hair was cropped at the sides like that, leaving a burgundy red layer flopping over the crown.

"Matt!" he hissed, shimmying up to him. "Am I glad to see you!"

282

Matt spun around in surprise before his frown changed to a smirk. "Watcher, mate. You've perked up since yesterday. Got lucky, did you?"

"Sorry, Matt, I ain't got time to explain but can I borrow your mobile?"

They boarded the train together yet still Matt seemed hesitant.

"Please," he whispered in his ear. "I gotta call the cops and fast."

"Yeah, but I'm only going as far as Barnham to see my nan," Matt faltered. "I'll need it back."

"Then I'll get off at Barnham with you," Joe said. "I can catch a later train to London but this is urgent. So just gimme your phone will you?"

He could wait no longer. While Matt frowned his way slowly to a decision, Joe snatched the phone from his hand and leapt into a toilet, locking the door behind him. What else could he do? The situation had become critical. His hands trembled as he turned on his own handset, and copying the number for Charing Cross Police Station, switched it off again. It seemed a good plan: call first, explain later, if he could just get through to DI Fitzpatrick.

"Hi, Joe, DS Mike Havers here. Andrew's in a meeting, what's happened?"

"I saw Mortimer last night," he shuddered. "Living in the same bloody house as Maisie but he looks different. Older, thinner..." Closing his eyes, he could still picture the man, stooped in front of him like a poisonous old spider. "Christ, no wonder he had her fooled - he goes under the name *Richard Lacey* now. Drives a fucking great white Nissan. Oh, and another thing. Schiller's there, too!"

"Okay," Mike responded firmly. "Well done, we'll get a local squad car around there immediately - so where are you now?"

"On a train to London," he kept whispering. "Any chance I could drop by? 'Cos I've got shit loads to tell you..."

By the time the call ended, he had secured an appointment. If everything panned out, there might even be an unmarked police car waiting for him at the tube station, but for now, he needed to stay vigilant.

Stepping out of the toilet and with the train picking up speed and then slowing, he felt the wheels lurch under his feet. He almost stumbled, at the same time winding his way along the aisle to reach an anxious-looking Matt.

"Jesus, you cut it fine," he muttered. "What the fuck's wrong?"

"Shh," Joe whispered. "Can it wait 'til we get off the train first?"

No sooner had they alighted in Barnham than Joe slapped a friendly arm around his shoulder. Urging him to walk a little further up the platform, this was his last chance to offload everything - from the sighting of his nemesis to that noxious text - the reason he dared not risk using his own phone.

But now seemed as good a time as any to ask Matt the one question that had been niggling him all morning.

"You know this phone you gave me at the charity shop? I think it's bugged.

Can you remember who dropped it in?"

Another frown crinkled Matt's forehead as he scratched the side of his head. "Hmm, it was a while back - um - I seem to remember some old bloke..."

"Old bloke?" Joe echoed.

His mind struggled to imagine what age Mortimer was.

In his seventies most likely.

"Was he a tall geezer? Scrawny with brassy hair and a beard?"

Matt nodded, his mouth dropping open. "Um - it's starting to come back now, but he said he wanted one of the volunteers to have it. Someone - um - who was homeless."

"That figures," Joe said, smiling, albeit wryly. "In that case can I ask one more favour and I'll get off your back, I swear. I want you to take a picture of this text and send it to the cops. Call Bognor. Ask for DC Mark Anderson and then at least it's on record."

"Okay," Matt nodded, "but whatever shit's kicking off, promise to be careful and stay in touch, alright?"

They departed warmly. Matt he could trust. Matt had looked out for him on numerous occasions, even if he could be a bit of a prat at times.

Awaiting the 8:17 train to London, Joe stared at his phone. He scrolled through his texts, wounded to see the last of Maisie's messages before all communications had been severed.

Only now, though, did he see this phone as a deadly weapon, a poison-coated gift his enemies had used to great effect.

Switching it off, he tossed it under the seat of a Portsmouth train, glad to be rid of the bloody thing before it could be used to track him any further.

Chapter Sixty-One

Where the hell was Joe?

I hadn't heard a word since he had tracked me down on Monday, and by Thursday I was beginning to panic. He'd looked so desolate when he had confided in me, his eyes filled with hurt. But it took one heated telephone exchange with Jess to confirm my suspicions.

She and Joe had split up, and it had been far from amicable.

"Bloody man!" she ranted. "You should have seen the way he behaved, Maisie, and after everything I did to help him... I was only trying to coax him into a more cultured circle but he was so bloody rude to my guests!"

I could have laughed, imagining the scene.

Hadn't I warned her he had endured a tough life?

However hard she tried to tame him, she was never going to gentrify him, and his story about Fontwell Racecourse said it all. I wondered if I should mention it; *how degraded he had felt.* And then she started bad-mouthing him.

"He's nothing but a scrounger," she added nastily, "a conniving bastard out for what he can get, and as soon as it doesn't go his way, he moves on."

I closed my eyes, the vitriol in her voice grating on me. Joe was my friend. Joe, a little rough around the edges but a genuinely lovely person.

"Stop it," I gasped. "Joe isn't like that. I know you were crazy about each other but mixing in each other's social circles was never going to be easy..."

"I knew you'd take his side," she snapped and with nothing more to say, hung up on me.

Her attitude left me breathless and in the wake of such acrimony, I couldn't help fearing how it would affect *our* friendship.

Overriding everything though, I felt so sorry for Joe. His face gleamed in my mind again, anxious and despairing, but with his relationship teetering on a cliff edge, hadn't I said he could move back into my flat?

Chewing my lip, I was on my way to Bognor anyway to see Hannah, curious as to why he hadn't contacted me.

Surely he would have given me an update by now?

But as I stopped in Annandale Avenue to check if he was there, the answer hit me in a flash. *My phone.* He seemed to be having trouble getting through to me, and I had completely forgotten to get it looked at.

Opening the front door, I let myself in. My heels echoed ominously and even before I unlocked my own flat, I sensed the desolation all around me. A pile of post had accumulated on my doormat, the sitting room clean and tidy. But as I ventured into the kitchen, I noticed a few differences.

Yes, Joe had been here.

A loaf of bread rested on the work top. Opening the fridge, I saw a fresh milk carton, packs of cheese, ham and butter, and cans of his favourite beer.

Stepping back into the lounge however, I stopped dead. Spotted his rucksack marooned on an armchair and an icy fear slid right through me. I tried not to panic, convinced there would be a perfectly logical explanation... *except if Joe had ventured out somewhere, why leave it behind?* I thought it followed him everywhere.

My eyes were drawn to my telephone. It would only take a minute, but was it worth trying his mobile? Hastily dialling his number, I was dismayed to hear it go straight to voicemail. This was so unlike him, but with no time to dwell and my appointment with Hannah looming, I didn't want to be late.

******

Hannah Adams. Registered Psychotherapist/Counsellor. West Sussex
Client: Maisie Bell
18th June 2015

"It's good to see you," Hannah greeted me softly. "It's been four weeks, but before we begin, how's the investigation going?"

I studied her face, the lines of concern etched around her mouth. She seemed on edge, just as before, as if fearing the consequences this would have on me.

"Nothing much is happening at the moment," I reassured her. "We're hoping the Met will send an update but sadly they hit a stumbling block after the death of Sam's social worker. Her name was Yvonne Draper."

A look of sorrow hung in her eyes. "I saw it on the news. Dreadful business, and it must be devastating for your friend, Sam. Have you seen him lately?"

"Seen him?" I whispered. "Oh, Hannah! You'll never believe this, but we're in a relationship now and I'm totally in love with him."

Regardless of the horrors surrounding the police investigation, how could I not mention the whirlwind romance in the aftermath of our pub lunch? So much had happened; Joe moving out, that abrupt spell of loneliness, not to forget the recurrence of my nightmare.

Sam had brought me out of that darkness and as for the rest...

"It feels like I'm living a dream." I let my head roll back, savouring the soft leather embrace of my chair. There was so much more I wanted to tell her, our first night together soothing away those niggling tremors of self-doubt. "The house we're staying in is beautiful. It's a shame we can't be together all the

286

time, given his job, but he does phone me every night..."

"This is wonderful news, Maisie, and I'm happy for you," she responded. Yet something about her body language suggested she wanted to press on.

"Thanks," I said, "but going back to your original question, all we know is the police are desperately trying to track down Mortimer."

"They still haven't found any trace of him?"

"I'm afraid not."

"I see," she said. "In that case, would you mind if I took you back to your story where you left it? Sam had gone and you were about to be fostered - but I was wondering if you could remember the day you left the home. What are your last memories of Mr. Mortimer?"

"It was a strange day. I remember one of the wardens telling me to pack my things and to wait downstairs in the dining room. We'd just had lunch. Joe was there, hanging around with me, but we had this nagging sense I was leaving. I mean, why else would I need my suitcase?"

"Can you remember any other feelings?"

"Confusion, anxiety, but most of all I felt sad. Over the last few weeks we'd been inseparable and I'll never forget the way he looked at me... as if he knew we were about to say goodbye."

Tears choked my voice. Yes, that last vision of Joe's face shone bright as a flame, unleashing a riot of feelings. His big brown eyes clung to mine, his smile as warm as it had ever been.

'Look after yourself, Maisie,' he said, 'I'm never gonna forget you.'

'But what about you?' I croaked. 'You can't stay here...'

'I ain't got a choice,' he shrugged. 'Where else am I gonna go?'

'Just find a way out, Joe. I'm scared for you...' My mouth felt so dry, I could barely force the words out.

But time was running out and no sooner had I hurled my arms around him, than something else happened...

"Oh my God! I remember now... That stupid girl kicking off."

"What do you remember, Maisie?"

"There was this girl in the room, throwing a hissy fit. Lucy I think her name was - all spiky hair and thick black eye-liner, and she was renowned for being a self-harmer. Yet there she was, waving a knife around. I think she might have stolen it from the kitchen but - but..."

"Go on."

"A squad of adults stormed in, Mr. Mortimer among them. They surrounded her, restrained her, had her pinned to the ground... It was the last thing Joe and I saw before we were separated, and I hate to sound harsh, but it ruined our

287

moment! All I wanted was a few precious minutes with him, but as soon as Mr. Mortimer saw us, he split us apart. Said he had a few words to say to me in private and ordered Joe to leave."

"Was this the last time you saw each other?"

"In Orchard Grange? Yes... but I couldn't go against Mortimer."

The memory arose blackly, filling me with dread.

Summoning me upstairs for a 'chat in his office,' there was little I could do other than follow him. My heart hammered like a kettle drum as he closed the door.

'Accursed animals,' he snarled under his breath. 'I'm sorry you had to witness that, Maisie, now please, sit down.'

'What's going on?' My voice sounded weak and it was hard to disguise the quiver in it. 'Am I leaving now?'

A smile lifted his lips. 'We've been in contact with Stewart and Mandy Reedman and they are on their way to collect you.'

'My new foster parents,' I murmured. 'Today?'

'Hmm, I realise it's a little sooner than expected but you are indeed going to be leaving us, my dear...'

I held my breath as his glassy eyes wandered over me. He took my hands, stroking them gently, and all the while, he was smirking.

'Look at those lovely hands, such perfection. It's a shame to see you go but you don't belong here, Maisie. You're not like those other kids. Most of them are rabble but you are so very special, so virtuous and pure...'

Hearing his voice thicken, I pulled my hands away.

'They're not rabble,' I whispered. 'I've made some good friends here, so what's going to happen to them?'

'They are no longer your concern, Maisie,' he drawled.

His smile turned wooden but what did I have to lose? I was leaving this place forever, and right then I hated him with every fibre of my being, thankful I would never have to look at his smarmy fat face again.

'P-promise you won't hurt Joe,' I shuddered, 'you can't blame him for being worried about Sam...'

'Shh,' he quickly stalled me, 'Sam is fine and Joe can look after himself.'

I wrapped my arms around myself, feeling cold, despite the warm air discharged from the wall heater.

'It's yourself you need to think about now. You're a lucky girl to be fostered by such good people. Live in a lovely house. I am sure you're going to be very happy.'

'I know,' I sighed.

There was little left to say as he sorted through the paperwork. Yet slipping the last of my documents into an envelope, it seemed he had not quite finished.

'I hope everything works out for you, dear girl, though there is no predicting the future. I won't forget you, and I'm certain our paths will cross again.'

Staring at him in disbelief, I felt a ball of fear rise in my throat.

Why would he say that?

"Strange," Hannah murmured. "Do you wonder if he was playing with you?"

"I-I'll never be sure, but the way the way he looked at me turned my stomach."

I could see his face now, piercing through the darkness. I didn't want to be reminded of him, but the image seemed real, so horribly real. His protruding grey eyes burned into me with such intensity, it was as if he were in the room with me, watching through the dark twisted labyrinth of my mind.

Frozen in panic, I clung to the sides of my chair. I could not bear his image swimming around in my head any longer, and it forced my eyes wide open.

"Maisie, what is it?" Hannah gasped. "You look petrified."

"I always said he was a nasty man," I whimpered, "but it feels as if he's here... in Bognor... and I-I'm sure I've seen him more recently."

Hannah's face turned rigid. "Mr. Mortimer could be in Bognor?"

Suddenly she was the one who looked petrified. It was hard to imagine the impact this was having but as I scoured the tunnels of my subconscious, I was still searching... where had I seen those eyes?

They flashed again, sending shivers through me.

Only this time I was imagining an older man. Those same grey eyes, no longer so bulbous but shrunken. Glinting with evil, they sagged in a recess of folds, a familiar creepy smile... Yet who did that face belong to?

289

Chapter Sixty-Two

It was a long time since Joe had seen the inside of a prison, but on this occasion he was determined to do some good in the world. *If Thomas Parker-Smythe was innocent, Joe had to clear his name*. But he was on a mission. A chain of monstrous crimes had been committed and now he had faced his enemy, it was time to redress the balance.

Before this most unusual situation arose, however, he had spent an intense couple of hours with the police.

First it was essential to describe Mortimer, and he didn't hold back. "You wouldn't recognise him now. Used to be a big fat bastard like a puffed up balloon, but it's as if someone's stuck a pin in him."

Looking at DI Fitzpatrick, he detected a twitch of amusement in his lips. But with every detail recorded by a composite artist, they might soon be able to release a photo-fit image.

"Good stuff, Joe," he reassured him, "and to keep you informed, we've done a little digging of our own. It seems *Richard Lacey* moved to Thailand in 1998 where he led a covert existence. That in itself is disturbing, given the sex tourism you read about in the Far East, but he was also a collector of books."

"What sort of books?"

"Occult books. He was obsessed with it - devil worship, black magic rituals... for all we know he could still be running a satanic cult."

As Joe absorbed the information, he felt his blood run cold. Yet it drew his mind to another dilemma that had been disturbing him: Lord Parker-Smythe.

"He vehemently protested his innocence," DS Havers enlightened him, "swore the material we found on his computer was planted."

"I wanna talk to him," Joe pressed and leaning his body forwards, he stared deep into Mike's eyes. "Please! I bet he knows more about Mortimer than he's letting on, and I wonder if that bastard had some hold over him."

"I wish I could help but our hands are tied," Mike protested gently. "I doubt if there's time to secure a visiting order at such short notice..."

DI Fitzpatrick, on the other hand, had surprised him.

"Well, I say we should agree to it. This is urgent police business and if Joe can get him talking, then what have we got to lose?"

It gradually came to light that the DI was relying on him implicitly - as if perhaps facing Mortimer could allow him to regress back to his own childhood, a boy who had survived Orchard Grange - the theory being that only someone in that position would be able to ask the right questions. In all those formal interviews Thomas had been cagey; would meeting a survivor release the valve? Joe, a kindred spirit he could confide in.

"We can get you in," he informed Joe later, having spoken to his superiors, "but on one condition."

Joe met his steely blue eyes with intrigue. "Go on."

"Would you agree to being fitted with a wire?"

Seeing the stark square towers of Wandsworth Prison looming would have filled him with dread under normal circumstances, but if anything, Joe felt a buzz of excitement. He would fight his enemies until his dying breath, though mindful of their last-ditch attempt to intimidate him. That in itself left one final fear flashing through his mind.

Dear little Maisie, all alone and being watched...

At least word had come through from Sussex Police, where to his heartfelt relief Matt had done everything he promised. With proof of Mortimer's threat on their system, he prayed they would act accordingly. Ensure she came to no harm.

Thirty minutes later, however, he found himself face to face with the man he had suspected all those months ago. As previously observed by Cecelia, Thomas Parker-Smythe had become a shadow of his former self. With his cap of silver hair gleaming, he stood out distinctly yet his face was cadaverous, his cheeks hollow.

"Well, hello," he croaked softly. "I've only ever had two visitors, and certainly not in private, so would you start by telling me who you are?"

"My name's Joe," he began. "I lived in Orchard Grange once, I was a victim."

"Does this mean you're one of my accusers?"

He inhaled a deep breath, priming himself for his reaction. "I saw you at the home with Mortimer and I'm sorry if I said you seemed over-friendly..."

"I see," Thomas whispered. Suspicion narrowed his eyes as he surveyed him. "I have a feeling I know who you are now. The police showed me a photo of a boy when they questioned me. I wasn't leering at you. I was concerned. Cornelius said you were 'trouble' but I saw bruises on your arms. Suspected abuse."

"Yeah," Joe sighed, "but I never meant you to be implicated." Fiddling with his cuffs, he was finding it hard to meet the older man's frosty stare.

"What else did you say about me?"

"Not a lot. I was suspicious of your friendship with Mortimer, that's all. Could never understand why a politician would wanna invest in his homes, and that's God's honest truth. I thought maybe you had some *personal* interest."

"Personal interest?" Thomas snorted. "As Minister for Education, the only interest I had was in the children's schooling, and those homes fell short. I was deluded enough to think injecting government funds would help matters."

"But why *his* homes?" Joe kept baiting. "What did he offer you in return?"

"Nothing," Thomas spat. "Now let me ask you something. Are you the one who accused me of partaking in some party?"

Joe lowered his head, heart racing. He could not ignore the lash in Thomas's voice, but he had to keep the man talking. "No. That was someone else. What I wanna know is why you never spilled the beans about Mortimer... and you suspected abuse?"

"I did, and we fell out because of it. I could not endorse his homes. What you need to understand, though, is he was not a man to cross. Cornelius had friends in high places, one of whom wielded great power."

"Right," Joe nodded, "but I'm still confused. If you're so innocent then why are you here? What evidence did they use against you?"

******

Evidence? Oh, the hours Thomas had spent mulling over this, his mind drawn inevitably to Pianissimo Café. That elegant English tea shop had heralded the advent of a new era, the ravishing waitress he had met there unforgettable.

"Her name was Poppy," he said. "Charming girl! If anything, she was the one who flirted with me..."

With his mind wandering down past avenues, reminiscing about meeting Poppy ultimately evoked memories of the cleaning firm she had recommended.

Gleam Gals.

"Even she laughed at that ridiculous name," he sighed. "Two young girls working as cleaners. Never once did I suspect anything, until they turned up wearing French maid's outfits."

"Did you wonder why?"

"I made some joke," he snapped, "some casual throw-away remark about how I'd love to see them dressed as French maids. What an idiot! I should have asked them to put their coats on and leave, but I didn't have the heart."

"So you left them in your apartment," Joe mumbled.

Thomas nodded sadly. Relating it again tied twists of shame in his belly; what had he been thinking? Swept up in his fantasy, the risk he was taking had never occurred to him. It was all a game to them, but the thought of what it had led to...

"It pains me to tell you this," he shuddered, "but I'm sure that's the day my computer was meddled with. I was on my way to the House of Lords, you see, and just as I was leaving, I spotted some character lurking around..."

His hand folded over his eyes. One notable characteristic about Pimlico was its tranquility; few cars, few people ambling about, other than the occasional passer-by. That streak of shadow on the pavement had barely been noticeable.

"At worst I suspected a journalist, but it was too late to turn back. The taxi had set off. I was due at the House of Lords by noon, and a decision I will regret for the rest of my life. When the police informed me of that filth on my computer, I felt sick to my stomach! That's when I recalled that figure hanging around; tall, thin, hunched over a mobile, baggy jeans, black hoodie... sadly, I never did see his face."

He inhaled sharply, pinned with the hope *someone* would believe his story.

"Ever since my home was raided, I've had a horrible feeling that person was a hacker and those girls let him in. He must have spent a good while loading that rubbish, not just images, but a whole fake browsing history. Strangest of all, they chose my oldest computer; an Apple Mac I'd bought in the nineties."

Raising his head, he captured Joe's gaze. He seemed to have frozen in the last few seconds, his dark eyes suddenly penetrating.

"What is it?"

Joe's eyebrows shot up into an inverted V. "This guy you spotted... by *thin* would you say gangly?"

"It's hard to say," Thomas frowned, "his clothes were so baggy they hung off him like a sack, but I assumed it to be some youth."

"So what was found in your browsing history?" he kept probing.

"Evidence I belonged to some fiendish newsgroup," Thomas said. A chill spread over him, the room feeling dark. "This was before social media of course, but a group set up by none other than Cornelius Mortimer... contents so awful, I cannot bear to tell you."

"Try me," Joe pressed.

He let out a long rattling breath. "I swear to God I'd never heard of it, but it had a lot to do with ritualistic abuse. 'Babes in the Wood.' Children were involved, sex parties and those last horrific allegations cemented it."

"Really?" Joe questioned. "But you were accused of downloading images, weren't you? How long had they been there?"

"That I will never understand," Thomas said. He discharged a sob, a sense of powerlessness running through him. "The police informed me they were downloaded over the course of a decade. Some as early as 1996."

******

"Do you wanna know what I think?" Joe said, keeping his voice steady. "That man you saw lurking about weren't no 'youth.' It was Mortimer."

"But that's impossible," Thomas whispered. "Why would you think that?"

Joe's eyes narrowed. "I've seen him more recently, and you wouldn't recognise him, 'specially if he was dressed up in all that baggy shit and a hoodie. How old would you say he was when you knew him?"

"Forties maybe? It couldn't be him though, surely, he was a giant of man."

"Yeah," Joe nodded, "'cept he's older now and looks like he's lost ten stone. So supposing it was him? Just say he really did get into your apartment and found your old computer, 'cos from what you've told me, something don't add up."

Thomas swallowed. "What exactly are you suggesting?"

"The age of the material," he muttered, "the years it's been there. There ain't no way that stuff could just be 'planted,' not without leaving traces..."

"That's what the police said," Thomas shivered. "So how is it possible?"

"If those images were copied into your hard disc, it would show in a log file. I reckon whoever did this spent years collecting this stuff, knowing you had a Mac. They didn't copy it onto your machine. What's more likely is they kept an identical hard disk, copied everything from *yours* and switched them."

"My God! How do you know so much about computers?"

"Used to dabble in 'em as a teenager," Joe said, fighting an urge to smile. He was almost tempted to tell him about the computer games he'd counterfeited in his youth, but remembered the wire the cops had fitted. "Shame I didn't keep it up really, I could have done a lot better for myself in the long run, but my life went tits up."

"That makes two of us," Thomas said, his expression softening. "Now why are you here? You hardly know me. What is the real reason for your visit?"

"Mortimer," Joe said coldly. "Last night I bumped into him and something inside me snapped. I want this sorted. I'm sick of hiding, sick of him and his goons stalking us, abusing me online and trying to murder me."

Thomas nodded. "So how do you imagine I can help you?"

"Maybe I'm the one who can help you," Joe replied. "Why rot in jail if you ain't done nothing? It's Mortimer who's behind this and I want as much info as you can spare, so come on, tell me... what did he have on you?"

Thomas flushed, as if on the verge of spilling his darkest secret. "A camera. One I used to carry whenever I visited schools and children's homes. I took pictures of kids in lessons, the classrooms, the facilities... but on one of those visits, I was foolish enough to leave it in his office. I should have been more careful, especially after expressing my concerns about abuse..."

"And I'm guessing that pissed him off?"

"Yes," Thomas nodded. "He took umbrage. So one of those vile guards grabbed my camera. Used it to photograph naked girls in the showers..."

"Bloody hell," Joe whispered.

"It gets worse," Thomas choked. "When the government refused funding, he was apoplectic... took pleasure in warning me that if anything was exposed about his homes, he would drag me down with him."

"Expose what," Joe spluttered, "that you suspected abuse? Do you think he's still got this camera of yours?"

"I assume so," Thomas nodded, "and it's covered in my fingerprints. So can you see how bad my situation is? Given what I've been charged with, this could be the final nail in the coffin. Those photos were taken in Orchard Grange, the very place at the heart of this scandal, girls aged around twelve..."

Joe shivered. His immediate thought of Maisie being in those photos turned him cold with dread but he pushed the feeling aside.

"Christ," he said. "So he *did* have some hold over you?"

"I'm afraid so, and I'm sorry to hear you were a victim, but I don't know which way to turn. Cornelius is a very clever man and has a powerful network of allies. It wasn't just my Mac they must have tampered with, you see, but my phone. They managed to hack into my Instagram account."

Instagram. Such words brought another spiral of fear.

"That's weird. I think the same thing happened with Maisie's phone and I haven't had a chance to warn her yet. Shit."

The words slipped out automatically but Thomas froze.

"Maisie," he whispered. His face turned chalky pale. "Dear God, not the girl the police mentioned, the one who's having psychotherapy? I gather part of her statement alluded to those parties he organised."

"Are you saying you knew about them?" Joe breathed in horror.

"Of course not," Thomas snapped. "Cornelius might have mentioned them at a time I was present - told her he'd ordered *pretty dresses* - and that is all. Yet like everything else in this charade, all evidence points to me. Did you know, for example, that memories recovered under psychotherapy can be fake? And I'm guessing *your friend* made up this dreadful story about me attending one of those parties?"

"She did not," Joe spat. "Can't you see we are *all* victims of Cornelius fucking Mortimer, so let's just concentrate on the truth, shall we?"

"Of course," Thomas relented. "I'm sorry to get upset, but that story is a wicked lie."

Joe nodded, while at the back his mind unravelled another thought. It seemed obvious why Thomas didn't want to voice anything negative about Mortimer.

Yet why was he still protecting him?

"I don't get it! Why didn't you just offload all this to the cops when you had the chance?"

"Of course you don't get it," Thomas sighed. "This goes right back to what I was saying from the start. The people at the top - and there was one in particular. Someone who is not just powerful but incredibly dangerous."

"How can anyone be more dangerous than Mortimer?" Joe scoffed.

"Because of his position. There was a time when this QC had the police force and the entire judicial system in his back pocket. He protected people like Mortimer. I wouldn't be at all surprised if *he's* the reason I'm here."

"QC," Joe said. "Not a High Court judge as well, by any chance?"

"I've said too much," he muttered sadly, "but that is all I am prepared to tell you, so please tread carefully. He is not a man you want to cross."

Chapter Sixty-Three

Returning to Charing Cross Police station, Joe was still reeling in the aftermath of that conversation, just waiting for the DS to debrief him. Deep in his mind the threads of a new idea swirled darkly, something he couldn't quite tie together.

High Court judge...

It took the soothing voice of DS Havers to shake him out of his reverie.

"Good work, Joe. There's not an officer who isn't impressed by what you've got out of the old boy, but before we investigate further, I'll update you on our own findings."

Joe blinked as the sergeant switched on a light.

"Word's through from Bognor. The house has been thoroughly searched inside and out but no sign of Richard Lacey or the man downstairs. Apart from a young woman living on the top floor, it appears to be deserted."

"Paula," Joe mumbled. "How is she?"

"Feeling very proud of herself, as it happens," he smiled. "She got a photo of Schiller on her smart phone and promises to be vigilant. If anyone sneaks back, she'll be straight on to us. Other than that, we've got patrols on the lookout for a white Nissan Qashqai and a silver Mercedes van... and last but not least, our photo-fit image is ready to go live across the media."

Joe nodded, half listening while a remote part of his brain was struggling to take it in. "But what about Maisie?" he murmured dazedly. "She's not safe."

Glancing at his watch, he was startled to see how many hours had passed as daytime merged into evening.

No wonder it was getting dark.

"Try not to worry," Mike said. "Andrew informed me that Sam has been in touch and he's driving down to Sussex to stay with her."

"Did you tell him about the text?" he blurted.

"We did," he nodded. "He's fully aware of the situation and will not leave her unprotected, not while that monster's at large."

"Good," Joe whispered. "Going back to my prison visit, though, there's something else I've gotta ask..."

"I know," Mike sighed, and the light in his eyes finally dwindled. "It seems there's another player involved. A man at the top, and that's our next line of enquiry. We need to identify which prominent QCs were around at the time."

"There is one that springs to mind," Joe said and felt a chill slip down his spine. But he could not hold back what his inner voice was telling him. "Alistair McFadden QC. Sam used to tell us stories, like when his mum took him to the Old Bailey. She wanted him to meet his father but he treated 'em like dirt, and from everything he's said since, I get the feeling he's still scared of him."

Mike looked at him with unease. "I hear what you're saying, Joe, but you can't jump to conclusions. This needs looking into with caution..."

"Yeah, but something in't right," he pressed. "What about that sick gathering Sam reported? None of it went on record, which means that somewhere along the line there's been a huge cover up..."

Sagging in his chair, he scraped his hair back from his forehead. Yet the more he analysed it, the more he was wondering what else Sam had told them.

"Don't you think it's strange? His father, this McFadden guy, wrenches him up to Scotland. Tells him to forget everything, and years later just when things are getting heavy again, his social worker ends up dead."

Finally Mike let go of his breath, exhaling a loud sigh. "You could be on the right track, Joe, but this requires deeper examination. A QC he might be, but he's not above the law. Would you leave it with me to discuss with Andrew?"

Joe shrugged, conscious there was little more they could do today.

"So what about you?" he added. "You weren't thinking of going back to Bognor tonight were you? I was going to suggest we moved you to a safe house."

"Thanks," Joe said quickly, "but don't worry about me, I'll survive."

Joe knew at least a dozen places where he could blag shelter for the night, but he was in no mood for socialising. There had been a time when blending back into homeless culture might have uplifted him; that powerful camaraderie among rough sleepers, some having survived on the streets for so long, it had earned them a badge of respect. Mundane conversation just wouldn't cut it tonight, though; he needed time to think. So hands buried in his pockets, he started walking, those earlier pangs of anxiety starting to resurface.

Alistair McFadden QC.

But it wasn't just his musings over the QC that were bothering him.

It was everything that had happened to Sam. Samuel McFadden. His son.

Going back to the day they had been reunited, he would never forget Sam's story. Why would he invent something so horrific? If Thomas Parker-Smythe was to be believed, he had never participated in any party. But the vision of Thomas's ashen face kept haunting him, the breath on his lips trembling: *that story is a wicked lie.*

Drifting on another mind walk, Joe could not help raking over everything they had discussed. Fearful of Maisie's therapy, Thomas had said something very significant: *memories recovered under psychotherapy can be fake*.

His footsteps slowed, his mind bursting with possibilities. Hadn't he suspected already that Sam might have been brainwashed? Talking to Maisie, he was dismayed she had brushed it off, but thinking back, it made sense. Sam had been isolated for years, with no-one but his control freak of a father and some half-brother for company. Between them, they had infused a sense of powerlessness - severed him from his friends - forced him to forget everything. Yet what if they had done worse? Joe shuddered, troubled by the direction his thoughts were leading him.

Could Sam's mind be polluted with fake memories?

By time he reached Victoria Embankment, darkness swamped the pavements. The temptation to jump on a train overwhelmed him, except he couldn't go back to Bognor, not yet. Where would he go, anyway? Returning to Maisie's flat would be dangerous in the dead of night. Although he would have to go back at some point to collect his rucksack. Fleeing in desperation, he had left it there.

"Oh bollocks," he cursed under his breath.

With night closing in, no phone, no wallet, nor his bank card, his choices were somewhat limited. Perhaps he should have taken up Mike's idea of a safe house after all. Weighing up his options, however, he had been in worse situations, his mind sharpening in a way that once again brought back his homeless days. Just thank God he had some cash; enough to pay for a meal and find a hostel for tonight. It would buy him a little more time to think and to plan his next move.

******

With the sunlight fading, Cornelius began to shiver. A creature of darkness, he cherished the night, but as the shadows grew deep, so a chill settled over the forest, biting into his bones. Gripping the edge of his blanket, he pulled it tight around his neck. His chest heaved, every breath escaping in loud rattling gasps: for how much longer could he endure this? Even with his medication, he was beginning to weaken, wondering if he would last another night.

So when the call finally came, he clawed for his mobile with eager hands. But nothing could prepare him for the rage hissing from the handset.

"What the hell is going on with Joe Winterton?"

"Your guess is as good as mine," Cornelius croaked, "but please don't take that tone. I'm as incensed he got away as you are, I thought we had him cornered..."

"So how did that oaf, Schiller, cock up this time?" his ally interrupted.

"He didn't. He was outside, ready to tail him as soon as he showed his face. Only we weren't counting on that fat cow upstairs interfering..."

Breaking off with a gasp, he struggled to catch his breath before another coughing fit took hold. A little compassion wouldn't go amiss, he thought savagely.

Yet the caller fell icily silent, as if waiting for it to pass.

"How did he get out then?"

"I'm guessing he used the fire escape," he rasped. "Got as far as the station. There was a final trace in Barnham, then nothing. He seems to have disappeared off the grid..." Yet with his words trailing off, his thoughts drifted back to Schiller.

Restricted to using a motorbike, he was no longer so conspicuous, and if the police were on the lookout for a silver camper, they were unlikely to find it now. Hidden deep in the woods under a shroud of scrim nets and pine branches, even their drones would have a job picking it out.

Reviewing Schiller's position, he felt the twitch of a smile.

"I suspect Winterton will be back soon, so have faith. He might think he's outfoxed us, same as that bitch. Yet for all her careful vigilance, there is one place she won't have thought of." His smile twisted into a grimace of pure hate as he pictured his nemesis again. "At least we have our treasured sacrifice in situ, which brings me to my next point..."

"What?" the other man drawled.

The tremors had resumed. Maybe it was excitement, his moment of glory nudging closer, yet he could not help but fear the veil of death hovering.

"I wonder if you could visit me before tomorrow."

"Are you joking?" the caller snapped. "I've got far too much to do! What do you want that cannot wait until morning?"

Acid rose in his stomach, leaving a bitter taste. It was different for him. His ally had no concept how it felt, having to survive like a hunted animal.

"Just join me," he said huskily. "All I ask is twenty minutes of your company to discuss the final preparations for our ritual."

"And what of the risk? If my cover is blown now it'll ruin everything!"

"And if I die tonight, it will have been for nothing," Cornelius growled. "Or have you forgotten how ill I am?"

He heard a dramatic sigh.

"Your days may be numbered, Cornelius, but mine are not. So don't drag me under, not after everything I have done for you..."

Cornelius nearly choked, astounded by such petulance.

"I have given up half my life to help fulfil your dream!"

"Yes," he whispered nastily, "and will spend the rest of it reaping the rewards, sir. So you might want to remember that before you mock me."

"I'm not mocking you," he protested, "but haven't you forgotten something? The Great One is joining us for the finale, and it is time we touched base. So try to relax, Cornelius, get some sleep. Conserve your energy for when it is needed."

As the sun sank lower, he felt his breath quicken again. He knew damn well who his ally was referring to, and could not wait to be reunited.

Chapter Sixty-Four

Leaving Hannah's house, I leapt into my car. Spikes of cold pricked at my skin, the fear that Mr. Mortimer could be close to home a more unnerving prospect than I could handle. With unsteady hands I delved into my bag for my mobile. My first instinct was to try Joe again. But before I had a chance, an unexpected text flashed up in my notifications from Sam.

Strange. I wasn't expecting to hear from him so early, my fingers fumbling for his text of their own accord.

> *Hi Maisie, I'm on my way down from London but where are you?*
> *Call me as soon as you get this will you, I'm worried. Love Sam xxx*

I stared at the message with a frown but before I started the engine, my curiosity got the better of me. Something about his message seemed different, filling me with an insatiable urge to call back.

"Sam," I blurted. "It's great to hear from you."

"Maisie, thank God," he spluttered. "Where the hell are you?"

The sharpness of his tone froze the breath on my lips, drawing my thoughts back to my earlier therapy session.

"I had an appointment with Hannah," I gasped, "I've only just left."

"Hannah," he echoed. "You're not in Bognor are you?"

"Yes. Why, what's wrong?"

A soft sigh shuddered from the speaker. "There isn't time to explain. Just get yourself back to East Lavant as soon as you can."

By the time I was threading my way through the secluded countryside, I couldn't stop thinking about Mortimer's last words.

I won't forget you, and I'm certain our paths will cross again.

It couldn't have happened in Bognor, surely?

Pulling up outside the cottage, I was on tenterhooks, the urgency in Sam's message making even the already-familiar surroundings somehow foreboding.

I had just stepped out of my car when he appeared at the door. The sun hung low in the trees, soaking the grounds in a pool of golden light, but it took just one glance at his striking silhouette for me to realise how much I had missed him.

"Sam!" I called out, running over to him. "This is a nice surprise!"

My first compulsion was to hug him but he seized my hands, tugging me into the house.

"What's going on?" I pressed. "You've got me worried now."

He didn't answer straight away, his grip strong as he guided me through the lounge towards the kitchen. Only when we reached the dining room did he pause to observe me properly. I stared at him in confusion. For not only had he made a special journey, I saw the meticulously made table, little flickers of candlelight reflected in his anxious brown eyes.

"Do I need a reason to come and see you?" he said softly. "Now sit down and make yourself comfy. I'll pour us a glass of wine."

I obeyed without question, perplexed by his efforts. With my gaze wandering further, I noticed a cut glass bowl filled with salad, a crusty baguette and a dish of green olives on the sideboard.

"Sorry if I seem tense," he murmured. "I didn't want you to be on your own tonight, but you never mentioned anything about seeing your therapist..."

Opening a bottle of chilled white wine, his expression turned more pensive.

"So what did you talk about this time?"

I watched in a dream as he passed me a glass of wine. Its crisp clean taste brought a clarity to my thoughts, my innermost fears finally liberated.

"She regressed me back to my last day at Orchard Grange. Saying goodbye to Joe before Mortimer turned up. He wanted to speak to me alone. It was scary."

Closing my eyes, I pinched the spot between my brows.

"I could picture his face but it spooked me! I almost imagined him standing there, struck with this feeling I'd seen him more recently!"

Sam nodded almost knowingly.

"You may well be right," he said, "and this is what I need to talk to you about. I've been in touch with the police..."

"You have?" I gasped.

"According to Andrew Fitzpatrick, Mr. Mortimer could indeed be in Sussex."

"Sussex," I echoed in horror. "So it's true then. Where?"

He raised his glass and took rapid gulps of wine, his eyes flitting, unable to meet mine.

"Don't be cagey. Tell me!"

"Shh," he whispered. "I don't want to scare you, but after talking to Andrew, it got me thinking about what Joe said. He's always been concerned for your security, which reminds me... Have you spoken to him recently? I tried calling him earlier but he seems to have gone off the radar."

"I don't know where Joe is," I mumbled, "and I don't suppose you've heard but he and Jess have split up."

Finally he looked at me, eyebrows raised. "Really? No surprises there."

"What's that supposed to mean?" Hand tightening around my glass, I felt a surge of irritation. "You're not going to start running him down, are you?"

"Not him," Sam sniffed. "Her! What a nightmare! I mean, she was a classy bird but talk about clingy. Every time I saw them, she was plastered all over him like a big octopus, yet they were poles apart."

"I'm glad you agree," I said, "but I can't help worrying for Joe now, especially if Mortimer's around."

He exhaled a sigh and moving towards the work surface, unwrapped a couple of salmon fillets. "You know Joe. He's tough as old boots! DI Fitzpatrick said he spoke to him earlier, so I imagine he's lying low... but let's not dwell. I don't suppose you've eaten, have you?"

"No," I murmured. My eyes followed him but I was still thinking about Joe, wishing there was another way of communicating with him.

Sam seemed unruffled, and grabbing a heavy-duty frying pan, he placed it on the hob. "Cooking isn't my speciality," he joked. "I bought a pre-packed salad but at least I know how to pan fry a couple of fish fillets."

His words snapped me out of my trance.

"Thanks, Sam, you've gone to so much effort and I wish I could relax... but you've got no idea how scared I feel with Mortimer in the county."

His aged and shrivelled features tore through the darkness of my mind again.

"If only I could remember where I'd seen his face, though."

Swooping back to the table, Sam topped up my glass. "Don't be scared," he said gently. "It's why I'm here, isn't it? Now sit back and enjoy the evening."

There was a special warmth in his eyes as he clung to my stare, and at last I released my breath.

As the evening developed, I cherished our precious time, never quite understanding the real danger that blackened the edge of our world. The notion of someone as evil as Mortimer prowling around Sussex had turned my blood to ice. But Sam made things right. He took extra trouble to make a fuss of me, and instead of switching the TV on, he proposed running me a bath.

"There's nothing on but the news," he said, "same doom and gloom."

Closing my eyes, I sank back in the bubbles as he lit more candles. He seemed happy to sit back and watch me at first, his face angelic and glowing.

Yet I craved his touch, insisting he join me in the water while it was caressingly warm. Watching him peel off his clothes, I couldn't tear my eyes away. The sight of his shapely torso left me melting inside.

Having him close allowed me to forget my fears, and with my head cradled in his arms, I ran my hands through the creamy bubbles, soaping him all over. He seemed eager to reciprocate and with the slowest of movements he picked up a sponge. Lathering it with shower gel, he smoothed it gently over my back and shoulders, massaging away my tension.

"This feels like heaven," I murmured, my eyes drawn to a swirl of steam suspended below the ceiling beams. The effect was hypnotic. "It's lovely to have you here, but really, what is all this in aid of?"

"Nothing," he sighed. "You deserve a treat. Sometimes I wonder if you should just live each day as if it's your last."

That stirring sentence stayed with me deep into the night, long after we had drifted into the master bedroom to make love. I felt as if we were climbing towards the pinnacle of our dreams, where every little gesture seemed tender.

Though in another way, his words shook me hollow. It was a blissful escape while it lasted, as if we knew we were living on a knife edge.

Mr. Mortimer could indeed be in Sussex.

But how long had he been here? Even from a distance I sensed his power, like a spider weaving its deadly web all around us.

Looking back, I see that I never knew how much Sam was trying to shield me. Had he been more truthful and revealed everything the police had discovered about that hateful man, it might have changed everything. With the weekend approaching, I might never have been coaxed into an agreement so easily. But the events of the following day, not long after Sam had departed for work, left me floundering.

Chapter Sixty-Five

Seven o' clock the next morning, I watched with a heavy heart as Sam slipped on his jacket.

"I've got to go," he said. "If I don't leave now, I'll never beat the motorway rush hour and I need to be in London by nine."

"It's okay, I understand," I murmured.

Lingering in the doorway, he kissed me on the lips. The crisp country air drew out the essence of his aftershave, the trace of coffee on his breath sending my head into a spin. But as his car faded from view, I forced myself to accept the reality. He would have to commute for the time being. Closing the door, I returned to the kitchen.

The delicious aroma of croissants, still warm from the oven, was next to hit my senses, and with plenty of time to kill before work, I made another coffee.

But as I tidied up the kitchen and put the plates away, my fears began to resurface.

Joe. Where was he?

With the turmoil of everything else unravelling, I still hadn't managed to get in touch with him.

Sitting bolt upright, I put my mug down. Hadn't Sam mentioned something about DI Fitzpatrick talking to him, and if so, why hadn't he contacted me? With a frown I switched on my mobile, but I was thinking about my flat. I had definitely seen traces of Joe's presence there, and if I couldn't get through to his mobile, then surely I could reach him on my landline.

Several rings later, though, I heard my own recorded message.

"Joe!" I shouted. "If you're there, for God's sake pick up."

Nothing.

"I'm going out of my mind with worry, Joe. I need to know you're okay."

The drag of silence felt even more crushing.

"Just ring me asap, will you?" I finished with a sob, but as my heart plummeted still further, I remembered his job.

Didn't Joe usually work a shift on Friday?

I could always ring Sainsbury's to check he was there, but if I couldn't trace him at work, then what? I'd have no choice but to contact the police.

Deep down, I knew Joe would never blank me, and as I drank in my surroundings, I felt the brush of a shiver. This house, for all its beauty, meant nothing to me in the absence of my dear friend. And right now it felt eerie, something about the atmosphere chilling me to the core.

Later in the office, when a colleague said there was a call for me, I leapt from my chair as if my desk were on fire. Of all the people who would contact me at work, though, I never expected to hear from Sarah.

"Maisie?" she began shakily, "I-I hate to call like this but I'm at the end of my tether and don't know what to do for the best..."

"Calm down," I tried to soothe her. "Just tell me what's wrong."

"It's Connor."

Tears splintered her voice. I thought for one horrible moment this related to the warning she had received; that darkly veiled threat via Facebook that alluded not only to the town she was living in, but the identity of her foster son.

"Oh no," I mumbled, "has something happened to him?"

"Not yet it hasn't..."

The story that transpired was like nothing I had imagined though. His school had threatened to exclude him, and all because of a girl he liked.

There had to be a lot more to this story, surely.

Yet with his strange behaviour, his social awkwardness and staring, some of the nastier kids had been spreading rumours; the notion *he was some psycho*.

"He followed her home, that's all! He only wanted to know where she lived so he could post a birthday card without anyone knowing. It was so harmless!"

"But that's hardly grounds for exclusion," I spluttered.

"No, except the parents have muscled in and completely blown things out of proportion. I hate to sound condescending, but talking to them on the phone, they weren't the most educated people. Read too many tabloids, spend half their time watching the Jeremy Kyle show... they've accused him of stalking her but with no understanding of his Asperger's."

"But can't you explain it to them?" I said.

"I've got no choice," she shuddered, "they're coming over tonight to have it out with us, and I know it won't be pleasant, but it's Connor I'm worried about. I don't want him to be here, not if they're going to start viciously attacking him. It will shatter his confidence and he's had enough knock-backs already."

I felt a shiver of dread, thinking how familiar this sounded, but with memories of Paula's confrontation charging back to me, I could see where she was coming from.

Worried about her daughter. Referring to him as a 'weird kid', where something as innocent as staring had been rapidly perceived as creepy.

"Oh Sarah, I'm sorry, I don't know what to say. I wish I could help."

"I-I was wondering," she stammered. "Is there any chance we can drive over and see you? I know you're at work, but when do you take a lunch break?"

By the time I made it back to the cottage, midday, I was feeling uneasy. What Sarah was asking of me seemed obvious enough, but the timing couldn't be worse.

Greeting them in the driveway, I was shocked by Connor's demeanour.

Where was that impassioned, inquisitive teenager who had visited the previous weekend?

Withdrawn into a shell of shame, he would not even meet my eye. His face looked pale, every delicate contour rigid as if carved from stone.

Several minutes later, I had arranged some chairs around the patio. Sarah had brought a picnic, wrapping us in the illusion we were enjoying a nice summer outing.

Connor, though, wasn't fooled.

"Am I allowed to hide here?" he mumbled. "I don't care if I have to sleep in the summerhouse."

I could have smiled, though at least the weather was on his side. Exceptionally dry in the last week and with temperatures barely dropping below twenty degrees, a blanket of warmth clung to the air.

"You don't have to camp in the garden," I said.

"I'm sorry about this," Sarah kept apologising, "but I don't know who else to turn to. Maybe you should check with Sam first to ask if he can stay?"

"For the weekend?" I frowned. "Sure! Sam said Connor was welcome any time."

"Not the weekend," Sarah added, "just tonight! I hate to impose at such short notice, but I'm hoping this will have blown over by tomorrow."

"Sam's already been here," I enlightened her. "He turned up last night, which reminds me of something else I need to tell you..."

She must have seen the way my face clouded over.

"Oh dear. Is something wrong? D'you know I'd almost forgotten about this police investigation."

The gears in my mind spun faster; if Connor was to stay in the area for the next twenty-four hours, it was essential he understood the danger.

"It's Mortimer," I shivered. "He's been spotted in West Sussex, and this is another reason Sam drove down... He thinks I might be at risk."

Exchanging a nervous glance, I bit my lip, charged with a sudden fear.

Connor, on the other hand, seemed unfazed. Staring into the distance with his blank expression, I wondered if he had even heard me.

"Connor, you need to listen... I'm going to have to go back to work soon, which means you'll be here on your own for a few hours."

Still avoiding my eye, he gave a silent nod.

"You can stay," I said more firmly, "but on one condition."

"What is it, Maisie?"

"Promise to stay indoors. This man I mentioned, Mr. Mortimer... He is a very bad man and could be dangerous."

Connor let out a sniff. "Really?"

"Yes!" I gasped. "You have to believe me."

I did not like his expression. He was looking at me in a way that suggested morbid fascination, his eyes two shining orbs in the sunlight.

"A bad man?" he echoed. He gave a cutting smile. "We should get on just fine, then."

"Connor, stop this," Sarah scolded him, "you're starting to scare me."

"But I'm not scared. All the kids at school think I'm a psycho, and it's true, isn't it? So why would I be afraid of this man?"

Sarah's face drained of colour. "I have no idea where you picked up this rubbish," she whispered, "but I don't want to hear it. Not now!"

"Okay," he sighed, disentangling his legs from under his chair, "just being honest, and yes, I do need some time on my own. Isn't this what you drove me down to Sussex for, so I could hide from all this *rubbish*?"

Chilled by the direction the conversation was going, I didn't know which way to turn. Staring each other out, like two prize fighters in a boxing ring, it was Sarah who broke the deadlock.

"Do you want to stay here tonight or not?"

"You know I do," he replied in a clipped voice.

"Then show some respect," she finished softly. "Please, Connor! All Maisie is trying to do is protect you. So I hope you will heed her concerns."

Chapter Sixty-Six

A creature of habit, Joe was accustomed to waking early on Fridays. So when the sun cast its first fiery rays across London, it didn't take long for him to realise he should have been at work. His life had taken an unforeseen twist in the last twenty-four hours, and after politely requesting to borrow someone's phone, he finally got through to Sainsbury's.

Unfortunately, his boss sounded none too pleased.

"Where are you, Joe?" she confronted him angrily.

Guilt pounded into him like a sledgehammer as he pieced together his words. "I'm sorry, Vicky, I'm in London and I've lost my phone. Things got a bit dicey but I had to visit the police station. Do you want me to work tomorrow?"

A nerve-wracking silence followed. Joe held his breath as she absorbed his words, yet by the time she found her voice, it resonated with sympathy.

"It's okay, I didn't mean to snap. Better you keep your head down and take the weekend off, then as soon as the dust settles, ring me back, okay?"

Her words had a momentary sobering effect and only then did he consider his predicament. Shuffling his way to Victoria Station, he figured he couldn't stay here for much longer. He had to return Bognor, if for no other reason than to grab his rucksack.

Using his last twenty pound note, he bought an off-peak ticket, but fearing the possibility of his enemies lurking, spent the next hour hidden in a cafe.

It was past ten o' clock when he tentatively approached the platform, and with the crowds swelling around him, he felt the tension drop from his shoulders.

The journey passed in a tangle of confused thoughts but somewhere in the maze, a solution gradually began to unwind itself. By the time he arrived, it would be nearly noon and with the pavements teaming with people, what was the likelihood of an attack in broad daylight?

Joe nonetheless kept his eyes peeled as he crept from the station. Footsteps dragging, he forced himself to keep going and as he turned the corner of Annandale Avenue, he could sense the proximity of the house.

Continuing north, he felt a wave of relief wash over him.

No sign of the silver van, thank God.

It could be a decoy, of course, but what choice did he have? With his thoughts flitting back to Maisie, he had to warn her. Alone and isolated, there was no telling what Sam had said to her; Sam who he couldn't trust, never sure of the lies with which his mind might have been poisoned.

Footsteps quickening, it was now or never. Joe glanced around, and shimmying up to the door, slid his key into the lock, making as little noise as possible.

Once inside, he froze again, listening for any signs of occupancy. The hallway yawned before him, the staircase lit under the bright yellow glow of a ceiling lamp. Yet not a sound emanated from anywhere.

So the first hurdle was crossed. If he could just get into Maisie's flat undetected. Breath quickening, he unlocked the door, and edging his way inside with as much stealth as possible, closed it gently behind him. For a few more seconds he dared not move, his heart thumping. A clock ticked on the wall, but other than the occasional passing car on the road, the place remained eerily silent.

Now he was here though, he could not waste a second. His first priority was to get a shower and change. Discarding his clothes, he stepped into the bath. The spray of hot water not only refreshed him, but soothed his aching limbs and feet, still throbbing from the hours spent running.

Clean, changed and reinvigorated, his next goal was to grab his precious rucksack. He could not manage another day without his wallet, and if he withdrew some funds, he could always purchase a 'pay as you go phone.' How else was he going to get through to Maisie? Or the police, for that matter, should his fate take a turn for the worst?

Joe sank into a chair. He didn't want to delay his departure, but the notion that his enemies were close toyed darkly with his thoughts.

That was when he spotted the light flashing on the answering machine.

Rising to press the play button, he jumped at the sound of Maisie's voice.

"Joe! If you're there, for God's sake pick up..."

Even he detected the alarm in her voice.

"I'm going out of my mind with worry, Joe. I need to know you're okay... Just ring me asap, will you?"

Backing away from the table, he gulped back the lump of panic in his throat before hoisting his rucksack onto his shoulders.

The thought of seeing her was the only light glinting out of the darkness, whilst in another corner of his mind flashed the notion that she was in danger. She still had no knowledge of the spyware on her phone. How could he hope to warn her? He had to find a way of reaching her.

Hadn't DI Fitzpatrick said that Sam was driving down?

Yet even if they were together, there was no guarantee they were safe.

"Fuck," he whispered under his breath.

Moving towards the door, he made up his mind. He had no option left, other than to travel to Chichester and locate her. He would get a taxi to East Lavant if he had to. Anything to protect her from Mortimer...

As he stepped back into the hallway, though, he had forgotten about his own safety. A creak in the gloom brought him to a crashing halt, his eyes darting in all directions. They latched onto his neighbour's flat, but the door was firmly shut.

So where had that sound come from, and why was it so dark?

It took another second to realise the lamp above the staircase was no longer shining.

Then a second creak tore the silence, louder this time. Joe couldn't move, his breath coming in shallow gasps as he searched madly for the source. By the time he had detected the squeak of a hinge under the stairs, it was too late.

A huge menacing shape emerged from the shadows, blocking his only avenue of escape. Joe backed into the wall, only to feel an excruciating slash of pain across his belly. Robbed of any means of defending himself, he buckled to the floor, helpless, staring at his attacker in dread.

How could he have guessed there was a cupboard under the stairs, a perfect place to lie in wait for him?

He let out a groan, wary of the man drawing closer. There was just enough light in the grey gloom of the hall to carve out his brutal features.

Schiller.

And only then did he see the knife in the man's hand, a shimmer of cold steel reflecting each movement.

"At last," the man growled.

His sadistic smile hurled Joe years into the past. He squirmed on the ground, watching in horror as Schiller ran his finger along the flat of the blade. It came away dark with blood. *His blood?* He let out another whimper, and clutching his stomach, felt a flood of liquid, warm and wet, streaming through his fingers.

His eyes met Schiller's in a flash of understanding, the man still smiling before he licked the blood off his fingers.

"How long I have waited," he laughed evilly. "Time for you to die."

Chapter Sixty-Seven

Something was wrong, I could feel it in my blood. I didn't like leaving Connor alone in the house in the mood he was in, fearful he would get up to something.

My colleagues shrugged it off glibly, insisting I should stop worrying. From their modern-day perspectives, he was just behaving like any other surly teenager, and they were complex creatures.

"He's just testing you, Maisie. Seeing how far he can push the boundaries."

But I couldn't return their smiles. None of them had seen the flare in his eyes I recalled from earlier, that irrepressible force of defiance.

Unfortunately it didn't end there. The sense of foreboding grew worse and at about three o 'clock in the afternoon, a terrible knot of anxiety gripped my stomach.

All around Chichester echoed the sound of police sirens. The wail of an ambulance rose even louder, pulling me unsteadily towards the window.

"Does anyone know what's going on?"

My harassed practise manager looked at me strangely. "Sounds like a police chase. I wonder if it's got anything to do with that old paedophile who was in the news, the one they spotted in Sussex. Maybe they're onto him."

My mouth turned dry. I tried to speak, except the words were imprisoned behind a wall of terror.

"Dunno," another colleague said, "but I reckon the police have got their work cut out. There's been a fatal stabbing in Bognor, it was on Spirit FM News."

An icy, leaden sensation froze me to the floor. I could hardly breath, my heart hammering in my throat. My immediate horror was for Joe. For three long days, I hadn't heard a word from him, so where was he?

"Are you okay, Maisie, you look pale?" Swooping to my side, my manager touched my shoulder, his expression laced with worry.

"I-I need to get back," I mumbled. "I'm worried about Connor..."

Guilt pricked my conscience when I thought about how much leave I had taken lately. I swore I would make the time up - though right now, fear was my driving emotion.

By the time I fought my way through Chichester, the roads were clogged with Friday holiday traffic. It was closer to four o' clock when I turned towards East Lavant, my biggest concern being Connor. I hadn't been kidding when I warned him of *a dangerous man in the area* - and my colleagues had just confirmed it.

But more than anything, I badly needed to know where Joe was. My next priority was to contact Sam and if he was none the wiser, I would call the police.

With my thoughts racing wildly, I didn't dare slow down. The enclosing tunnel of trees seemed particularly dark and threatening. But with my foot down on the accelerator, I flung myself down the secluded road, desperate to reach my home and only when I swerved into the driveway did I stop.

Letting myself into the house, though, I sensed the emptiness I was walking into. The silence was unearthly and as I turned to close the door, the first thing I noticed was Connor's coat missing. I felt the breath drain from my lungs but kept walking, never once breaking step.

Typical.

My colleagues were right. He was determined to push the boundaries this time, though it did nothing to ease my anxiety.

I wondered he had gone gallivanting off on some adventure.

Hadn't he voiced an urge to explore the woods the last time he was here?

My feet ferried me through the lounge towards the back of the house and into the dining room. Maybe he was in the garden, unless he was hiding somewhere inside. Nothing he did would surprise me. Yet at the same time, his absence stirred a riot of emotions.

I didn't need this.

Frozen by the patio door, I saw no sign of him in the garden, either. Every minute dragged on in agonising silence, until my ears picked up the purr of another car engine; one I recognised.

Spinning around, I gaped in disbelief as the door burst open and Sam materialised in the lounge. *Sam. I hadn't even had a chance to tell him about Connor...* Yet catching the startled look in his eye, I was once again rendered speechless.

"Maisie," he spluttered. "You're home early."

I watched in a dream as he strode into the kitchen and without even looking at me, opened the fridge. Grabbing a bottle of wine left to chill, he unscrewed the cap and poured two glasses. Then at last, he met my gaze. There was no denying he looked pale and shaken as he pushed one of them into my hand.

"What is it?" I mumbled, my voice feeble. "Has something happened?"

"Sit down," he ordered curtly, "and yes, I've got news but I'm afraid it's not good. Drink your wine. I think you're going to need it."

A terrible fear wormed its way through me again, no matter how hard I tried to suppress it. "This is going to be about Joe, isn't it?"

He remained very still, his eyes never leaving me. Glancing at my wine, I took a hefty gulp without thinking.

"I-I thought he'd be in my flat," I kept rambling, "but he's not even answering the landline..."

I took another gulp, dizzy with fear, then lowered my glass to the table.

What was it Sam wasn't telling me?

Then at last he exhaled a sigh. "No, Maisie, he wouldn't be. I've been in touch with St Richard's Hospital and I hate to tell you this, but... Joe is dead."

I stopped breathing, refusing to believe what he had just said to me. The next thing I saw, though, were dots flickering before my eyes, little sparkles like dust motes. Thicker and faster they swarmed, clouding my vision.

I could feel myself weakening. An onslaught of giddiness I could no longer fight, a horrible suffocating feeling, before I completely blacked out.

******

I was beginning to come around, but where was I?

My head felt so leaden, anchored to the floor, my brain thick with fog. All I could recapture was some distant grain of memory, something so devastating I could not bear to face it...

When I finally managed to prise my eyes open, I found myself in a very dark place. Lying on my back, I stared up in dread at the gloomy brick walls surrounding me. Tiny flickers of light illuminated them, shadows dancing.

This could not be real.

But as the fog in my mind began to thin, it dawned on me I was in the basement.

I let out a gasp, as other details began to register. The lights for example. Secured to the wall in sconces, those flickering bulbs resembled torches. I started to shiver, feeling the hardness of the floor beneath me.

"What the hell?" the words slipped out as I struggled to move.

Yet my body felt paralysed, like a fly caught in a web. With some effort, I managed to wriggle on the floor, and felt the resistance of cords cut into my flesh. Not only were my hands tethered, my ankles were too, and something constrained my neck. With my eyes wide open, only then did I grasp the horror. For there, glinting in the shadows, I saw long metal spikes hammered into the floorboards.

Five of them.

And they marked the points of a star.

A pentagram.

I whimpered in terror, my breath rising faster. With the onset of hysteria, my panic rose in waves, prompting an ear-splitting scream.

"It's no use," a chilling voice resonated from behind me. "No one will hear you down here."

Jerking my head upright, I felt the tug of satin around my throat and nearly choked. But I didn't have to look to know who had spoken. The pain of betrayal cut deep.

"Sam," I moaned in shock. "What sort of sick game are you playing?"

"It's not a game, Maisie," he said.

I detected movement. Then at last his shadow towered over me, but as my eyes took in his features, I saw a man I no longer recognised. Devoid of all beauty and compassion, his face had hardened into a wax-like mask.

"Joe was right to suspect me. You think I didn't know about your cosy little lunch date in ZiZi's on Monday? So he believes I'm damaged, does he?" He released a ripple of laughter. "He wasn't even close!"

"Sam, for God's sake, stop this! Just tell me what's going on!"

"Okay, I'll let you in on a little secret. Ever since we've been together, I've been tracing your every move. It began with our date in Bognor. Do you ever wonder why you slept so late next day? I sneaked a sedative into your brandy, because I needed some extra time that morning. Time to install spyware on your phone, so when you finally came to, you wouldn't suspect a thing."

"Suspect what?" I said numbly. "My mobile was in the lounge. I don't remember leaving it there... b-but why would you do that?"

He looked at me with a smile.

"Why not? We always knew you and Joe would talk about me behind my back, so I needed to know what was said. Do you want to know something else?"

"We?" I whispered. I could hardly breath, waiting for the next bombshell to land.

"His phone's been bugged even longer. Ever since he got it, in fact. I knew he and Jess had split up. You didn't have to tell me that, I had the pleasure of eavesdropping on all the drama at their dinner party. Oh, you should have heard it, Maisie, it was classic! And that's another thing. Were you even aware of fake apps designed to look like Instagram? That's how I installed the spyware without you knowing, so how could I resist putting a few posts up? I wish I'd seen Joe's face though. I was rather hoping you'd see them before he did, but Jesus! He proper freaked out!"

"I don't know what you're talking about. What posts?"

"Well," he sighed, "you did drop that little hint about forests. I didn't know about your phobia but I'm guessing *he* did, so I put up some pictures. Some really creepy pictures of woods and oak trees did the trick, especially on a misty night. I thought they were quite atmospheric really... albeit the stuff of your nightmares."

"I see," I said with a resigned shudder. "So you've been playing nasty psychological mind games with both of us. Joe was right, you're not the friend we knew. What the hell happened to you, Sam, to fuck you up like this?"

"Woe, steady!" he laughed. "D'you know, that's the first time I've heard you use the F word? Sweet little Maisie. So innocent and pure..."

The tutting that followed turned my stomach, and that was when I became aware of how chilly I was, my arms and feet bare. Writhing on the floor as he stood over me, it struck me I was no longer in my work clothes but wearing a long satin gown. He had not only bound my wrists and feet, but dressed me up. Even as I struggled to glance at myself, I knew that gown would be red.

"Anyway, I'm digressing. Let's go back to the night of the dinner party. Joe saw those posts and panicked. They had a blazing row and he dumped her! And how kind of you to give him a key to your flat. I knew he'd go back, but the rest is a mystery. You haven't spoken to him lately, have you?"

"Joe," I whimpered. A sob caught my throat as the worst memory of all came charging back at me like a tornado. "What happened to him?"

The smile dissolved from Sam's face, filling me with dread.

"He came face to face with Mr. Mortimer, that's what," he hissed. "He always was a meddling bastard but no one counted on him racing up to London to go blabbing to the Met. He shouldn't have done that, he was warned not to... Remember Schiller, do you?"

"Schiller," I echoed. "Mortimer's thug. How could I forget?"

"We laid a trap," he added coldly.

"Who's we?" I finally dared myself to ask.

"This may come as a shock, sweetheart, but I'm not on your side, and I never have been. Sorry to deceive you, but Joe always was a pain. He should have listened to the warnings when he had the chance and just buggered off!"

"How can you say that?" Tears blurred my vision as I struggled to speak but the horror of Joe's murder was ripping me apart. "He was your friend!"

"I know," he continued, "but we could never go through with our plan with him in the way, so he had to die, and this time, Schiller did not fail. He was hidden under the stairs when Joe came back. Did you hear about the fatal knife attack on the news earlier? It was him."

"You bastard!" I could hardly find the breath to splutter the words out.

If only I'd thought to contact Mark. In all those days when I couldn't reach Joe, I should have known something was wrong. Yet I hadn't acted on it.

"How could you leave Joe at the mercy of that monster?" I screamed. "Have you forgotten how much he cared for you? We were kids, Sam... Joe, Maisie, Sam, three kids too young to protect ourselves. He'd have done anything to protect you!"

"I know," he sighed.

The next time he looked at me, I saw the tiniest flicker of pity.

"And *Sam* was very grateful!"

His words punched into me with devastating force.

"Oh my God," I gasped. "You're not him, are you?"

"No, Maisie," he smirked. "Would you like me to put you out of your misery and tell you who I really am? I'm not Sam, darling. I'm Duncan."

Chapter Sixty-Eight

Maisie was in fact very much in DC Mark Anderson's thoughts. From the instant Matt had warned them of the chilling screen shot taken from Joe's mobile, he had agonised over her safety. If only his colleagues could do more. But after scouring her residence in Bognor and the remote woodlands around East Lavant, not a trace of her enemies could be found. Furthermore, he had left several messages, urging her to get in touch, and was surprised she had stayed so silent.

And now a fatal stabbing had occurred.

Mark chewed his lip as they fought their way to St Richard's Hospital. Dressed in plain clothes, he was happy for his partner, DC Anthony Monroe, to take the wheel.

Just thank God they had kept the victim's name out of the news, for Maisie's sake.

"Harold is such a dick," he growled under his breath, "I don't know why we couldn't have just visited her before this happened."

"Calm down, Mark," Tony said, "you know he's got her down as something of a hysteric. He didn't want to cause undue panic."

Angered by such complacency, Mark fired him a look of irritation.

Had they forgotten Maisie and her friends were central to a major investigation? Had it slipped their minds that the perpetrators were still at large?

"Is this for real?" he snapped. "You saw that text!"

"Sure, but it could easily have been a bluff," Tony argued. "Winterton's the one they were putting the frighteners on. Isn't he the one we should focus on?"

Swallowing back his frustration, Mark didn't get a chance to reply. The traffic lights had turned green, and with a clear view of the A&E department, where staff would be awaiting them, it was time to mentally prepare himself.

"Let me do the talking," he said.

A mist of sweat clung to his brow as they were led down a corridor to a room. Only now, though, did his thoughts turn to the *second* man involved in the knife attack, the core of steel in him growing as they marched up to the door.

Yet the sight of the man resting in the hospital bed brought him to a skidding halt.

Mark's mouth fell open. "Joe!" he breathed

"That's right," whispered Joe, through gritted teeth, "now for God's sake, please don't let on it was Schiller who died in the attack."

Inching his way to the bedside, Mark left his colleague hanging back.

"Can you bear to explain what happened?"

Adjusting his position, Joe winced, but with his torso laid bare, it was impossible to ignore the swathe of bandages around his middle.

"I'll tell you," he hissed, "but we ain't got a lot of time."

Terror flashed in his eyes, a look of pain buckling his features. Yet Mark recognised the fight in him, of a mind to let him say what he had to.

******

With the hands on the clock turning faster, Joe wished he didn't have to describe the bloodbath he had left in Bognor. He was still in shock. But it seemed unlikely the police would take any further action unless he told them what had happened.

All things considered, he was lucky to be alive. He might have guessed they would lay a trap for him, too rash in his departure to prepare himself... but when Schiller had slashed him across the belly, he had genuinely believed his life to be over. The pain had been excruciating, draining the breath from his lungs.

Yet when Schiller licked the blood off his fingers, something inside him had snapped. He had listened to the thug's taunts in outrage, listened to the man list the things he intended to do to him, and a murderous red mist filled his vision.

At that point, he knew he needed to act fast if he was to survive. So the next time Schiller brought the knife down, he had flung out his elbow to shield himself, taking another nasty gash to the forearm.

The pain had barely registered then, his attacker caught off guard. Joe had used this to his advantage, and hooking his feet around Schiller's ankles, succeeded in tripping him up.

"H-he went down with a crash," he stammered, the scene playing out in his head like a horror film, "d-dropped the blade..."

He pressed his eyes shut, fighting another wave of nausea, but every grain of hate he had ever felt for that man had brought out his killer instinct.

Yes, Schiller had gone down like a sack of shit.

Schiller's roar of outrage still resonated. Joe could picture the knife as it went skidding across the floor to the edge of Maisie's flat, his hand out quick to grab it.

In no way was Schiller about to give up the fight, though. Disentangling his legs, he had struggled to his feet enraged, and Joe needed to up the offensive immediately. Wasting no time, he drew back his knee, and regardless of the pain ripping through his innards, delivered a hard kick to his groin. Maybe it was his bellow that drew attention but the rest was a blur.

'*Piece of scum! I will gut you like a fish!*'

The last memory he recalled was of the man leaping on top of him, using his body weight to pin him down. Yet both had forgotten the knife clenched in Joe's fist, its lethally sharp tip pointed upward. Schiller landed heavily, knocking the breath out of him, but in that same pivotal moment, had been impaled upon his own knife.

As the blade thrust deep into his heart, even Joe guessed the wound would be fatal, a fountain of blood soaking him. But in that final frantic struggle, he had hauled himself out from under Schiller's bulk, and within a few torturous seconds, the man was dead.

"I-I didn't mean to kill him," he whimpered.

Tremors wracked his body as he finalised his story. He looked up, amazed to see such compassion radiating in Mark's eyes.

"Don't beat yourself up, Joe," he said. "It was self-defence and I doubt Schiller would be having any regrets if it had been the other way round. Now try to get some rest. You've had a very lucky escape."

"Rest?" Joe spluttered. "Are you kidding? It's Maisie we should be worried about... I-I was desperate to try and reach her before this happened!"

Mark shook his head as if struggling to make sense of it. "What are you talking about? I haven't heard a peep out of Maisie."

"What?" Joe murmured under his breath. "Oh shit."

Clocking the confusion in Mark's eyes, it seemed obvious not one of them knew the truth. He exhaled a shuddering breath, flinching at the tug of stitches. But shoving aside his pain, he swung his legs over the bed, determined to act before the worst happened.

"We have got to get her out of that house," he snarled. "Haven't you lot sussed she's in danger? I'll go myself if I have to..."

"You can't," Mark insisted, "you're in no fit state to do anything right now, so why don't you just leave us to handle this?"

Joe clenched his teeth, fighting an urge to slap him. "It's too fucking risky, that's why. Surely you saw the text I got. If those bastards even get a whiff you're onto 'em, they'll have no qualms about killing her."

"I did see it," Mark gulped. "Officers did a thorough search but found no one. They concluded it must have been a bluff, just to throw *you* off the scent."

Joe dug his nails into his palms, the frustration in him soaring to boiling point.

"Bollocks!" he retorted. "How would Mortimer know she was *all alone* if they weren't watching her? We need to get to her now but without them knowing, 'cos if they find out I'm still breathing..." he broke off with a shiver. "Any news of Sam? He was gonna drive down and protect her, but do you trust him? I know I don't!"

Mark turned to his colleague, braced by the door. "Do me a favour, Tony, and check this out, will you? See if you can get hold of Maisie and failing that, try Sam. Let's see what he has to say about this. If anything."

******

Mark was beginning to feel the onset of panic. Even more so when a few minutes later, his colleague returned to the room white-faced. The only news he had to report was that *Maisie had left work early to go home.*

"She's not answering her phone," he said, "and neither is Sam."

Joe turned to Mark, the dread in his expression growing more profound by the second.

"That's it," he gasped, "there's something going down at that place, and you can bet it involves Mortimer. Please, Mark! Call the guys at the Met if you have to and they'll fill you in, but I've got a really bad feeling about this."

Mark swallowed. "They've already updated us. Confirmed what you said about Sam driving down to Sussex..."

With his words trailing off, however, he felt an icy chill crawl right through him; a growing suspicion he had never had the chance to voice until now.

"What is it about Sam you haven't told us, Joe?"

The next time Joe stared at him, he saw the fear in his eyes.

"I'm worried he moved her into that house to isolate her, but I haven't figured out why. She could be in there, unprotected, and left to chance, anything could happen. Do you really wanna take that chance?"

Absorbing his words, Mark was rocked by another wave of panic.

He had always wondered about Sam, and was intrigued to hear Joe's view, having never forgotten their reunion in Charing Cross Police Station.

Joe had been gawking at Sam's i-Phone, almost oblivious to him sauntering by his side. Mark caught a glint in Sam's eye, lit with cruelty. It passed in a flash - perhaps he was the only one who felt a shiver roll over him, but it was there - that tiny flicker on Sam's lips, and with it a smirk that had left him cold.

As Harold often cautioned, though, police investigations had to be based on more than just a hunch.

Mark frowned. He could not see how they would ensure Maisie's safety without giving the game away. But looking at Joe now, he felt a wave of understanding pass between them; that whatever they decided, he was going to sneak his way out of this hospital to save her. With or without their help.

Chapter Sixty-Nine

Tears filled my eyes, the lights on the wall blurring into surreal shapes as the words of my tormenter sank in.

Words that changed everything.

"Duncan," I echoed in horror. "Duncan, as in Sam's half-brother?"

I so badly wanted this to be a dream, but knew the man pacing around me was no illusion. He was very real. A man I had fallen in love with, and he had transformed into my enemy.

"So for all this time, you've been spinning a lie."

His face turned stony. "Not all of it was a lie. Sam *was* adopted by his father, and brought up to Scotland. You saw the photo of Galbraith Castle, home to the McFadden family. I showed you at the police station, remember? Sam was in that photo, and exactly as you remembered him."

"Yes, I remember," I whispered.

"Sam, my annoying little screwed-up half-brother," he sneered. "The boy I was forced to look after and watch like a fucking hawk..."

Staring at him spellbound, I could hardly believe what I was hearing.

"It's like I said all along, I had no choice. *'If anything went tits up, Duncan took the flack'* and boy, did I suffer. That story about him sneaking into the garden for example. I was the one Father grabbed by the throat. It was my head he bashed against the wall. I wasn't lying about Hogmanay, either. I missed out on the best celebration of the year because of that little prick."

"Maybe you should have stood up to your father," I replied in my naivety.

"Yeah, I could have done," he nodded, "but on the other hand, I had far more to lose by not following his instructions."

"You were scared of him, weren't you?" I tried to empathise.

His eyes gleamed in the shadows. "Not scared. I was in awe of him. He drew me into a secret pact, you see. He promised me that if I spent the next years getting to know Sam and learning everything there was to know about him, I would be richly rewarded. As his heir and successor, I couldn't really wish for more."

"I don't get it. Why assign you to be Sam's minder if you hated him?"

"Ah, I thought you'd ask that," he said, "but this is where it gets complicated. So allow me to explain the true reason the respectable Alistair McFadden QC rescued his bastard son. It all goes back to Cornelius Mortimer.

The sad fact of the matter is, Sam knew too much..."

"The party," I shivered. "Does this mean everything you said he witnessed was true?"

"That's right! I wasn't lying when I gave my statement to the police, only the story I fed them was Sam's story. He was so traumatised. But once I'd gained his trust, he told me everything, from Joe being drugged, to the punch he spat out. But do you want to hear the most scandalous part? The satanic ritual he witnessed was real enough, but it wasn't Lord Parker-Smythe in the background... It was our father!"

Every muscle in my body froze.

"Your father?" I gulped. "So the politician was innocent?"

Duncan shrugged. "Someone had to take the fall. According to Cornelius, he broke his promise about funding. Got suspicious, until eventually they fell out. Cornelius swore revenge, but that's another story. The closure of the homes was never really down to lack of funding, but a lot to do with what Sam witnessed."

"So for all this time you conned us into thinking your father tried to stop the ritual when the truth is he was a participant!"

"Yes."

A surge of terror shuddered down my spine. *Sam had always maligned his father, but not once did I imagine anything of this barbarity.*

"When Cornelius formed his cult, Hooded Shadows, it was bound to attract men like my father. The highest ascension of power, something that not only violated every written rule but enabled men in authority to cross the barriers of morality. Like drugging and raping children. They thought they were above the law."

Holding my gaze, he exhaled a pitiful sigh.

"He aspired to the role of High Priest, you know. The man at the top. The Great One. Yet that party could have destroyed him. The instant he recognised his son lying there, he panicked. He had to stop the ritual, in case Sam recognised him too."

"That's horrible," I shivered, "although I never doubted your story."

"No, I don't suppose you did - and those nightmares of yours backed it up very nicely - another nail in the coffin for Thomas."

I shook my head, fighting to bury my contempt. *How dare he mention my nightmares, given the hell he was putting me though now.*

"Anyway, going back to that night, Father had to act fast before Sam started bleating, and as a judge he had contacts. Enough to persuade the authorities Sam was better out of care, especially with the protection of his real family. Christ knows how he did it but within a few hours, the police had turned up to collect him, and you already know the rest. I spoke the truth about Sam's isolation but you must understand why we had to do that - sever his connections from his friends – more specifically, you and Joe."

"Joe..." I choked. Tears sprung to my eyes at the mere mention of him, but I saw not one flicker of compassion in return.

"Joe was the biggest pain in the arse out of the lot of you, as far as Cornelius was concerned," he snapped, "but the day after that party he was bricking it."

A tear rolled down my face, the horror of Joe's fate magnifying the pain.

"It makes sense now," I blubbered. "Mr. Mortimer was so threatening towards him but why? He said you'd been adopted but something didn't tally. Just thank God he ran away when he did..."

Taking a step back to observe me, he tilted his head to one side.

"Yes, well now you know why, because *he's* the reason Cornelius had to close Orchard Grange. Joe bloody Winterton! Couldn't keep his trap shut, could he? Forever taunting him about Sam, insinuating he might have been killed. Okay, I don't blame him for running away, I'd have done the same, but consider the consequences for Cornelius. He saw Joe as the ultimate whistle blower, never knowing when he'd start shooting off his big mouth. So he shut the place down. Got rid of them all, chose a new direction in life and fucked off abroad. But he swore to my father he'd hunt Joe down and deal with him..." A look of loathing narrowed his eyes. "The only problem is it took a little longer than expected."

"Don't!" I gasped, struggling against my restraints. "Please... stop torturing me! I can't bear to imagine Joe dead."

"But I haven't finished," Duncan goaded, "there's more. You see, it wasn't just Cornelius who had to cover his tracks, but my father. He thought he was on top of his game when those boys were returned to the homes, unharmed. Quick to 'rescue' Sam and invite him into the family fold - convinced that once Sam was spirited up to the Scottish Highlands, people would forget him... but there had to be procedures and paperwork, which is where that sodding social worker got involved."

"Oh no," I whispered. "You're talking about Yvonne Draper, aren't you?"

"Yvonne Draper was a problem he never expected," he said brutally. "He'd guessed Sam would be traumatised after what he witnessed. He just never considered the possibility he would blurt it all out to his social worker."

"But she kept quiet," I argued. "Another thing Joe couldn't understand."

"Ah, Joe, always the curious one. I suppose he wondered why she didn't report it?"

"Did your father put the frighteners on her?" I challenged him. A lump tightened my throat, but I had to ask.

"Too bloody right he did!" he replied. "Sam's account was everything he feared, so he had to nip it in the bud before word got out, and yes, there was a cover up! He warned the Draper woman that if ever she repeated a word of what Sam had said, her family would suffer big time. He wasn't just protecting himself, but Cornelius. Anything to avoid a scandal, and for a while, it paid off. A secret they suppressed for years."

A dangerous tone had crept into his voice but as the threads kept unravelling, I hankered to know more.

"So she didn't dare speak the truth..." My words came out as a whisper. "Even when the investigation was underway."

"Oh yeah, the investigation," Duncan muttered. "Shame she had to die, but when the cops cranked up the pressure, the last thing we needed was her falling apart. You were sat in the pub when I contacted DI Fitzpatrick to arrange an interview."

"I remember," I said numbly, "and did you?"

"Of course! I did whatever it took to throw Joe off the scent, but what you didn't see was my text to Cornelius. Joe's phone might be bugged but I had to be sure Cornelius knew what I was about to do. He was clever to arrange her death so speedily. Or rather, Schiller was."

"Schiller," I breathed. My fear turned to hatred as I glared at him. "Christ, how many people have died to protect your father and that pervert, Mortimer?"

"Does it matter?"

The chill in his eyes unnerved me, but I had nothing more to lose. "It does to me! And what about you? What was your role in all this? You mentioned a pact..."

"I'm glad you asked, because the answer brings us full circle, so to speak. So let's rewind a little and go back a few years. Back to the time Sam lived with us. My father ordered me to be in charge of him, as you know, but there was a little more to it than that. I had to watch him, observe his behaviour, listen to his stories until I knew them off by heart. He said plenty about his mother, but I was more interested in his life at Orchard Grange. His friendship with you and Joe..."

"So that's how you knew so much about us."

"Yes," he said, "and I meant it when I said how *grateful* Sam was for Joe's protection. That story about having his head forced down the bog, that did amuse me, and as for Joe's face when I repeated it! I had a feeling he'd want to test me, though I was particularly intrigued to hear how much Sam adored you, Maisie. In fact, I think he was in love with you, and that proved to be of even greater value!"

"I see," I murmured. A thread of tension drew the atmosphere taut as the impact of his words hit home. "So for all the years Sam was isolated in your castle, you were planning to impersonate him? I don't understand..."

"No, I don't suppose you do, but you will. This entire charade has had far reaching consequences. I wasn't just in charge of Sam, see, I had to copy his behaviour, learn everything about him and ultimately *be* him."

"But why?" I whimpered. My wrists burned as I tugged against the cords again, helpless.

"It was all part of an ingenious strategy devised by Cornelius," he said, "and my father went along with it. Sam was contained, but they were never going to be safe with you and Joe walking free. So he kept an eye on you, especially you, because you were the one thing he desired more than anything, a girl so special, he wanted to save you for his final ritual..."

"What?" Suddenly it was hard to focus as a wave of panic swept over me.

"Call it 'unfinished business.' From the day you were fostered, he had you in his sights, but perhaps it's better to let *him* tell you about that. All I understood is they needed Sam to get to you, and I was perfectly placed to play the role..."

Pausing for effect, he ran his fingers through his hair.

"See this? I even had his fucking scar carved into my forehead, another wound my father inflicted to carry out his master plan!"

"So where is Sam now?" I dared to whisper.

The silence hung between us like fog. I held my breath, waiting for him to divulge the truth, though deep down I already knew.

"Where do you think?" he said, his voice a shard of ice. "Cornelius was in it for the long game, and by the time Sam reached his fourteenth birthday, we'd extracted every little drop of information we needed. He was of no further use."

"You killed him, didn't you?"

"I did," Duncan gloated. "My father had no qualms but it had to be me. I was the only one Sam trusted, so imagine his feelings the day I invited him to come on a hike with me. He was ecstatic! I knew exactly where to take him. Following the path from the grounds, we ventured into the mountains, and he loved it! All those years cooped up and finally he was out in the fresh air, seeing the views. The best were at the top, and when we finally reached the vantage point we were over three thousand feet up. I dared him to look over the edge, and smiled one last smile at the whining brat, sure that the best day of my life would be the day I ended his."

I blinked, unable to fathom his expression. With flickers of light reflected in his gleaming eyes, he looked as triumphant as he did dangerous.

"At least he died happy," he added softly. "*Goodbye little brother* I said, and one hard shove sent him toppling over the edge."

"How can you say that and smile?" I cried out but as the tears started flowing, I recalled every devious trick he had used to woo me.

The drive in the countryside, this house... Sam, Joe and now me. Oh, how cleverly we had been reeled in by his lies.

"You're a monster," I shuddered. "No wonder Joe couldn't warm to you.

You stand there, boasting about your brother's murder, when all the while you were impersonating him to lay a trap? And I thought you loved me!"

"It wasn't easy," he responded. "There were times I felt so stressed, I wasn't sure I could go through with it. Keeping you happy, while hopping backwards and forwards to indulge Cornelius's every whim. It was tearing me apart, but he's the one calling the shots here..."

"You're as evil as he is," I choked through my tears, "and to think, this was all for Mortimer?"

"All for Mortimer," he repeated coldly, "but it was his dying wish. He's terminally ill now, so what can I do? If it's any consolation, I am sorry."

"Sorry?" Pressing my eyes shut to stem my tears, I could not look at him.

"I mean it, Maisie. These last few weeks have been fun, and I truly enjoyed getting to know you. Shame that autistic kid had to come along and disrupt things, but as soon as you mentioned the authorities checking me out... well, you must realise how upset I was. They'd have blown my cover. That's what put me in a bad mood, and I hoped after that you'd back off. But then you threatened to go back to Bognor! I could have wept when you said that, thinking I'd lost you, so I had to turn the tables. Anything to stop you from leaving me..."

Waves of hate spread like flames through my heart, but muddled up in his speech, he had drawn someone else into my thoughts. *Connor.*

I kept my eyes shut, fearing any emotion would betray me.

Or was it hope? Connor had not been in the house or the garden when I'd got home, and going by what Sarah hinted, had probably gone wandering off somewhere. Wherever he was, I just prayed the police would find him. But with my life dangling on a thread, I had to forget about him for now.

"These last days have been hell," Duncan persisted, "and I don't like where it's going but I'm in too deep..."

"You m-might as well k-kill me then and have done with it," I said, struggling to breath between my sobs. "Joe and Sam were the only boys I-I ever trusted and if they're dead, then what have I got to live for?"

"Oh, Maisie," he murmured. "I can't kill you."

Dropping to his haunches, he stroked a tear from my face. The gesture seemed tender but I cringed from his touch, his next words making my skin crawl.

"Cornelius has to be the one to do it."

"What?" I whimpered. "You're going to invite that sadist here?"

"It's time to put his plan into action, and there is nothing I can do to stop it. Sacrificing you was his ultimate goal and this, I'm afraid, is how it must end."

Sacrifice. A cold sick feeling rose from the pit of my stomach.

"No," I gasped, "you can't let him do this!"

My mind raced as I wondered if there was anything I could say to change his mind; but before I had a chance, I saw him reach into his top pocket. He withdrew a syringe, his eyes dark with threat as he took my arm.

"I don't have a choice," he said. "At least this will sedate you. But I'm going to have to leave you for a while, so you might as well drift off to sleep..."

I felt the scratch of a needle in the crook of my elbow before his voice faded away; the last thing I heard, before the darkness took me again.

"Cornelius is waiting."

Chapter Seventy

"Finally," Cornelius murmured with unrestrained pleasure. "I do hope you're calling to say that everything is ready."

"Oh yes," his ally purred. "After all my efforts trying to lure her here, did you think I was going to let you down?"

"You've done well," Cornelius indulged him, "and you'll be pleased to know your father has arrived to congratulate you..."

He felt a smile cross his face. Two hours earlier, a sleek, cross-terrain vehicle had swept through the village undetected. Following the winding road into the countryside, the driver had pulled over by a concealed forest opening, the trees dividing into a narrow, leafy track.

With the metal gate left open, he had carved his way through the woods, seeking out the exact co-ordinates where Cornelius had been hiding.

"Now before we proceed, tell me what you've been doing."

"I set up the basement as you instructed," Duncan whispered, "locked her car in the barn. Right now she is out cold, which gives you about an hour."

"Good," Cornelius croaked. "Very good."

With a sigh of ecstasy, he imagined her anchored to the pentagram in her beautiful red gown, auburn hair like a flame against her flawless white skin.

How could he forget the night they had stolen her virginity? An innocent twelve-year-old on the cusp of puberty. Pity she hadn't been fully unconscious, though, her frantic shrieks as Alistair clambered on top of her a flaw in an otherwise perfect night.

'Silence her!'

He remembered severing her scream with the palm of his hand, one speedy injection all it took to paralyse her... and for the rest of the ritual she had been theirs. It was the same night he swore vengeance on Joe Winterton, given his attempts to disrupt their gathering; but Joe no longer mattered. Joe was history. One of three prying children, whose inevitable fate had caught up with him.

That left only Maisie...

Twenty years he had waited for this, and as his eyes sprung open, he saw his dearest and closest ally gazing back at him. Cornelius sighed again. With his head rolling back, he took a last look at his surroundings. The trees stretched overhead like a canopy and as the sun gleamed through the leaves, they formed *an intricate mosaic against the sky.*

"Are you alright, Cornelius?" Alistair frowned.

"Just thinking about what lies ahead... Heard from Schiller, have you?" he muttered into his mobile.

"Not yet," Duncan answered. "I suspect he's lying low after that knife attack but we can touch base when this is over. You need to start making your way through the forest if you intend to be here by six. Let yourselves in through the patio and I'll be waiting for you in the basement."

******

By the time Sussex Police had formulated their tactics, Joe was beginning to fear they would be too late. With early evening approaching, Maisie could be dead soon if the premonition gnawing inside him proved correct. Two turbulent days had passed since he had recognised Mortimer and the shock had not worn off.

Yet still the police had failed to apprehend him.

"Anything happening?" he dared to whisper.

Faced with initial resistance from his superiors, Mark had doggedly persuaded them to let him accompany them on this operation. Perhaps they didn't fully trust him, but seated in the back of an unmarked car, he was an additional asset. He could still tune in to their radio alerts, where any information would be useful.

"Well?"

"I'm not sure," Mark muttered. "As far as I know the specialist unit has set up distance surveillance in the woods but..."

His words were cut short as a volley of shouts erupted from the speaker.

"The house appears empty and there are no signs of activity - over."

"Any vehicles parked near the property? Over."

"Just one car parked in the driveway... A turquoise Audi S3 - over."

"Sam's car!" Joe blurted before he could stop himself.

"But no sign of Maisie's," Mark frowned to his colleague. "I thought she went home early."

"According to her manager, she left at about three-thirty," he muttered darkly, "so what do you reckon, Mark, is it worth a quick circuit to check this out?"

Five minutes later, having finally been granted clearance from OPS1, Tony started the engine. Joe watched with a pounding heart as they entered the heart of the village; the mossy flint walls just as he remembered, bursting with a tapestry of flowers. Vehicles clogged the lane, reducing traffic to single file; given they were in the height of summer, progress was bound to be sluggish.

Once released into the open countryside, however, they sped up, Tony's foot firm on the accelerator as the road twisted, merging into an area of woodland. With the trees in full leaf, Joe felt the touch of a shiver, unnerved by the thickening forests. The trees sapped out the sunlight, plunging them into shade.

"The house is coming up," he said. "It's around the next bend."

Dread hung in his voice as the boundary hedge rose ahead of them. But he was already picturing the house in its seclusion, the thought of Maisie trapped in there sending a chill through his blood.

"Can you slow down a bit?" Mark mumbled.

Tony kissed the brake, enough to steal a glance towards the house. There wasn't much to see beyond the hedge, apart from the driveway, the house mostly hidden from view.

Sure enough though, the Kingfisher blue gleam of Sam's Audi peered out of the shadows.

"If Sam's there, then where the hell is Maisie?" Joe spluttered. "She drives a silver Toyota but I can't see it!"

He kept his head low, hands twisting in his lap as he considered their options, and with his fear for her safety spiralling, it took every ounce of willpower not to jump from the car and kick the door down.

He had to heed Mark's advice, though.

Any rash heroics could wreck the entire operation, and until they knew what they were dealing with, there was nothing he could do.

Tony, meanwhile, kept driving. Passing the house, he followed the lane to the junction where it joined Goodwood Estate, but with no wish to travel any further, he stopped in the nearest lay by.

The next phase was a waiting game, the wooded countryside around Goodwood Estate sufficiently remote for them to linger in the area without detection.

Twenty minutes passed in unbearable tension, an eternity before the radio hissed into life again.

Joe held his breath.

"We've tried calling the occupants," a voice crackled. "Still no reply from either mobile but the surveillance team have touched base. There appears to be some suspicious activity in the woods surrounding the property..."

"Where?" Joe exploded.

"Shh," Mark hissed. "Just listen... Can you repeat that? Over."

The interior of the car buckled into silence as the report continued. But the gist of their findings turned him cold with shock.

Two figures had been spotted sneaking through the forest on foot. Quick to slip into the garden, they had let themselves into the house via the patio doors at the rear.

"Shit," Joe whispered.

He could visualise it in his mind. A solitary oak tree towering above the hedge, and the hint of a hidden track. Nudging his head close to listen, every breath began to race faster.

From the descriptions given, both men looked to be in their senior years, although it was the frailer of the two who drew attention; a man who matched the appearance of their suspect, Richard Lacey.

Joe felt a lurch of panic.

"Mortimer! So why haven't they gone round there to arrest the fucker?"

"Calm down, Joe," Mark counselled him softly. "I told you what the Force Commander Control said: any proceedings must be handled with caution. Now consider what we know so far..."

Joe sat up sharply, and immediately wished he hadn't. Spears of pain ripped through his middle, reminding him of the wound Schiller had inflicted.

"No one can be certain if Maisie is in the house," Mark continued. "Her car is missing and she's not answering her phone, so we need to find out."

Turning his head, he met Joe's eye with a look of despair.

"Given what we know about Mortimer, though, the police are seeking his arrest for a number of crimes. But if your theory is correct and a hostage situation is imminent, they need to act with extreme stealth. Panic makes people react badly."

"What are you saying?" Joe breathed. "That until they know the state of play, they ain't gonna do nothing?"

"Just hear me out," Mark pressed. "Any form of dynamic entry is risky, so in order to avoid a life threatening situation, it has to be slow and methodical."

"Then what?"

"There is one other clue to consider. Where does Sam fit into all this? For all we know, he could be in as much danger as she is. Maybe the best approach would be simply to knock on the door. See if he answers..."

"And if he doesn't?" Joe interrupted.

"They may have to consider a forced entry," he finished gravely.

Joe took a moment to absorb this. The revelations conveyed by the surveillance team brought him out in a cold sweat, but he still had one more roll of the dice to play; something none of them had thought of.

"Then why not use me? Let me be the one to knock on the door. That'll shit 'em up, especially if they think I'm dead."

"Are you serious?" Mark gasped. "If your enemies are in that house, there's no way you can put yourself at risk. You've already narrowly escaped death!"

"Yeah," Joe sighed, "but it's worth a shot, and I'm guessing there's other police officers on standby?"

The more he thought about it, the more it made sense.

If his theory was correct, the sight of him turning up at the door would spring a surprise not one of those bastards would be expecting.

Chapter Seventy-One

I woke to find myself immersed in the same evil world. Flickers of light danced behind my eyelids, my bare arms crawling with goose pimples. Staked out on the floorboards, I was dimly aware of the cramp in my shoulders, but only when I tried to move did reality strike hard.

This was no nightmare.

Trapped in this hellish place, I started trembling. I heard whispers. Hissing through the darkness, they sent shivers racing over my skin - but as I focused on the sound, those short sharp breaths began to form consonants.

"Morf su revi led tub-no itat-met otni..."

My eyelids fluttered open, my senses sharp enough to realise I was not alone down here. The first thing to register were the torches on the walls. Only this time, those glowing flames illuminated the shapes of three hooded men.

A gasp tore my throat as I squirmed under their gaze. As the chanting receded, a sinister silence replaced it. I held my breath, dreading what was to come as somewhere from the fog of memories arose the concept of a final ritual.

Sacrifice.

Twisting my head sideways, I cringed as one of the figures approached me. He rolled back his hood.

"Hello again, Maisie," Duncan murmured.

My heart thumped, a sense of dizziness overwhelming me.

But I had no words left to say to him. I hated him.

"I don't believe you've been properly introduced to my father."

The next man to step forward was taller, and as he pushed back his hood, I clocked the resemblance. The square-jawed face was similar, the high forehead, but there the resemblance ended. With receding white hair, a glossy complexion threaded with broken capillaries that gave it a slightly red flush, he scrutinised me through eyes like chips of black lead.

"So you're the great Maisie Bell," he taunted. "I gather my son was quite infatuated with you..."

The unctuous drawl of his voice turned me sick with loathing, his eyes crawling over me from my bare feet to my throat. But it took one sharp flinch to remind me of the ribbon secured around my neck.

"Very well done, Duncan. I can tell how much you liked her and you've excelled yourself in fulfilling your end of the pact..."

His Scottish accent echoed with a chilling resonance as I remembered Sam's fate.

"You're a murderer!" I hissed. "Sam was one of the sweetest boys I ever met and you snatched him away! Killed him in cold blood just because he witnessed one of your sick rituals!"

"Ah, she has spirit," Alistair laughed. "I like that, but allow me to enlighten you, dear girl, because whatever you think, Sam didn't have a bad life!"

"It was cruel to cut him off from the outside world," I protested, "separating him from his friends, keeping him locked up..."

"Maybe. But in all the years he was under my care, I gave him books to read and board games to entertain him, finer food than he'd ever tasted. I installed Sky TV. Got him watching the History Channel, the Discovery Channel, opened his eyes to the big wide world all around him. At least we gave him an education, which is more than can be said for that whore of a mother, Stephanie, too busy earning a living on her back to help him with his school work!"

Hate narrowed my eyes as I flung a glare in Duncan's direction. "What the hell did it matter if you were planning to kill him?"

"He didn't know that though, did he?" Duncan said.

"Sam had to die," his father intervened harshly. "We did consider using him as bait to entrap you, but it would never have worked. Whereas Duncan here..." His smile was calculating as he turned to him. "With the same good looks and charm, we created a perfect pawn to replace him when the time was right."

"And that time has come," rasped a different voice.

Raising my head, I could barely breath as the third hooded figure crept towards me.

Mortimer was nothing like I had expected. Shadows masked his face as he inched a little closer, thin to the point of cadaverous.

For some reason I had imagined a larger man, but then, all adults seem huge when you're a child, too small to defend yourself.

"Finally we meet again, my dear," his voice slithered through the darkness. "You don't recognise me, do you? Though I've kept a very close eye on you."

I fought back a shudder, appalled by the things Duncan had told me. But that voice... There was a sinister ring to it that sent my mind hurtling into the past.

Then slowly he peeled back his hood. I didn't relish gazing at his face, but I knew I had to, and it was truly the face from hell. Not only did I recognise his tanned, heavily lined complexion, but his eyes, splinters of ice, glinting under bushy brows. For all this time, the leathery folds of loose skin had concealed them.

"No," I burst out. "It can't be..."

I knew in a flash where I'd seen his face now, a face that had haunted me since my last therapy appointment. And he had been living right on my doorstep.

"Mr Lacey?"

"Sweet naive little Maisie. I tried to keep my distance, wary you might identify me..." His voice oozed with pleasure.

"But you look so different!"

"Yes," he sighed, "but I've been ill for years. It began in the Far East, some dreadful disease, and I shed several stone, but the weight kept on dropping, until I was diagnosed with cancer. I've endured surgery and chemotherapy but my illness is incurable. My hair grew back white, so I dyed it gold. Grew a beard, a moustache to enhance the disguise and last of all, I invested in solid brown contact lenses."

A cruel smile curled into his slack withered lips.

"Winterton recognised me instantly. We came face to face on the landing when that slut next door invited him round. Regrettably, I had taken the lenses out by then."

"Joe," I mumbled. "Oh my God..."

"Don't you want to know how I found *you*?" he taunted.

Taking another step towards me, he lowered himself unsteadily to his knees.

"For the past twenty years, I have never stopped monitoring you, not even when I left the country. I had people assigned to keep an eye on you, told them how special you were and that after meeting you at Orchard Grange, all I wanted to know was how your future would pan out."

His drawling words made my flesh crawl.

"Stop it," I gasped, "I don't want to hear this..."

"Shush," he interrupted, "I am proud of you, Maisie. Delighted you went to college and pursued a career, and out of all the paths you could have chosen you worked in fostering. How virtuous! Helping vulnerable children. When I think of all those unruly, damaged brats I took in... yet despite your own trauma, you rose above it to help others. I admire that!"

I felt the stab of his eyes as he leaned over me, pale slits in the shadows.

"It's why I became obsessed with you, my dear girl, so innocent and pure..."

Icicles of dread pounded into me as his words sank in, that final scene in his office replaying itself.

"Imagine my joy when I discovered you had moved away from your foster home to settle in Sussex. Did you know I attended one of your fostering evenings in Chichester? You were probably too preoccupied to notice me..." he gave an unpleasant snigger. "And do you like this house? Alistair bought it! A

337

good investment, don't you think? Especially when I wanted to move nearer to you."

A wave of nausea welled up inside me.

No wonder the atmosphere unnerved me at times; that for all its splendour, this house was infiltrated with his evil.

"In January, though, a flat in Annandale Avenue became vacant," he gloated. "I couldn't resist, having never imagined I could get so close."

"January," I shuddered, "the same time my nightmares came back."

Everything snapped into place. I thought of the day he had been carted off to hospital. In the weeks that followed, Joe had kept me safe, but it wasn't so much *him moving out* that had resurrected those dreams, as *Mr Lacey moving back in.*

"Oh yes," he drawled in amusement, "I heard about your nightmares from Duncan here. Very intriguing."

"My foster parents suggested psychotherapy," I whispered aloud, "then other memories started to surface. I had flashbacks..."

Maybe his voice had triggered them, some tiny subconscious window opened as if to alert me.

As my eyes rose to meet his, he could barely contain his glee.

"It was your *psychotherapy* that spurred us on. We had you followed. Read stories in the news about some sex abuse ring linked to children's homes... I began to fear it was only a matter of time before there'd be an investigation into *my* homes, and I was right, wasn't I?"

He narrowed his stare.

"We were primed and ready to move in on you, but that was before someone else reared their ugly head. That meddlesome creature, Joe Winterton."

"Joe did nothing wrong!" I yelped.

"He was better off on the streets," he added nastily, "like the vermin he was! But you, ever the Good Samaritan, had to invite him to live with you. Now that *did* cause a problem, and the only reason I sent for an ambulance, but I needed a decoy. Nobody questioned my so-called collapse, but when you're as ill as I am, medical attention comes swiftly. It wasn't difficult."

"So why threaten him?" I hissed through clenched teeth. "Why did your thug try to run him over? Because that's what launched the investigation. All Joe was trying to do was turn his life around!"

"Calm down, Maisie," Mortimer smirked, "you're beginning to sound quite hysterical. Now let's forget the investigation, since it's irrelevant now, what with Joe and Sam dead - and you – well. We did our groundwork and we were already in the process of setting Thomas up..."

"But he was innocent!" I retorted.

"Thomas was a pompous prick," Mortimer growled, "lecturing me on how to run my homes. Come March, however, we had our own network in place, including those slutty cleaners. Alistair was the one who introduced them to that waitress Thomas liked. Our long term goal to gain access to his home."

I closed my eyes. As if what they had done wasn't terrible enough, the sight of his smug face looming over me turned me sick to the core.

"Thomas was an easy scapegoat," he continued, "and as soon as he was on remand it was time to resurrect 'Sam', our pièce de résistance..."

"Sam." His name froze on my lips, stirring memories.

How could I forget that forlorn figure staring at me bolt-eyed along a dark drizzly road in February? Perhaps he had been a ghost after all, reaching out from the grave to warn me of impending danger...

As I opened my eyes, though, my gaze shifted to Duncan. He met my stare, his expression empty - but the picture that leapt out at me was the moment he and Mr Lacey had shaken hands. *The night of our date.* Maybe, I thought, they were sealing their own pact, his words from last night flitting back.

'Sometimes I wonder if you should just live each day as if it's your last.'

He must have known I would meet my death tonight. Tears filled my eyes as I opened my mouth to speak, but the words wouldn't come.

"Which brings us to you," Mortimer continued. "So pure and virtuous, you were destined to be our sacrifice. Twenty years may seem like a long time, but the faster my health deteriorated, the greater my obsession grew and now finally here you are. A perfect offering to the Dark Lord, before I finally meet my death..."

I cringed in terror as his bony fingers reached down to stroke my neck.

"Why?" I found the strength to gasp. "What's in it for you?"

"There is a pattern to rituals, which must be finished," he said, "and by the time I closed my homes, it had never been completed."

His cold hand coiled around my throat.

"My life-long ambition was to find you again. With Sam, Joe and you gone, there would be no more traces of our deeds. But it was my dying wish to complete the circle, whereby sacrificing you will grant me supreme power and immortality."

"You're insane," I breathed. "How can you believe in such rubbish?"

"Do not dare mock the power of the Dark Lord," Mortimer retorted, his voice thick with menace.

His hand tightened around my throat, turning me rigid, and as his face loomed close, I saw the satanic flare in his eyes.

"Nothing you say will stop me, Maisie Bell. I am going to kill you."

There was a beat of silence as he delved into the folds of his robe.

The next thing I saw was the dagger in his hand. Shock widened my eyes, but even after all I had seen and heard, nothing could prepare me for the horror yet to come, his hand clawing my gown, tearing the delicate fabric.

"Get your hands off me," I sobbed, although I knew my words held no power.

"I might have made it quick and painless," he sneered, "but your friend, Joe Winterton, had to get in the way again, didn't he? I warned him not to go to the police... that if he did, you would die in agony."

My throat turned dry as he flaunted the dagger before my eyes. He gave a cold, twisted smile.

"I could stab you through the heart, you know," he added thoughtfully. "End your life in a single blow. But that seems too merciful..."

Frozen in shock, my eyes were fixed to the blade, its razor sharp edge reflecting little glints of light as they bounced off the walls.

Mortimer was still smiling. "Your heart is a precious gift. So precious, in fact, that I would like to carve it from your chest while it is still beating."

"N-no..." I was shaking so much, I could barely find the breath to stutter the words out. "Please!"

Glancing across the basement, I caught Duncan's eye again. His face crumpled in despair, a look I had seen before, but it was to him I appealed directly.

"Help me!" I cried out. "You have to stop this!"

"I-I can't," he said through shaking lips.

"What's your problem, Duncan?" Mortimer mocked, twisting his head around. "You knew this was how it would end when you agreed to your pact. Don't tell me you've developed feelings for her."

"B-but i-it doesn't have to be messy..." he faltered.

Sadly, it took just one savage glare from his father to weaken him.

"Just kill her, then," he finished, "and get it over with!"

A slick of fear ran over me, any last hopes fading.

Mortimer released a laugh. He looked dangerously insane now, as he raised the dagger high. The unbearable silence hung for another second and I squeezed my eyes shut, bracing myself for the worst.

Chapter Seventy-Two

"Tonight, Dark Lord, we present a sacred offering," Mortimer's voice whispered from above. "Ridding the world of a woman so virtuous, we serve you well. And in order for evil to triumph, we deliver her to you as our ultimate sacrifice..."

Powerless to fight, my heart crashed so wildly, I thought it was about to explode in my chest. My breaths became shallow, and to my eternal shame, I felt a warm wetness between my legs; but with a horrible death looming over me, I could no longer hold my bladder.

All I could pray for was a swift release. That when death came it would be quick; that it would sever the cord that bound me to life without unmerited pain.

I waited for the slice of cold steel in my heart.

But of all the scenarios that might have delayed this nightmare, I never expected to hear the ring of the doorbell.

"Who the hell is that?" I heard Duncan gasp.

"It doesn't matter," his father hissed. "Just ignore it."

My eyes flew open, drawn to Mortimer's face. The hatred in his eyes blazed brighter than the torches now, his teeth bared. Yet that tiny seed of hope was crushed in an instant, his knife jabbing into my throat.

"Not a sound, bitch," he seethed.

The next time the bell rang, it was impossible to ignore, a prolonged and piercing vibration that reverberated across the ceiling like nails down a blackboard. Nobody moved, the air choked with tension.

"Why don't you let me answer it?" Duncan pleaded, "and whoever it is, I'll get rid of them."

"Dressed like that?" Alistair sneered. "It could be the police, you imbecile."

"You're not going anywhere," Mortimer added, his voice icy with threat.

My mind spun into overdrive, the point of his knife at my throat holding me suspended, as I battled to wonder who could be out there.

My immediate thoughts turned to Connor.

Yet no sooner had the idea struck me, than I caught a movement on the back wall. Staring at Duncan, I read every conflicting emotion as it writhed across his face. Confusion turned to panic, fury and then hate, while on the periphery of my vision flickered the silhouette of another person. The faint glow was enough to reveal his outline, before the shadowy figure froze.

That was when I realised Connor had been hiding here all along.

His eyes met mine across the web of gloom, two familiar glowing orbs dilated into circles of shock. With my gaze anchored to Duncan, I dared not move a muscle for fear I would give the game away... except the game was about change.

Whoever was outside started pounding on the door.

The atmosphere in the basement shifted, the men exchanging glares. The sound was unrelenting. Thump after thump, shaking the house with its intensity.

"Sam!" A muffled voice bellowed. "It's Joe! What the fuck is going on?"

My breath shook as I stared at Mortimer. A look of insane fury twisted his face as he turned to Duncan.

"Oh, shit," Duncan groaned in disbelief.

"Joe?" I bleated.

Hearing his voice seemed like an impossibility. Yet as I yanked at my cords, a sense of panic thudded into me.

If they let him in now, he was doomed.

But Duncan was still talking, his words shuddering with hate. "It's not him, it can't be. I called the hospital on my way over here and the victim of that knife attack definitely died..."

"But did you find out *which* victim?" Mortimer whispered.

"Sam!" The voice hollered from above. "Open the fucking door!"

"Best let him in then," Duncan whispered, a smile folding his lips.

"NO!" I screamed.

Too busy squabbling among themselves, they had failed to spot Connor creeping along the back wall. Flitting in and out of sight like a ghost, he caught my eye for just a moment, and held a finger to his lips. I saw him crouch behind a crate, his hand feeling along the wall. But as my eyes explored further, they picked out the shape of a fusebox; a single row of switches embedded in the brickwork.

And suddenly I knew what he was about to do.

The lights in the basement dimmed, before plunging us into darkness.

I screamed again, and amid the chaos erupting all around me, several things happened at once. The pounding outside had ceased but a violent crash replaced it, an explosion of splintering wood and glass. Various doors clicked open. And even as the confusion rose, I was aware of something else unfurling in the basement.

A loud clang caused me to flinch, the thud of a body hitting the floorboards. The next sound I heard was shuffling.

Mortimer.

342

He had finally backed off, purging my personal space of his presence. I drew in a deep gulp of air, relieved that I could no longer smell his cologne, nor feel the heat of his foul breath on my face.

"Duncan!" a voice resounded around the basement.

I heard a sob, just as the trapdoor flew open. The fading sun painted a rectangle of amber light onto the floorboards, though its gleam didn't quite reach me.

The powerful beam of a flashlight was the next thing to divide the gloom, but all I could see was Mortimer, struggling up the stairs. The beam must have startled him, as he froze like a deer in headlights, and that's when I noticed Connor again. Sneaking up behind Mortimer, his hand coiled around his ankle. The shock caused the older man to topple and he landed heavily on his back with a howl... and that was the last I saw of Connor, his shadow flitting through the aperture.

As far as I could tell, all hell had broken loose, and now there were many men entering the basement. *Police, by the sound of it*. Torches swept over the floorboards until at last my position was illuminated.

"Sweet Jesus," one of the men breathed. "What's going on here?"

Shapes clustered around me. I felt the welcome release of my hands and feet, the cords cut, freeing me from that macabre pentagram. I was trembling so much, though, it took more than one of those officers to help me to my feet.

Yet there was still so much going on.

So much, it was hard to figure out what was real.

"Cornelius Mortimer, you are under arrest for the historic crimes of running a paedophile ring - a satanic cult involving child abuse - and perverting the course of justice..."

But Cornelius Mortimer did not move, and neither did Alistair McFadden. Crouched over his son, he was weeping uncontrollably, and watching him, I spotted an ominous dark pool radiating from Duncan's head.

I gasped in shock.

The last thing I recalled, before they finally coaxed me out into the daylight, was a heavy brass lamp lying on the floor beside the stricken, bleeding man.

At first I had to squint. Shafts of hazy evening sunlight beamed through the trees but after the claustrophobic darkness of that basement, it took a while for my eyes to adjust. Creeping into the driveway, however, I slowed to a pause. The first person to greet me was Mark, his face pinched with worry. A female constable accompanied him, and moving to my side, she draped a blanket around my shaking shoulders.

"Thank you," I babbled, fighting tears.

Glancing at my surroundings, only now did it dawn on me how many police cars were scattered around. Mark said nothing as he led me to his car, but my eyes kept roaming, and nothing delivered more joy than the next man to appear.

Joe, mercifully, still alive.

His face looked ghostly pale, horror buckling his brow as he stared at me. I guessed I must have looked awful, the front of my gown ripped. I was yet to discover the rivulet of blood staining my throat - but that tiny nick beneath my chin was Mortimer's last legacy, the kiss of his deadly dagger with its razor sharp point.

"Joe," I sobbed. "Thank God!"

As he inched his way towards me, the smile creeping onto his face was warmer than sunshine. I would have thrown my arms around him if he hadn't cringed in pain, his arm folded around his lower torso.

"I thought you were involved in a knife attack!"

"I was," he said, his smile draining away, "took a gash across the gut, but it weren't life-threatening. I-I was more worried about you."

I shook my head, at a loss where to begin, but our moment of quiet reconciliation was short-lived, as Mark soon intervened.

"Let's get you to the hospital," he muttered. "It's time for you to convalesce now, Joe, and as for you, Maisie... you need to be checked over, too."

Staring back at the house for what I hoped was the last time, I felt a shudder surge down my spine as one more person leapt into my thoughts.

"Where's Connor?" I gasped.

Joe frowned. "Sarah's foster son? What's he got to do with this?"

My eyes flitted from Joe to Mark. "She brought him over at lunchtime because he was in some sort of trouble. He's sixteen. I said he could stay but... Oh no, and to think he was hidden in the basement all that time!"

Mark froze. "Then he's a witness," he responded.

"You've got to look for him," I shivered. My eyes were drawn to the woods at the back of the property, the most obvious place he might have fled.

A look of intense curiosity tilted Mark's features, and at the same time he was nodding. "Don't worry, we'll find him. There's enough surveillance in those woods to root out a terrorist cell, so I am sure they'll find a teenage lad without any problem."

"Good," I murmured and charged with reassurance, I slid into his car.

His colleague took control, wheels crunching on the gravel as he reversed the car, ready to ferry us to St Richard's. Yet something pierced the air, something that suggested this wasn't quite over, the blare of an ambulance emerging from the opposite direction. Joe stared at me, his mouth dropping open, and in the instant our eyes met, I knew what he was going to ask me.

"What was going on with Sam, then?"

"Sam," I echoed. My lips started quivering. "Sam is dead. The *real* Sam, that is. He died years ago, but if you're referring to the man I was living with..."

Tears splashed from my eyes as I shook my head.

"It wasn't him, Joe! I need time to explain, but it's a horrible story."

"Ssh," he whispered, sliding an arm around my shoulder. "I ain't letting you out of my sight 'til I'm discharged now, so take as much time as you want."

Chapter Seventy-Three

St Richard's Hospital, Chichester

Joe spent a turbulent night with Maisie by his side. Huddled in an armchair under her blanket, it seemed a very long time before she stopped shaking. The horror of her ordeal had left her in deep shock, and even after the nurse administered a tranquilliser, she could not bear to be parted from him.

Side by side in separate beds, they had talked into the early hours. But regardless of Joe's suspicions, neither could have predicted how *close to home* their enemies truly were.

Come morning, the first person to appear was DI Fitzpatrick. His steely eyes flashed as he peered around the door, but at the same time he seemed somehow guarded.

"Morning, Joe," he greeted him, "and Maisie. How are you feeling?"

Unsure who the question was aimed at, Joe eyed him warily.

"I'll live," he said. "S'only a couple of knife wounds, but imagine what it was like for Maisie, trapped in a basement with them psychos."

"I know," Andrew sighed, "and I am sorry. I'm as horrified over what happened as you are, but before we go any further, there's someone else who wants to talk to you. Is it okay if we come in?"

Joe nodded, his hand folding over Maisie's as she rested in her chair by his bedside. But when the door swung open, he was intrigued to see a petite, silver haired woman accompanying him.

"Hannah!" Maisie expressed with a gasp.

Joe frowned.

Hannah, as in her psychotherapist?

"I don't believe you've met Joe."

She observed him with a smile as Andrew dragged two plastic chairs across.

"It is lovely to meet you, at last," she said, "after everything Maisie's told me about you, but to clear up any confusion, it's Connor I came to assess..."

A shadow passed across her face, and straight away, Joe sensed her unease.

"So I already know what you've been through."

Maisie met her eye with a shiver.

"How is he?" she whispered. "I've been so worried about him."

"Connor is okay," Andrew intervened, "a very brave young man, to act so

346

fast. Sarah is on her way. But what about you, Maisie, are you ready for this? Because I might as well cut to the chase... we've got an awful lot to discuss."

Joe adjusted his position. With everyone's eyes on Maisie, he felt an ocean of tears welling that would have to remain unshed for now. The thought of what she had endured shook him hollow, but they were yet to hear Connor's version.

"You see, it wasn't just Connor we found in the woods," Andrew continued, "but the silver camper van Schiller was last seen in, so no wonder it disappeared off the radar. Mortimer was using it as a hideout. But enough about him, let's go over what Connor witnessed."

"He's asleep now," Hannah said, "after a long session of psychotherapy. By the time the police found him, he was in such a state he couldn't speak. So I had to calm him down and regress him."

Connor had, in fact, been in the house all along, curled in a hidden corner at the top of the stairs when Maisie had let herself in. There was a lot he wanted to say to her, and he had nearly crept down to apologise. But a moment later Sam burst in and from his startled expression and clipped voice, Connor guessed something was afoot.

Frozen on the landing, he did not dare move a muscle.

He remained there, motionless, until a thud sharpened his senses. From his elevated position, he caught a reflection in the patio door, thinking Maisie must have fainted. Yet if that was the case, then why was Sam dragging her into the basement?

"He said Sam left you there and went out," Hannah added. "He sped down to the basement and found you unconscious, but before he had a chance to do anything Sam came back, by which time he was trapped. He didn't panic, though, just hid himself behind some crates along the back wall..."

It was with some difficulty that Connor had described the next scene.

Watching in confusion and with no clue of the ritual about to be enacted, he witnessed the man he knew as Maisie's boyfriend hammering metal pegs into the floor. He sensed there was something creepy about the star painted on the floor; something creepier still in the way Sam dressed Maisie up in a red satin gown, and bound her hands and feet before securing the cords to each point.

"He even began to wonder if it was for a horror film..."

Hannah's expression darkened as she glanced from Maisie to Joe.

"You were right to be worried."

Caught in the midst of something far more sinister than he had imagined, Connor remained hidden until eventually Maisie awoke. She had been hysterical at first. Yet he had tuned into their dialogue; a painful untangling of secrets that left him cold.

"He heard every word, Maisie - from Duncan admitting who he really was to the horrible things his father did - right up to the day they killed Sam."

It stood to reason that by the time Duncan left her a second time he had been frantic, though ever more determined to seek a solution...

"The next time the trap door opened," Hannah shuddered, "he saw three cloaked figures approaching, whispering strange words... some sort of chanting."

"Chanting," Maisie choked, "I know."

Her bottom lip trembled and Joe dropped his gaze.

It must have thrown her into orbit, her worst nightmare brought to life.

A murderous hate savaged his heart as the truth unravelled, but keeping his thoughts to himself, he relished the next part of the story: how Connor had derailed them, his gaze zooming in on a fuse box.

"He guessed those flickering torches ran off electricity."

Crouched in the shadows, he had watched the most horrific scene play out, yet not one of those men had detected his presence. So nudging towards the alcove where the fuse box was located, he considered the next part to be a waiting game... Mortimer raising his dagger, the instant in which everything turned surreal.

"He said he felt detached at that point," Hannah murmured, "as if he was floating on the edge of another world, looking in. I could almost imagine his mind emptying, every emotion suppressed as he calculated the exact moment to turn the power off."

"So clever," Maisie whispered, "anyone else would have panicked."

Joe nodded, Hannah's covert smile reassuring him.

"The ring of the doorbell caused panic, but you shouting Sam's name turned out to be a real game changer."

He felt the breath stream from his lungs, unsure he could handle much more, although she seemed to be reaching the end.

So Connor flipped the power switch. Maisie screamed; but with the lights extinguished and the basement drowned in darkness, the timing could not have been better for the police to smash their way in.

It had since transpired, however, that this was not his plan.

No one knew he was there, other than Maisie. So he had grabbed a heavy brass lamp and tiptoed a few steps to where he imagined Mortimer to be crouched before pitching his deadly blow.

If only Duncan hadn't got in the way.

For it was Duncan who took the hit. Duncan who dropped to the floor like a stone, his father crying out his name.

Joe could no longer stay silent, a black mist rising as he pictured his face. "If

I ever see that fucker again, I'm gonna kill him," he snarled.

Andrew, on the other hand, was quick to catch his eye.

"Forget it," he said. "The ambulance crew pronounced him dead before they got to the hospital. His skull was so badly crushed he would never have recovered."

"Wait a minute," Maisie gasped. "Does this mean Connor killed him?"

The inspector's face turned stony, his mouth pursed into a knot. "I'm afraid so, but there's more... Duncan McFadden was not the only man who died last night. Cornelius Mortimer passed away too."

Joe narrowed his eyes, unsure why he felt so deflated.

How he would have loved to see that monster brought to justice.

Although in another way, it came as some relief knowing he was dead, if only for Maisie's sake. Her face lingered on the shore of his vision, her expression laced with dread, still swimming in the horror she had been put through.

"If it's any compensation," Andrew added, "the end was not at all peaceful. He was not just suffering from advanced cancer but sustained a broken back when he fell from the stairs. He was trying to escape when Conner grabbed his ankle."

Maisie squeezed his hand. Looking at her now, she had regained a little colour in her cheeks, but neither of them could bring themselves to rejoice this news.

"Let's just say he was the one who died in agony," the DI finished dryly.

"Right," Joe sighed, thinking he deserved nothing less.

They took a moment to absorb this, until the wall of silence became crushing. Tearing his eyes away from Maisie, he sensed the weight of Andrew's gaze, and it seemed obvious he had more to tell them.

He exhaled an uneasy sigh. "So, finally we come to Duncan's father, Alistair McFadden QC. You were right to suspect him, Joe: a man reputed to be very dangerous and with contacts in the criminal world. It's even been suggested he played a hand in the assassination of Stephanie Ellis, Sam's mother, but I digress. By the time we were probing into his affairs, he was on a flight from Inverness to Gatwick. Hired a four-by-four cross terrain vehicle, the last transaction we traced before we lost him. Other than that, mobile phone data suggests he was in the area by five o' clock."

Maisie's eyes widened.

"The same time Connor was hiding in the basement," Hannah added, "and we know the rest, from the story I extracted earlier..." She broke off with a swallow, her eyes flitting to Andrew. "There's one more thing we should mention though, and you're not going to like this."

"Alistair McFadden is in police custody," Andrew said stonily, "but threatening to bring charges against Connor for the murder of his son. He has already drafted his own press release."

Chapter Seventy-Four

I turned to DI Fitzpatrick with a gulp, hit with wave after wave of panic as the contents of the press release sank in. But this story, this vicious slant on the truth, had been tainted with everything I had feared.

TEENAGER MUST FACE MURDER CHARGE

Sussex Police have detained a teenage boy for a series of actions that resulted in the deaths of two men. The sixteen-year-old (who cannot be named for legal reasons) suffers from severe mental problems which have been verified by a professional team of social workers who dealt with his care since early childhood.

On the two occasions he was placed in foster homes, his behaviour was deemed challenging, which at times led to violence. Early warning signs were recorded in 2013 when the police were alerted to an incident. Although no charges were brought, the damage caused inside his foster home could have been life-threatening. He has since been assessed with high functioning autism, but concerns remain that he may develop psychopathic tendencies...

"They can't print this," I started spluttering, "it's outrageous! How dare he twist the truth, when he was trying to save my life?"

Three pairs of eyes zoomed in on me but of all the people in the room, one face stood out in particular: *Hannah.*

"Tell them," I urged her. "Tell them about Sam!"

"I will," Hannah nodded, "but first and foremost, we need to explain what he witnessed."

A weight closed around my chest, every breath dragged painfully from my lungs while I struggled to grasp this most chilling part of the story.

"The party..." I could hear my voice wobbling, the horror flooding back in a deluge, but they had to know the truth.

Sam.

Suddenly I started crying, as I recalled how this nightmare had begun.

Maisie, Joe and Sam. That's how it began.

351

We were three kids in a care home, too young to protect ourselves.
Three kids who were inseparable until the night Sam went missing.
And all we had ever wanted to know was what happened to him.

"Hang on," Joe interrupted, "I think you're missing a point here. How does McFadden know so much about Connor?"

Andrew did not move, his expression steely as ever. "Like I said, Alistair McFadden has his fingers in so many pies, I wouldn't be at all surprised if they include the local authorities. If he wanted to dig up dirt, he found a way."

"Sarah was threatened!" I gasped and as I wiped away my tears, another bubble of memory popped up. "Someone warned her not to go probing into Sam's case or there would be consequences."

"When was this?" Andrew frowned.

"The day we met in London, though none of us dared report it. Whoever sent that threat contacted her through Facebook, but they definitely mentioned Connor."

The DI leaned forward, his stare hardening.

"There's more," I gulped as pictures came flashing into my head. "They sent an image of the house in East Grinstead where Sam's social worker lived..."

"In other words, they used powerful scare tactics," Andrew finished, "and I'm betting McFadden had something to do with it. Anything to guard his secret. Think about it, they set up this charade with Duncan, so the last thing they wanted was someone like your friend, Sarah, getting too close to the truth."

The palms of my hands felt clammy as I clung to my blanket, but the more I reflected, the more I realised how deeply Connor had become entrenched in this mystery.

"But you can't let McFadden bring charges against him," I uttered aloud.

"I couldn't agree more," Andrew nodded, "and I hope what I am about to say will reassure you, but there is no way Connor can be held responsible for what happened. It was a life-threatening situation. You were inches away from being murdered. The former QC might think he's clever, but he's not going to pull any strings this time, and I shall personally make sure of that."

"How?" Joe frowned. "With his power, won't he just deny everything?"

"He can try," Andrew muttered and sneaking another glance at Hannah, I saw a glint in his eye. "He assumes Connor has no proof, but he's wrong. You've got to credit that boy's intelligence. He recorded every word on his mobile app."

My head started spinning with the immensity of it. Here I was, recalling every scene, every horrible disclosure they had hurled at me: the things Sam witnessed, the despicable way they boasted about killing him... and suddenly we had turned full circle again.

It all came back to Sam.

"Furthermore," the DI continued, "we have Hannah's assessment in his favour. Would you like to share your findings?"

"Of course," Hannah consented. "Connor needs to undergo a full psychiatric assessment, but in the period I regressed him, I delved deep into his emotions and I can assure you he is not unhinged. His greatest anxiety stems from abandonment, from his mother rejecting him when he was small. He is otherwise a well-balanced, perfectly healthy boy and with no psychopathic signs."

"I never doubted it for a moment," I said to her.

Her expression turned as serene as I remembered from my own therapy, but I was thinking about Connor, and the special rapport we had developed.

"Even his Asperger's could be considered a gift," Andrew intercepted. "From what I understand, kids on the autistic spectrum have a communication barrier, but they see the world through different eyes. In Connor's case, analytical eyes."

DI Fitzpatrick left us after that, while Hannah remained a little longer. She too had played an instrumental role in this story, teasing the threads of memory out of me until they fused into something tangible. It stood to reason her notes from my psychotherapy would provide the final back-up if needed.

"Now what about you, Maisie?" she sighed. "You've been through a terrible ordeal, and not for the first time." Her eyes wandered to Joe's bed. "I guess you both have."

"I'll be okay," I said, "I'm looking forward to seeing Sarah, and my foster parents are on their way, too. They've invited me to come and stay with them but..."

I felt a smile lift my lips as I turned to Joe.

"I'm not going to abandon you, Joe, so I've sent them a text, suggesting they book a couple of hotel rooms in Chichester."

With his hair ruffled against the pillow, his face pale and unshaven, it struck me how vulnerable he looked. Yet regardless of his discomfort, his eyes gleamed with a warmth that had my heart melting.

Eventually Hannah left too, and I cherished a few minutes alone with him before anyone else turned up.

"Sweet," he murmured, "you didn't have to do that for me."

"Shut up," I whispered. "It's my choice and I'm not leaving you. You took a couple of nasty knife wounds yesterday, so don't try putting on the tough guy act."

"I'm not," he protested gently, "but you should take up their offer to stay

353

with them. It'll do you good to get away for a couple of days."

"Then we'll both go, but only when you're fit enough. Don't worry, Mandy and Stewart are lovely, and they've always wanted to meet you."

"Okay, well in that case, you're on. I'd like that."

The silence swelled between us, the room turning warmer as the gaps in the blinds drew the sunlight in. They painted white stripes across Joe's bed, and as I struggled to tear my eyes away, I could guess what he was thinking.

"So what happens next? Are you going back to your flat in Bognor?"

"I guess I'll have to," I shrugged, "but that's not all. I need to return to East Lavant some time, to collect my things."

A black cloud rolled into my mind as I thought of it. That house had seemed like a dream once but now... picturing it, in its creepy surround of woods, it represented my darkest nightmare, the place my demons had finally come for me.

"I wish I didn't have to go back. I'm not sure I even want to live in Annandale Avenue, come to think of it, not after what I know. The thought of Mortimer living there is never going to stop haunting me. Suppose I terminate my contract? We can always find some other place to rent."

Joe turned very still, his eyebrows steepled. "We?" he repeated.

"Yes, Joe," I said, as I rehearsed my next words. "Because whatever the future holds, I want us to be together..."

How strange that it had taken the events of yesterday evening for me to realise it was Joe I loved all along.

354

Epilogue

Six months on, and we are still together – in fact, we couldn't be happier. I love the flat we rent in Pagham. A first floor property with massive front windows and such a glorious view of the beach further away. It has everything we cherished in Bognor yet without the cobwebs of the past clouding our vision; the freshness of the sea breeze around us, a couple of good pubs and plenty of places for walking.

If anyone has been around for me, though, it is my dear friend, Sarah.

I feel a warmth fold around me as I picture her face but in the last few months we've grown even closer. No surprises there, when you consider the deadly web we were caught up in. The icing on the cake is how quickly Connor bounced back. He won't be facing charges after all. DI Fitzpatrick saw to that. Sarah and I often wonder but... what would have happened if Connor hadn't been around that day? The thought makes me shiver and I push it away. Something I don't wish to think about!

Going back to Connor, I'm pleased he never went back to his old school, that shortly after the holidays he embarked on a fresh start. He attends an academy now, one specially geared towards gifted kids with special needs. I know he's happy and as for his new schoolmates... they think he's awesome.

Jess, on the other hand, was never there for me.

It took that terrible week in June to realise what a truly toxic friend she had been. Looking back, Jess only ever got in touch when she needed a shoulder to cry on. I always knew she was a drama queen, using me as a sounding board to offload her problems, while not caring about mine at all. But the way she treated Joe disgusted me, and that was the final straw.

Glancing at him as he sleeps, I can see why she was attracted.

His unruly dark hair falls like feathers around his face, and with his head tilted sideways, I trace the angle of his jaw with my fingertips, loving the roughness of his stubble. A glow fills my cheeks when I think of the intimacy we share. For not only did he save my life, but by the time his wounds healed, he turned out to be a perfect lover – although those are thoughts I keep to myself.

But going back to Jess, there was something else I never knew; that according to her friend, Imogen (who cornered me not long after the incident in

East Lavant), she thought she was onto something big with Joe's story.

And Joe was right all along about her intentions. There was nothing sympathetic about her interest in his traumatic past, just the opportunity for some publicity, and even a little notoriety. According to Imogen, Jess harboured dreams of being a journalist, and this would be her big scoop. Even Imogen was shocked. Our story, when it finally did hit the news, was like nothing she had imagined, even after the little aperitifs she had sampled at Jess's dinner party.

I could hardly be surprised at her shock. Who would have thought this idyllic corner of West Sussex could conceal crimes of such evil?

I glance away, biting my lip as other faces begin to materialise.

Suddenly I feel a creeping sensation, but it's too late... thoughts of our enemies are stuck inside my head, so I might as well deal with them, starting with the man at the top.

Alistair McFadden QC was charged with multiple accounts of murder and conspiracy to murder. Now he is awaiting trial, though, he's singing like a canary.

Joe begins to stir, as if conscious of my thoughts. In the aftermath of Mortimer's death, McFadden named four other men involved in his satanic cult (all public figures), and admitted that he owned the mansion in Buckinghamshire where the rituals had taken place.

All things considered, the investigation has only just begun.

As for Duncan, I shed no tears over his death. Goose pimples crawl like insects over my arms when I think about what he did to Sam. For regardless of the iron rule of his father, murdering Sam was a horrible revelation in itself, and his lack of remorse showed him to be as much of a monster as Alistair.

I take deep breaths, willing my heart to slow down as my fears threaten to take hold again. There are times I could kick myself for letting Duncan into my life so easily. But only now do I realise those powerful feelings I harboured were nothing compared to what I have with Joe. It was never love, more infatuation. Because despite everything I know about him, he reminded me so much of Sam. The Sam I adored. Perhaps my feelings were the result of some self-fulfilling prophecy; that my yearning for Sam to be alive made Duncan's illusion seem so real.

Joe doesn't hold it against me, and I can't say how lucky I am that he has stood by me! I don't know how I could have got through the last six months on my own. Hannah, too, plays an essential role in helping me battle my traumas. I still visit her for therapy and she's got me writing things down lately...

Skimming over my ramblings, my newly acquired reading glasses sliding down my nose, I chew the end of my biro in deep thought.

For there, lingering on the shore of my mind, gleams one other person.

Sam.

The real Sam, that is, the boy we lost twenty-one years ago.

Hardly a day goes by when he doesn't pop into my thoughts, and Joe has said the same. Police in Scotland were faced with the grim task of searching the mountains surrounding Galbraith Castle, where sure enough, they did eventually discover human remains, scattered among the rocks and ferns. Those bastards didn't even give him a decent burial, something we vowed to put right.

When Sam was finally laid to rest, it was an emotional day. After consulting the authorities, it was agreed he should be interred alongside his mother, at a grave in Brompton Cemetery, Westminster, which seemed very small and insignificant.

A ball of sadness forms in the pit of my stomach as I picture the scene. It was hard to imagine that simple wicker coffin contained the bones of our fourteen-year-old friend. Sarah and Connor attended the funeral with us, as did my foster parents. Officers from the Met turned up too, Mark from Bognor Police Station, and although none of them had known Sam, they wanted to pay their respects, if for no other reason than to honour a child whose life had been brutally cut short.

One person I never expected to see, though, was Thomas Parker-Smythe, mercifully released from prison and acquitted of all false accusations. He and Joe have forged a cordial, if not awkward camaraderie in the wake of his prison visit, but it forced a deeper investigation into his story.

Most astonishing was the authenticity of the Apple Mac they seized. It turns out it wasn't even his! It had a completely different IP address, proving without a doubt that his real computer had indeed been switched for an identical model: one that bore the hallmark of Orchard Grange.

This is the moment I stop writing. The air feels cold, and I don't want to think about the men who stole Sam's life, but they are there nonetheless, crouched on the edge of my consciousness like gargoyles. As Mortimer's face flickers briefly, I sense a black fog pushing into my thoughts before Joe opens his eyes. It seems like telepathy.

He holds my gaze before a slow, luscious smile slides its way onto his face. Our fingertips connect beneath the duvet where they entwine.

"What are you writing about now?" he murmurs.

"Just stuff," I murmur back. "Memories, things I need to get off my chest... Like Hannah says, it helps me purge my thoughts, instead of suppressing them."

With a contented sigh, I set down my notebook and turn to him. Bury my face in his chest hair, inhaling his sweet manly essence.

"I was just thinking about Sam's funeral service..."

Joe nods, his hand caressing the back of my neck.

"D'you fancy going for a wander, then?" he says. "Take another look at the harbour?"

"Yeah, I'm up for that," I smile.

He's excited, I can see it in his eyes, something that pulls in a more recent memory. Because if anything good is to come out of this saga, it has to be Joe's prospects, and now the dust has settled, he fantasises of a career working with youngsters; troubled kids like him who have ended up in care, knowing what it was like to have no family around the corner to fall back on.

The only problem is that he needs a qualification, and after missing so much schooling, hasn't a single GSCE to his name. But all that is about to change.

For if anyone has come through for Joe it is Thomas: Thomas, who feels indebted to him for seeking out the truth when he was on remand; Thomas, who has pledged to do whatever he can to guide him onto the right path. The first step would be to get Joe onto an Access to Education scheme. If successful, that brings him a nationally-recognised Level 3 qualification, with which he can go on to study for a Diploma in Health and Social Care.

A strange swimming sensation passes over me. Following the exposure of those homes, no one could have been more devastated than Thomas. Yet when he talks of a broken society, he genuinely thinks men like Joe can make a difference.

It's something we discussed after Sam's funeral, and if the past is bleak, the future looks rosy.

Returning to Sam, though, we have dreams of creating our own tribute right here in Pagham, a place we can hold him in our hearts.

We've written to the Parish Council, and requested permission to install a memorial bench close to the nature reserve.

So this is where we're heading now, a sheltered lagoon embracing a glittering expanse of water. Swathes of reeds stretch beyond the footpaths, nesting grounds for migrating birds and the tiny white herons known as egrets. It seems so perfect; the place in which Joe and I have established our home; a place of beauty, where Sam's spirit seems destined to be, and to beam a special piece of his sunshine into our lives.

And if they agree, all we will ask for is a simple brass plaque:

In Loving Memory of Sam Ellis
Never to be forgotten

THE END

Author's Note

Thank you for reading *Lethal Ties* and I hope you enjoyed it. If so, please could you leave a review? Reviews are the life blood of authors and help other readers to discover new books.

The idea for this novel arose in 2015 when a series of stories appeared in the news concerning the historic sexual abuse of children by people in power, including TV celebrities and high establishment figures. That many of the victims were deemed vulnerable only exacerbated the scandal, the more so when it emerged that the allegations centred on the abuse of children in residential care homes nationwide. But in 2018, a high profile case (Operation Midland) collapsed when claims of a VIP paedophile ring were proven false. Police had no choice but to investigate allegations made by Carl Beech against known public figures, a case widely publicised in the media before any concrete evidence was found. This put a different slant on my story, so for this reason, I chose to write it from two perspectives. The central perspective is that of the abused, and the long term damage they suffer, including anxiety, low self-esteem and in some cases victims feeling suicidal; but I also had to focus on the effect allegations may have on those who are falsely accused, on how lives can be ruined before they are proven innocent. This story is entirely fictitious but aims to be a chilling psychological thriller with a police investigation at the heart of it, and although there are references to the news stories that appeared in 2015, I included them for no other reason than as a discussion point among characters.

Acknowledgements

I would like to express my thanks to everyone who assisted me. Andy Kille, Ops Controller with Sussex Police whose career spanned three decades, was happy to advise me on the finer details of police procedures. Furthermore, I spoke to Phil Lickorish who joined West Sussex Constabulary in 1964 and held several posts, ultimately working in CID. Phil also kindly put me in touch with DI Jez Prior from the Metropolitan Police. Jez dealt with cases of child abuse in the 90s and we spent a considerable time talking about his work, from the treatment of victims and taking statements, to the gathering of evidence including home searches. The underlying message he wanted put across is that children who have been exploited sexually should always come forward, report their abuse and be listened to.

Focussing on the police investigation was a factor that really drove this story forward when I was struggling. During the first UK lockdown, it began to take shape, but in addition to the police officers who helped me, I have many other people to thank for sharing their knowledge and providing insights into child care and fostering I might never have otherwise discovered.

One of the first people I spoke to was Rosemary Conroy-Smith, from West Sussex County Council Child Care and Fostering Department, generous with her time explaining the processes of adoption and fostering. She described the various roles in their department, then invited me to attend one of their Fostering Information evenings in Worthing. I was lucky enough to meet even more people in this field, watched a very moving film and came away feeling enlightened. The vital service they provide for families and children needs to be recognised.

Next, I enjoyed an informal chat over a coffee with one of our dog walker friends in West Park, Bognor. Nicola Elridge and her husband, Carl, adopted their son when he was a baby but have opened up their home to other foster children. She had some captivating stories to tell, and as a result I came away with a better understanding of the fostering process and some real life cases of parents who have been there and done that. This paved the path of a much deeper journey.

My author friend, Dan Jones, worked in a number of children's care homes in the 1990s, and when I briefly mentioned my WIP on Twitter, he was quick to offer advice and share his own experiences. Dan has written about parenting techniques and managing challenging behaviour, and was kind enough to send me a comprehensive email (and documents) about his work in children's homes, some of which did not make pleasant reading. Children in care frequently hail from unhappy backgrounds, have abusive parents, suffer low self-esteem and exhibit behavioural problems. Thus, the care home environment can be a hostile one.

I greatly appreciated his help, most of all for introducing me to his friend, Graham, someone who lived through the care system yet turned his life around.

In fact, it is Graham I have to thank for inspiring this book more than anyone. Not only was it a pleasure to meet him, but in the brief time we talked, he told some amazing stories about living in care and in foster homes. I pledged that when my book was published I would include him in the credits - and he said he would be interested in reading it. My deepest regret is that day never came. Graham tragically passed away on October 29th 2020 before I had a chance to convey my thanks, but the information he shared was priceless, so I chose to dedicate this book to him. The next page includes a tribute to honour his life, and he must never be forgotten.

Having other authors to network with has always been a boost, and none so much as my friends at Chindi Authors for their continual support (especially Jane Cable and Carol Thomas whose uplifting emails were of great help when my inspiration was flagging). I also have my beta readers to thank. I could not have completed this book without them, so a big thank you to Ray Green and Rose Edmunds, both talented thriller authors, and to best selling author, Joel Hames, for being my editor. With Joel's help, my final draft was shaped and polished to make it flow better; a book I now feel proud of.

Last of all, I would like to make a special mention of my talented niece, Carys, who has battled with Asperger's since primary school. A spate of bullying in her first year of secondary school led my sister to a decision to home-school her for a year; but with no interaction with other kids, she expressed a desire to go back to school to study for GSCEs. It emerged she was 'on the spectrum' and after diagnosis, her parents managed to get her into a good school, offering her the specialist help she needed. Little was known about Asperger's until recently and only now do I understand the inherent traits, from the frustration of not being able to read people and non-acceptance by peers, to social withdrawal when they feel threatened. Those I have met with autism see the world differently but are intelligent, intuitive and creative. No two people are alike, even my own character; a boy who exhibits behaviour some might consider 'strange,' while balanced with compassion and bravery. In 2020 Carys graduated from Southampton University with a class 2:1 degree in English Literature and Creative Writing, a proud moment for our family. Her dream is to write screen plays and it would be wonderful to see her work brought to life in a film or TV drama series, maybe even this story... who knows?

For further information about my writing, please visit my website where you will also find my social media links and blog:
www.samefacedifferentplace.com.

Thank you all,
Helen Christmas

Tribute to Graham Levell

As mentioned, I have many people to thank for inspiring me, but none more so than Graham Levell, who I interviewed in the Waverley Pub on Bognor Seafront, September 12th 2019. Our meeting happened by chance when author friend, Dan Jones, related his experiences of working in children's care homes in the 1990s. Graham was his best friend.

Before I begin my tribute, I should mention the characters, specifically the male lead, Joe. I had no difficulty writing Joe's back story; from living in a children's home, running away, serving a prison sentence, battling with depression, drug addiction and paranoia to ultimately ending up on the streets, homeless. The difficulty arose in creating Joe's complex character.

So when Dan mentioned his friend, I was intrigued:

"He would have stories to tell you, he did drugs, drank, spent time homeless, missed education, mixed with all sorts of people, yet turned things around. So he knows what the scene was like here in Bognor during the 1990s for teenagers in a difficult home environment and in the care system..."

Introducing me to Graham felt like fate, and in the course of an hour, I gained some fascinating insights into his life.

Graham's story began when he worked at Butlins but at the age of fourteen, decided to leave home and spend the next fortnight sleeping under Bognor Pier. At no time did I get the impression this was traumatic, more an adventure, as he colourfully alluded to the homeless culture in Bognor.

"That was before they put down anti-homeless alarms. Sit on a bench for too long, it makes a horrible noise so you can't sleep."

Graham had dreams of going to college, to avoid the predetermination he would follow the path of many local youngsters and work at LEC. The more he talked, the more I got the impression he was unhappy with his life. Working at Butlins however, the next turning point was Dan's girlfriend discovering he was sleeping rough; as a result, they invited him to come and stay with them. This was 1997, at a time when he had been gravitating towards other troubled youths, getting into drugs and alcohol. He described himself as quite a suspicious, cynical person.

"I mean I don't have any lasting relationships and Dan was just about the only person I had a long friendship with."

Shortly after this, the police got involved. His mum had reported him missing and Social Services intervened; said he couldn't stay with Dan (19) and his girlfriend, and that as a fourteen-year-old runaway, they felt uncomfortable about it.

In the next part of Graham's life, being in care, some really enlightening stories began to emerge. I asked him about the process of being fostered, which he described as being *"really scary... where they used to force us into these gatherings. It was all well-intended, but all a bit weird and false. Social workers present, theatre groups... others were just 'happy clappy' Christians."*

During these gatherings, he would meet all sorts of people - girls who had been sexually abused - but with the lads, he remembers a sense of brotherhood, the usual teenage dominance (chest beating), and then laughing and joking about the different foster carers they'd had.

"There were some right bastards out there caring for people... One couple used to have the kids living in a caravan at the end of their garden and then drag them indoors for bridge games every Wednesday night, and the kids would be made to work this huge great big garden and were generally slaves and dogsbodies around the house. These days, they wouldn't pass the fostering board."

An interesting transition from being in care arose when Graham ended up working in care himself. But before this could happen, he needed an education. He missed a lot of schooling, messed up his GSCEs (was even threatened with suspension) but turned things around in the sixth form and finally achieved his dream of going to college. It was amazing how fast he adapted, joyfully describing how this was the making of him; first studying a National Diploma in performing arts and a Diploma in vocational education in business.

"They worked me ragged for four years but I had some wicked tutors and started mixing with people who were fairly decent."

364

Best of all, Graham achieved a National Diploma, went on to do a Professional Development Certificate, then a Professional Development Diploma (which is a level 5 certificate) and was hailed as 1 in 10,000 kids to come out of care with a degree level qualification (in Health and Social Care).

I feel blessed to have had this one-to-one with Graham, who gave up his time entertaining me with his stories and accomplishments. To an author this was gold dust, and as the conversation gathered momentum, he became more animated, describing his work in care homes with troubled youngsters, one of which was for young offenders and substance misusers.

"They would get wrecked and come back late after staff had locked the doors... and I was a bit of a soft touch, because one of the rules was 'three warnings and you're out' - and I wanted to keep the kids with me until my dying breath. There was no way I was going to let anyone else look after my kids, because I knew what it was like to have no one you could depend on around the corner. I mean, they used to throw me through doors and everything... I got the shit kicked out of me loads of times BUT no one else was going to look after them. Not as good as me and my team."

So when did Graham turn his life around? He was quite frank.

"When I got my ex-wife pregnant. With a little baby on the way – the first of my three daughters – I got a job selling mobile phones to retail. Business supplied the learning and I found myself taking on a lot of what they taught me in terms of sales and communication. Knowing Dan, too, was a massive help."

Graham won various awards in quality of business (still has the glass statue), and even Dan said he felt like a proud father to see him achieve success. This was the start of his professional development.

A darker side of Graham's musings emerged in some of the stories he came across about kids in care; from a high functioning autistic boy left to fend for himself in a studio flat who became almost feral - to a three-year-old child raped by his adoptive father. He ended up in a foster placement and it completely went undetected, but he used to sleep in the same bed as his foster father and nothing was ever said.

"He was schizophrenic when he came to me, because this had been a repeat pattern with every placement, but looking after him around 2007, he became

the abuser. If it happens from an extremely young age it becomes a sense of normality..."

This was one of the last things Graham spoke of, the referral files he used to read, which would make him cry; cases of abuse that emotionally floored him:

'Awful. Absolutely awful. This is why I would never let my kids go, because I'd seen what they'd been through... I could never be a social worker because I would KILL people.'

I will never regret meeting Graham, not only to hear his amazing story, he became the biggest inspiration behind Joe's character. I've even included some of his quotes, one being that kids in care have a huge chip on their shoulder.

"You're either a victim or a fighter."

Anyone who knew Graham might recognise a little piece of him in Joe, from his flickers of insight to his sunny personality, his compassion and sense of humour. For all the while we were talking, I sensed neither bitterness nor regret. Graham was a genuinely lovely guy – had the gift of the gab, portrayed life in a colourful, humorous way and had a wicked laugh.

What I did not know at the time, though, was that he had mental health problems and battled with bi-polar disorder. Sadly in 2020, with his existing problems exacerbated by the impact UK lockdown had on single people during the coronavirus pandemic, Graham died from an overdose of his medication. It broke my heart to discover the loss of this inspirational man, but he often spoke of suicide among males and took his life before I had a chance to properly acknowledge his help. My time with Graham is a memory I will forever hold dear. So I hope I have, in some way, kept his spirit alive in sharing this emotional tribute.

Printed in Great Britain
by Amazon

67333288R00220